The
BIRDCAGE

ALSO BY EVE CHASE

The Daughters of Foxcote Manor

The Wildling Sisters

Black Rabbit Hall

The
BIRDCAGE

Eve Chase

G. P. PUTNAM'S SONS
NEW YORK

PUTNAM
— EST. 1838 —

G. P. PUTNAM'S SONS
Publishers Since 1838
An imprint of Penguin Random House LLC
penguinrandomhouse.com

First published in the United Kingdom in 2022 by Michael Joseph,
an imprint of Penguin Random House UK.

Library of Congress Cataloging-in-Publication Data

Names: Chase, Eve, author.
Title: The birdcage / Eve Chase.
Description: New York: G. P. Putnam's Sons, 2022.
Identifiers: LCCN 2022019009 (print) | LCCN 2022019010 (ebook) |
ISBN 9780525542414 (hardcover) | ISBN 9780525542438 (ebook)
Subjects: LCSH: Detective and mystery fiction. | LCGFT: Novels.
Classification: LCC PR6103.H45 B59 2022 (print) |
LCC PR6103.H45 (ebook) | DDC 823/.92—dc23/eng/20220420
LC record available at https://lccn.loc.gov/2022019009
LC ebook record available at https://lccn.loc.gov/2022019010

Printed in the United States of America
1st Printing

Interior art: Birdcage © fran_kie / Shutterstock
Book design by Alison Cnockaert

For Ben

Of all lies, art is the least untrue.

—GUSTAVE FLAUBERT

The
BIRDCAGE

7 JANUARY 2019

Breaking news: The police have confirmed reports a swimmer was recovered from the sea near Zennor this morning. The individual was later pronounced dead at the scene. Exact circumstances of the incident are not yet known. Devon and Cornwall Police has appealed for eyewitnesses.

1

LAUREN

| | |

Three days earlier
4 JANUARY 2019

THE SNOW IS still falling, feathery flakes whirling in the golden light of the train window, then sucked into the black. But the 14:04 London-Penzance keeps hurtling west, drawing Lauren closer to Rock Point, the house she fled one summer's day twenty years before. Her gaze flicks to the carriage's emergency stop button, away again. Ridiculous. It's only three nights. And she has a promise to keep.

With a metallic screech, the train lurches. Lauren grabs the back of a seat, her hands small, strong; nails clipped short to disguise the biting and painted the sort of pale pink she hopes won't show chips. Since offering her seat to a mother and her toddler an hour ago, she's been stuck swaying in the crowded aisle, wedged between dandruffy shoulders and boxy sales bags advertising department stores she can't afford. Lying across her feet, a gym holdall never used for its intended purpose, hurriedly packed, quite possibly without her phone charger or enough knickers. And almost certainly the wrong clothes for a reunion with Kat and Flora, the half sisters she rarely sees.

Her father's email had landed on Boxing Day, knocking the air right out of her. She'd had to read it three times, sunk to the floor of her Whitechapel kitchen, emptied of flatmates over the holidays. Pinning her hopes on the invitation being some sort of awkward mistake, she didn't reply. But Dad left voicemails. He texted: "Charlie Finch will not take no for an answer!!! You must come, Laurie. I have an important announcement to make. P.S. Kat and Flora think this reunion a MARVELOUS idea."

Ever since, Lauren's tried extremely hard not to think about the last time they were all together at Rock Point: the thrilling, appalling summer of the total solar eclipse, 1999. But whenever she drifts or blinks, there it is: *Girls and Birdcage*, the portrait they sat for that August, in their artist father's Cornish studio. She dreamed about the painting last night, tossing and turning as the London snow fell. And she can still see it now, like a hologram projected on the carriage wall.

Caught in meaty gouges of their father's oils: her younger self—a scruffy shy scribble of a thing—and her older half sisters, Kat and Flora, with their fearless gazes and rich-girl glitter. The three of them glowing from sea and sun—the delirious freedom of cliffs and coves; those precious days before the eclipse—squished on a white sofa next to the black dome of a large empty birdcage.

Charlie Finch's masterpiece, the critics agree. But really, it's a piece of them. As they were. The girls in that painting climbed out of its gilt frame—and into separate lives—long ago.

"Excuse me?"

Lauren startles, and the painting pops like a soap bubble.

Sitting in the adjacent window seat, the man is studying her with navy eyes. He has one of those roughly cut, craggy faces that don't reveal themselves straightaway. Something about him pings in Lauren. She hasn't the foggiest why.

"You've been standing for ages." He speaks with an unmistakable Cornish burr, just in case she needed a reminder of where she's headed. "Here, please . . . my seat." Rising to his full rangy height, he sloshes takeaway coffee on his jeans. The woman sitting beside him irritably yanks her handbag to her knee.

"I'm good. Thank you, though," Lauren says after a beat, stupidly flustered. She's spent too much time alone over Christmas, lost all her social skills. Grief has opened her up like a whelk.

The man nods, lowers again. But his gaze sticks, like a handshake that goes on too long. Feeling exposed, Lauren stares hard out of the window, her mind turning with the clacking wheels to childhood train journeys—same line, same destination, same migratory path—that once bookended August. Back then the view rolled past lush green, hazy with insects, heat, and hope. Now: smears of light from country houses and distant villages. Superimposed upon them, her winter-pale city face: hollowed eyes, dark as mineshafts; a slightly regretted cobalt streak in her blunt fringe.

She's swaying, twisting, digging in her handbag for her mobile—better tell the others she's nearly there; no, she's out of charge—when a passenger tugs open a nearby window's top partition. Lauren's unprepared for the cold salt air, the way it streams into the carriage, flushing away the gamey fast-food stink—and drawing in the heartstopping smell of *sea*. With it, fragments of their last Rock Point summer: linseed oil; her sisters' laughter; the burned-out eye of eclipsed sun. Fear and longing.

For all Lauren's mind has blocked, deep down her body remembers. And in the reflection of the train window, she sees the man who offered his seat staring intensely, his hand over his mouth, like he might too.

Local or not, he can't possibly recognize her, Lauren tells herself, panic prickling up the back of her neck. It was so long ago, and they'd been too young to be identified in the papers. She meets his gaze with a defiant flash, then turns away, steeling for the reunion. With a diesel hiss, the train picks up speed, syncing with Lauren's racing heartbeat, and plunges to the far edge of the map.

2

KAT

| | |

AS THE SMALL plane bucks toward Newquay airport, Kat wonders what the hell her father is playing at. She's struggling to focus on work—Spring's subscriber data marches across her laptop screen, awaiting analysis—her thoughts maddeningly, compulsively looping back to her father. Rock Point.

When she'd first read his email, her inner voice yelled, "Do. Not. Go." Instead, she'd listened to her mother as they were squashed together in a booth at the Carlyle, Manhattan. Kat's treat every year, even though any sort of holiday makes her twitchy. Still. Anything to escape the minefield of Christmas. Dad had similarly slipped away to Paris, sparing Flora the agony of how to seat him and her mother at the same lavish table. And if Lauren's mum—RIP, Dixie—hadn't lost her battle in October, Lauren wouldn't have volunteered at the hospice but hunkered down with Dixie in Oxford, eating nut loaf in a cloud of incense.

When there are three half sisters and three rivaling mothers with some overlap, it's complicated.

"So, the old wolf is inviting you all to *Rock Point*?" Sipping her Virgin Mary, Blythe had brazenly read the email over Kat's shoulder. "Oh, hello. 'An announcement'? Charlie's not getting any younger. Maybe he wants to hand over the house. Don't do that skeptical thing with your mouth. You'll get marionette lines. Look! He says Flora and Lauren think a reunion is a marvelous idea! Frankly, if Lauren is brave enough to go back . . . and Flora's probably camped outside already, that mother of hers crouched behind a rock, egging her on." Blythe's hand gripped her glass tightly, historic grievances surfacing. "I'm not having my girl missing out. We deserve something from that man, Kat. We really do."

We? Charlie Finch had been her mother's lover. (And, at that point, married to Flora's mother, Annabelle.) But he is Kat's father, even if he doesn't always behave like it. "For all we know, Dad's going to announce what he ate for breakfast. And I really can't take any more time off, Mum. It's mental busy. I've got a shareholder meeting, a big eff-off early the following week. Seriously, no bandwidth."

"Well, find it, honey." Blythe's shellacs furiously tap-tapped on her phone and magnified an aerial view on Google Maps, making the hairs on Kat's arms lift. "Rock Point. Prime real estate, Kat. You want to be the only daughter who is too busy to show? Who pisses off her narcissist father and gets *squeezed out*?" When Kat rolled her eyes, Blythe moved in for the kill. "This is not about a house. Or money; we all know you've made a stack of that. This . . ." Righteous pause. ". . . is about *fairness*, my darling."

And just like that, Kat's childhood insecurities were expertly detonated. Whatever it was—even if just her father's attention for a freezing weekend in January—Kat needed to have her slice of it, ideally the biggest.

Only now she's irreversibly on her way—the jaunt no longer theoretical, or some sort of inheritance TV drama, scripted by her actor mother—it feels like she's shooting through time, not space. And that by returning to Rock Point, there's a possibility she'll regress into her teenage self; she and Flora their old glorious savagery.

Also, the whole thing is just odd, even set against their father's low bar, Kat thinks, stretching a long leg into the plane's aisle. Until last month, the house was long-term tenanted by a retired couple, charged a peppercorn rent; their role was to inhabit the place uncomplainingly. Dad never talks about Rock Point. None of them do. Well, they wouldn't. And they haven't slept under the same roof for years, let alone that roof. Flora will no doubt slap on a sepia filter and insist they're all having A Lovely Time. But Lauren? Kat won't blame her if she bails at the last minute and stays hiding in Whitechapel. Rail disruption, the perfect excuse.

What's hers? Unlike Lauren, Kat doesn't carry the weight of that summer. She's not sure she even recalls what happened the day of the eclipse, not accurately. All anyone remembers from their teenage years is what they mythologize as adults, isn't it? In a similar way to how a faked emotion starts to feel real if you keep the pretense going long enough. And it was a different millennium. Analog: pre-smartphones, Twitter, and smashed avocado. A time of her life that, set against the ever-scrolling present, seems hazy, discontinuous, and remarkably undocumented.

Ridiculous then that she's been barely able to eat for days; her stomach fluttery, not with nerves but something else, an emotion she can't identify. Then there's this sweaty, caffeinated feeling. For the third time on the short flight, she dabs a skein of sweat off her nose with the scarf she keeps hidden, scrunched at the bottom of her handbag. Scarred with rips, wine stains, stiletto heel punctures, and cigarette burns, the Dior silk scarf belonged to her mother at her most chaotic in the late nineties. Kat always travels with it, a sort of discomfort blanket; the photographic negative of her hard-won success. A reminder of how far she has come.

"Whoa!" The plane takes an ear-popping dive. The woman spilling over their shared armrest squeals, dropping her tube of Pringles. Someone whispers a Hail Mary. The pilot broadcasts a brisk order to buckle seat belts and prepare for landing.

Kat calmly puts away the laptop. As a kid, flying alone between her mother's TV sets and disparate American and British relatives and schools, she taught her petrified self to enjoy turbulence. The cabin crew would fuss over her and offer extra dessert. When Kat told them who her parents were, they'd pretend to have heard of them, and say, wow, that's so cool, and she'd crackle with pride and loneliness.

"We're all going to die!" screams the Pringles woman, as the plane rolls.

"Not today," Kat shouts into the woman's ear, trying to reassure. "It's just physics! Thrust, drag, and a severe weather warning . . ." Then through the porthole window, a wavy hem of malachite-green sea. Dark gold sand. A patchwork of fields.

Kat sucks in her breath, Cornwall's rapid approach registering as one tiny shock, then another, until it's like dozens of acupuncture needles bristling on her scalp. The rest of her life—her six a.m. runs through streets of glass and steel; the industrious murmur of the Spring office; all the likes and shares and tweets—fades away, unreal.

And something small and scared inside Kat—normally bolted tightly down—loosens. As the plane bumps to the runway, tears blur her eyes. She wipes them fiercely on the ratty scarf, wondering what's going on. She hasn't cried for years—and no effing way is she about to start now.

3

FLORA

| | |

"YOU HAVE ARRIVED at your destination," announces the satnav. Oh god. Reluctant to leave the warmth and safety of the SUV, Flora listens to the Atlantic raging two hundred feet below. With a four-year-old in the car, it feels much closer. Like the ocean might rear up in a monstrous wave and suck them off the cliff to their deaths any minute. Her stomach registers this with a small convulsion.

Rock Point isn't quite the elegant Victorian villa she remembers; more a lonely old house that's been swept against the rocks, quite possibly with its tenants skeletonized within. Light thrown down by the windows bores across the drive and the wind-gnarled hawthorn tree to the rocky edge of the raised bank. Beyond that, it vanishes over the cliff edge, into the velvety dark. As might a young child. You wouldn't hear the scream.

Flora sucks harder on her antacid. They'd been so unsupervised here as girls. Left to roam. Build bonfires on the beach. Trusted not to run across the hot embers or fall or drown. She's not felt that free since. Giddily, stupidly free. It's a miracle any of them survived, frankly.

Rock Point too. While it's still standing, the salt has eaten into its white façade like acid on a tooth. What a costly restoration that's going to be. Adding jobs to an imaginary builder's list, her gaze travels from the keystone—dated 1841—to her childhood summer bedroom on the first floor then to the art studio at the very top, with its brow of small square windows squinting at the horizon. The hipped slate roof is as symmetrical as the house: you could fold it in half, like a napkin, and its corners would meet. But there any sense of order ends. Above Rock Point, the bruised uplands of fields and moor hunch under a vast cold sky.

Flora is struck by a powerful urge to reverse. Drive back down the potholed ribbon of lane, edged by steep banks of rock, past the abandoned mines and collapsed cottages—caved in, like warnings—away from this desolate place. Three hundred miles back to Surrey, her husband, Scott, and their smart house in its leafy, gated cul-de-sac of executive homes, with its gentle microclimate of heated driveways and steamy Nespresso machines.

But she's run out of bribery treats. Her ears are still ringing from listening to the same children's audio stories on repeat—"Again, again," Raff demanded—until she thought her brain would explode.

Also, she's promised Raff adventures. ("I don't like adventures, Mummy." "You will.") And she'd never let down Daddy. Whatever her mother says—"selfish bastard"—he's always been there for her, at least when she really needs it. And she's got a gut feeling something's not right. For the last few months—since Dixie's funeral, really—he's been vague about his whereabouts, only the international dialing tone announcing he was in Paris—*Paris!*—on Christmas Day. When she has managed to see him in person, he's seemed guarded yet excitable as if he'd pulled off some sort of secret criminal heist. All compounded by this short notice, out-of-character, out-of-the-blue, season-inappropriate invitation to Rock Point.

But . . . if Kat and Lauren think the reunion "a marvelous idea," she certainly does too. It's a rare opportunity for them to hang out as sisters again rather than three women who happen to share half their DNA, whose draw to each other is usually overcome by its opposite repelling charge. Yes, they *will* make new Rock Point memories. Overwrite the old.

Nothing can go wrong. Not this time. She's brought notes on rainy-day excursions; directions to the nearest A and E; a menu plan. Emergency supplies: Children's ibuprofen, aspirin, pinworm treatment, loo roll. Unwaxed lemons. Clothes to cover all weather events. Even a bathing costume she's zero intention of using. ("Bring swim stuff," Kat messaged last night. No kiss, no emoji, nothing). Most importantly, she will stay stone-cold sober and on high alert for signs that anyone is on the verge of talking about *it*. For the sake of harmony, the day of the eclipse must stay sealed, unmentioned. Like an affair if a marriage is to survive.

But first, game face. Grabbing a hairbrush from the glove compartment, Flora smooths her shoulder-length blond hair—carefully blow-dried that morning—applies a slick of nude lipstick, and inspects herself in the mirror. Christ. How did the lithe, spirited creature in *Girls and Birdcage* turn into this? Knackered. Puffy faced. No, she'll call it: fat. A thirty-something mum with an inexplicable digestive issue and a bladder that, to her deep shame, leaks. She will never tell her sisters this as long as she lives.

Raff was a humongous baby: almost ten pounds. Forceps. Thirty stitches, like a zipper. She's forgiven him now. In the rearview mirror, she eyes her mini bullock of a son, his clenched fists and cross frown. (First word: "No.") Her heart squeezes. He looks pitifully alone in the carapace of this giant SUV, the seats either side of him empty, awaiting siblings. A reminder it's the wrong time in her cycle to be away. Scott hasn't worked that out yet. But he will. She knows he will.

Pushing open the car door, Flora lurches into a rushing wall of air, a briny pong mixed with wood smoke. The wind slaps her cheeks. Sucks at her sheepskin vest like a rabid hoover nozzle. The weather is an affront, a rude shock.

What was she expecting? The smell of Ambre Solaire and coconut-sweet gorse. Well, yes! In her mind, this place *was* summer.

"Hi, stranger."

"Kat!" Flora whips around. Her jaw drops, the cold clinking against her fillings. They've not seen each other since that charged, difficult drink after Dixie's funeral back in October. Kat's work phone had flashed in the center of the table, like some sort of air traffic control radar charting all the unspoken issues flying between them.

Has Kat had something done? Clearly, *she's* not spent her holidays face down in a tin of Celebrations. Kat looks sleek, skinny, and international. Her jacket's hood is extravagantly trimmed with fur—Flora disapproves yet longs to stroke it—showcasing her sharply drawn features, a delicious Roman nose, the sort of androgynous beauty that gets better with age. Lean runner's legs. Thighs that could crush a jackfruit.

There's a peculiar moment when Flora—who prides herself on being able to make small talk with anyone at any time—cannot think of a word to say. They are now close enough to hug, like normal sisters. But it doesn't quite happen. Because they're not normal sisters.

Flora slid into the world first: no one can take this from her. No one. Five months later, Kat was born, in secret, at the exclusive Portland Hospital. As the legend goes, Blythe Stein, Kat's American-born actor mother—debuting during what critics call "Finch's fertile L.A. period"—knocked on Flora's mother's Kensington front door, baby Kat in her arms: "Didn't he tell you there was another?" Charlie forewarned his ex-wife and ex-mistress the next time. It didn't help. Thirteen months after Kat, Lauren was born, six weeks premature. And in Lauren's mother, Dixie—Charlie's young, pierced, left-field lover—Annabelle and Blythe discovered a common enemy. Little wonder Dixie only introduced Lauren into their lives when she was nine. Oh, Dixie. Dead at fifty-eight. Even Flora's mother wept.

"How are *you*, Kat?" Flora always emphasizes the "you," to prove she's interested in the answer.

"Lauren's still going straight to voicemail." Kat doesn't feel the same need to deal in social niceties. Her voice is deep, husky, sure of itself. "My money's on a no-show."

"Oh, no!" But Flora suspected Lauren might lose her nerve since her sister is all nerve, like a rescue animal with a bit of history. Their canary down the mine. You don't get over damage like that, not really. Why else would she snub Flora's offer of hospitality over Christmas? Volunteer at the hospice where Dixie died instead? Not that Flora's smarting. Not at all.

"Mummy . . ." The first snuffling wail. Flora rushes back to the car. "Hey, sweetheart, we're at the seaside!" Because Kat is watching, she makes a mess of unbuckling the car seat and twists Raff awkwardly out of it, and he screams.

Kat steps back.

"Always a bit cranky when he wakes up," she says, feeling judged, struggling to hold on to her smile. "Say hello to your amazing Aunty Kat."

Raff buries his face into her neck, crushing his sweaty curls against her chin. "No."

Flora can't help but be a little gratified by her son's rebuff. Even if it is lost on Kat. Her sister is so busy these days. So unneedy it's selfish. Flora can't find a way in. How is it possible to be standing inches from somebody and miss them horribly?

"Wow," Kat says. "He's got so big, Flora."

"Four-year-olds have a habit of growing." Flora sniffs. Kat's not seen Raff since the disastrous Hyde Park picnic in September; a red ants' nest, a Tube strike, two cancellations—Lauren and Dad—and an indecent amount of wasted food Flora pretended she'd just "cobbled together" but had spent hours preparing.

Kat is back on the phone again. "Oh, answer, Lauren."

Flora feels a small sting of jealousy since an actual phone call with Kat is a rare privilege. If Kat does pick up—Flora's tactic is to ring repeatedly until she does—she answers with "Sorry, not a good time, I'll call you right back." Then doesn't.

"I need to warn her," Kat says, flicking her hood down, revealing a chic crop, shorter, more severe than ever.

"Warn . . . ?" Flora says blankly. When they were young—or *before* as she thinks of it—she was able to read Kat's thoughts. But theirs is a faulty connection now.

"Unexpected guest." Kat winces. "Bertha."

Flora almost drops Raff. "You're not serious?"

"Yep." Kat hangs up. "The parrot's foster carer dumped her at

Dad's flat yesterday. No, Dad didn't tell me either. He's in the conservatory right now, trying to settle the diva into her old cage."

Berthingham Palace. The large, tiered birdcage hinges open in Flora's mind, the eclipse summer spinning inside it, a cyclone of tiny yellow feathers. She clicks it shut with a shudder.

"Bertha is an African Grey, Raff." Kat waggles his foot, and his half-hanging sock is ripped away by the wind. "A parrot. A *talking* parrot. Like an Alexa!"

"Don't like Alexa," says Raff flatly. "I like sharks."

Kat grins. "Well, Raff, if you like scary biting things, you'll love Bertha."

Raff's hands tighten around Flora's neck.

"Aunty Kat is teasing," Flora says quickly, cupping his bare foot and worrying whether Lauren's bird phobia might have a genetic component. "Bertha's terribly old, sweetheart."

"No, she's a boomer. African Greys can live sixty years," Kat says. "In fact, Raff, Bertha was at Rock Point last time we . . ."

"*Kat . . .*" Flora warns, with a shake of her head. For a held beat, a funny sort of charge crackles between them. An understanding, she hopes. Rain starts to fall, accelerating from drizzle to downpour in seconds.

They shriek and laugh and run toward the gabled porch, the promise of warmth spilling out of the door's fanlight. Under its shelter, Kat, struck by something, touches Flora's arm. "It's weird being back. Deeply weird. And I am just . . . well, I'm actually really glad you're here, Flora," she says, almost sheepishly, as if she might have just changed her mind on the matter. "That's all."

"Oh." Flora blinks, momentarily floored. "Well, I . . . I'm glad too, Kat." With the collapsing sensation of a dawning truth, she realizes she's spent weeks telling dozens of people—Scott's relatives, the neighbors who complained about her garden fairy lights, the school mothers who never invite Raff back for playdates—how lovely it is to see them when it isn't. When, deep down, all she really wanted was this. Her sister. Raw salt air and rain and wood smoke. Rock Point.

4

LAUREN

| | |

Rock Point

1 AUGUST 1999

twenty years earlier

D AD BURST OUT of the porch into the evening sunlight and
threw open his arms. "Ha, my very best creations."

I held my breath, like at the top of a roller coaster, just before
hurtling down. Kat and Flora ran to him, kicking up clouds of
sandy dust. I hung back holding the digging-in straps of my army
surplus rucksack, awaiting my turn, heart drumming, excitement
and shyness rolling over me in waves. I guessed he'd been waiting
for our mothers to leave, that this was what Mum called "parallel
parenting"—lines that never quite met, like me and my sisters didn't
much either, not the rest of the year. Rock Point brought us together.
Like a stage set erected just for us, then packed up at August's end. I
couldn't imagine it in winter.

Flora threw herself at Dad. Tiny explosions of jealousy and awe
popped in my chest. She looked too big to be spun around but Dad—
wiry and strong—lifted her easily. Flora screamed, her sunshiny hair

flying out. He planted her down, staggering and laughing. Kat grabbed Dad, hugged him tight, with her eyes screwed shut. Like she'd never let go.

My turn? I wasn't sure. I'd rehearsed it too many times in my head. Wanted it too much. Crossing off the days in my Greenpeace calendar, all year I'd counted down to the moment the huge white house would rise on the cliff—and I would be a Finch sister again. But I couldn't even think how to hold my arms. So, I tracked a kittiwake as it flew toward the moor where my pen pal Gemma lived. Unlike the hot blue sky above Rock Point, inland it was black, ugly and swollen with rain. You can have two weathers in the sky at the same time here, Gemma always said. And it can change in a bleeding blink.

My sisters had changed too. Since I'd last seen them at Dad's Soho flat, three days before Christmas—eating from plates on our knees; "Fairytale of New York" playing over and over—they'd got taller and bustier, more dazzling, bolting somewhere out of reach. The girls who'd turned cartwheels across the lawn in previous Rock Point summers had gone.

Flora walked differently, boiled with beauty. She wore a flowery mini dress with dainty straps that tied around the neck. White-blond hair tumbling down her back. Eyes blue as summer. Kat was spikier and cooler, a mouthful of braces. Thicker shorter hair, a mix of blond and brown, like Weetabix. Strong swimmer's shoulders in a tie-dye vest top—on show, leopard-print bra straps; I could only dream—and denim cutoffs with frayed edges, the insides of the pockets hanging like tongues. A CD Walkman in one hand. Head-phones around her neck. No self-doubt. The gap between us had got even wider.

At thirteen, I remained the least Finch. I had Mum's Molloy sur-name, her pale Irish skin and dark bushy hair. Also, a Pepsi-colored birthmark on my cheek, like a baby's handprint. My teeth were not straight like Flora's; like Kat's soon would be. My clothes were wash-faded with other people's names written on their labels. Apart from the odd bargain, my stuff came from charity shops. Better for the planet, Mum said. Back in Jericho, Oxford, a scruffy sort of place, it didn't matter. That summer, facing my half sisters from London—Flora lived in Chiswick, Kat in Notting Hill, like the new movie—while wearing secondhand scout shorts and a banana-print T-shirt, it mattered a lot. Luckily, I'd packed my new Hennes dress—bought in the summer sale—which I'd purposely not worn so it still smelled of shop.

Other differences I'd never admit to Mum stung more than ever that summer. Kat and Flora had arrived in cars. With piles of smart suitcases. We'd turned up on foot, sweaty, having hiked from the bus stop after a six-hour train journey, and my tatty rucksack was stuffed with books. (My biggest fear at that point was still running out of things to read.) Mum wore her faded denim dungarees and Glaston-bury Festival 1994 T-shirt; silver nose stud; henna tattoos lacing her wrists. Worst of all, I hadn't dropped her hand fast enough: my sisters had spotted us.

They'd also stared when Mum wouldn't stop hugging me good-bye; "I love you big as the world, Laurie, okay?" Like I was six. But Kat's mum, Blythe—voice like the movies, huge black sunglasses—just blew kisses from an open-top car, like she couldn't get away fast enough. Flora's mother, Annabelle, pregnant as always, rushed in to use the toilet, hug Granny—"Thank goodness for you, Pam, organizer-in-chief, I'll leave my teen in your capable hands! Good luck!"—then, ignoring my mum, like she didn't exist, squeezed her beach-ball belly back into her Range Rover, stuffed with dogs and squealing blond children—Flora's infant half siblings from the new marriage—and zoomed off. Mum was the last to leave. Refusing a lift from Grandpa, she strode back to the village, piercings sparkling, retracing our long route home. Even though I knew I'd miss her badly, like I always did, it was a relief when she'd left. At Rock Point everything was bigger. Skies. Rooms. Feelings. There was more to go wrong. And to survive it I had to leave Mum behind.

With a plasticky clink of bangles, Granny's hand landed on my shoulder. "A nice cold glass of homemade lemonade?"

"Yes, please, Granny. I'd love that. Thank you very much," I replied with terrified politeness.

It was my fourth summer at Rock Point but my worry about appearing badly brought up hadn't faded. I was desperate to prove myself, out of loyalty to Mum, who'd homeschooled me until I was eight, and mostly on the road, in vans and yurts and hostels because she'd taken me traveling around the world. "Like some sort of wretched little circus animal," Granny once said.

Deeply tan, Granny's cheeks were textured like a walnut. She'd tucked green and yellow budgies' feathers into the ribbon of her straw hat, which almost covered a whip of thick rock-gray hair, and wore a long swishy turquoise dress, with a row of shells, like milk teeth, sewn around the V-neck. In one hand, she held a wicker trug full of eggs—brown, stippled with chicken poo—that the farmer would leave outside the front door: a promise of the huge Rock Point breakfasts to come. "Bertha will be terribly pleased to see you, Lauren," she said, smiling, which was her way of saying she was too. Granny's heart was like a sea anemone. It closed if you reached for it. And although it played dead a lot, it was alive. "Ah, here's astronomer Finch."

"Laurie!" Grandpa appeared from the lane where he'd been waving off the cars.

Granny didn't do hugs—I had never even seen her kiss Dad; Mum said she had "a lot to answer for"—but Grandpa did. His nailbrush mustache spiked my cheek. He smelled warm and woody, like the inside of a violin case. I had started to love Grandpa properly by then. But I'd known from the first time we met at Rock Point that we'd be friends: he told me he had nine little presents waiting in his study—books, sweets, a shark's tooth—to represent all the birthdays he'd missed.

"I say, Charles . . . Charles?" Granny called out shrilly. "Aren't you going to say hello to Lauren?"

Everyone turned to stare. A bit of me died.

For an awful moment, Dad looked surprised to see me, like he'd forgotten he had three daughters turning up for August, not two; a reminder that I'd once overheard Granny say, "For the love of god, Charles, how many more are there?" and she'd only fully accepted I was related after some sort of test.

Until four years ago, I hadn't met my grandparents in person or Kat and Flora. I'd spoken to Granny and Grandpa on the phone, and knew that mythical half sisters existed and things were "tricky" between my mum and their mums. Although I'd often fantasized about having siblings—they'd look just like me, we'd share all our secrets— Mum was my whole world, and we'd lived abroad, far away.

Mostly, I fantasized about Mum and Dad being together. They were when I was born. I had evidence, a photo: Dad cradling me in his arms, against a T-shirt saying *The Clash* and Mum, head on his shoulder, looking much younger, wearing one of his splattered painting shirts, and a huge smile. When he did "the bad thing" Mum wouldn't talk about, me and Mum set off on our travels, and I didn't really see him much. Mum said it was too upsetting if Dad blew into my life, then out of it again, that he was only reliable in his unreliability. But I sensed this wasn't the only reason, that a spiky big thing sat between them. The sort of thing grown-ups like to pretend isn't there and children can reach out and feel. And all this history— the photo, the mythical sisters, the bad thing—whooshed through me in the second between Granny calling Dad's name and Dad calling mine.

"Laurie!" he shouted.

Grandpa stepped back as Dad ran across the stony drive, the wind inflating his white shirt. I could feel Kat and Flora watching, frowning. Like there was only so much of him to go around, and I was about to steal something of theirs.

"Come here, you." A short, longed-for hug. Painter's arms. Turpentine. Sweat. Camel cigarettes. "Ah, little Laurie. Good to see you." His eyes were gray as pencil lead. A smudgy, soft one, like a 4B. His smile was wide enough to see pink gum. "It's been a while, right?"

Eight weeks. Three days.

"Wow, you're looking so much like Dix," he said. Out of the corner of my eye, I saw Flora and Kat glower, like any mention of my mum was an insult to theirs. "You've shot up too."

I instantly felt taller.

Dad raked his wavy blond hair—longer than I'd last seen it, hitting below his shirt collar—and beckoned Kat and Flora over. We stood in a little circle, not looking related—mismatching dolls from different sets—and stared hungrily at him.

Funny and warm and vivid-alive, Dad was one of those people who made you feel like it was your birthday, even when it wasn't. When I visited him in London, he'd take me to galleries, smoky cafés, and arts clubs for lunch. But he was still quick to vanish, for weeks sometimes. To London or New York or Paris: his work was exhibited all over the world. He always left you wanting more of him. We weren't the only ones either.

Dad had what Mum called A Reputation. "The bad boy of portraiture. Let your wife sit for him if you dare," said *Tatler* magazine: the scissored-out profile was stuck on his red toilet wall in Soho alongside rude cartoons by artist friends and a stuffed deer head, one eye missing, cigarette jammed in its mouth, hanging above the cistern. The article's words were inked on my brain too, although I didn't really understand them.

"Listen, your old man has laid on some special entertainment. A total eclipse. How about it? The first since 1927. On August the eleventh, this place is going to be mobbed. But my girls have a ringside seat. Also . . ." He nodded at our grandparents, shuffling through the gate that led to the garden. "I'll warn you now, Grandpa is *extremely* excited and has been mining facts on umbral winds, occultation, and pinhole cameras all summer. Just for you."

Flora groaned. Kat slipped on her headphones. Dad pointed at the low sun, a fat glowing ball, impossible to imagine going out. "The Incas would offer a human sacrifice to the sun god after an eclipse. Who shall we pick?"

My sisters' eyes made a minuscule flick in my direction.

"The other thing—take those things off your ears, Kat—I'm going to paint you all this August. Together, you know, a portrait. What do you reckon?" It wasn't a question.

A smile spread inside me.

"What's our hourly rate?" Kat punched Dad's arm.

"You'll go far, Kat." He laughed. He laughed a lot then. Didn't take anything too seriously, just his art. "Come on. Studio."

"*Now?*" Flora widened her eyes, edged by the longest, thickest lashes I'd ever seen on a human. "But I will literally die if I don't jump into the sea in the next thirty seconds."

"I need to see you all in situ. It won't take long. The Atlantic isn't going anywhere." Even Kat knew there was no point arguing. When it came to his work, Dad had a rushing energy that pulled you along with it—and you never knew quite where you'd end up.

———————

THE STAIRS GREW narrower. The air still. Old servants' rooms, then a junk room, the top floor was turned into an artist's studio back in the 1970s or something like that, when Dad was starting out and didn't have any money. A small pendant light, its frosted glass shade like a flower, swung in a draft. A few steps behind me, Kat and Flora whispered and laughed, and I could tell they'd seen each other recently. Maybe they'd had sleepovers in London, where I wasn't.

It always took time for them to get used to me again, I reminded myself, trying to stay cheerful. At the end of August, our mothers would come to pick us up and comment on how tanned we all were—Granny didn't trust sun cream; "You know where you are with a sunhat"—and how well and happy we looked. Me, Kat, and Flora would beam at each other, the long summer days tying us together for another year, like a beautiful blue ribbon wound round and round. That was how I liked to imagine it anyway. How I wanted it to be. There was some way to go.

"My studio has missed you, little Laurie." Dad held open the green door and I threaded through into the sky. Dazzling and light, the studio stretched half the length of the house: ocean on one side, the moor on the other. Outside, gulls glided, barely moving, dangling on wires. The sound of the waves was a conch-shell-to-the-ear whoosh, and the sunset had turned the sea candy-floss pink.

Unable to stop smiling, I drank it in. Dad's guitar propped against the wall. The paint-gobbed floorboards. The heap of rags in the corner. On the trestle, half-used tubes of paint, brushes, palettes, a hammer, tape, and sandpaper blocks. Metal clamps screwed to the table edge. Around the big sink, jars. On the shelving, more jars: varnishes, glazes, oils, binders, resins, thinners, epoxies, solvents, and rabbit skin glue pellets. The animal skulls I collected from the moor. A narwhal's tusk. All a jumble, waiting to be tidied by me.

Dad's proper studio was an old button factory in London's East End. He painted important people there, and he had proper assistants. But at Rock Point he "mucked around" and I'd seized the role of helper, mixing things, washing brushes, organizing. It was the only part of the house where I felt at home. Unlike my sisters, I'd learned its language: scumble and saturation; fat over lean; filbert and fresco; top-tone and tooth; gesso and ground. The stories sat in the fat metal tubes of paint. Bone Black was made of charred animal bones. Cobalt gave you cancer. Lead White sent you curly whirly cuckoo.

Kat sniffed. "Has something died in here, Dad?"

He patted his jeans pocket for his cigarettes. "Quite possibly."

The smells were the best bit: oily, metallic, like a slipped bike chain, thin and chemical, that raw rubbing-alcohol scent. "Don't sniff anything or you'll end up high as a kite," he'd mutter, cigarette balanced on his lower lip. He wasn't allowed to smoke in the studio either. Too many flammables. But he didn't care about things like that. "It's Cornwall," he'd shrug.

"Tunes." Dad turned on his stereo, a silver tower, with speakers that moved in and out like black lungs. David Bowie. He'd played his songs so many times we all knew the lyrics. But it was the first day so it was a bit awkward, and no one sang along to "Changes," like we would by the holiday's end.

"Sit, sit." Dad gestured at the white sofa. To the left of it, he'd positioned the big birdcage my sisters had shut me inside my first Rock Point summer, feeding me crackers through the bars—"You can be our new pet," Kat had said—until Grandpa intervened. I tried not to think about that. "Flora, center," Dad said, frowning. "Kitty Kat, right. Lauren on the left." I was glad to be closest to the window. It meant I could keep an eye out for Gemma, who would surely call round soon.

As we fidgeted—flicking hair, adjusting elbows, Flora trying not to squish her thigh against the seat in case it looked "flabby"—the sofa's loose covers slipped about, releasing the smell of sunbaked cloth and hot cars.

Dad adjusted the cage, pushing it with the toe of his trainer. Tapping a cigarette out of its squashy packet, he stared at us, turning from Dad into Charlie Finch the Artist, his gaze a force you could feel. We were objects to position in space. Like fruit in a bowl. He lit his cigarette, then planked it across the top of a dirty mug and picked up his camera. "Lauren, shift closer to Flora."

Flora's thigh was soft and warm. She smelled clean. I worried I didn't. Mum refused to buy deodorant: we used a crystal thingy that didn't really work. A second later, Flora moved her leg so we weren't touching.

"Seriously." Dad lowered his camera. "Kat, what's with the feral vibe this summer?"

"Please don't say 'vibe,' Daddy." Flora piled her hair to the top of her head. "You're too old to say 'vibe.' It's horrible."

Kat smiled, baring her metal braces. "And we're too old not to be paid."

"My subjects generally pay me, darling." He lifted the camera again. *Click. Click.* "All your mothers take a pretty cut, don't you worry."

The checks didn't always arrive. But Dad would always send Mum flowers for Mother's Day. Fancy London florist bunches, with curled ribbons and honking lilies—exotic flowers to remind Mum of her travels—or white orchids in pots, with gray tangled vine roots. Mum's bestie, Becca-from-the-barge-with-pink-hair, would insist Mum refuse them on principle. She didn't. "If life throws you something beautiful, take the gift," she'd say. And I'd wonder if that was what she said when she fell pregnant with me too.

"Lauren, this way. Not the window." Dad snapped his fingers.

Caught out, I blushed. My thoughts had drifted disloyally to the moor. Gemma.

"*Et finis.*" The camera swung down on its leather strap. He was Dad again. "Thank you, Finch Sisters."

A sweet sense of belonging melted over me. I wanted him to say it again. *Finch . . .*

"Half." The word shot out of Kat staple-sharp. "We're only half sisters, Dad. It's totally different."

5

LAUREN

| | |

2019

THE METER'S GLOWING digits climb in the gloom of the
taxi. Less than a mile from Rock Point, Lauren can bear the
unnecessary expense no longer and asks to be dropped off in the village, assuring the nice old cabbie she's fine, knows exactly where she
is. After the long journey she needs to walk. And work out how she'll
avoid the trip wires at Rock Point. She cannot risk having a panic
attack in front of her high-functioning sisters. The humiliation of it.
If she is to freak out, she'll do it alone.

Head bent, the wind moving inside her puffer coat like a live
thing, she edges past the little church and onto a winding unlit lane.
The surrounding fields have a tremulous sheen, like the silky flank of
a panting black horse. But she's not scared. Not of the dark anyway.
Herring gulls are another matter. And possibly that bloke on the
train. She'd felt a spike of alarm when he got off at the same stop,
then hovered on the platform, as if wanting to ask her something.

She'd hurried away, taking no chances. He didn't follow her taxi: she checked.

She looks around again, just to be sure. Lights twinkle in the village pub but no one else is out in this, a batten-down-the-hatches, boisterous sort of night with a storm snarling at its edges. After five minutes or so, the lane twists left, and the horizon blows open, reaching into all directions, a fish-eye lens. The sea is obsidian, smudging into the sky. It takes her breath away. Fills her heart. The landscape is ancient, yet in the first days of this new year it also feels fresh and unwritten, like a blank sheet of paper.

And tomorrow she will indeed click the lid off her favorite ballpoint and write. "Dear G, Are you sitting down? You'll never in a million years guess where I am . . ." She'd give anything to see Gemma opening that letter in the Greenland science station. Her disbelief. The big wonky smile that presses a dimple into her left cheek.

Finally, Lauren has something to report after weeks of, well, nothing much. Working in the back rooms of the National Gallery's exhibitions department; at weekends, the coach to Oxford, back and forth to the hospice where Mum died and Lauren now volunteers, feeling at home pressed closed to life's tremulous fragility, its last prismatic shimmer before it all goes dark. Only the mosaic has kept her busy in her bedroom, sticking bits of glass to a board. Unable to face any parties, she completed a satisfyingly big mosaic section on New Year's Eve, absorbed by the jewel-like chips, the emerging pattern, as fireworks tore through the London sky. She'd probably have carried on like that, burrowing into her sadness, weeks muddying into months, if it weren't for Dad's invitation. Her dying mother's words chased her here too.

"I can't bear the thought of you alone, Laurie," Dixie had rasped very near the end. "Promise me you'll reach out to your sisters. Your

Finch family. Promise me." Of course, Lauren had given her word, never suspecting a reunion at Rock Point would soon test it.

And there it is. A glowing lantern on the cliff top.

Fighting the urge to turn back, she walks on until she's caught in a wrinkle of time, gazing up at the big white house again, enthralled and terrified, the leviathan thump of the waves vibrating through the soles of her boots. She's not sure how long she stands there, transfixed, slipping between the shores of girlhood and adulthood, before snapping back—it's January 2019, and she's thirty-three years old—and remembering her plan. She needs to get on with it. Seek out the spot she most fears.

The garden gate never was locked. There was little point since its wrought-iron spikes were undermined by the circular aperture in its upper half—designed to frame the moon; "the rock," as Grandpa called it—the width of a burly man's shoulders. Lauren hesitates, her heart thrumming in her ears, then steps into the alley of ivy, weighted with fat winter berries, and into the garden. It smells loamy, mineral, wet. Solar lollipop lights run alongside the main path, weakly illuminating clumps of hydrangeas, their dried flowers gray as skulls. The conservatory spills a skirt of light across the lawn. She must avoid this, lest her family spot her skulking and think her a basket case. More than they do already.

The sundial is still there. A cordyline palm. Spines of towering, desiccated echiums. Further on, the collapsed greenhouse, where Grandpa once grew his tomatoes. The old swing seat swims out of the gloom, its canopy shredded. And at the back of the garden, sheltered against the wall, under the shade of the pine, Lauren sees it. Feels it. A rectangle of black. A void, like an empty tomb. Her heart rackets, full of blood. The aviary.

Approaching slowly, she takes little sips of air. Feels tiny budgie feathers stuck in her throat, pointed hollow quills, sharp as fish bones. A familiar tightness in her chest is anxiety's warning sign. *Breathe.*

Peering inside, Lauren half expects to see her younger self, bony knees pulled up, balled in the corner. Instead, just a deserted playground of rotting swings and perches. She can picture the budgies still: the sickle markings on their feathers, like the scales on tropical fish. But the morning of the eclipse is fragmented, incomplete: she's never been able to hinge it fully open in her mind. All she really knows is what Kat and Flora—perhaps not the most reliable witnesses—told her afterward.

Breathe. Touch it. Take away its power, Laurie: her mother's voice in her head.

The cold metal fizzes against her fingertip. In her ears, a rushing sound. It takes a moment or two to process that she's okay. The aviary hasn't swallowed her. Exhaling with relief, she glances up at the sky and hopes her mother is proudly watching, nose stud glinting like a star.

On the front porch, Lauren drops her bag with a thump, flicks her fringe out of her eyes, and reaches for the doorbell. An avian screech stills her hand in midair. From *inside* Rock Point? It can't be. Which means the bird—some sort of monstrous gull, oh god—is nearby. Desperate to get to safety, she presses the brass bell with a frozen pink finger, and rings twice, long and hard.

6

KAT

| | |

THE PARROT CANNONBALLS across the entrance hall with a flash of blood-red tail feathers and another hellish squawk. Despite the maturity of her years, Bertha's livelier—and less obedient—than ever. "Oh, crap. Dad?" Kat shouts up the staircase. "Do something! Lauren's rocked up and the bird's gone completely mental."

Lauren's turned to stone. Her eyes big as eggs.

Kat tugs Lauren—bent double, hands clasped over her head, as if under enemy fire—down the central hallway of the house that leads to the kitchen, and the smell of burning. Kat slams the kitchen door behind them.

Lauren leans back against the wall, terrified, panting. With her enormous dark lemur eyes, the bright blue streak in her damp hair, she radiates skittery electricity, a thrum of the wild.

"God, I'm so sorry," Kat says, shocked by the force of Lauren's reaction, wishing she knew how to help. "We weren't sure if or when you'd arrive, you see, and . . . long story short, Granny's immortal parrot is back in Dad's care. He wanted her to have a fly about 'to settle her in,' which obviously went brilliantly." She steers Lauren to a chair and wishes Flora would hurry up—seriously, how long can it take to put a kid to bed?—and do her maternal thing. Kat's no good at it: HR recently sent her to a god-awful soft skills workshop. "Can I get you a glass of water? Tea? Vodka?"

Shaking her head, Lauren does a weird thing with her thumb, squeezing it tight with her other hand. "I . . . I can't believe I'm here," she stutters.

"Bloody hell, nor can I, Lauren." Kat marvels. Where did she find the courage? It's as if Dixie's death has emboldened rather than broken her sister. Or left her with little to lose. "I'm so impressed you came," she says honestly. "Good on you."

"Well, if I'd known about Bertha . . ." Lauren manages a trembling, transformative smile. She's got one of those plush French movie mouths with a slight overbite that can only be carried off by someone gamine, with psychological complexities. Dixie didn't believe in braces. (Unlike Kat's own mother, who also tried to give Kat a nose job for her sixteenth birthday.) Dixie didn't want to laser off Lauren's birthmark either: the café au lait stain seems more obvious than ever, intensified by her bereaved pallor. The sweet quirkiness Lauren's always worn like a floaty blouse now seems to be constructed from a denser, heavier fabric. "Right, coat. So you can't bolt."

Glancing anxiously at the kitchen door, Lauren peels off her jacket.

"So any intel about this"—Kat makes quote marks with her fingers—"announcement?"

"Sorry, no. No idea."

"Bah." Turning her attention back to her sister, Kat clocks the knee-faded black jeans, plaid lumberjack shirt, and chunky brogue boots, the laces frayed and the heels worn down. She reads a tumbleweed existence of flatshares in edgy postcodes and fleeting affairs with man-bun baristas; hollowing Hinge dates; a heart full of intense longing yet terrified of the irreversibility of its choices. A lack of disposable income. Because it makes her feel better, and she hates, really hates, the thought of her little sister alone, Kat tells herself Lauren's got a family of friends—skint, young, arty—who look out for her. But the grim fact is cancer has claimed Dixie. And Dixie and Lauren were close. Almost too close. The sort of co-dependent mother and daughter who went on holiday together—not out of a sense of duty, or to escape Christmas—and spoke two or three times a day. After that summer, Dixie was tiger-mum protective and held Kat and Flora at arm's length, as if she didn't trust their influence. Kat can't really blame her, not after everything that went down.

Her conscience fidgets. She wishes she'd made more effort since the October funeral, the last time she saw Lauren, that she hadn't so readily accepted Lauren's excuses of being busy. But as she and Lauren mostly message, Lauren too easily becomes abstract, reduced to ellipses and emoticons and notifications that carry a nagging low-level chase of guilt, like the sort of toothache that only hurts when you think about it. Yet in person, Lauren's just her lovely little sister again, random, offbeat, smelling of wind and earth and wet cloth, the sort who'd give you the last tin of tuna in her cupboard. And their relationship is not so complicated after all. Well, not quite.

"This house . . ." Lauren looks around with wonder. "It's a portal into the nineties, Kat."

"Ha, yes." Kat's short, awkward laugh comes out like a crack. "I keep expecting Granny to walk in any minute. Gin in hand. Bangles clanking."

Rich Tea biscuits. Cola ice pops from the freezer, smelling of fish fingers. Quiche. Farm eggs in wicker baskets. Don't sneak your broccoli to the parrot, girls. Heavens, jam first then cream, we're not in Devon! Now where is that hopeless father of yours? Wipe the sand off your feet. Kat, you'll have seconds of syrup pud, won't you?

"I know," says Lauren, as though she's being assaulted by the same déjà vu.

The large, airy room's sunflower-yellow walls have faded, bleached by the Cornish light. But the pine farmhouse-style kitchen looks little different, so too the rustic dining table where they ate many hearty meals, kicking each other under the tablecloth at private jokes; sat on those same rush-seated chairs. In the corner nook, the Lloyd Loom sofa, tatty and blue, piled with dusty ticking-stripe cushions: Kat had felt so cozy and cosseted there, nibbling Granny's oven-warm shortbread, a pilled blanket on her lap. Stacks of dated cookbooks—*Dessert Techniques, Jams and Pickles, Italian Feast*—still march along the shelf beneath the butcher's block island. And there's the same grubby radio, and the plastic cooking timer Granny would slap to silence.

All distracting reminders that Kat's hundreds of miles from her London office and Thames-side apartment, with its smart fridge and pristine stainless-steel kitchen she rarely uses. Marooned in a house with a disconnected landline, an erratic mobile signal and abominable Wi-Fi. A critical investor's meeting Tuesday morning. Her heart does a two-beat skip just thinking about it.

"I wonder . . ." Lauren murmurs, twisting in her chair and scanning the slab of pea-green kitchen dresser that's always loomed behind the dining table. Kat can't think what Lauren's searching for.

The dresser shelves are cluttered with the same flotsam that floated through her nightmares after that August: mismatched floral teacups; Granny's cabbage leaf–style bowls; a limb of driftwood; a striped jug full of dusty seabird feathers. All things she'd once found immensely comforting—her mother didn't do "crockery"—but turned into symbols of a golden world Kat helped shatter.

"Coming through with the beast!" Charlie bellows, knocking Kat out of her darkening thoughts and making Lauren gasp, "No!" He charges into the kitchen, his cloud of curls disheveled, his red-framed glasses askew, and his shirt hitched up over his belly, as if he hasn't so much caught the parrot as boxed a round with her.

Perched on their father's hand, Bertha fixes her merciless gaze on Lauren, who is rigid. "Ice and a slice, dear," the parrot squawks in Granny's shrill voice. *"Ice and a slice."*

"Christ," mutters Kat. "The bird forgets nothing."

"And no one." Charlie sweeps out of the French doors and into the wrought-iron conservatory. A few moments later, he strides back into the kitchen, rubbing his hands triumphantly. "The pterodactyl is safely back in solitary."

Still thinks he cuts a raffish dash, Kat thinks, with a mix of affection and irritation. Like one of those aging rock stars whose snake-hipped youth and predatory energy has been buried under a good cheese board. Still, she's glad he's in good spirits. Dixie's death hit him far harder than she expected. But what's with the spanking new red Nike Airs? The bleached teeth? The whiff of a desperation that makes her heart ache a bit. Or maybe it's just that the last time they were all at Rock Point, he was in his late forties, and everything was so different.

"Hey, you." Charlie kisses the top of Lauren's dark hair. He didn't kiss Kat's hair, she notes, not that she wants him to. "You're shaking, Laurie," he says. "Come on, Bertha was your best buddy once, remember?"

Of course, she bloody remembers, Kat thinks. But he has a way of handling Lauren.

"You're all bones." Cupping Lauren's shoulders, he examines his youngest daughter. Kat fights an unseemly spiky feeling when she registers the tenderness in his eyes. "I'm going to feed you up," he says. "Get some meat on you. So Bertha gets a tasty bite."

Lauren laughs. She actually laughs. If Kat had made the same joke, it'd have gone wrong. She's always offending somebody.

"Speaking of food." Kneecaps clicking, Charlie bends down and flings back the oven door. Smoke. "Damn. Where's Flora when needed?"

"Upstairs. Settling Raff. What can I do, Dad?" Kat asks vaguely, glancing at an alien landscape of pots and stained utensils and prehistoric spice racks.

"If a woman learns to cook, she ends up in a kitchen," her mother would say. When Kat was a kid, her meals were either fishcakes and frozen berries at the Ivy, or bagged salad and hummus from Tesco Metro; Saturday nights, a four-poster in a five-star hotel or a few hours sleeping, forgotten, on a nest of coats at a party. Rock Point was her safe place—clean sheets, regular mealtimes, a wicker picnic hamper lugged down to the cove, heavy with fruitcake—a refuge from Blythe's domestic chaos. An air pocket. A kind of bliss.

Charlie crashes the smoking enamelware pot onto the hob and lifts the lid. "Can someone light the candles? The less we can see of this carbonized chuck the better."

"Pimp it with herbs or something?" Lauren says doubtfully, peering over his shoulder at the bubbling, smoking casserole.

"Good idea. I'll rewild it. And it can sit for a bit. Luckily, I've stocked up on fizz. That'll distract the taste buds, eh? Do the honors, Kat."

As Lauren chops parsley—the knife looks unsettlingly large in her small childlike hands—Kat tries to decode the champagne. Two rows of gold foil noses in the fridge—what exactly are they celebrating? She lights candles stuck in old wine bottles and hurricane lamps, with dusty, dirty wax pooled in their bases and bumblebee skeletons from long-gone summers. The room starts to flicker and glow. But her mood is still sodium lit, city-primed, stuck on a different setting. "So, Dad, your announcement . . . ?" she asks, impatient to know why they're there. Maybe then she'll be able to relax into it.

"What announcement?" He insouciantly leans back against the kitchen counter and crosses his arms. The buttons on his denim shirt gape slightly over the barrel of his stomach, revealing thick, white whirls of hair.

Lauren looks up from the flashing knife with a bemused smile.

"But, Dad, you said . . . oh, very funny." Unable to leave it alone— she *hates* not knowing something—Kat goes in again. "Come on, is it about the future of Rock Point?"

"Ah. My clever Kitty Kat." His mouth twitches with a maverick smile.

A regressive thrill blazes through Kat. Still the smartest sister. Still always right. Still got it.

"Nothing gets past you, does it?" But there's a dangerous glint in her father's eye as he says this. A funny sort of truculence in the way he tosses handfuls of herbs into the pot, disguising the blackened, smoking mess beneath.

7

FLORA

|||

SHH. THE STORY'S about to start." Flora presses play on the audio book. Raff glares reproachfully from the single bed she's dragged closer to her own. She wants to hear Raff's snuffling at night here, not just those waves rampaging on the rocks below. The bare boards creak underfoot as she pads across the room in her 50 deniers, trying to ignore the mouse droppings, the damp draft slurping at her ankles.

Outside the window, the sky shakes. Sea spume flicks against the glass. As a girl, she'd loved these Atlantic storms; always the first to run outside, spinning, arms wide, mouth wide open to catch the rain-drops. Now she worries a slate will whip off the roof and smash into Scott's new SUV.

Who the heck is that? A colossus of a man, with a dog. Just stand-ing in the lane, hunched against the wind, hands in his pockets, hood up and brazenly staring at the house. Hating the thought of being mistaken for an unfriendly emmet—as the Cornish call tourists—Flora waves enthusiastically. But he ignores or doesn't see her, turns his shoulders, and melts away into the turbulent night. The sting of disquiet is followed by a small frisson.

"I don't like it here, Mummy."

Clenching her jaw, Flora stays facing the window, trying to channel the patient mother she constantly tries and fails to be. "Yet. Raff doesn't like it *yet*." She grabs the curtains, habit making her rub the soft nubbly linen between finger and thumb. Before Raff, she'd worked for an interior design company, a small, barely profitable outfit that she'd loved, earning far less than her childcare costs if she returned. Every day she thinks of that life rolling on without her, like a favorite series that's recast its lead character. "You're doing the most important job in the world now, Flo," reassures Scott—an insurance risk specialist—who nonetheless refuses to consider the post himself.

"House is ghosty."

"Oh, Raff." She swishes shut the curtains, returns to her little boy, and brushes the curls off his forehead. Refusing to look at her, Raff clings to the grubby Tiny Tears doll he bought at the school fair and sleeps with every night, unsettling his father. "No ghosts here, I promise," she lies, tucking him up in a patchwork quilt snatched from her own childhood summers: she'd fall asleep counting the fabric hexagons, paisleys, checks, and stripes, loving the way they all slotted perfectly together.

"Don't go, Mummy." He pulls on her hand, her gold wedding band, which doesn't swivel. Is it possible to put weight on your *fingers*? Kat will be able to tell. Kat can see if you've put on a gram. It's one of her superpowers. That's it. Decided. Flora will wear her fun fake pearl necklace. She'd worried it was too much. But she needs a decoy. Yes, and her sparkly bag.

"Grown-up time now, Raff. I love you. Night-night, sweetheart."
When she kisses his cheek, it's hot with the resentment of being deserted in a strange bedroom. He sulkily turns away to face the wall.
"I'll leave your lamp on, okay?" she says gently, trying to hide her
impatience to get downstairs, and swiping at the clothes moth hovering above her dress.

On the landing, Granny's antique Swedish tall-case clock—sky
blue, gilt accents—grabs at her heart, just as it always did. She runs
a finger up its flank, which feels cold, sapless, and dead. Its loud,
musical chime used to punctuate the drift of languid summer days.
But its hands are frozen in time now. Its song muted. Probably for the
best. Sound is like smell, the way it chucks out memories. If Britney
Spears's ". . . Baby One More Time" ever comes on the radio, she
leaps to turn it off. Bowie's "Changes" is another. "Changes"
kills her.

Cupping the newel post, Flora pauses, mentally preparing. She
peers down the staircase, with its steep risers and wainscot paneling,
and thinks how easy it'd be to trip. Especially in this fitted claret
dress—has it shrunk?—and wedge heels, which demand an ungainly
sideways crablike descent. Gripping the banister, she vows to train
her mind on the present: she's no longer the girl who'd seek out sensation and drama and, finding none, would create it without thought
of the consequences. Because life's grown-up lesson—always, by its
nature, learned too late—is about consequences, mostly the unforeseen ones.

The entrance hall is fogged with wood smoke. Trying not to anxiously fixate on when the chimney was last swept for nests, if there's
a working carbon monoxide alarm, Flora arranges a big smile—her
default setting—and advances from the hall into the firelight flicker
of the front room. "Well, isn't this just lovely?"

Christ on a stick. Everywhere she looks, the past! Like one of those trick birthday cake candles you blow out only for them to flare again. It's a dusty, sun-bleached diorama of their childhood. Same chintz sofas they'd curl up in after a swim. The fireplace fender, its brown leather cracked and shiny like a saddle. Wooden shutters: folded back, exposing the gash of night. The window seat where Lauren loved to sit, arms wrapped around her bony knees, waiting for Gemma. On the shelves: small antique birdcages, books, binoculars, Scrabble, Monopoly, and VHS tapes of the classic movies—*Grease*, *It's a Wonderful Life*, *The Sound of Music*—they'd watch over and over. Her grandfather's brass telescope. Above the fireplace, the big glass jar of seashells they'd empty in a sandy, salty heap and rank according to prettiness, just as they'd secretly rank themselves. And the same distinct Rock Point smell—sea, damp plaster, and, oddly, self-rising flour. Sweet nostalgia sweeps into Flora . . . then something more disquieting. Collecting herself, she opens her arms as wide as the dress's tailoring will allow. "Woo-hoo! You made it, Lauren." She envelopes her sister in an overcompensatory embrace. "You look *so* well."

Lauren looks dreadful. Much too thin. Dark shadows under those extraordinary eyes. "It's been far too long," she says, truthfully, rubbing Lauren's arms. A memory sparks like static. Lauren's first summer at Rock Point; Daddy, walking into this same room, holding Lauren's little-girl hand—tiny, sticky with nerves—and slipping it into her own, saying, "Flora, look after your new sister." The conflict she'd felt, torn between pleasing her father and begging him to send this scrappy little girl away again. She'd just escaped three new half siblings at home—toddler twins, and a baby, who stole all her mother's attention—and didn't want another. Especially not the child of a woman who'd trapped her dad and got pregnant on purpose to fund her hippie lifestyle; the gospel according to her mother (and Kat's). A few years before that, Flora had asked her mother, "Is it true I have another half sister like Dad says?" and she'd stiffened and replied, "Technically."

Flora grows aware of Kat and Dad watching tensely from the sofa, and that her hands are still gripping Lauren's arms, as if trying to hold her safe—or push her into the fire. She whips them away.

"Can I read Raff a story?" Lauren's smile is hopeful, warm.

"Oh, no, thank you. I've just settled him," Flora replies far too quickly. Still, she's right to be cautious. Until she gets the measure of things, where Lauren's head is at. "His aunts are still a bit of a novelty," she adds, making it worse. She feels bad. Lauren may have snubbed her invitation to Christmas—the first, since Flora hadn't been able to mix her mother with Dixie; it should have heralded a new chapter—but she did drop off a rucksack of presents for Raff (many homemade). It's Kat who just dumps into Raff's savings account every year, as if her nephew were some sort of sponsor-a-white-tiger scheme. Kat never comes for Christmas either; oddly, she's always away. Her father the same. Although Flora's festive table is always rammed with her other half siblings—much younger, they grew up with a reserved banker as a dad, secure childhoods bereft of notable traumatic events—and Scott's relatives, it's the absent, troubled Finches she misses with an ache, year after year.

"Right . . ." Her father tugs up his shirtsleeve, checks his watch. Oh, the announcement, Flora remembers uneasily. She's not keen on surprises. Sucking in her belly, feeling a dress seam strain, she lowers to an elderly chintz armchair next to the footstool where Lauren's perched, elbows on her knees, grasshopper light.

Not wanting to sink too far into the musty chill of the seat—or the house itself—Flora sits upright, keeping her wits about her, clutch on her knee, legs crossed. Her tights catch. She glances around with a bright smile, trying not to mind that no one has complimented her outfit.

"Right, drinks." Lazily tucking his shirt back into the back of his jeans, Charlie walks to the small round table by the window—she remembers that too, the chip on its mahogany edge after Kat sent it flying during a ferociously competitive game of Twister. He pours a glass of champagne. "Bubbles, Flo?"

Flora inwardly tussles, forces her lips around the words "Not for me, Daddy."

A moment's confusion, then "Aha!" A delighted smile. He tilts the glass to her belly. "How many months?"

"I *knew* you were pregnant!" Kat grins. "From the moment I saw you, Flora."

"Congrat . . ." Lauren stops, her smile fading, mirroring Flora's own.

"I'm not pregnant." A wave of humiliating heat. "I'm doing Dry January."

A deadlocked hush. *Don't cry, don't cry.*

"Abstinence in Cornwall?" Her father laughs: she knows he's clumsily trying to make her feel better. "You'll get booted back over the Tamar. Anyway, you rather look like you could do with a glass."

Flora bristles. She wants to rush upstairs and grab Raff. Exhibit one: *this* is why I look fried. He still wakes in the night. Screams at the school gate. Has anyone else in the room scrubbed vomit off a sisal carpet? Or have any understanding of the sheer overwhelm of a mother's love? No. Especially not Kat, who ditched the best thing to happen to her—Kofi—simply because he loved her back. Flora never asked to be the only functional member of the Finch family. The only one to work at a relationship. To carry the weight of happiness for all of them.

"Here," Charlie presses a glass into her hand. "Blame me."

"We do," says Kat.

"I suppose one glass won't hurt." The drink works. It always does. Flushing her darker thoughts into the recesses of her mind where they live, dormant, like the tubers overwintering in her Tuscan pots at home. Her mind skips to her father's ultraviolet teeth—are artists meant to care about the shade of their enamel? Is this some sort of cry for help?—and then her sisters' outfits. Lauren's buried under a man's baggy plaid shirt—hip or hideous, Flora honestly couldn't say—boyfriend jeans and heavy boots, while Kat's wearing velvet trainers and a black boilersuit, which Scott, a frock-and-heels man, would loathe, and Flora suddenly desperately wishes she owned. In comparison to her sisters, her dress is too neighborhood-drinks-party. She hates it. And the stupid pearl necklace.

"Ah, a full set of daughters at last. Do we have a collective noun? A jury of daughters?" Charlie raises his glass. Behind him, the storm glitters, a whirl of wind and rain and stars. For a moment, Flora's not sure if someone's out there in the slick liquid shadows or if it's just the thrashing of the hawthorn. "Anyway, I've herded you down here for a few reasons," he continues, thumbing his red specs up his nose. "Apart from the most obvious one, which is, well, why not?"

There are *plenty* of reasons why not. Flora pulls at a loose thread on the armchair's brocade, imagines tugging and tugging, the house unraveling around them. The birdcages bobbing out to sea like lobster pots.

"First things first. This is not my announcement by the way, don't you worry. It gets better. I'll warm up. But . . ." Charlie sighs. "I've had a few physical issues. A bit of heart trouble. Minor. Survivable. Nothing to worry about."

Flora skims a puzzled, frightened glance at Kat. Lauren starts to gnaw on her thumbnail, and Flora has a ridiculous urge to slap her fingers down, tell her she'll ruin her polish.

"Then there's this." He gestures at his head.

Flora grips the chair's arms. Aneurysm. Brain tumor. Daddy cannot die; she simply will not let him.

"My hair," he says solemnly.

"Your *hair*?" Even by her father's standards, Flora's astonished by his vanity: his frizzy silver Neptune's curls were once wavy and flaxen, like Jude Law's in *The Talented Mr. Ripley*.

"Because of the messing around with paint I've done over the years, my doctor insisted on having a strand tested while I still have a thatch," he goes on.

"Oh. Oh, I see." A quiet devastation creeps over Flora. Out of the corner of her eye, she sees Kat's knee start to bounce: Kat's legs always betray her, escaping her steely control. Only Lauren sits still, rooted, listening carefully.

"Fascinatingly, it transpires I've got so many heavy metals in my body I should be a corpse." He laughs, rests his interlaced hands on his mound of belly, and waggles a foot gleefully, revealing jaunty striped socks. They are not ill-person socks. "Cadmium. Lead. Polyester resin. I'm a walking chemistry lab, girls. Med students will fistfight for my autopsy." His brio falters. "And it may have fed into the heart thingy-ma-jig. The doctors aren't sure."

"Jesus, Daddy." Flora squeezes her eyes shut.

"You should have painted wearing gloves," Lauren says, exasperated and gutted.

"You know I like to feel my materials, Lauren." Charlie shrugs, a nonbeliever in self-preservation or self-pity.

Their silence ripples outward, a physical thing. Flora can't work out how bad this news is, or what else there is to come.

"Well, nothing more boring than an old fart's medical condition, is there?" he says, brushing it aside. "And we all know you can smoke twenty fags a day and still live to a hundred, do everything right and . . ." He stops, caught in a twist of private pain, and Flora knows he's thinking of Dixie. "Anyway . . ." Flipping the mood, he smiles warmly again. "Looking on the bright side, at least I didn't let you girls finger-paint with the Lead White, eh? Poison you all too."

The word "poison" lands like a hard slap to the cheek. Flora startles. Upstairs, the tall-case clock rings out a random chime; like the past, not so dead after all. She shakily drains her glass. *It. Will. Be. Lovely.*

8

KAT

| | |

KAT HOLDS HER inscrutable poker face. What's the point in Flora trying to enforce a code of silence, then looking like she's stuck her finger into a plug socket when she hears a triggering word? She needs to get a grip. Lauren noticed; her searching gaze immediately tipped to Flora, where it remains.

"Well, I'm glad you did those tests, Dad." Kat kicks the conversation back to his health. "Knowledge is power, right?"

But, of course, this jars too—and Flora flinches again—since knowledge has never been equally divvied between them. For Lauren, 11 August 1999, sits in a penumbra of shadow, and there it must stay.

"All I know is that at my age it's like a bloody sniper's alley." Charlie checks his watch once more. Puzzling. This is a man who can be a week late for lunch. "Which means . . ." A solemn pause.

Outside, the wind builds like a drum roll. ". . . I've decided to live out the rest of my life exactly as I please."

"No shit," Kat splutters. "Who the hell were you trying to please before?"

"Kat," warns Flora, levering herself out of her armchair—necklace swinging, noosed around her neck—and weaving toward the champagne. Kat vaguely wonders when her naturally beautiful sister, who needs no adornment, started to wear aging ropes of pearls; a thought shredded by Bertha, who starts to shriek from the conservatory, adding to the lunatic air. Lauren's eyes magnify into inkblots. Three nights, Kat thinks. Christ.

"Which brings me to the other reason I wanted you all here . . ." Charlie nods at Kat, as if acknowledging their earlier conversation.

"Oh?" Flora frowns, clearly not liking their father's collusive nod, a suggestion of a chat she's not been party to. Rolling her champagne glass against her cheek, she lets out a small random laugh.

"Well, as you know, the old McKees—our trusty poet tenants—have deserted us after fifteen years. Despite their negligible rent, they claim Rock Point is too much," he says, put out by this. "So we have an empty house again. Burning a hole in my pocket." Tenting his fingertips, his gaze roves over them gently.

How those famous gun-gray eyes used to spark. Kat can still see him pacing back and forth from the easel, brush in hand, ceaselessly in motion, unstoppable, like he had hot coals in his Dunlops. Where did that creative zeal go? That egotistical burning molten core she'd so resented. With an unexpected swell in her chest, Kat realizes how much she misses it. Her father's alley cat heat. His messianic indomitability.

He hasn't produced a major work for years now. None of his paintings have sold for more than *Girls and Birdcage*, now in a private collection in London. It still hurts Kat that he flogged it. "Oh, it's flawed," he will say when pressed, a tiny muscle quivering under his eye.

Before they split last year, Kofi dared suggest that Kat's drive was ignited by the sale of their portrait, the realization that everything had its price, and some people were so rich they could buy a bit of you. The sale also proved that her father—a master of compartmentalization—was capable of detaching from anything. "So, you're putting Rock Point on the market?" she asks, speaking her thoughts aloud.

"No," he says slowly, heavily, with the air of someone who has considered this and cannot face it. "No, I'm not."

"Kat! How could he? It's been in the family *forever*," Flora says, as if Rock Point were Downton Abbey rather than a villa bought in the early sixties with profits from their grandfather's booming electro-domestics company. "And it should be kept for the next generation." She rolls her powder-blue eyes upward, drawing attention to Raff, and the children that Kat and Lauren haven't organized yet.

Kat opens her mouth to argue that the cleanest way of closing their family's darkest chapter—and to end the headache of owning a house so far away, perched on a bit of rock, battered by biblical storms—would be to sell. Then she zips it again. On some unconscious level, perhaps Dad doesn't want to close that murky chapter. Or he cannot. And would she trust him not to peddle the house for half its value just because he likes the cut of someone's coat? He's always been cavalier with money, oscillating between stinginess and excessive generosity, disinterest and obsession. She can only imagine the accounts on this place, if he's kept any at all. He stubbornly refuses her fiscal advice, even though she's the only member of the family with a numerical, analytical brain. She founded Spring, a digital health platform—"Wellness is the only true wealth"—five years ago and it's now valued at over ten million, employing eight members of staff (twelve including the interns). She works seven days a week. She's proved herself. Made it. Dad hasn't noticed.

"The tenants kept this place like a museum. Everything as Mother left it," he continues, cupping his knee with his hand. "Which is what Ma wanted. But she couldn't take it with her. So, a skip calls." Fingers piano-playing the air, he gestures around the firelit room. "I want rid. All of it. Birdcages. That highly disturbing stuffed fish."

"Not Ugly Humphrey!" Flora squeaks, and they all turn to stare at it, mugging in its dusty glass case on the wall. Who named it Ugly Humphrey? Kat can't remember now.

"I want a fresh start, Flo. And that means Rock Point being dragged kicking and screaming into the twenty-first century. Paying for itself with a proper rent, you know, a luxury let, like the reality shows on Netflix," he adds blithely, making Kat wonder if he's done any serious research at all. "I plan to split my remaining time on planet Earth between London and Paris and defer to a smart letting agent."

Bertha shrieks loudly from the back of the house.

"Oh, her days are numbered too," says Charlie. "I'm trying to find a new parrot parent, obviously. If you know anyone."

Flora leans back into the window seat, with a faint ripping sound.

"I invite you to take anything you fancy from the house this weekend." Distracted, he peers out of the window. "Rummage around. Rescue what you want."

A quicksand silence. Well. Certainly not the inheritance Kat's mother had in mind. She feels unexpectedly wrenched by the dismantling of their childhood summer haunt. The invitation to stick their hands right into the past and yank bits out. Resisting the urge to self-soothe with a Twitter scroll, Kat sneaks a glimpse at her phone. Eight missed work calls. It never stops.

"Kat, put that damn phone away for once." The table lamps start to flicker, threatening to plunge them into darkness. "I'm also going through my old sketches upstairs. They'll pay for the roof, septic tank, all that malarkey."

Lauren is staring at him in disbelief. "You've left sketches *here*, Dad? In the studio?"

Something unreadable travels across their father's face. And the funny undertow Kat's sensed since she arrived tugs harder, a sort of mistuning, like the crackle of a public radio when it picks up a private channel. "Odds and sods," he murmurs.

Rain starts to finger-tap at the windows. And Kat remembers the sound exactly, the soft, slightly metallic timbre of it, nothing like London rain; the way it made her feel warm and safe behind the stone walls. Rock Point hosted her happiest childhood memories—but also her worst. Unable to collate her feelings effectively, she springs up. "I'll grab a shower before we eat."

"Well, if you're quick," says Charlie, checking his watch again. "You'll need to run the water for ten minutes before you get a second-degree burn. The water system is all fire and ice. Mostly ice."

"Good." She takes a cold shower every day. It quiets the chattering in her head. "Speaking of which, who's swimming in the morning?"

Lauren sinks back on the footstool with a shy smile, like a pupil in a classroom who doesn't want to be picked out by the teacher.

"But you've got no subcutaneous fat!" Flora refills her glass. "You'll freeze like an ice pop! I bet you run in and straight out again."

"Er, when have I run away from anything?" Kat says, annoyed.

"His name begins with *K* . . . ends with *I*." Flora is always less conflict averse after a drink.

"Well, my reply begins with an *F* . . ." Her six-month relationship with Kofi was a glitch, a system crash, a joyous chemical delusion. No dating site would ever have matched them. "Not everyone lives in a rom-com like you and Scott."

This disarms Flora, who mistakes it for a compliment. "Gosh, you're right," she says after a beat, looking horrified. "I'm so sorry. I never should have . . ."

"Well, *I'd* just like to say," Charlie cuts in, and stands up slowly, with an odd smile. "It's never too late to fall into a rom-com."

"What? That's possibly the least Charlie Finch thing you've ever said, Dad." Kat studies him uneasily. "I am worried about your hair shafts now."

"So, *the* announcement . . ." Charlie takes a breath, visibly bracing. Out at a sea, a clap of thunder like a starter pistol. "I'm getting married in Las Vegas next month."

They shout over each other, *"What?" "Who?"*

"I've met someone." Charlie holds up his hands, flapping back their questions. "Rather, three months ago I met this someone again. I haven't seen her for twenty years. It's been a . . . a whirlwind. A joy. And she's just . . ." He shakes his head, boyishly awestruck. ". . . lit up my life."

On cue, an arc of car headlights sweeps across the living room. "I think you'll remember her," he calls over his shoulder, rushing to let in his new fiancée—and a violent blast of the gathering storm.

9

LAUREN

| | |

1999

A CAR COUGHED INTO the drive. Bertha's talons, light and strong as paper clips, tightened around my hand. Her scalloped gray feathers puffed. She had a sixth sense about people. Swiveling on the window seat, I parted the shutters with my fingers.

The car was dented like a tin can, with bits parcel-taped on. A woman emerged into the mirror-crackle of morning sunshine and just stood there, staring up at the house. Youngish—younger than a mum anyway—with wavy, Fanta-orange hair, she wore a white dress. With the sun behind, it was see-through, revealing the shape of her legs and a bright dot of light at the top of her thighs.

"One of Dad's friends, I bet," I whispered to Bertha. Me, Kat, and Flora called these friends "the hangery-ons." The sort that called him "Charlie, darling" and touched him unnecessarily. Every summer one or two turned up uninvited, not realizing Rock Point didn't run on the same rules as Dad's Soho flat. Granny patrolled the edges of August—"Finch family time"—like a grizzled guard dog. "Just passing," the hangery-ons would say even though Rock Point wasn't on the way anywhere but the sea. Dad would whisk them to the studio. Cigarette smoke, music, and laughter would roll down the stairs. But Dad didn't have sleepovers at Rock Point, not when we were there. Granny made sure of that.

The doorbell rang. Bertha mimicked it. She also did the telephone, dog barks, and sea shanties. Kat was teaching her Britney Spears's ". . . Baby One More Time." But Bertha's best trick was repeating overheard phrases in the voice of the speaker. The day before, the woman Grandpa called Cross-Cressida-from-Zennor popped over to complain about eclipse watchers "swamping the place," and Bertha squawked in Granny's voice, "ghastly woman," and Flora snorted lemonade out of her nostrils.

African Greys are smart as a human three-year-old. But Bertha was gifted—"Cleverer than Flora," Kat said—with an amazing memory and piercing mango-yellow eyes. Parrots need to remember complex navigational paths in the wild. When she flew across the entrance hall—her wings were never clipped—the jungle streaked through her. Granny had surrounded Berthingham Palace with potted palms, so she felt at home. It was still a cage, though. My parrots are born in captivity, Granny would say tightly, and you don't miss what you don't know.

I wasn't sure this was right, since a bit of me had missed having sisters before I met them. But I knew better than to say that.

The front door slammed. Bertha clicked her half-moon beak.

"It's that awkward age, of course," I could hear Granny saying. The visitor had penetrated the first line of defense and was in the entrance hall. "The girls come every August. It's the only time we get them, and it's like negotiating the Good Friday Agreement on an annual basis. Different mothers, you see." A sigh. Maybe Granny didn't understand why our mothers couldn't just be friends either. "And I'm still waiting for my new hip—us oldies don't matter to shiny Mr. Blair, it seems!—and I can't go chasing after girls on the cliff tops willy-nilly," she continued. "Herbert, my husband, can only think about this eclipse business. And their father's preoccupied with work. He's an artist." She sniffed.

Granny had wanted Dad to be a doctor. She'd sat for him once, years ago, around the time he met my mother. When Dad unveiled the portrait Granny was so offended, she didn't talk to him for four years.

"Is he painting here right *now*?" the woman asked, excitably. "Charlie Finch?"

My heart sank. She knew his name. She was a fan.

Granny wouldn't approve either. She enjoyed an exhibition opening, the fancy ones on Cork Street—hair done, long dress, gliding around as if on casters—but she didn't like Dad bringing "it" to Rock Point in August. Luckily, he took no notice: he couldn't turn his art on and off like the garden sprinkler. "Through here, please."

I tensed, watching the brass doorknob turn.

"Oh, there you both are. Step up!" Granny instructed.

Bertha flew, rippling the air, showing off her scarlet tail feathers, and landed on Granny's outstretched hand. African Greys are "one-man parrots," and that man was Granny. Bertha took dislikes to certain people. Last summer, she'd bitten Flora's finger, drawing blood. Granny smiled. "I did mention . . . ?"

The woman shook her head, shocked. Nothing prepares you for a parrot.

"Budgies too. Our noisy little ladies travel down from Hampshire with us and summer outdoors here." Sat deep in her deck chair, a cocktail in her hand, Granny watched the garden aviary as if it were the telly.

"Wow." I could see how much the woman wanted to edge away from Bertha's murderous stare, but she stood her ground. I respected this.

Also, she was interesting to look at. A big face and even bigger hair, red-gold. Her eyes reminded me of Granny's cocktail olives: green, glossy, with a notable convex bulge. There wasn't a straight line on her.

"It's amazing," she said. "Like being in a cruise ship or something."

"Oh, Rock Point is unsinkable," Granny said with a small laugh, like people do in movies moments before the ship hits an iceberg. "Angie, this is Lauren."

"Hi." Angie smiled at me, revealing a pearl of gum wedged against tooth and cheek. "You can call me Ange if you like."

I already knew I wouldn't.

"Lauren is the youngest of my son's three daughters." Granny's voice always went squeaky whenever she veered near the subject of our close ages. "Kat and Flora still swimming, dear?"

I nodded, suddenly wishing I'd stayed in the cove too. But I'd returned to wait for Gemma to call round.

"Now how are you in the water, Angie?" asked Granny.

"I'll be straight with you, Mrs. Finch. I sink like a sack of potatoes. Big bones."

"Oh." Doubt ran across Granny's face, then disappeared. "Well, Flora's done her lifesaving badge. Kat's won galas, all sorts. They look out for you, don't they, Lauren?"

I nodded. They didn't. Mum had no idea how unsupervised we

were at Rock Point either. I just told her Dad took us swimming, which he had done in other Augusts, hurling us into the water from the rocks, trying to get me used to the Atlantic: Mum had taught me to swim in warm exotic seas. And now that I was older I looked after myself, staying in my depth, away from the jellyfish and the deep swell.

"You're lucky having sisters." Angie's smile slipped slightly. "I'm an only."

I almost said I'd been an only once. But it'd have been too complicated to explain. Sweat itched the back of my knee.

"Angie's here about a job, Lauren," Granny said.

My heart sank further. I could feel the summer changing shape and had no idea how to stop it.

"I must confess," Granny said to Angie. "I haven't had a chance to check your references."

Angie's relief was obvious. But Granny didn't seem to notice. I realized she and Angie weren't actually talking, just trying to get something from the other.

"You've au-paired a bit?" Granny stroked Bertha's head with a fingertip.

"I've done a lot of assisting in art studios too." Angie's words shot out fast, like they'd been waiting.

"Remind me." Granny's gaze swept over Angie's filmy dress and stuck on the silver chain around her ankle. She frowned. "How did you hear about the job again?"

Angie tossed her hair, releasing the fruity chemical smell that blew out of hair salon doors. "I was at art school with one of Charlie's assistants."

"Ah, I see." Not the answer Granny wanted. "May I ask where you're residing?"

"With friends in St. Ives." Angie glanced around the big, comfy room. "On their sofa."

"Well, you're young."

I breathed out: Granny wasn't about to offer a guest bedroom.

"I'm twenty-six," Angie said.

"Young, dear." Granny took a sharper look at Angie, as if something about her didn't add up. "A long way from the razzmatazz of London for a girl like you."

"A load of us came down." Angie rubbed the side of her nose: a sure sign someone was lying, Mum always said. "The eclipse, you know."

"Ah, yes," Granny said, brightening, like this explained everything. "Well, the job is yours. Cash in hand. Until the end of August. Or the last girl is collected. Kat's mother usually gets the wrong day."

Angie looked surprised, like she couldn't believe it'd been so easy.

"Sort out their laundry. Bedrooms. Snacks. And you know, keep an eye out, what with all these eclipse watchers descending and the general brouhaha."

A funny little silence opened up. And a shaft of sunlight struck the papery skin of Granny's cheek, like when you put a hand over a torch and the blood glows red inside, and you realize there's only a layer of skin sealing you in. Yet on that day I still couldn't imagine Granny—or anyone close to me—dying.

"Shall I go and introduce myself to Charlie Finch?" Angie shifted her weight from one sandal to the other. Bertha's tail started to fan, her equivalent of a warning growl.

"I suppose you should," Granny said reluctantly. "Lauren . . . will you?"

"Our bedrooms are down that landing. Kat's is on the left . . ." I pointed into the tunnel of leafy wallpaper on the first landing. Kat's door was open, a bikini on the floor. But Angie wasn't interested in our bedrooms. She was staring at the studio stairs. "Is he up there, Laura?" she whispered hotly. Her cheeks were pink roses.

I nodded. "I'm Lauren, though." We climbed up the narrow steep staircase—Angie's sandals slapping behind me, her breath quickening. On the other side of the studio door, I could hear Dad moving about. A particular shuffle that meant he was wearing his painting shoes, grubby green-and-white Dunlops, unlaced, their backs crumpled under his heels. I hesitated, gripped by the feeling that if I let Angie into the studio, my Rock Point world, I'd never get her out again. "Well, go on, Laura," Angie hissed, with minty gum breath. "*Knock.*"

10

FLORA

| | |

FLORA INCHES OPEN the downstairs toilet door. The entrance hall is clear. Slipping off her noisy wedge heels, she creeps past the living room—where her father and Angie are laughing and talking in hushed voices—to find her sisters. After an agonizing half an hour or so in which they were forced to repeatedly toast the lovebirds and pick their jaws off the floor, the three of them fled like startled stomping cattle after a lightning strike. Only she'd peeled off to relieve her bladder. And try to process what she'd just seen.

The Campari-red plume of hair. The triumphant smile on that sensual mouth. The starburst of lines around those blown-out mad-green eyes. The surreal cruelty of Angie, now in the pneumatic badlands of her mid-forties, wearing Cuban-heeled ankle boots— silver!—and a leopard-print fake fur, sashaying into Rock Point, looking like she's spent the intervening years at a sordid party. She even moves in her own pocket of warm, sweet musky air: that smell when you strip clean bed linen after sex.

Flora's phone rings. She fumbles to silence it: a missed call from Scott. The screen is blurred. She wipes it on her dress. Still blurred. Okay, she's sloshed. And if she speaks to Scott, he'll know. "Etting dinnr. Will cal back. Miss u!!!" she texts, buying herself time.

Swaying in the kitchen doorway, heels in hand, a dress seam split, she feels like the hostess of a dinner party gone catastrophically wrong. But does she detect a new siege unity too? Kat and Lauren are huddled over the table, next to an open bottle of red, and lit by a guttering candle; while physically dissimilar—Kat's got the Finch wide cheekbones and Grandpa's nose; Lauren's a birdlike version of Dixie—Flora sees echoes in their tight jawlines, their expressive hands, and this pleases her. For all their distance in recent years, there's still a lot to lose.

Angie knows too much. And she'll kill any chance of her, Kat, and Lauren finally putting the sorry summer behind them. The past will be inescapable now. It'll be like having a dead body in the corner of the room, buzzing with bluebottles, and trying to eat lunch.

Also, Angie fled that August day. How can Dad forget that? Are they *all* meant to claim amnesia? The moment—"Where's Angie?"— is seared on Flora's brain. Similarly, the sight of Dixie screeching into the drive in a battered VW van, driven by her friend with pink dreadlocks. The way Dixie had asked in her soft kind yoga voice that made Flora want to confess immediately, "Tell me what happened." They didn't. Not everything. They'd been too scared.

"There you are, Flora." Kat spins around. "Engaged to Angie? I mean, fuck, right?"

"Right." Flora wants to climb on her hands and knees up the stairs, curl beside Raff, and tumble into one of her dreamless drunken sleeps, and for the next day to begin as it was meant to, according to her itinerary. Instead, she slumps to a kitchen chair and spreads her palms on the faded William Morris print tablecloth. With the candles, the wind yawning outside, it feels séance-y. A strobe of moonlight spills across the table, powdery and potato-pale. The blinds that had once hung at the windows have gone, she notices, plucking a sugar cube from the small pot on the table and pushing it against the roof of her mouth with her tongue.

"Cadmium!" Kat barks with such force it blows out the candle.

"Cadmium?" Flora repeats blankly; she's always a step behind her sisters. Growing up, she'd read so slowly she didn't bother. She couldn't spell. Or do math. Only Kat can do math: numbers make Flora's brain melt. Ironically, she discovered books after the eclipse summer, searching for escape, anything to take her away from herself. Her thoughts paddle drunkenly, with a sharp physical tug of yearning, to her book group.

"Dad used to joke about it, don't you remember?" Kat continues. "Lauren, you know about this stuff . . ."

Lauren nods, presses her fingertips against her eyes. "Cadmium can disrupt neural processes, but . . ."

"Oh god!" Finally, Flora gets it. She coughs on the sugar cube. "Maybe that explains why he's throwing Granny's things away too?"

"No, Angie will be behind that, bet your bottom dollar. Out with the old . . ." Kat slams back in her chair. "Did you catch that he bumped into Angie *the* night of your mum's funeral, Lauren? In the arts club. Think about it. He'd have returned to London emotional, vulnerable, ripe for the picking. And rich. Angie would have moved in like a heat-seeking missile."

Flora sloshes red wine into some dusty goblets. She doesn't normally drink red—it plays havoc with her gut biome—but this counts as an emergency. Despite never meeting, Dixie and Angie are now connected, invisibly sutured together, the death of one woman bringing back another in a horrible way.

No one had expected her father to be quite so devastated at Dixie's woodland funeral in October. He'd sobbed, shoulders heaving, as he scattered a handful of earth into that ghastly hole. It'd been painful to watch, not least because she'd known he'd never cry like that if Annabelle, her mother, had died. Even as girls she and Kat had sensed—and deeply resented—that it was young, feisty Dixie their father loved most. Lauren's mum, not theirs. But then Dixie was the only one to reject him, wasn't she? Dixie left him, taking baby Lauren. Annabelle and Blythe—whom he'd deserted for Dixie; what goes around . . . —always loathed Dixie for being *wanted* by Charlie when they were not.

"Do you remember how Angie couldn't swim?" Kat says after a beat. "She'd just stand in the surf, terrified if the water went over her knees. Maybe we can tempt her back in."

"*Kat*," Flora admonishes, even though for a fraction of a second the idea glitters in her mind too. Kat always nudges her to darker places.

Kat raises her hands. "Joking."

Lauren shoots Kat a slightly wary look, then strikes a match with tremulous fingers, relighting the candle, filling the room with that sulfur cigarettey smell.

Flora could kill a cigarette. She hasn't smoked since meeting Scott, who believes smokers should be refused NHS cancer treatment. She was thinner when she smoked. "We *have* to fix this." She leans forward, invigorated by the wine and the sheer scale of the family crisis. "How about I call Mum and you call Blythe, and we stage some sort of intervention?"

"The cavalry?" Kat shakes her head. "I think not."

"And what if Angie makes Dad happy?" Lauren suggests quietly, her eyes black and soft, the candle flame dancing inside them.

"But he wasn't *unhappy*, Lauren!" Flora groans. "Isn't the absence of unhappiness enough? At his age."

"You're both missing the point." Kat breaks off a drip of candle wax, rolls it between thumb and finger. "This is a white male midlife crisis, very late onset, supercharged by a terror of his own mortality and artistic and cultural irrelevance." She flicks the wax ball away. "Being generous, I'd say he's trying to capture those unreconstructed anything-goes golden days of his own roaring talent, the *Girls and Birdcage* summer, the pinnacle of his fame."

"Seeking what's lost," murmurs Lauren heavily, as if this makes sense to her too.

"But it's no excuse!" Flora's a firm believer in making your bed and lying in it, however uncomfortable the mattress.

"It's not. He should have warned us, rather than dragging us to Rock Point during an extreme weather event. It's a stitch-up." Kat pinches the bridge of her nose with her fingers. "A cluster fuck. He's going to marry Monster."

"Gosh. I'd forgotten we'd called her that." When Flora thinks what they were like, it makes her grateful she has a son. "*Monster,*" she says, relishing it once more.

"I guess it takes one to know one."

Flora turns and, to her mortification, there's Daddy standing at the kitchen door, his expression thunderous. She dreads to think how long he's been standing there, what else he might have heard.

"Well, you lot regress pretty damn quickly." He stomps over, slaps a scrunched piece of notepaper on the table, making the wine slosh greasily up the sides of Flora's goblet. "Who knocked this out?"

Before Flora or Lauren can react, Kat swipes it. Her eyes move from left to right, then widen. Her left leg starts to bounce. "Shit," she mutters under her breath.

"What?" Flora has a bad feeling. That leg.

"Feel free to share, boss." Their father's expression is cold now, with that detached artist's gaze Flora's always hated. Then, down the corridor, the *clip clip clip* of ankle boots—like the ticking crocodile in *Peter Pan*!—and Angie appears, planting a hand on his shoulder. "What's up, babe?"

Kat's trainer taps out a tattoo. Flora anxiously twists her rope of pearls.

"Don't be shy, Kat." Charlie's low voice swells with fury. "Read it out. No secrets between me and Ange."

Kat inhales to speak. But Flora's necklace snaps, explosively, and the pearls hail down, spinning, rolling into the room's dusty, darkest corners, out of reach.

11

LAUREN

|||

1999

FOUR DAYS TO go, and handwritten notes were stuck up in shop windows: "Eclipse goggles—sold out!!" Towels tiled busy beaches. Tourists wandered lost and sunburned down the lane. Others put up tents and speakers in a nearby field, until the farmer's wife irritably moved them on. The briny air had an itch to it. I started spotting mini eclipses everywhere: in the shape of Kat's fingernail clippings around the bathroom sink and the small coves at the base of the cliff. Granny started on her "sundowners" at lunchtime to ease her hip, which was stiffening: "Us girls, we're linked to the rhythms of the moon, aren't we?" Me and my sisters stared at the tablecloth, mortified to be in the same category. Granny had hairy toes.

At the sittings, Kat and Flora were restless, funny, and excitable. I struggled to understand their ventriloquist conversations, whispered out of the corners of their mouths. Mutterings about eclipse parties. And "The Plan." When I asked Flora—sitting in the center, leaning closer to Kat—what it was exactly, she just winked and smiled. A dumb Mona Lisa smile, Dad called it, cigarette dangling from his lip. "What's the hell's the matter with you all?"

Maybe it wasn't the eclipse. Maybe that summer would have gone wrong anyway. But the things we usually did those first few days of August, the way we normally got to know one another again—swimming, bonfires, sleeping in Grandpa's scout tent in the garden, our three heads by the open front flap, staring up at the stars, or sunbathing on the swing seat, legs extended, turning krill-pink—seemed small and boring, at least to Kat and Flora. Until the eclipse, we were killing time. Snuffing out those last hours one by one, not realizing how precious they were.

We longed for something to happen.

Which was why we were crammed into Granny's dressing room that baking morning, a week after arriving. The eclipse, Flora had decided, was "a dress-up opportunity." I wasn't sure what this meant, only that I needed an ally. So, when Gemma called round to go swimming, I'd pulled her upstairs instead. Never keen to come into the house—it felt weird, she said, what with her mum being the cleaner and everything—she looked awkward, uncertain in a way she never did outdoors. The dressing room was very Finch, very fancy. It smelled of perfume counters in department stores. There was a dressing table made of mirrored glass with cotton wool puffs arranged in a pink bowl, like meringues, and a row of life-sized ceramic hands, chopped off at the wrist, wearing rings and bracelets. So many clothes.

Mum said storage was a privilege of the rich—the rest of us had IKEA plastic boxes jammed under our beds—and Granny could afford to not throw anything away. And she didn't. There were crocodile handbags. Dead-fox scarves. Jewel-colored shoes with satin-covered heels. Dresses from her hard-to-imagine "glad-rags days"—London in the eighties—in a paintbox of colors. Many were wrapped in plastic. Others hung freely, sleeves sticking out, as if a thinner, younger Granny were still inside them.

Thankfully, she wasn't. Lying in the sitting room, gnarly bare feet up against a wall, resting her hip, she didn't want to be disturbed, "unless it's a matter of life and death or parrots." Grandpa was in the study, cursing the constantly dropping dial-up connection. Dad had gone out: no one knew where. And Angie was running so late we were convinced she'd get fired: "Basically, she's been drinking and overslept," said Kat, who was surprisingly knowledgeable about such things. "It's just us." Whitney Houston's broken heart trickled out of Kat's CD player, propped against a hairbrush. "We're free!" Kat declared.

This meant my sisters were now in charge.

"Is this The One?" Flora held a green flowing dress against her underwear. A bee thrummed against the windowpane.

"Perfecto, Flo." Kat stepped into a Ferrero Rocher–gold column dress and her mum's American accent. Lifted one hand. "Taxi! Claridge's!"

I laughed, pretending I knew what Claridge's was, and glanced at Gemma, who was tugging a loose thread on the dress she'd put on that morning. Pleasingly, it was the same as mine—navy jersey, star-print, Hennes. Without knowing it at the time, we'd both picked the same dress from the sales rack the week before. "You two are like freaky telepathic twins," Flora said earlier, which I took as a compliment.

Me and Gemma met three summers ago, when I still woke every morning at Rock Point with a pulpy homesickness in my chest. Still the only granddaughter who didn't know which fork to use first. A random who'd joined the family, like one of those quiet, unpopular girls you're forced to invite to a party because your mum knows her mum. Then Granny hired Viv, who'd moved to the area. One early morning Viv, in a fluster of apology, brought her daughter along to work because she had a chest infection.

Gemma was ordinary, like me. Six months younger. With a wonky smile, a dimple on one cheek, silver-blue eyes flecked like mackerel skin, and shyness that lasted about five seconds. We'd sat on the bench by The Drop, sharing a blanket and a packet of crisps, our lives crackling out between crunches. By the time Viv had finished her shift, I longed to live on the moor too. In a cozy cottage, hugged by gorse and circled by hawks. With a big brother, who sounded a lot easier and simpler than half sisters. A fisherman for a dad, who'd take me out on his growling boat. We sent letters the rest of the year, full of doodles—hers brilliant—and truths scraped from the bottom of ourselves. When I worried that I'd arrived in the Finch family too late and didn't know how to be a sister, Gemma wrote back, "It's Kat and Flora who need to learn, not you."

"And what will Lauren Molloy wear?" Kat said, using my surname when she didn't have to. Flora unclipped her bra, so her breasts swung free, full, shock-white next to her tan and gestured at Kat to fasten her dress at the back.

I grabbed a ball gown, crinkly fabric, yellow like a sherbet Dip Dab. Trying to hide my own body, the throbby nipples that felt like they didn't belong to me, I slipped it over my head, leaving my jersey dress underneath. The ball gown was way too big. "Gemma?"

Gemma shook her head. "Mum will do her nut if she finds out I've tried on your nan's stuff." She picked up the little rucksack she carried everywhere, ready to leave, and shook her hair off her face. It didn't matter how she combed it; her parting was always a zigzag. (Both Kat's and Flora's fell naturally straight, like stripes on a perfect lawn.) "I'll get in all sorts of trouble."

Kat rolled her eyes. "No more than the rest of us."

"I'm not one of you," Gemma said quickly.

No one said anything. Kat started moving her hips, threading her arms in front of her face. Flora grabbed Kat's hands and they swayed together, rippling gold and green, like seaweed underwater. "We don't think of you as the cleaner's daughter, you know, Gemma," Flora said over her shoulder, confirming the opposite.

Those words blazed in me too. Mum had cleaned houses, done all sorts of jobs to get by. I grabbed a periwinkle-blue dress. "This matches your eyes," I said, pleading with my own. "Your mum's not working today. She won't find out."

"No. Wait." Flora dropped Kat's hands, turned, and started flicking through the hangers. The dress she pressed against Gemma's body was ruffled, ugly and lilac, the color of veins on the underside a wrist. It made Gemma look ill. "This." The music stopped. "Don't you think, Kat?"

It felt like Flora was asking something else.

"Yeah. The lilac," Kat said, as the bee dropped to the sill with a bristling flutter.

"I want the blue dress." Gemma lifted her chin. "Lauren's pick."

Kat and Flora exchanged a look and held it. A new song started playing. Something else too, a different sort of noise, and one I wouldn't stop hearing for months after, even with a pillow clamped over my head.

————

THREADING THROUGH THE moon gate, we bumped up against each other, shushing stifled laughter. In the drive, the wind blew away the crackly mood of the dressing room. Our shadows touched at the edges, like paper cutout figures. We were united, a group again.

As we scrambled to the beach, it felt like we were outrunning something, not charging toward it. Laughter rolled out of us. Our dresses swelled and snapped against our legs. When I stumbled, Kat helped me up, her hand in mine, and we were a flock of tropical birds, the smallest two at the back, sucked along by the stronger ones at the front. For a few seconds, everything was perfect: the sunshine, Gemma, my sisters. Then, by the ruin of the hermit's hut, a terrible sound. We stopped and marveled breathlessly: Gemma's dress had torn right up the front, revealing her "Tuesday" knickers. "I stepped on it," she said, clamping her hand over her mouth.

"Wrong day of the week." Kat pointed at Gemma's underwear.

Gemma colored and tugged at the cloth to hide them.

"That blue dress is Granny's favorite," Flora said, with a cruelty that shocked me. "You should have worn the lilac."

From the top of the ridge: "Gemma? Are you there?"

"*Mum.*" Gemma's eyes popped. "I'm for it."

We all ducked behind the hermit's hut wall.

"Gem?" Viv again. Closer. Gemma grew teary.

"Look, I'm wearing the star dress under this." I pulled out a spaghetti strap to prove it. "If we swap dresses, Gemma, she'll never know. We can change inside . . ." I nodded at the ruined building and Kat and Flora bolted, scrambling down the ledge.

Gemma hesitated. The hermit's hut crawled with ivy and stories of black magic. A man had been found dead inside ten years before; not fresh dead either, his eyes pecked out by gulls. The roof was just beams crisscrossing the sky. There were cigarette butts in one corner, an empty beer can. Me and Gemma crouched under the flaking stone sill, spiky grass tickling our ankles. After a while, I peered over the top of the hole that was a window and started.

A few steps away on the cliff path, a teenage boy, squinting right at me from under a baseball cap. I shot down again, relieved it wasn't Viv.

"What?" Gemma whispered, picking up on my fluster.

"Nothing," I said. Gemma was anxious enough. "Come on. Let's switch." I yanked my jersey dress out of the gown's neckline, twisting a strap around my shoulder, getting stuck. Unzipped from her dress, Gemma tried to help but made my strap tangle worse, and we sank to the ground in a heap of fabric, entwined, wheezing with suppressed laughter—until we saw the face in the window, very still, a portrait in a frame. And our laughter died.

12

LAUREN

| | |

2019

LAUREN PAUSES ON the cliff path, struck by a nettle-prickling sense of being watched. She glances around uneasily. But the rocky crags and the early-morning fog rupture any sightline. Create places for disturbed note writers to hide. Slippery nooks for her imagination to fill.

"*We remember. We know what you did*" read the note Dad found by the living room door last night. They had to point out that it must have been pushed through the letterbox and blown across the hall floor in a stormy draft.

Well, *what* do they remember exactly? Lauren wishes the note's author—or authors—had knocked on Rock Point's front door and called out the accusation instead. She wouldn't have freaked, unlike the others. Kat's voice had wobbled as she read the note aloud. Angie's face turned an Elizabethan lead white against that cochineal hair. And Flora clamped her hand over her mouth, staring mutely at the pearls scattered on the floor. For Lauren, it was like being slapped awake. And she'd felt her mother's spirit in the kitchen, right beside her.

"That summer, Laurie . . . it wasn't the whole story." Dixie had started to morphine-drift by that point, lucid one minute and unintelligible the next, as if she were swimming underwater and then coming up for air, the time under the surface growing longer and longer. "I couldn't tell you . . ." Her mother never finished that sentence. Afterward, Lauren wasn't sure if it'd been the drugs talking, or if, in her own sleep-deprived state, she'd misheard. But as the weeks have gone on, at random moments she'll stop what she's doing—gluing on a chip of mosaic glass, typing a work email about the loan of a Caravaggio—and there's a moment of clarity, like a clearing in a cloudy sky, and she'll wonder, what *was* her mother trying to say? Yesterday's note has brought back that question with full force.

As she'd written to Gemma last night, sitting at the little desk in her bedroom under a buttercup of lamplight, *"Reckon this is one of the many differences between me and my sisters, G. They've always had this propulsive thrust, haven't they? I think that's why their lives are so successful now. They'll take what they fancy from Rock Point—Granny's prettier antiques I guess, Flora's oohing at the copper pans—then move on. Whereas I'm beginning to wonder if a bit of* ME *is stuck here and hidden in some dusty cupboard or whatever—and I need to find that bit to be complete again. I know you know what I mean."*

At breakfast—painfully awkward—it did occur to Lauren they might also all recall events differently; the story of that summer like studies for a painting, endlessly scribbled over, revised, and drawn from different perspectives. Not even Dad could pin it down. The surface of *Girls and Birdcage* built to an impasto hide, the paint layering ever thicker, as he tried to capture a truth that slipped through his fingers, the tapered hog hairs of his brush.

Squawking beats back Lauren's thoughts. Panicking, she looks up. Gulls are quarreling overhead. Too close. She grips her left thumb—as Janet, the therapist, taught her years ago—and, trying to contain her anxiety, that urge to scream and run, continues her winding descent into a landscape not wholly unlike summer's, too hard-boned for seasonal flightiness, with its slabs of rock and hip-bone hollows.

Cr-unch. Lauren slips, then steadies by clutching a clump of heather as the path turns into a stream of scree, stones, and shells, sweeping down to the tiny, heart-shaped cove.

Hugged by an amphitheater of cliff, it is studded with boulders the size of small cars. The protruding ribs of an abandoned rowing boat are exposed: low tide. As she walks toward the sea, grains of sand slip and shift so the forward motion of each step is countered by a small movement backward: exactly how life has been since Dixie died. Everything taking such an effort; the ground unstable under her feet.

Close to the water's edge, she kneels to inspect the brainless, bloodless lump of a stranded jellyfish, wondering if it's still alive and she should give it a helping hand back into the sea. Gemma once explained how jellyfish can regrow amputated body parts, regenerate after injury. She will do this too, she vows—as a great force whacks her from behind. Lauren stumbles, hands slapping down on the sand. A dog yaps excitedly. A second later, someone is helping her up. "God, I'm so, so sorry," he's saying. "Are you okay? She's a ten-month-old nutter. Rocket, *sit*."

"Don't worry, I'm fine." Lauren straightens, flicks her fringe out of her eyes—and starts.

Tall. Same ferrous blue eyes. He smiles, says, "You refused my seat on the London train?"

She should leave. A rough sweetness hums off him. She doesn't trust it.

He tugs down his hood, revealing shaggy hair and a large robust head. "I'm Jonah."

"Lauren," she says, then regrets it because recognition ripples across his features, and he glances at her birthmark, away again. But she just cannot place him. A face from an old painting, perhaps. The same facial features repeat over the centuries. Young Rembrandts strut down Whitechapel Road in Nikes; Botticelli's Venus applies lippy on the Central Line. Jonah's got an Italian Renaissance face, she thinks, with those deeply cut features, olive skin, slightly pitted. Or she's been working at the National Gallery too long.

"Good to meet you. Again." There's a funny sort of intimacy in his gaze.

Coloring, she strokes his dog—a Lab, black, glossy as wet paint— and fixes on the horizon. The storm has passed but the sea is still choppy, with giant waves dumping seaweed on the beach.

"Tempted by a swim?" he says, conversationally.

"I'm too much of a wuss." She smiles at the optimism of packing a swimming costume. "But my sister definitely will. Kat's a wild swimmer." She hears the small hitch of pride in her voice.

"Ah, one of them." He sounds amused rather than scornful. As he leans down to ruffle the dog's ears, his hand is suddenly close to Lauren's leg. She feels a fiery tingle at its proximity, which is confusing. Since Mum died, she's felt too shelled, too raw for sex; her body switched off below the waist. "No one dares tell Kat anything," she says.

"I've got a sister like that too."

The tide is starting to frill toward them. Something else.

"Londoner?" he asks, in the manner of someone who already knows.

Too many questions. *Leave*, she thinks again. But she stays, weakening, feeling as though, at any moment, the brutal beauty of this place might carry her away from the grief-flat monochrome inland in which she's been hunkered. "Very much so."

"My sister loves London. Wheels me in every Christmas to remind my nephews of their Kernow roots. Like they care." She sneaks another glance, registers the bulk of his shoulders, the fullness of his upper lip, and feels a pluck of desire.

"Luckily, I've got another week off work here to recover," he says. Their eyes catch. A moment passes. "Staying at Rock Point?"

Lauren stiffens, last night's ugly note unfolding in her mind's eye.

"Hard to miss," he adds, as if reading her alarm and trying to reassure her. "I mean, lit up like that on the cliff."

"Ah, yes." Her body unclenches slightly.

"Good to see a bit of life in the place again." He digs his hands into his pockets. "Wrong to have houses empty when the locals can't afford them."

"Absolutely." She thinks of friends who, like herself, have little chance of getting on the housing ladder, let alone in a half-decent postcode. "Same problem in London."

"It's different here," he says quickly, an unexpected heat in his voice.

Her heart starts to race. "Some nutty local, pissed off at second-homers," her father said last night, after accepting that the note wasn't an in-house production. She glances over her shoulder at the lonely cliff path—the only way out—that forks further up, one side in Rock Point's direction, the other a cut-through to the fields, the uplands. But she stays. There are things only a local can tell her. "What about those old cottages on the moor?" she asks, and he double-takes. "Are they second homes now, I mean," she blunders on, not sure if this is what she means at all.

"Depends on the cottage," he says, weighing his words.

"Well, there's one . . . I can't remember the exact address." She hears her own voice pitch, its tight knot of emotion. "But there's a track leading to it. And it's near two upright stones." Still Jonah says nothing, letting her reveal herself. "That's like the most hopeless description ever, isn't it?" she says, embarrassed, unnerved. "Well, I better go. Bye, Rocket." Walking away—suddenly knowing exactly which fork in the path she'll take—she feels his eyes on her back, hears him shout, "Take care, won't you?" and wonders if it's a threat or a warning.

13

KAT

| | |

K AT'S SKIN IS scarlet and screaming, her fingertips numb. "You two don't know what you're missing," she says, towel-drying her hair. Her gaze is drawn to the salt-crusted window, left ajar to air the studio. She wonders where Lauren's got to. Better if she doesn't come back right now. Not with Angie in the drive smoking— what sort of idiot *smokes*?—and tossing her hair like a circus horse. Not until she and Flora have had a chance to talk some sense into Dad, whom they've followed up to the studio for this purpose.

With a small "oof," Charlie sinks to the swivel stool at the trestle table. Switching on the swing-arm lamp, he takes a sketch from a pile and inspects it with the intense focus of a watchmaker. On the adjacent shelves, a beam of watery sunlight strikes the congealed jars of cleaners, varnishes, and other nasties that now sit in his hair shafts. Kat will be relieved when they're all in the skip.

"Raff, for god's sake." Flora is kneeling on the paint-pocked floorboard, grabbing Raff by the ankles, trying to stop him from crawling inside the infamous birdcage. She looks up at Kat, her eyes glassy and pink, as though she didn't sleep the previous night either. "Is the sea as cold as it looks?"

"Colder. Crazy cold, Flo." Outdoor swimming shocks Kat into a calmness she can't find anywhere else, each dip a conduit to the heavenly sea swims of her childhood summers here. The water had held her then. And it still felt like an embrace this morning, albeit an icy one, rinsing away her disquiet about the note, at least for a minute or two. But as she thaws, its wondrous effects are rapidly wearing off: the note feels, once more, like a devastating message in a bottle that's spent twenty years bobbing about the high seas before washing back to their shore. And then, of course, there's Angie.

At supper last night—the casserole inedible; they'd ended up with heavy pasta—Kat stealthily interrogated her father's new fiancée. She dug up a six-month childless "starter" marriage to a Russian art dealer and a patchwork of slightly made-up-sounding careers in the art and nightclub worlds. Kat, who'd been aware of her father nervously watching—willing her to be civil—tried to smile and nod, like it was a normal conversation. But it felt like she was stuck in one of those awful, claustrophobic escape room things, with nasty surprises, written clues, a strange soundtrack—wind, waves, parrot—and no easy method of extrication.

"Does it burn fat?" Flora interrupts the scratch of Kat's thoughts. "The cold, I mean. I'd have to lose at least a pound for every second I was in the winter sea to make it worth it."

"Always worth it, Flora. You'll feel better afterward. Less stressed." It's quite hard to see what her sister has got to be stressed about, but she *is* stressy under the surface of that slightly weaponized smile. Kat sinks to the sofa; her spot on the right, same as the sittings, realizing it'd feel strange settling anywhere else, like carrying her handbag on a different arm. "*And* it's rocket fuel for the brain. Cognitive speed. Creativity. Science backs it up."

"Does it now?" Charlie swivels on the stool, his interest piqued. "Well, I could certainly do with some of *that*." He holds up a sketch of a nude's torso, thick-waisted, an elderly lady. Just a few lines—hair, hip, waist—but extraordinarily alive. "This might earn me a tenner or two. I was good once, you know."

"Bloody good, Dad," Kat says, encouragingly, silently despairing that he let his talent slip away. She wonders if all humans are born with a finite amount of talent—like women are with eggs—and you can use or waste it but when it's gone, it's gone. If so, her father could be in some sort of creative postmenopause.

"Annie?" he murmurs, trying to identify the life model, head on one side, scrutinizing the sketch. "Yes, I think so."

One of many. Working the studio circuit in St. Ives, life models would visit Rock Point if Charlie was in residence. Kat had been wary—Dixie had been a life model, after all—but also intrigued. The women were comfortable in their own skin, however slack or dimpled, in a way her diet-obsessed mother wasn't. The *Girls and Birdcage* sessions gave her a new respect too. Sitting was hard work—pins and needles, cramps, itches—and it was boring. Staying still is anathema to her now. All the desks at Spring are standing workstations, or treadmills, a decision that's proved mystifyingly unpopular.

"Maybe I will do that swim," Charlie mutters to himself, turning back to the pile of sketches. "Yes, yes, I will."

"Your doctor might have something to say about that, Daddy," clucks Flora.

"Bah. I'll do what I damn well like, Flora. I'm an excellent open-water swimmer." He harrumphs. "I taught you all to enjoy the sea, didn't I?"

"You did too." Taking them out, probably too far out, when they were little, clumsy with armbands, Kat remembers. Making them dunk their heads under the water to remove their fear of its salty sting. And then, later, with newly arrived Lauren, whom he'd carry from the surf in his arms, a scrawny thing, and bundle up on the beach, like he was trying to make up for missing her younger years. That put her and Flora on edge. They hadn't liked that at all.

"I want to swim," announces Raff, grabbing the cage bars and heaving forward.

"Want to come with Grandpa?" Charlie says.

"With sharks!" Raff shouts as Flora picks him up, telling him not to be silly, to get out of that grubby birdcage, and holds him, wriggling, protesting, on her hip.

"Ah, a healthy shark obsession." Charlie slides another drawing off the pile; dismisses it, takes another. "I think we've got *Jaws* downstairs."

"Daddy, he's four," Flora says breathlessly. "Ow! Don't kick Mummy."

Charlie sticks a pencil behind his ear. "I let you two watch the movie around his age."

"Hey, how about a parenting manual? *A Creative Guide to Child-rearing*, by Charlie Finch. It could be a side hustle to your art." Kat scrolls her phone, flickering with notifications, each one a spike of adrenaline. "Like we were."

"God loves a trier, darling," says Charlie.

"Here. You take him, Kat. He's your nephew." Flora drops Raff on her knee.

Kat and Raff stare at each other in mutual bewilderment. He's unexpectedly soft and cushiony—he looks so blocky, like a baby rhino—but then Kat's not sure when she last held him, or any child. Circumspectly, she lowers her nose to his hair and sniffs. What is this elixir that keeps stealing her girlfriends and the best Spring staff? Milky, sweet, an undernote of laundered sock. From a spectator's point of view, parenting seems to involve an enormous amount of stress for very little payoff, like running a failing business. But it makes more sense when you hold a live one, she decides.

"Kat," whispers Flora. She taps her watch.

Kat nods. It is time. "So, Dad . . . out of all the women in the world, why Angie?"

Their father tenses, shoulders rising, then spins on the stool to face them. "I realize you're deeply cynical about such things, Kat, but I love Angie." He rolls up his shirtsleeves with precision, a calculated restraint. "We connect. We have history."

"You can say that again." Kat can't help it.

"I'm damn lucky to have found love again at my age." His face darkens. "I'm not going to balls it up this time. I'm not going to lose her," he mutters, barely audible.

Kat exchanges a look with Flora, who pulls a face before reassembling. They both feel Dixie in the room; their father's regrets stirred up by her death. And that's the problem with "love," Kat thinks. It's a reaction, a corrective, to the loves that precede it. Although she's not yet sure how her ex, Kofi, fits into this theory—he always did defy easy definition—their mothers prove it.

Charlie had felt stultified in his marriage to Annabelle—only marrying, according to Blythe, to please his mother—and Blythe was the medicine, with her hedonistic airbrushed American glamour. Then along came Dixie—passionate, political, earthy—the palliative to them both.

"Maybe you should take a bit longer getting to know each other, Daddy?" Flora suggests, picking her way around confrontation, always in thrall.

"Why wait? We know each other inside out. We hide nothing from one another."

Raff drops off Kat's knee and pulls her by the hand toward the window to spot killer whales. "What about from us, Dad?" she asks over her shoulder. "Any more secrets we need to know about?"

It's his expression—that visible flinch, the muscle spasm under his eye—that tells Kat she's onto something, that there's more, muzzled.

"You can be a piece of work, Kat, you know that?" Charlie starts flipping angrily through another pile of sketches.

Kat flinches. "Er, excuse me?"

"Leave it, Kat," whispers Flora. "Not on the first day. Let's have a lovely first day."

She won't leave it. People are always telling her to dial down, back off. A man would be applauded for asking difficult questions. "Okay, I'll be blunt, Dad. When you planned this reunion, did you even consider Lauren? For one minute? Dixie's barely been buried three months. There's a live parrot in the house. And now you want her to deal with Angie too? Because that's going to help her mental health, isn't it?" She lowers her voice, aware of the window being slightly open. "What if this sends Lauren into another . . . spiral?"

Her father freezes, a sketch in his hand, considering this awful possibility. Out the window, Kat sees Angie, standing at the edge of The Drop, gazing out at the boiling sea. She pictures her slipping, the carmine mane lifting, swirling, as she falls. A silence stretches.

"Well, I think it's time I consulted my menu plan, don't you?" Flora says brightly, reaching for Raff. "And we'd love a little poke through the vintage kitchenalia, wouldn't we, Raff?"

"Wait." Charlie holds up a hand resignedly. "I acknowledge I may have sprung Angie on you all in my enthusiasm, okay? I'll speak to her. Suggest she return to London tomorrow so you three can get used to the idea. She'll understand. But give her a chance?" He drums his fingers on the edge of the trestle. "What happened here that day wasn't her fault."

Kat catches Flora's eye. The wind bucks outside the window, as if channeling the energy in the room, fluting in a sharp gust, lifting a sketch off a pile on the trestle. It rocks down to the floor, landing face up, nudging the tip of Kat's trainers. She hears her father draw in his breath sharply. They both reach down to pick it up; Kat gets there first.

A recumbent nude, a small, private smile on her lips, legs crossed at the ankle; charcoal, age-dappled paper. Kat frowns, head on one side, trying to read the spidery, scrawled date in the left-hand corner—1980?—when her father snatches it aggressively from her hand. "What the . . . ?"

Charlie doesn't answer. Flustered, his fingers tremble as he buries the sketch at the bottom of a pile, out of view. And a tiny amber warning light starts to flash in Kat's mind.

14

LAUREN

| | |

2019

LAUREN STOMPS ACROSS the moor, memories expanding in small, spasmodic shudders underfoot; hidden here all along, just below the acidic topsoil. Wind at her back, blue sky above, she's adolescent again. Undamaged. Sun-scrubbed. Grandpa's slipping his binoculars around her neck, excitedly pointing up at a circling hawk. She's running in flip-flops—*slap, slap, slap*—with Gemma, sharing a bag of Skittles that leave sticky rainbow stains on their palms. If you come to this place as a kid, she realizes, it never leaves you. It stirs inside, restless, waiting for reconnection. It is so good to be back. Funny how forgotten details are rapidly coming into focus— and in the house; a particular loose floorboard outside her bedroom, a salad bowl with daisies painted around the rim—while the bigger picture remains hazy, slowly breaking up, like a shipwreck underwater.

Sweating now, she climbs a stone stile—one hand on a wooden

post, the other holding her hair off her face—and squints, smiling, at the rolling heath, the dips and dents of ancient barrows. There are no other walkers around and she feels safer for this emptiness: Jonah's ominous words, "Take care, won't you?" have followed her from the cove. Her heart lifts. There they are. Two fingers on the horizon, the upright stones: an eleven, the date of the eclipse. She has her bearings.

Should she? It's their first morning at Rock Point, and she's been out too long already. But it's hard to resist the welcoming draw of the Heaps' home—and the letter she'll be able to write to Gemma afterward. Jumping down from the stile, as she walks farther away from the sea, the smell grows loamier, like a freshly dug hole. Bracken flicks water against her legs. She can see the cottage now, the rust orange of its front door. Getting closer, she imagines Gemma's brother Pete at a window, watching her approach.

A few meters away, Lauren stops, puzzled. Something's not right. A huge crack, wide enough to fit a hand, zips like a lightning strike up the cottage's front. The windows are dirty, ivy pressed up on the wrong side of the glass. Still, out of politeness, she knocks, and, to her surprise, feels the door give slightly under her knuckles. "Viv?" she calls, ridiculously. No one could possibly live here. Certainly not house-proud Viv, who was always sweeping back the invasion of mud and burrs from the moor. And yet, it's not like the hermit's hut. The cottage looks abandoned rather than ruined.

Lauren curiously pushes the front door, meeting resistance. There's a scuffing sound, something scraping along the ground. A coir mat and clump of decomposing post, she realizes, pushing harder. The door opens directly into the living room. The sight shocks her.

Mold blooms on the walls, stamped with pale rectangles where pictures once hung. A sofa has split open, its foam spilling out like fungus. Lumps of plaster powder the floor. The air smells dank, subterranean. It all brings a lump to her throat, and a yearning for a bowl of soapy water and a scrubbing brush. She cannot resist walking inside, drawn in by the cottage's deep familiarity, its strangeness, and through to the little kitchen at the back, where she and Gemma would sit parched and giggling, downing glasses of orange squash, lurid and delicious with chemicals, the stuff her mum would never buy. She can almost hear Viv's music, the off-beats and octave jumps of reggae and lover's rock. Taste the fish paste sandwiches, the lovely white sliced bread that would compress to nothing between her front teeth. She's wondering where Viv might have moved, if she's still local, when a sound makes her stiffen. Animal? *Bird?* Please not a bird. When there's no further noise, heart pounding, she peers back into the living room, her hands half-raised, ready to protect her face. Her stomach drops. Standing in the cottage doorway, his hood up, his coat flapping, one hand reaching down to restrain his dog: Jonah.

15

LAUREN

||||

1999

W E WERE TRAPPED. Scrunching the evening gowns against our half-dressed bodies, me and Gemma listened to the brush of feet moving through the grass. Angie's shadow slipped across the hermit hut's doorway first.

"You dirty little so-and-sos." She shook her head and smiled. Our shocked faces blinked in the screens of her mirrored sunglasses. "Butter wouldn't melt, eh?"

I knew some sort of misunderstanding had taken place, just not what. "Me and Gemma were swapping over dresses," I explained. Even though this was true, it didn't sound it.

"I may be a bit worse for wear today." Her lips looked swollen, redder than normal. "But I'm not a total moron, Lauren. Not on my watch, okay?"

I nodded, agreeing to something I didn't understand just to make her go away. The hot sun sliced through the roof beams to my exposed shoulders, the softness of early morning gone. And the dresses no longer felt magical or glamorous but shiny and scratchy, like something from a dressing-up box.

"Well, don't just blink at me like bunnies in the headlights. Make yourselves decent."

We were quick. Gemma grabbed her rucksack off the ground. "Thanks for lending me your dress," she whispered, with a small grateful smile, handing me the blue one, which I bundled in my arms, trying to hide the rip.

Outside the hut's walls, everything was too harsh, too bright. The boy in the baseball cap I'd spotted from the window cavity had gone. Yet I could still see him on the exact spot where he'd stood on the path, like he'd left a bit of himself behind.

"I'll let someone else do the bollocking." Sweat popped above Angie's upper lip. "But I'll do you a favor and tell you, Lauren, that Mrs. Finch mentioned she doesn't want you and Gemma hanging out all the time. You're here to spend time with your sisters, she said."

Heat rolled over me. I told myself this was the sort of thing Granny might come out with after one of her gins, a throwaway line, not really meant. But Gemma wouldn't meet my eye.

"As for that ripped dress . . ." Angie glanced at the bundle in my arms, then Gemma. "Best not lose your hardworking mum her job, eh?"

"I can't believe you said that!" I hissed to Angie as Gemma, red-faced, hared away up the path.

"Well, she should think first. And so should you. You've got a good gig here, Lauren." Something raw and hurt streaked across Angie's face and for a strange moment I thought she might cry. "The big house. Sisters. Whatever you want. One day you'll grow up and see how most people live, that's all I'm saying."

I opened my mouth to explain, then shut it again, not knowing where to begin. Homesickness swelled against my ribs, a solid, physical thing. I wanted Mum's laugh and chickpea curry, her bare foot tapping when she played the fiddle. Our rescue cat, Pumpkin. The fat bold robin I fed cornflakes every morning. Even the toilet that didn't flush properly without pouring in a saucepan of water, carefully, so you didn't get splashed. Noises. Smells. Home.

"Speaking of which, where be Lady Kat and Princess Flora?" Angie turned to face the horizon, her sunglasses flashing. I thought of the wreckers of old, how they'd trick boats to dash on the rocks with their lamps. "Any idea what they're up to?"

I shook my head. First rule of Finch sisters, never snitch. A second later, I caught Kat's laugh on the breeze, just a snippet of it, like you can hear one note of music and immediately recognize the song.

I expected Angie to hear too. But she didn't. "Charlie asked me to herd you all back for an impromptu sitting. Something about feet, you know, getting them right."

I didn't like the way she used his name rather than "your dad" or "Mr. Finch."

"If I fluff my first session for him because of . . ." The expression on my face must have stopped her short. "What?"

"Session?" My heart started to hammer, like it already knew.

"Art assistant, Lauren. Between my household shifts."

A dizzy, tipping sensation. "But you can't. That's . . . that's my job," I managed.

My first day at Rock Point rushed up at me; the staring half sisters, the new grandparents, the strange, too-big house until Dad said, "Come with me, kid," and took me by the hand up to the studio and asked if I'd help him melt down some rabbit skin glue on his camping stove. I no longer felt like a grubby castaway pulled out of the hold. And afterward he kneeled down and said, solemnly, "Tell me, Laurie, how did I ever manage without you?" and I thought I might die of happiness.

"Don't look at me like that, Lauren. It's not personal. I'm a proper studio assistant, that's all. Trained. Charlie needs me this summer. And this painting . . . well, you wouldn't understand, but it's not some little holiday project. *Girls and Birdcage*, it's going to be mega, honestly." Angie flicked up her sunglasses, as if she wanted to let me in. Not somewhere I wanted to go: her pupils were enormous and tadpole-black, the whites lacy with red. "Charlie Finch is on *fire*. Take it from me."

I wouldn't. He was my dad. "The stuff he does here is never little holiday projects," I said fiercely, as Granny's ball gown tried to blow inside out.

"If you say so," she said, amused, disbelieving.

I took a breath and mentally drew up the *Tatler* article on Dad's London toilet wall, reading the march of little black letters. "'Finch's pencil and charcoal life studies, the bounty of his Cornish studio, are spare, almost painfully intimate and eminently collectable, if you can get hold of one. Or persuade him to sell. Forget the oils of the great and the good, these private drawings—and sitters—are a peek into Finch's heart.'" I exhaled. My photographic-memory trick didn't always work, but I knew I'd pulled it off.

"Blimey. Ever thought of being an art critic when you grow up?" Angie cocked her head on one side, interested in me for the first time. "So, apart from you lot, who else does he draw here?"

"Life models," I said, still distracted by my own small triumph. "Friends. Anyone who's game really."

I could see an idea land in her eyes, just before she pushed her sunglasses back down. "Let's hoof it. See if Kat and Flora are already back at Rock Point, shall we?"

Glad to leave, desperate to get changed out of the dress, I followed a few steps behind on the stony path. Angie's blouse blew up in the breeze, revealing a gecko tattoo inked on her lower back. There was something lizardlike about Angie too, I thought, the way she emerged into the light and you could see who she was, just for a moment, and then she'd vanish down a crack again.

"Wait. Before we go in, Lauren." We stopped in the drive. "Sorry about what I said to Gemma, okay? I meant well. But it was out of order."

I looked away, embarrassed by this unexpected apology, suspecting she was just worried about me saying something to Dad.

"And the other thing . . . one assistant to another." She was smiling, her voice gentle, kind. She'd changed again. "You've done a brilliant job in the studio. I'm dead impressed. Your dad says you're a natural."

Trying to hide the burn of pride in my chest, I said nothing, stared at my feet, the torn bracken frond caught in my sandal strap.

"Hey, you're almost airborne." Angie leaned over and, like a big sister might, patted down my dress to stop it from ballooning in the wind. "One other thing. Since you're the studio mistress, where does he keep those private life drawings?" She winked. "I'd like to check out the competition."

I hesitated. The sun gunned down.

"Ah, so the studio mistress doesn't know *everything* . . ." she teased, playfully.

Unable to resist showing off my knowledge, I regretted telling Angie immediately. But, like so many things that summer, by then it was already too late.

16

FLORA

| | |

IT'S STILL SALVAGEABLE. If Angie leaves straight after lunch, Flora might just save this reunion from being a damage limitation exercise. Their father, grounded by his close, loving family, will realize his priority should be his health, not gallivanting off to Las Vegas. Standing by the cooker, briskly stirring the tomato and basil soup, she vows to persevere with Blitz spirit, as if Angie had never landed back in their lives—and that nasty little note hadn't slipped through the letterbox. At least their father no longer suspects them of writing it. That's something. Funny then that she keeps getting these sharp stabs of misgiving—a sort of physical reflux—as if she *had* penned the thing, which must be some sort of deflected guilt.

She's apparently alone in this.

Angie certainly appears untroubled by a conscience. Like she never appeared at Rock Point's door in a transparent white dress, snapping gum, twenty years ago; played no part in that fateful summer. In middle age, she's solidified somehow, and seems even more a force of nature—Storm Angie?—compared to their waning, love-doped father. Sat at the kitchen table, laughing too loudly at one of their father's asides, she's all raucous hair—clearly dyed; telltale gray roots—and sun-creped cleavage. The "Angie" of her gold name necklace nicks at the wattle of her throat, as it sticks in Flora's. Granny will be spinning in her grave.

Flora could do with some sisterly solidarity, frankly. A bit of emotional reinforcement. But Lauren's still not back from her walk. (Should they be worried? And who was she talking to on her phone so early this morning? Although Flora couldn't hear the conversation its rhythms were peculiar, one-sided; Lauren doing all the talking, barely a listening pause.) Kat isn't exactly present either, sat on the Lloyd Loom, eyes drilled to her laptop. A bomb could fall, and she'd still be there, covered in rubble, determinedly banging out weekend work emails and orders, like some sort of half-crazed military commander. Or perhaps she's trying to make the point that she's got bigger things to think about than whether she'd like one of Rock Point's Howard & Sons armchairs—Flora offered to share her little black book of upholsterers; Kat didn't even pretend to look interested—or any of Granny's beautiful old French linen, monogrammed with a swirly blue-threaded *F* and stored in the airing cupboard upstairs.

Clearly out there, in the world, Kat matters. Before this trip, Flora hadn't realized quite how much. And it kindles a confusing conflict of pride and jealousy, even though she'd rather die than admit either sentiment to Kat. Pouring a glass of water—it spurts from the tap in spasms—she vaguely wonders how it is that her own life has got smaller and smaller while Kat's has expanded globally, hot and light, like some sort of astonishing gas.

Flora can't help but feel slightly diminished by her sister's success.

Caught off-guard. Who knew decisions made in their midtwenties—or subliminally perhaps, after that eclipse summer—would have such an exponential effect on their lives? Hers to marry doting, dependable Scott; a man who, in five years of marriage, hasn't read one novel. (When she jokingly mentioned this to her book group, Louise from number nine said, "I'm so sorry, Flo," with such tenderness that Flora had to hide in the loo for a small, drunken sob.) And Lauren . . . ? Well, Lauren may not have found her life partner, but she's found her calling, working her way up the grand stone staircase of the National Gallery, from the information desk to the exhibitions department, while Kat's invested everything—savings and soul—into building Spring, tragically sacrificing her own personal life in the process. So, either Kat cleverly saw through the romantic fairy tale—Flora was a believer, she's still a believer—or she's grown a hard rind over her heart and she needs . . . *fixing.*

"Flo?" says her father, looking at her curiously, as if he's already addressed her and she hasn't registered it.

"Yes!" she says, glad to be stopped from further torturous comparisons with her sisters, a bad childhood habit. Raff barrels past and she reaches for him, instinctively wanting to restrain her clumsy boy, slow him down, but he's already in the conservatory, arms outstretched toward Berthingham Palace, which seems to exert an unexpected pull. "Fingers!" she yells after him. She'll never forget the pain of Bertha's bite, all those years ago. How she'd rolled on the floor, screaming, and Kat said, "And the Oscar goes to . . ." and Granny, rummaging in a drawer for plasters, shook her head. "What do you expect, dear? You're not part of her flock yet. You don't put in the hours like Lauren."

"So, Flora. Rock Point?" Daddy pours coffee, slopping it over the tablecloth. He's jittery, pale; the strain of reintroducing Angie to their lives clearly draining him. Or there's something else he's not told them. Kat has apparently got "a hunch" about this: Flora very much wishes she hadn't. "Any instructive thoughts about its future?" he says, when she doesn't answer.

"Well, I . . ." Flora's brain is jumbled by a punishing hangover—she has a hazy memory of taking a mug of red wine and a lump of cheddar to bed—and her need to tell her father not to booze so much, and to go easy on the caffeine, swap full fat for skimmed.

"I'm thinking wellness retreat, Dad." Kat muscles in, blindsiding Flora.

"Ooh, there's an idea, Charlie," says Angie, sitting straighter in her chair.

An insane one. Wishing Angie would butt out—none of her business—Flora sips her water, which tastes faintly saline, as if seawater has leaked into the pipes.

"Raw food. Meditation," says her straight-faced sister, used to selling concepts like "wellness loop data" to a room of suits without giggling, as if they were actual real-life *things*, like console tables. "A place for people to unplug."

"Rock Point not off-grid enough for you, Kat?" Charlie says, lifting an eyebrow, stoking things. He uses a different voice when he speaks to Kat, harder-edged, but with a wary respect. It's no wonder Kat, despite being five months younger than Flora, has always refused to subordinate, always jostled to be the one in charge.

"We'll sell digital detox," says Kat, looking a little too pleased with herself.

"But you'd not survive it, Kat." Flora twists off a chunk of the nearby loaf and stuffs it in her mouth with a twinge of self-loathing. Bread plays havoc. "You'd sneak off for a data hit every five minutes."

Kat ignores this and goes on about raising investment, "circling back"—here, really?—and "moving the needle" and, worse, far worse, cold water immersion therapy.

"Sounds like a Victorian psychiatric treatment," Flora says, palming her thorax.

"You're not our customer," Kat says brusquely, frowning into her laptop again. "You're more spa, Flo."

"*Spa?*" she repeats, outraged. (She adores spas.) Damn it, she'll swim in the freezing Atlantic if it kills her. That'll shut Kat up. "Well, it all sounds a bit woo-woo to me. It'll certainly keep our local note writer busy."

"Can we not waste breath talking about him?" Charlie says abruptly. And a small charge of fear rushes into the room.

"Hey, mister. Who says the troll's a man?" Angie gives him a playful shove.

Flora hadn't considered that. Yes, yes. A pillar-of-the-community type, perhaps? Her mind keeps slipping uneasily to the guy who was staring up at the house yesterday evening. If they must be targeted by a poison-pen writer—and the note doesn't necessarily mean what she dreads it does; it could be a coincidence, it could be nothing—she'd rather it was a woman. An old frail one, preferably bedbound.

"Jobs. Local investment." Kat starts to pace around the room, pausing under a framed yellowing map of Cornwall. "And the sort of tourists who'll pay serious money to be deprived of home comforts."

"Not everything's about money," Flora says in the gentle, moral voice she uses with Raff. ("Was biting the bully the right thing or the wrong thing to do?" "Right thing.")

"Funny how it's always those who've never had to worry about money who say that." Kat traces the coast path with a finger, as if plotting an escape route.

"I think we can all check our privilege, Kat." Her sister grew up with unimaginable glamour—celebrities literally popping round for tea! Lauren had neither money nor glitz. But she did get Dixie, who put her in the center of her world. Whatever Flora's mother said about Dixie—"Probably hasn't paid a penny in tax, ever"; some wounds heal, some hearts, not Annabelle's—Flora couldn't help but feel envious of Dixie and Lauren's obvious closeness. After her own mother remarried, their relationship felt like a sort of distracted surveillance on Annabelle's part. Money was thrown at Flora; she was never allowed to forget this. Private schools, pony club, ballet, tennis; she excelled in precisely none. Her stepfather referred to them as "Flora's running costs."

"You know what, Dad? I think I'll take these antique maps," Kat muses, her head on one side. "I do like a map."

Flora hadn't wanted the tatty maps. She does now. "Daddy's legacy is more important." I raise you, Kat, she thinks hotly. "Even if we modernize the rest of the house, the studio should be conserved. The old brushes. The paint tubes. The sofa from *Girls and Birdcage*." Seeing her father's flush of pleasure makes her feel slightly cheapened, knowing she's played directly to his ego. "And the birdcage, of course."

"*Preserving* things, Flora?" Kat's question thins the air in the room.

And that's when it happens, the rupture in the fabric of their first morning. *The circling back.* Lauren on the aviary floor, twitching, eyes open, glazed, unseeing. The blood at the bottom of the staircase, red as the soup bubbling on the stove. Flora's stomach heaves nauseatingly. She steadies herself, hands braced on the marble pastry slab, lights like floaters at the corners of her vision, pulsing on and off.

"Right. Anyone for a bracing ocean dip after lunch?" she hears her father say.

"Babe," says Angie. *Babe.* "Just no. I'm not letting you in there either. Not in this weather."

"God, you all fuss so," he says, sounding both irritated and pleased. "A walk, then? Or might that finish me off too?"

"I've made a list of local excursions . . ." Flora begins, and her voice comes out woozy. No one notices. They presume she's okay. Everyone always presumes she's okay. And they're right, of course. She's living her best life. There was no justification for hurling the Nutribullet across the kitchen last week and gleefully watching the green gunk—Scott's post-workout smoothie—slide down the metro tiles.

"Good call. I could do with some air." Out of the corner of her refocusing eye, Flora sees Angie examine her reflection in the selfie mode of her phone and ruffle her hair with her fingers. "Before I get on the road." She flashes a pointed look in Flora's direction. "Leave you good people in peace."

Flora perks. Her father *has* kept his promise.

"Zennor Quoit?" Charlie moves a hank of hair off Angie's face and rearranges it over her shoulder, as if perfecting a composition. "Shall we go disturb the dead, my darling?"

Kat looks up from her laptop and opens her mouth to say something witty and explosive, then wisely shuts it again.

"I'd like that, babe," Angie coos. They gaze at each other with such indecency, Flora edges away and into the conservatory, where Raff is standing far too close to the cage. The parrot, a witness to that terrible day, glares at Flora as if she remembers it, her, everything.

In the front pocket of her cream corduroys, her phone beeps, signaling another missed call. Scott. Again. Scott sweetly checking that she's okay; that her family hasn't upset her, which, of course, they have. She still has no desire to leave.

Bertha mimics the beep, then dips her head and rips a feather from her chest.

Watching the cloud-gray plume float to the cage floor, Flora winds one of Raff's curls around her finger and, with it, thoughts of the quoit, the megalithic burial chamber on the moor. A tale of the ancients laying out cadavers on the lozengelike stones for their flesh to be pecked clean by birds before burial. They'd loved the goriness of that story, drawn to the quoit because of it. Lauren would usually disappear off with Gemma, but she and Kat would stay and sunbathe, turning in the heat like rotisserie chickens. Lying there, the sun on their skin, whispering about the imminent eclipse—a cosmic event surely orchestrated for their entertainment—the cobalt sky soaring above, their lives ready to unfurl like shiny spring leaves, she'd felt so powerful. Shameless. Capable of anything.

She's changed.

And yet. Here she is, back at Rock Point, away from her marriage, her grown-up life, and aware of a puzzling new sensation: a tiny inner agitation, a cellular jostling, nowhere near her lower colon, but closer to her heart. Almost as though that younger self still lives within her—and is starting to stir.

17

LAUREN

| | |

2019

S CRAMBLING BACK FROM the deserted moor cottage in the
mizzle, her head thick with Jonah, Lauren nearly misses the flapping scrap of paper, impaled on the wrought-iron spikes of the gate.
She pulls it off and shelters in the alley to read it.

LEAVE. *Leave us in peace.*

Oh. Okay. Nothing ambiguous about *that*. Same handwriting as
last night's note only more manic, the letters slanting in different
directions. A sign of a troubled soul: it takes one to know one. Her
handwriting was almost illegible in the weeks after Mum died, and
her letters to Gemma became rambling, smudged scrawls of ink. Because of this Lauren feels an unexpected connection—and a rush of
compassion—to whoever wrote it. But she also knows she must take
it seriously. The others will.

One note can be brushed off as a tasteless prank. Almost. Two is more sinister. Likely to achieve its aim, *Leave*. But it's too soon to go. It'd taken so much to return in the first place—and she's not fulfilled the reason she came, her promise to Mum. Will she, Kat, and Flora get a chance to be together like this again? She doubts it, not for years anyway. Instead, they'll slot back into their normal lives, at a safe distance from one another. The process of them turning into strangers will continue; time shunting them further and further from the girls in the portrait. Maybe a part of her isn't ready to say goodbye to Rock Point either.

Unlike her sisters, Lauren sees why their father drew them here. He must have known that once at Rock Point it'd be hard to wriggle away with a "something's come up." It's different in winter too. They can't easily leave given the storms causing chaos on the roads and rail in the rest of the country. Instead, they're trapped in their own weather and forced to look one another—and Angie—in the eye. Or not. Flora often seems to smile brightly at a point between Lauren's brows, as if she's wary of directly meeting her gaze. She senses Kat's sidelong glances too. And it feels like she's being assessed as much as Angie.

So, no, probably not a good idea to mention the Heaps' cottage just yet, nor that oddly charged meeting with Jonah. "I thought you were someone else," he'd said, standing in the doorway, and she hadn't known whether to believe him. "I didn't mean to scare you." Startled, embarrassed, she assured him he hadn't. But beneath their almost comically polite exchange, she'd felt another conversation lay between them waiting, forming, like the dot-dot-dot ellipsis of a typed message when someone is writing on a phone. Did he feel it too?

Bang. The slam of a door in the wind knocks Lauren out of her thoughts. It's followed by the waft of cigarette smoke. Angie. Unable to face her, Lauren slips into the garden where the air is sweetly scented with pine needles and something warm and tomatoey— lunch, hopefully—that's fluting out of the house's air vents. Trying to work out what to do next, whom to tell first, if at all, Lauren leans against the cold stone of the wall and reads the note again. Her thoughts slide back to Jonah.

Is it his work? He doesn't seem the type but it's possible. People are never quite whom they want you to believe they are; she knows a bit about showing one's most acceptable face to the world, the curation of self. Also, and this shouldn't be a factor, it really shouldn't, but he's disarmingly attractive in an elemental way—his presence as tangible and physical as a hand on the plane of skin between her hip bones—which is going to cloud her judgment. And he could have stuck the note on the gate *before* she set off, then trailed her down to the cove—"Take care, won't you?"—and cottage. Gouged into this exposed landscape are shortcuts and hiding spaces only a local would know—and Jonah looks like he's been carved out of a slab of its rock. He's seeped in the place.

Enough. Stuffing the note into the pocket of her cargo trousers, she weighs up the unappealing choice of entering the house via either Angie or the parrot. Having survived one night in a house with a resident bird, albeit caged, it's dawning that she doesn't hate Bertha. She hates her fear of Bertha, the phobia that crouches inside. Earlier, when she noticed the small bald patch on Bertha's chest—stress plucking; probably missing her foster carer—and the feathers on the conservatory's brick floor, it was like seeing her grief in feathered form. Not just for Dixie, but for her own younger self, the Lauren who'd trust Bertha to nuzzle her earlobe. The Lauren that would have sat by Bertha, settled and consoled her, fed her chopped fruit and bits of newspaper to shred with her beak. Even the grown-up Lauren who keeps one of Bertha's red tail feathers, shed that last summer, a memento she cannot bear to either touch or throw away.

The conservatory. She will be brave. Before her resolve can waver, she walks around the corner of the house, stopping by the dilapidated swing seat when she hears Flora's telephone voice.

"I miss you too, Scott," her sister is cooing. "So, so much."

Lauren allows herself, just for a second or two, to imagine how it'd feel to be Flora: settled and loved. The sheer relief of it. Dixie brought her up to be independent, but occasionally, especially since her mother's died, and existence seems both unbearably beautiful and painfully fragile, her roots hacked away to stringy tendrils, she's ached to be held by someone familiar, known, safe. Someone who will reliably be there in the morning, and the morning after that.

"Scott, you know I'm doing Dry January," Flora says with a taut laugh. "No, not drinking! Absolutely not."

Lauren sucks in her breath: Flora put away more booze than all of them last night. Then she wonders if she's too puritanical and idealistic, if it's the little white lies that keep a marriage alive. Flora's not adulting, she's fully nested, with a child, a husband, and a mortgage, a grown-up life of which Lauren—and most of her friends—can only dream.

"Yes, I know I promised. Of course, I love you," Flora continues. "I couldn't love you more."

Lauren cannot stop listening, transfixed by this glimpse into Flora's charmed world. And yet, there's a strain in her sister's voice that gives her pause.

"It's just one month we're missing." Flora's voice grows increasingly wrought, almost tearful. "It doesn't mean . . . Of course, I'm keeping an eye on Raff! No, I'm not *not* telling you anything. It's just lovely family time. All good! Yes, I know you're looking out for me . . . please, Scott."

Lauren is torn now, wanting to check that Flora is okay, not wanting to admit she's listened in on a private call. The longer she stands there, the more she hears, the more damning it'll be. She chews on a nail.

Flora is unlikely to appreciate Lauren sticking her nose into her private business. And what does she know about marriage anyway? Her longest relationship—Franciszek—lasted six months, ending when he moved back to Poland a year ago. And she's always largely judged men on whether her mother would like them; if she can imagine them sat with a bowl of Dixie's spicy tagine on their lap in her Jericho courtyard; their kindness to manky rescue cats and stamina for circling art galleries. It's no wonder she's single.

The note has made her hypersensitive. That's it. The empty husk of a cottage has unsettled her too, especially the absence squatting inside it like a question: Where's Viv? She's projecting, interpreting Flora's phone conversation through her own anxious prism. Van Gogh painted the demented-blue night sky twisting through his own troubled mind, she reminds herself, slinking through the moon gate and out into the wind-whisked drive. Unfortunately, Angie's still there, an unavoidable obstacle, hand on one hip, frowning at Lauren then back at her car. "I was meant to be leaving for London after our walk. But look. Just look at that, Lauren." She points at the car's front wheel, its flat tire. "Puncture marks, too."

"Christ." A chill sweeps through Lauren.

Angie stamps out her cigarette. "Seriously, who'd do a thing like that?"

Lauren glances around for any sign of the guilty party. But all she can see are obfuscating rocks and distorting, ballooning sprays of water, the optical tricks of air, sky, and sea. A fine veil of rain. A landscape hiding its own.

18

FLORA

|||

BENT DOUBLE ON the toilet seat, her belly cramping, Flora listens to the commotion outside the bathroom window. Angie's voice. Lauren's. Daddy's. Something about a tire? But loudest of all is still Scott's. His phone call repeats on her. "I want you home now," he'd said, in a low, wounded tone. "It's day fourteen."

She knows it's natural for him to want another child as soon as possible. And it's fairly normal for a husband to follow his wife's ovulatory cycle—well, isn't it? But she feels interrogated, and there's a quiet teenage voice rising to the surface, one that wants to tell him to fuck off, frankly. After the miscarriage last summer—the rusty stain on her knickers that thickened into horrifying meaty globs— Scott had grilled her about what she ate and drank, desperate for "a reason": to blame something. She's still haunted by the wedge of Brie she ate in the early hours of the morning, standing at the altar of their pastel-blue larder fridge. She tearfully confided to her

GP—who assured her it was extremely unlikely to be connected—but never told Scott. Not about other stuff either. Her deep buried longings.

Right now, she'd be happy never to have sex again, let alone the scheduled "baby-making" sort, as Scott calls it. What she wants is an antacid. A painkiller. A vat of white wine. And she's starting to realize how much she aches for the little things Kat and Lauren take for granted: dressing for work, gossiping by the coffee machine, examining other women's shoes on the Tube. A grown-up world outside her house, the school gate and local park, the small radius she grazes day after day, like a tethered goat.

Her sisters wouldn't have any sympathy. Nor would she expect it! Lauren's lost Dixie, and lives in a grotty flat above a kebab shop. Kat's a childfree comet, trailing brilliance, Bitcoins, and the remains of Kofi's broken heart: she'd just say, well, I told you so. When Flora announced the engagement—when Kat should have been happy for her—she'd said, "But you are not *you* around Scott, Flo." And Flora had screamed that Kat didn't know who she was anyway because Kat was a workaholic, with an ability to say *exactly* the wrong thing at the wrong time. But a little voice had whispered, what if Kat's right? Kat's always sort of right, someone who approaches a simple equation in an unnecessarily complicated way but still digs up the correct answer. Flora wipes away her tears on her sleeve and tries to rally to get up and serve lunch, or care about lunch, fighting the urge to throw back her head and howl for her sisters, like a lost wolf for her pack.

"Mummy?" A little worried voice.

"Won't be a sec, love."

Raff's lumpy shadow shifts in the gap of the closed bathroom door. Raff, her dear, bonkers boy whom she loves more than life itself;

her atonement; her captor. She's no longer at all sure it was right to bring him.

"A bit of a crazy ask, isn't it?" Scott had snorted when she first mentioned her father's invitation. Really a summons. (And her husband's name wasn't on it.) "Obviously, you're not taking Raff," he'd added. But it was one of those rare times she dug in her heels; a battle she dared pick. Partly, it was because her father cherished Raff, and she'd sensed something wasn't right with Daddy, and thought Raff's company might help. But mostly, it felt wrong that her little boy had run across the sun-bleached sands of France, Portugal, and Florida but had never rock-pooled on a windswept Cornish beach, bumpy with worm casts, ripe with seaweed. Nor had he ever spent time away with his Finch aunts, or her father.

Scott had pointed out that it was she, Flora, making all the effort again, like it always is with her Finch relatives. And that Charlie, Kat, and Lauren had snubbed her at Christmas, not for the first time. "You deserve better than that, Flora," he'd said gently, reaching down to cup her buttock. Although on one level, she'd agreed with him, she also believes you only get permission to criticize a family if you're part of it. And he belongs to a different part of her life: the functional bit, the sunny world above the waterline, not the ugly hull beneath the surface. Which is why she's never told him the truth about the eclipse summer either. She often wonders what would happen if she did. If he'd still love her in the same way.

Raff knocks on the bathroom door. "Is Mummy sick?"

With a physical jerk, Flora realizes she hasn't taken her pills. Rock Point's thrown her routine. "Oh no. Not at all. But can you grab my handbag, sweetie? On the bed."

She listens to the purposeful scuff of his feet. The sound of him dragging the handbag's brass base studs across the floor. He wants to please her, she realizes, welling up. At home it so often feels like he wants to eat her alive, that he's furious to have ended up with Flora as his mother. The bathroom door opens a few inches, and he shoves the bag through.

"You are such a good boy, Raff." She doesn't tell him often enough. Rifling through her handbag, she panics when she can't see them, a film whirring in her head: the dash to A and E, the awful call to Scott. There. There they are. Just the sight of the pills makes her abdominal cramps subside. She's retrieving them when the bathroom door flings open and her heart leaps to her throat.

"Oh my god, what have you . . ." She bends down, wipes Raff's bloody face with a tissue. Just lipstick, red lipstick. For goodness' sake.

Raff giggles, delighted at her reaction, escapes from her grip, and runs out. Standing on the landing, leaning over the banisters, checking his progress, she watches him scamper down the stairs. "Don't run," she yells, the lipstick, the steepness of the stairs, all mingling messily in her mind's eye. "Slow, Raff!"

When he's safely in the hall, she turns back along the landing, then hesitates, her gaze catching on Kat's and Lauren's closed bedroom doors. It moves her in some indefinable way that, like homing pigeons, without discussion, they've gravitated to their old summer rooms. Their bedroom doors were left ajar then. They'd tiptoe across this landing at night and end up top to tail, cramped in a bed, giggling, kicking each other's shins because it was more fun together than alone. Recently, back home, those nights when Scott's away for work, she's started to wonder if it's because she grew up with so many siblings, that the things she's so lucky to have—a detached house, a silent street, a super king-size bed—feel lonely.

Unable to resist a nose, Flora opens Kat's door a few inches, and her heart sinks. She hopes this room is not reflective of her sister's inner life; snaked ugly cables, chargers stuck in every plug point, and a fitness mat unrolled on the floor. No sign of a book, she notes with a tut, recalling how Kat would hoover up bonkbusters and read the juicy bits out aloud (in retrospect, setting Flora's expectations a bit too high).

Next to her own room, Lauren's, although you'd not know it, she thinks, peering around the door. Little evidence of its guest apart from a gym bag on the rug. Oh, and a pad of writing paper on a rather nice Georgian desk, with a pen lying diagonally across it. Wondering to whom Lauren's writing—the possible lover she over-heard Lauren talking to on the phone earlier that morning?—she moves curiously toward it, only the sound of someone on the stairs bringing her up short. She darts back to her bedroom, her bathroom, where she attacks her T zone with powder.

Eyeing herself in the mirror, Flora experiences the unpleasant sensation of being scrutinized by her teenage self and found wanting. She imagines a hidden history of reflections, all the pouting faces over the years, young to old, like rings in a tree.

The mirror's thick oval frame is crusted with seashells, a favorite of Granny's. "Since you are our family's Area of Outstanding Beauty, Flora, you must have it," Granny would say. Only now does she realize quite how divisive this must have been. How her sisters must have secretly hated her for it. And yet the mirror had felt rightfully hers, almost earned. Back then, she hadn't been able to differentiate between how she'd looked and who she was, her soul and her face, or rather other people's reactions to her face, the double takes and intimidating building-site whistles she bore as her lot, as well as proof of a secret power—and a ticket to future happiness. She knows better now, of course. But she fears that her self-worth is still bound up with how she looks, her weight, the desire she ignites—or not—in others. Trying to ignore the pores on her nose, she wonders who she'll see in the mirror at fifty, or sixty, or eighty. What she *wants* to see. A different sort of power, that's what.

Her fingers slide into her handbag's discreet internal pocket, somewhere even Scott would never think to check, and pulls out her blister pack of contraceptive pills. She swallows one down with a decisive gulp of water. Better. Relieved, she rushes downstairs to ladle her tomato soup into Granny's cabbage leaf bowls, determined to rescue lunch.

19

LAUREN

| | |

1999

GRANNY'S LEATHERY HAND bore down with the cabbage leaf bowl, pillowed with cream. "You really won't, dear?"

Bertha squawked a repeat of the question. A wasp circled the sticky pot of red jam. The scone waited, glossy on my plate. I was too full of feelings to eat.

"No? You need a bit of meat on you." Granny passed the bowl to Kat, who spooned out fat dollops, and Granny gave her an approving smile. "You've not gone whatsy-a-ma-doodle faddy have you, Lauren?"

"Mum has made cream illegal in our house now," said Kat, her mouth full. Unlike Flora, who nibbled around the edges of biscuits in case she accidentally became fat, Kat always ate with ferocious hunger—at least two eggs for breakfast, second helpings, and puddings—like she'd been starved between Augusts. "Also bread. And cake."

"Good god," said Granny, patting Kat's hand. "You poor creature."

I loved the cream teas normally, just as much as Kat. The cloth napkins I'd learned to drape across my lap. Milk in a dainty jug, never a carton like at home. The cake stand with the long stem and frilly edges. The way each cream tea was a Russian doll containing all the others we'd ever had. But that August had broken off from the ones before it. Rock Point felt like a slippery, confusing place to be.

Dad wasn't at the table—he preferred working hungry—and I knew Angie was in the studio that very minute, washing his brushes, cleaning the palettes, burrowing her way into the one place in the house I truly belonged, wasn't at the edge of things. Kat and Flora didn't care. The less Angie was around, the better. Their conversations were all about the eclipse—and the rumors of beach parties. Like Grandpa, their eyes were on the sky. Mine were on the moor. I hadn't seen Gemma since she'd bolted away from the hermit's hut two days ago. I'd tried to call her from the phone in the hall, but Granny had hovered, and no one answered the phone at Gemma's anyway.

"You do look pale, Lauren." Granny's eyes jabbed, then softened. "I hope you're not coming down with something. Or is it the reading? I've seen your light on far too late."

"Explains why Flora's never ill," Kat said.

"I'm just not hungry today for some reason." I tried to smile. But I felt watery around the edges.

"Don't worry. It'll be this oppressive heat, Lauren," said Grandpa kindly, patting my hand. "A storm's brewing."

The air did have a stick-and-suck to it, like skin on drying oil paint. Berthingham Palace had had to be moved out of the tropics of the conservatory into a cooler spot in the corner of the kitchen. But it was the atmosphere in the house that was wrong.

I'd begun to suspect Angie of saying something to Granny, who kept asking questions about my "plans," as if checking Gemma wasn't involved in them. "As things are no easier between your assortment of mothers, Lauren, enjoy being with your sisters while you can. That's why I've got you girls here after all. And you know how August just flies?" (And I knew not to tell her where I was intending to go after that tea.)

Granny hadn't even seemed upset about the wardrobe raid at the time. When Kat and Flora hurtled back into the house, their dress hems crusted in sand, Granny's hand leaped to her throat, and she'd hooted with laughter and said it was a great improvement on denim hot pants. Waiting in the studio, Dad hadn't been so happy. "Take off those ridiculous dresses. I'm not Joshua bloody Reynolds."

The kitchen filled with the sounds of chewing and tea sipping and clinking cutlery, until Bertha squawked, super loud, in Granny's voice, "I've got a most terrible suspicion, Herbert."

Either the light changed outside the window or the color drained from Granny's face.

"A most terrible suspicion!" Kat was delighted. "Ooh. About what, Granny?"

"Mrs. Peacock in the library with the candlestick?" said Flora.

I started to smile too because Granny looked so flustered. Although I'd never dare tease her, I loved it when my funny, fearless sisters did. Then it dawned that this terrible suspicion might be connected to me.

"It's just parrot nonsense, girls. Shush, Bertha," Granny said sharply, exchanging a charged, private look with Grandpa.

"Bertha, our oracle." Kat twisted on her chair and clapped for the parrot, who puffed her feathers. Granny's forehead smocked with a frown. I stared at my uneaten scone.

"Bertha doesn't know if she's coming or going right now. Not with the eclipse. She'll sense it, all animals do." Grandpa drained his tea, keen to move the conversation on. "Only two days, Kat, and the birds will start flying backward."

Granny got up abruptly and started clearing plates with a noisy clatter.

"A total eclipse can make people behave in unexpected ways too." Grandpa adjusted his mustache with his fingers and raised one eyebrow at Kat and Flora. "Don't say you haven't been warned."

———

HEAT PUFFED UP from baked ground. Rabbits scattered. A hawk circled overhead. On the horizon, two stones. I ran and ran, over clover, dandelions, valerian, and grass, up and up, inhaling the green smell, lighter and lighter.

The moor swept under the Heaps' rickety fence like a prickly, heathery sea. Rock Point had its clouds of hydrangeas: this cottage had yellow gorse. I preferred the gorse. In the scrubby front garden, Viv, belly down on a towel, wearing a brown bikini, the tiniest strip covering her bottom, which gleamed with oil, like a seal's wet skin. "Hello." I didn't know where to look. "Is Gemma in?"

"Oh, hiya." Viv lifted her face from the towel and smiled, squinting in the sunshine. A line of sweat threaded into the groove between her breasts. Next to her was a book, a can of Coke. "Gemma's a bit under the weather today. I've ordered her back to bed, I'm afraid."

"Oh." Movement sucked my eyes to the cottage's ground-floor window. Two faces, just for a flash. Gemma's brother Pete and, I was pretty sure, the boy who'd stared back at me at the hermit's hut. They bundled, laughing, and dipped down below the sill. I felt very hot.

"All okay, love?"

My gaze shot back to Viv. I nodded, scuffed my sandal into the grass, startling a cricket, turned to leave, then stopped. "Can I talk to you?" I asked shyly, without knowing exactly what I wanted to say. But there was something about Viv, like you could tell her anything, a bit like Mum. And I couldn't face returning to Rock Point, all the words jangling inside.

"Me?" Viv hesitated. Something zipped behind her eyes. "Sure. The rain's coming, I can smell it. Can't you? Here." She patted the towel.

I sat on the farthest edge, near Viv's foot. Purple shiny varnish, nails like mussels. Long brown legs: iron filing dots where she'd shaved. A small waist, wide hips, like the cross-section of two circles of different sizes. I suddenly understood why Dad would watch Viv from the studio window as she walked across Rock Point's drive at the end of her shift, untying her apron. Dad was fascinated by shapes, like a mathematician was numbers.

"So, Lauren." Viv propped up on her elbows and glanced around, checking that no one else was there, and said quietly, "Is this about the ball gowns . . . ?"

I caught my breath. "How did you know?"

"A mate of Pete's spotted you all. Said something." She brushed an ant off her ankle.

Him. The boy on the path. In the cottage right now. For some reason, I felt betrayed. Like he'd broken an unspoken promise. "Viv, it wasn't Gemma's fault, I swear. I ripped the dress."

"Ah, you're a fine friend, Lauren. Don't worry. She's not in trouble." Viv offered me some of her Coke and I shook my head. She tapped a little finger on the metal top. "So, nothing else?"

I couldn't stop it all from rushing out then: Angie saying we were dirty little so-and-sos, Granny saying I should spend more time with my sisters, the funny atmosphere in the house.

Viv listened with her whole face. Talking and talking, I wrapped my arms around my legs, dropped my chin to my knees, wanting to sit on that towel with Viv forever. But then I ran out of stuff to say and already the big things were smaller. The hush was soft, lively with wind, something else too.

"Leave it with me, Lauren." There was something about how Viv said it, her jaw set. I couldn't really imagine how she'd bring it up with Granny but was relieved she was on my and Gemma's side. A moment passed. Closing her eyes, Viv raised her face to the sun, with a frown that hadn't been there earlier. It felt like the end of the conversation.

"I hope Gemma feels better soon." I stood up, the skin of my legs sticking.

"Thanks, love." She peered at me through half-shut lashes. "The Finches are lucky to have you. Don't forget that."

I fought the overwhelming urge to ask for a hug. As I got to the gate, she called out. "Oh, wait. Gemma made something for you. I was going to bring it over to Rock Point on my next shift. You should take it now. Give us a sec."

I watched Viv's oiled flesh jiggle toward the door, then dash back out, clutching a paper bag. Far out at sea, thunder rumbled. She nodded up at the sky. "Uh-oh. Looks like the eclipse has turned up early." Cloud masked the sun, smoldering at the edges. "Get your skates on, Lauren. You don't want to be out on the moor if there's lightning."

I ran back, digging into the bag as I moved. A bird? I stopped, breathless, delighted. A bird, like a corn dolly, woven out of straw. A budgie, I realized. Like the ones in the aviary Gemma loved. The nicest thing I'd ever been given by anyone ever, its woven cavities filled with our friendship, every letter we'd ever written, all our meandering conversations and jokes. I was still grinning as I reached Rock Point, the corn bird warm in my hand. A fork of lightning struck the sea, turning it gold. *Boom.* Seconds later, another and another. *Boom, boom, boom.* I watched spellbound, the forks of lightning cracking the wall of sky.

20

KAT

| | |

LOW WINTER SUN bounces off the mirrors her father would use to manipulate the light in the studio. Kat can't help but wonder if he's still using shiny things—talk of heavy metals in his hair, Rock Point's refurb, a Las Vegas wedding—to distract their attention from murkier matters, or worse, further "announcements" to come. Searching for the nude sketch that had so ruffled him, she tugs the lowest cabinet drawer again. Locked. Damn. Was it a nude of Dixie, one he's feeling too upset to share? Only that wouldn't tally with the date—1980; Dixie was mideighties—or the panicked urgency of his snatch.

Kat's mobile shatters the studio's hush, piercing her thoughts. Is her phone always this loud? How does she bear it? The bloody lawyer. Again. On a Saturday as well. She flicks it to voicemail. Her left leg starts to move, her trainer sole rhythmically scuffing on the floorboards.

Quite a few calls to return now. And she can't face any of them. Even ignoring the capricious signal—she needs a satellite phone, like a deep-sea trawlerman—Rock Point is a vortex, messing with her head, slowing the ticker-tape rush of her thoughts. The constant crash of the waves has become a numbing, hypnotic white noise that makes Spring's data—click-through, engagement, advertising revenue—seem oddly meaningless, a spray of digits, not the patterns she can read faster than anyone else. She needs to get her shit together. Her priorities straight.

A run might help. Just her, pitted against Strava and the universe, all breath and thrust, legs like pistons. Another black coffee. And a garage that's open and able to fix Angie's bust car. So they can wave her off into a treacherous blizzard. Dad can love whom he likes—he always has, with extravagant abandon. But marrying? No. Just no. Marrying brings ugly inheritance issues. And not just of Rock Point. There's his art collection, his Soho flat and East London studio. Possibly other boomer treasures—stocks, investments—squirreled away and forgotten. If he marries and then dies before changing his will, Angie will get the lot. Likely Angie, no fool, knows this, and will not be shooing him into his solicitor's dusty Marylebone office anytime soon. Flora is naïvely certain Dad will sort it out, and says he's recently muttered a couple of times about "needing to update" his will. But Kat can sniff out fiscal disorder, and this has a pungent whiff. Her father's affairs have always teetered on the edge of chaos, life's admin of no interest. And she's not sure he'd even care if he did leave a steaming legal mess behind. Still. It'd be too inflammatory to dive into the touchy subject of inheritance with Angie still at Rock Point. For this reason alone, she could throttle the person who screwed that tire, delaying her departure.

And why target Angie? She can't work out why Angie's scruffy

Kia was picked over Flora's ostentatious SUV, or Dad's distinctive yellow Porsche ("The Blonde" Kat's mother witheringly calls it). Someone local—the note writer, presumably—must have nursed vengeful thoughts about Angie in the corner of their mind all these years. With that lurid flume of hair, she's instantly recognizable.

The police should be called. But Angie refused: "I don't want *them* involved!" she'd said, appalled, like some sort of gangster's moll. Dad agreed with her—channeling the nonchalance of Cockney ex-crim friends who'd long ago swapped lives of crime for arts club notoriety—insisting the "Keystone Kops" wouldn't be interested at this time of year anyway. Kat suspects he's secretly worried about jogging a local policeman's memory. Disturbing old ground.

Speaking of which . . . She presses her hip bones against the trestle table and curiously opens a thick sketchbook. Hearing the click of the studio door, she whips around.

Lauren's surprised gaze slides to the sketchbook in Kat's hands. "What's up?"

Kat feels both guilty and faintly ludicrous then, searching for some random old sketch. Chasing shadows from the past. Better not to mention it. She doesn't want Lauren to think she's snooping—there's a possibility she might tell Dad—and she doesn't want to add to Lauren's hefty psychological load either. Her sister is delicate enough right now. Yes, she'll keep it to herself. If in doubt, say nothing. "Just checking out Dad's roof repair funds."

"Ah, yes." Unquestioningly swallowing this line, Lauren pads over in socks, bringing a waft of salt and earth; smells Kat remembers carrying back to her mother's Notting Hill flat years ago, like the gritty sand in her shoes and straggly sun-bleached hair that smelled of bonfires and sea. On her first days back in London—the city revving into September, new school shoes, new starts—Kat refused to wash, not wanting to lose that last bit of freedom and summer. Not wanting to grow up again.

"Lauren, tell me." Kat folds over another page, sending a mite scurrying. "Isn't it reckless to have left all these drawings here?"

"Totally. It's too damp and they should be properly archived." Lauren picks up two stray dried-out brushes from the table and slips them into a battered metal pot, neatening the place, just as she did as a girl.

In the studio, their sibling power balance always did turn on its head. Lauren had an assurance in this room she didn't elsewhere. And it was her opinion their father sought here, as though her unconventional childhood—or, more likely, Dixie's influence, Dixie's genes—gave her a prized perspective. Kat and Flora had resented her for this. They'd also tried to crush it, Kat realizes with a jolt of shame. Behind Lauren's back, they'd called her "the studio pixie."

Kat points to a drawing. "What do you think?" she asks uncertainly, deferring to her sister. "To my hopelessly untrained eye, works in progress?" A torso, just a few lines. A doodle really. "Half-finished?"

"No, don't think so." Lauren tilts her head on one side. "Life model sketches. Or studies for a bigger work."

"Oh, okay. What do I know?" Kat thinks of the muddy-gray blank spaces that often surround figures in his portraits, or coalesce in corners; negative space, Dad calls it, as important as any sitter. A lot of the stuff in *Girls and Birdcage*, as if there was something he couldn't quite portray or resolve. "His paintings always look kind of unfinished to me too."

"If an artist says a work is finished, it's finished." The smile in

Lauren's eyes catches the petrol-blue shimmer of sunlight. "Picasso used to say to finish a work is to kill it."

"Ha. I will use that line at the shareholder meeting."

Lauren laughs and Kat thinks what a wonderful laugh it is, bigger than you'd expect from her frame.

Another sketchbook: she turns its pages carefully. "It's a bit like rifling through Dad's head. Or bed." Wrong thing to say. "Sorry. I didn't mean Dixie . . ." Kat blunders. "You know what I mean. I'll stop now. So, is this stuff any good?"

"Yep," Lauren replies without hesitation.

"Worth something?" She wishes she could put a figure on it.

"Definitely," Lauren says, distractedly, head on one side, more interested in the drawings.

"Here. Take this." Kat closes the sketchbook and presses it into Lauren's hands. "Before Angie does."

"Oh no, I can't take it." Lauren looks baffled.

"Dad said take anything you like."

Lauren places the sketchbook down again. "Not these."

"You, out of all of us . . . you deserve it," she says, possibly too forcefully, as if emotional debts from childhood can be repaid materially. The holes stuffed with sketches and banknotes. "No one would blame you if you left early either," she adds, trying to be kind, making it worse. "This must be a nightmare for you. Angie. The parrot . . ."

"I'm not going anywhere," Lauren says quietly. "Mum made me promise to reach out to my Finch family after she'd died." Her voice wavers slightly, grief bubbling beneath it. "Dad's invite felt like a sign."

"Okay," Kat says, trying extremely hard not to sound skeptical.

But life is about cause and effect, action and reaction. Mysteries unusual events without analysis. One of her favorite throwaway quips is that everything, ultimately, is code. Knowing it'd be a horribly insensitive thing to say at that moment makes an awful part of Kat want to say it. Decimate everything. Edging away from the delicate, intimate turn of the conversation, she takes her phone out of her pocket and rolls her eyes. "Work calls," she says, with a small excusing groan.

But Lauren just stands there, refusing to take the hint. A loaded silence presses against them. Kat can sense what's coming.

"Kat, the eclipse summer . . ." Lauren's voice lowers, as if the words might crack on contact with the air.

A ripped blue ball gown; Gemma's "Tuesday" knickers; a black gunshot sun. "Oh yeah?" she says absently, her heart starting to hammer.

"No one ever talks about it."

"Well, that's the Finch family for you."

Lauren picks at a hardened lump of glue on the table and explains that in the days before she died, Dixie tried to tell her something important—some sort of secret—about that summer. Outside the window, gulls scream and wheel, and it feels like they're inside Kat's skull.

"But Mum lost her thread and drifted off," Lauren continues. "And I never found out what it was, this secret. Do you know?"

"I just know what you know, sorry." She tries to sound neutral. But her voice comes out too high. "And what was in the newspaper."

In the years afterward, if a journalist ever dared ask Dad about it, he'd walk out of the interview. Eventually, the story ran out of oxygen. But, of course, it didn't, Kat realizes. It's still alive, and currently shuffling around the studio.

"Kat?" With perfect timing, Flora shouts from the bottom of the studio stairs, "Lauren? Are you up there?"

"Yeah!" she shouts back, relieved to be interrupted.

"Kat, wait. Quickly, I need to show you something." Lauren reaches into the pocket of her combat trousers. "I should have mentioned it earlier, but I didn't want to freak out Flora and . . ."

A thunder of footsteps. "Where's Raff?" Her face flushed, Flora bursts into the studio. "Please tell me he's up here with you."

21

LAUREN

||||

2019

LAUREN LEAPS BACK as Angie throws open the master bedroom door. "What's the kerfuffle?"

"Have you seen Raff?" Lauren peers over Angie's shoulder, catches a glimpse of ruffled bedsheets, and quickly averts her gaze. "He's hiding somewhere." And so is the note that she'd been a second from sharing with Kat and is still in her trouser pocket. She desperately wishes she'd told her sisters straight after she found it now, rather than hesitating, worrying it might spook them away, its menace compounded by the stabbed tire. "Flora's worried."

"Where is he?" Flora walks over, grabs Angie's sleeve, as if she might be responsible.

"Hey," says Angie softly, glancing down at Flora's hand. "He won't have gone far."

"We'll find him, Flora," Lauren says, trying to reassure her sister as she spins in blind panic on the landing. "He's probably rooting through the cupboards for treasures to take home or something."

Flora stops. "Yes. Yes, he will, won't he? But . . . but . . . oh god."

"What's this business with Raff?" Charlie appears in his bedroom doorway, his shirt askew, his hands on Angie's shoulders. "Oh, he's being a monkey, is he? Flo, don't worry. You lot would disappear for hours—hours!—at Rock Point some days." Flora blinks at him incredulously.

Lauren tries to think of the places and nooks that drew them as children, the places one might hide—and get stuck. Rock Point's not the sort of place you want to lose a four-year-old. Not for a minute.

"Right, where was he last?" Angie asks, bending over, pulling on her silver boots.

"I . . . I left him downstairs playing with the shells, the jar in the living room, and went upstairs to take a call from Scott. We were talking, I don't know, twenty minutes? And I came down and . . . and the shells were there, on the floor, and Raff wasn't." Flora can hardly speak now, wiping tears from her eyes with the heel of her hand. "Oh god."

"The dressing room?" suggests Lauren.

Flora flings open Granny's wardrobe, revealing its soft stale belly. The hangers screech on the brass rail as they rummage through the forest of their grandmother's dresses they'd once pillaged and worn, gallivanting over the cliff tops. No Raff.

As each room in the house is checked—the chilly scullery, the warm laundry cupboard, empty closets in empty bedrooms—it becomes less likely Raff's in the house or playing some drawn-out game.

The house starts to fill with rising urgent voices, "Raff? Raff, are you here?" and shake with footsteps, as if the floors were drum skins, and hundreds of feet are running, besieging it, splitting it apart. Lauren returns to the studio, just to be sure he's not sneaked up here while they were looking elsewhere. She prizes open the under-the-eaves cupboards of tools and paints, releasing a clotted scent of undisturbed things. Pushing a wicker picnic hamper aside, she sees a box labeled "Photos." At any other time, she'd fall on it, attempt to fill in the lost frames of that last summer. But Raff must be found first. The only discovery that matters.

"His wellies! His wellies are missing!" Flora shouts from downstairs. Raff hates the wet and cold. He wouldn't wander out alone, she's sobbing. Never, never, never.

Lauren's heart crashes as she traverses the conservatory—Bertha screams and squawks excitably—and straight into the bleak January garden.

The aviary. It seems to radiate cold like a block of ice. For a snip of time, she can see a figure lying there, balled, hands over their head. But it's a trick of the low light, the moisture in the air, and she turns away, back to the house.

Bertha's squawking. Talking. Lauren stops, listens harder. Yes, there it is again. "Shark!" Bertha's mimicking Raff's voice. "Shark!"

Lauren runs through the alley, the dripping ivy, into the savage expanse of sea, sky, and rock beyond. In the lane, she turns and squints up at the moor. If Raff has wandered up there it could be very dangerous indeed, and he'll need retrieving quickly. But if you want to see sharks you don't head away from the water, do you? Deciding that Bertha's tip-off is worth following, she scrambles toward the cove, not sticking strictly to the path since a boy probably wouldn't either, crisscrossing the ridges and ledges, slipping and skidding.

Halfway down, she spots Jonah—his tall bulk, coat hood up, his black dog—walking on the cliff top, the other side of the cove. She waves frantically to get his attention—he might have seen Raff. But he walks away, head down. Her spirits plummet. She wonders if he's blanking her after their encounter in the Heaps' cottage, and why, and then feels bad for thinking about herself at such a time.

The fog starts to roll in, curling around her boots, clinging to the cliff face in little clouds. Resting gulls explode upward, stealing her breath; poised to dive-bomb, razor-beaked, and attack her as they would a freshly hauled fishing net. Her heart scuds in her chest, her slickening palms. Stupidly, she's left her phone in the house. A couple of times, she's struck by that sense that someone else is around, watching. She hears a footstep, the knuckle crunch of small rocks moving against one another, unseen behind an outcrop. When she stops, the noise does too. "Raff?" she shouts into the torrent of wind. Nothing.

Where *is* he? She pictures the cave at the bottom of the cliff, that dark wet throat where the incoming tide seeps, playfully slow at first, then in a lethal flooding gush. "Raff?" she yells again, cupping her hands around her mouth. His name seems to cling there a moment before the wind steals it.

There's one place she hasn't checked. A few meters down.

That ledge. With its perfect panoramic view. And vertiginous drop. A memory starts to twist into life—the same ledge, a boiling summer day, the world tipped upside down. She stumbles, cutting her steadying palms on a seam of raised white granite. More gulls lift with a bellows-beat of air. And that's when she sees Raff.

A few feet below, a small lump on the ledge, like the back of a hunched puffin. She inhales to call out, then stops, not daring to startle him, realizing, with a gut flip of dread, why she cannot see his legs.

22

LAUREN

| | |

1999

THE LEDGE WAS the sort of thing grown-ups warn you about. Only no one did. Not that we'd have listened. To get to it, you had to scramble down facing the cliff, checking that the rocks held firm before releasing your full weight, grabbing the tough tussocks of grass like handfuls of hair, hoping the person above didn't dislodge a stone onto your head. I wasn't as bold as my sisters but was still, at that point, without real fear, foolishly trusting. It was the holidaymakers who got in trouble, bobbing out to sea on inflatables. The newbie surfers. Oh, and the tourists' dogs, who'd chase rabbits off the edge. Still, it was best not to look down until you reached the strip of flat smooth rock that protruded from the cliff wall like a rock climber's camp bed. And then it was the best place in the world.

Our dangling feet kicked into the breezy nothing. The next day's eclipse seemed like a hoax. The morning sky was still the brilliant chemical blue of a grow-your-own crystal. The molten sun. Close to shore, we spotted dolphins and held our breath, tracking their inky shadows vanishing into the deep. And as the tide sucked out, rock pools flashed like small round mirrors, and the cave's mouth grew. That evening, we'd build a driftwood fire on its sandy floor. The sparks and embers would glow against the rock walls, and we'd toast marshmallows, cindery and gluey-sweet, and plait each other's hair and talk in low voices.

But at that point, we were still wearing damp costumes, having grabbed a sweet slice of time between swims and a studio sitting, out of reach of Angie. After the dolphins had gone, Kat cracked us up with Granny/Bertha impressions: "A most *terrible* suspicion!" Every few seconds, Flora extended her legs to check on the progress of her tan. And Gemma's little corn bird sung silently in my hand. Unlike on the studio sofa, I was in the middle for once, and enjoying being squished, guarded by my sisters. It'd begun to feel like our August would turn out okay after all, that any wrongness would right itself.

I lifted the corn bird to my nose and sniffed it—sunbaked hay bales. Marveled at its sharp beak. The airy swell of its woven straw chest. Gemma's deft fingers had given it life, and the pulse in my own palm was its heartbeat. But I still hadn't seen Gemma to thank her or ask if she was feeling better, or where she'd watch the eclipse tomorrow. My sisters' plans, which seemed to revolve around gatecrashing beach parties, still came with an unnerving fizzle, and, partly because of this, I wanted Gemma there too.

"Did Gemma really make that thing?" Flora said suddenly, jamming right up against me, her ribbony hair blowing into my mouth. She gave the corn bird a wary prod. "You don't think she found it in one of those junk shops where they sell horseshoes and passed it off as her own?"

"She'd never do that." I lifted my chin. "Doesn't need to either.

Gemma can make anything." I could feel my sisters' gazes hook together over my head.

"That's worse." Kat leaned in from the left, braces flashing in the sunlight. "Come on, it's kind of witchy. It so is, Lauren! Hang on a minute, is Gemma some kind of . . ." She threw her hands up into the air in a fake silent scream. "Did she whip up yesterday's lightning too?"

They started to laugh, and I caught it, disloyal, giddy from the heat and height.

"First she tries to electrocute us. And now she's trying to roast us alive." Flora lifted her hair off her shoulders. "It's boiling. Anyone got a scrunchie?"

Kat tugged one off her wrist and flicked it at Flora, but a gust caught it, sending it flying over the edge. I peered down; crags of rock, staggered like stairs; snaky ripples of sand. When I looked up, my sisters were staring greedily at the bird in my hands, and the mood had changed.

"Toss the witchy corn dolly, Lauren," teased Kat. "Dare you. Let's see if it flies."

I held the bird tighter.

"Of course, it'll fly," said Flora. "Gemma made it."

I laughed, just to prove I wasn't taking them seriously, then leaned back, starting the delicate maneuver of standing up. Escaping them.

"Don't leave us!" Kat pulled me down again, her strength a shock. "Toss the bird off the cliff, Lauren. Do it, do it."

"No." It came out too fiercely. "Gemma made it especially for me."

Kat did jazz hands. "Introducing the amazing Gemma Heap!"

"Perfect Gemma." Flora winked. "Told you they were in love, Kat."

Just from Kat's huge grin, I could tell this was a joke that was already alive and had been running without me knowing. And the more I defended the bird, the more they'd fight for me to throw it. A test of loyalty, I told myself even though I knew there were other things going on too. A sort of rubbing friction—like a tight shoe in the heat—that sometimes blistered up, and was always there, and had been since my first Rock Point summer.

"You prefer the cleaner's girl to your *sisters*?" Flora said.

"I did wonder," Kat said in a way that was both affectionate and yet also not. And that's when she lurched, trying to grab it out of my hand.

"Get off," I shouted, half laughing. Yet also not. We wriggled, twisted, fierce and playful, joking not joking, until I was leaning too far out of balance, and the bird slipped from my clammy palm. "It's flying!" hooted Flora. I instinctively lurched sideways to grab it and everything tipped and wheeled, and the warm August air flooded my throat as I screamed.

Through my hair, a centimeter or two from my nose, I could see a lone pink thrift flower growing in a crag on the vertical cliff wall and, directly down, a kaleidoscope swirl of beach and rock. My blood was in my head. My weight too. My left buttock was still in contact with the ledge but at the wrong angle and I knew I was only held there by my sisters' sweaty grip on my shins. I tried to push against the rock with the flat of my palms and leverage back but didn't have the strength. "Pull me up!"

Flora started giggling, a nervous, stunned giggle, like she couldn't quite believe what was going on either.

Kat said, "How much is it worth?"

They weren't scared for me because life was a game to my sisters. Bad things didn't happen to girls like them.

"Please," I panted, wriggling, trying to find the stomach muscle that would right me, save me. Instead, I suddenly descended, my cheek brushing against the flower's petals.

"Kat, I'm losing my grip," Flora called above me, panic in her voice.

But Kat didn't reply. Nor did they pull. And I realized how much they resented me for showing up in their lives aged nine. For existing. And I could feel something cruel and out of control rushing through Kat and Flora. The way they gave each other permission to do things they'd never do alone.

"Please." A sob cracked my voice.

"Oi!" A voice boomed from the cove below. And I glimpsed him, the boy from the path by the hermit's hut, and, later, Gemma's cottage. "You idiots. Pull her up!" he called.

"What's it to you?" Kat bellowed back. But they started dragging me backward slowly. My T-shirt rode up, grazing my stomach. I was gasping from the inversion and fury. "I can't believe you didn't . . . you didn't . . ."

"Hang on, *we* saved you." But Kat looked like she'd shocked herself. "Didn't we, Flo?"

"You fell. We pulled you up," Flora said shakily, trying to rewrite it.

I rubbed my calves where Kat's and Flora's hands had left flaming bracelets. Even then I somehow knew they'd never quite vanish, that what had just happened had marked me. Despite the sunshine, a chill traveled over my skin, like the eclipse had already started. A shadow. First contact. No one said anything.

Then Kat touched my arm. "You know we'd never actually let you fall, don't you, Laurie?"

But I didn't know that at all.

"Don't turn this into something it's not, Lauren," said Flora quietly: she meant don't snitch. "I think Grandpa might be right, you know, what he said about the eclipse making everything go a bit mad? And it's tomorrow. Tick-tock, right?"

Fearing I'd blub if I spoke, I stood up, grabbed my towel and flip-flops, and scrambled away to rescue the straw bird from the beach, Kat and Flora calling me back, shouting sorry. The bird's lightness had saved it. Carefully brushing off the sand, feeling like it'd fallen instead of me, I glanced around for my savior. I didn't want to thank him exactly since I was humiliated by what he'd witnessed. I didn't know what I wanted. But he'd gone. I shakily made my way back to Rock Point, trying to put it behind me; not knowing then that I'd feel that tip from the ledge, over and over.

Nearing the house, I spotted Viv and Dad by The Drop. Talking intensely. Rather, Viv was talking, Dad listening, nodding, a hand over his mouth. Wearing her bleach-splattered cleaning overall, she was clearly setting him straight—*"Leave it with me"*—all the things I'd confided sitting on her towel. I breathed out: Viv was on my side. But Kat and Flora? I wanted to believe they were, I really did. But as I slipped through the moon gate, unseen, a new fear of my sisters had started to burrow inside me.

23

FLORA

|||

NO ONE'S DIED. It's all completely fine. Look. Raff's strutting around the kitchen in his brown bear onesie wolfing cheese on toast, burned to a carcinogenic crisp by Daddy. She's curled up on the Lloyd Loom with a packet of Oreos. Now that Rock Point is inhabited again, it's no longer hypothermic. Not one bit of her is cold. Hanging on the rack, the glint of the copper pans she'll soon take back home. Gingham tea towels drying on the cooker's rail. Pots of wooden spoons. A full fridge: there is so much comfort to be found in a full fridge, and the radio's shipping forecast's dulcet tones—"*There are warnings of gales south in Viking, North Utsire . . .*"

But, oh, the domesticity and normality only intensify the horror.

One can live carelessly one minute—in a world where the sugar content of raisins matters, and she can lovingly dust Granny's old pickle jars—and not exist the next. Lurking innocently in the diary, passed every year until it's not, a last breath, an end of what-ifs and maybes, to-do lists and tomorrows. And this will happen to her. Far, far worse, it will happen to Raff. And she will not be able to stop it. Oblivion is inevitable. It is too much to bear. She reaches for another biscuit.

Dad wanders back into the kitchen wearing Moroccan slippers and Angie, draped like a shawl around his shoulders. "How is my little wild man?"

Raff Tarzan-beats his chest with his fists. And her father does the same.

"Daddy, please don't encourage him." But she's touched by how much he loves being a grandparent, the surfeit of worship, the lack of responsibility. But mostly for how he accepts her little boy for who he is, rather than trying to mold him as Scott and his parents do.

"Shall I tell Flora about the noseprint?" Angie whispers loudly.

"I wasn't going to . . ." Charlie eyeballs Angie.

"What?" That yawning dread again. "Tell me. Tell me immediately."

"Angie noticed a little greasy mark on the living room window," he says, swatting it away with a hand flap. "Almost certainly nothing."

"Sweaty forehead. Or the tip of a large greasy nose," Angie says.

"Oh god." Flora grabs Raff, cuddling him to her knee. He smells animal. He needs a hot bath. A good scrub and shampoo. He still has a smear of red lipstick beside his ear. Normally, she'd have sorted this straight away. But a draining heaviness has rooted inside her, and her son's cleanliness no longer feels terribly important. "I think it's probably best I take him home now, Daddy," she says apologetically.

"Raff *not* going home." He tries to wriggle away. "Raff staying with talky-talky parrot."

Charlie throws himself down on the sofa, knits his hands over his belly, rising and falling under his cobalt shirt, straining the buttons. "Listen, Flora, it always takes a bit of time to adjust to Cornwall. Take a leaf out of Raff's book—you were the same as a kid, adaptable—and just go with it. You're not in Surrey now."

"Clearly not." Her hopes for this reunion—hearty hikes along the cliffs, cozy sisterly chats, card games around the fire—now feel absurd. From the conservatory, the sound of Bertha tearing up newspaper in her cage, one of her favorite games: it might as well be Flora's meticulous plans shredded and tossed to the floor.

"And you, young man." Charlie picks a bit of thistle out of Raff's hair. "Have you told your ma what happened yet?"

"No, Daddy, he hasn't." What she does know: alerted by Bertha's squawk—"Shark!" in Raff's voice—and the logic of a four-year-old's mission, Lauren found him and coaxed him off the ledge. When Flora heard this, her legs went weak. Because what if Lauren had taken revenge for what Flora and Kat did on that ledge years ago? The bitches they'd been? The next moment, she was—and still is—filled with self-loathing for such a thought, rather than feeling straightforward gratitude, as a normal sister would.

"We're dying to hear all about your expedition, Raff," says Angie.

"Please don't glamorize it." Flora takes a shuddery breath, goes in again, trying to pinpoint the exact moment her mothering disastrously failed, and she hadn't sensed—not even the faintest maternal instinctive hunch—that her little boy was in danger. It was after the aborted game of Scrabble. Before Scott hung up on her. "So, let's rewind, Raff. Mummy went upstairs to take a call from Daddy. You were playing with the shells in the front room. But . . . then you put on your wellies." Just this breaks her heart. "And opened the front door?" She turns to her father crossly. "You need to sort out a proper lock. It's not 1950."

"I'll do that, Flo. But don't be cross with me. Or him. Sometimes we all need to go walkabout," Charlie says, one who knows. "The urge to venture forth, it's in us."

"It wasn't in Raff! Not before we came here. He was afraid of heights." She blinks back angry tears. Angie offers her one of Granny's linen napkins—used; from lunch earlier—and she snatches it and wipes her eyes, humiliated that Angie should be seeing her like this, ugly crying, when she's tried so hard to keep up appearances for everyone's sake.

"What would you do if you weren't afraid, Flora?" Angie asks, leaning back against the yellow wall, eyeing her curiously. "That's the killer question. Everyone should ask it of themselves."

"What? What on earth are you talking about?" And yet the answer to that question nibbles at her edges: she knows she knows it, which makes it all the scarier. "Raff could have *died*, Angie," she says, returning to the main point.

"But he's very much alive." Charlie strokes the top of her hand with his gnarly painter's thumb, trying to do that thing of his: like she's the only person in the universe who matters; whatever is broken he can fix. "Have a little faith in him. He's just a kid looking for an adventure."

"Doesn't sound like he gets too many at home," mutters Angie, her gaze snagging Charlie's.

Flora's mouth opens and shuts. The cheek of it! When she thinks what they got up to here back in the day. Benign neglect, her Granny called it, jollily, like this was a good thing. Like predators and accidents didn't exist. Everyone presumed they were okay. And they were . . . right up until the moment they weren't! She *knows* what can happen. How quickly things can go wrong. And her father and Angie damn well should too.

"Raff wanted to pat the nice doggie outside," Raff says suddenly. He has their attention.

"A dog?" she repeats. Raff loves dogs. Scott's not keen, though. And they have pale carpet. "I see."

"Did he have an owner?" Angie asks.

Raff fiddles with a button on her father's shirt. "Big man."

Flora's abdominals do a swoop, as if she's dropping very fast in a lift. "You know, I saw a man with a dog from my bedroom last night. Staring at the house. I waved and he didn't wave back."

"Big geezer?" Angie pulls out a kitchen chair, and sits on it back to front, legs either side. "Black Lab. He was in the lane this morning. I borrowed a light for my cig."

Flora grabs Charlie's arm. "That's it. Enough. We've got to call the police!"

"Nee-nah, nee-nah," sings Raff.

"Flora, darling, it's the land of the Labrador." Her father shrugs. He actually shrugs. "Maybe it ran up to the house? You can't arrest someone for letting a kid stroke their dog."

"But . . . but . . ." Her mind spins, unable to detangle it all. How will she tell Scott? He will freak. She won't tell Scott.

"Parrot." Raff slides off her knee and tugs at his grandfather's fingers. "Come on."

Charlie stands up with a knee-crack, grabs Raff, and swirls him upside down in a way that might easily end in a head injury for either party. "Come on, let's feed those fingers to Bertha."

Flora can feel Angie's assessing gaze sweeping over her. It's the sort of uncomfortable, impolite sort of visual weigh-in that precedes a comment Flora would rather not hear. Wishing Kat hadn't gone for a run—venture forth, as her father might say—she mutters, well, she'd better get on.

"Hold your horses. I need to show you something." Angie pulls a folded bit of paper out of the top pocket of her denim shirt. "I don't think it's right to hide it from you."

Flora reads this note—"*LEAVE*"—with a weakening sensation. "My god. Where did you find this?"

"Fell out of Lauren's pocket. Yes, Lauren's. Really. Saw it with my own peepers. As she was coming back with Raff. Afterward, when I asked her about it she said . . ." Angie raises an eyebrow incredulously. ". . . it was spiked on the garden gate. That she was about to show it to Kat, when you guys were in the studio, but then you interrupted, Raff was missing. Et cetera."

"Gosh," Flora says, uneasy at the confidence, wondering if it's just a brazen attempt to forge intimacy, or create a wedge between her and her sisters.

"Look, I don't mean to meddle," Angie adds, unconvincingly. "But I happen to think you're a big girl now. I told Charlie I was going to tell you and Kat. If we're all to move forward here, like a family . . ."

Flora recoils at the turn of phrase. "I don't see why Lauren didn't mention it straightaway."

"Nor did I. Then I walked past her room, and she's up there, Flora, like a little Jane Austen, bent over a desk, scribbling away," Angie says, her voice hushed. The kitchen grows smaller and brighter and more intensely, sickeningly yellow, like the inside of a hangover. "I mean, I'm not implying anything, but what is Lauren writing? And to whom?"

24

KAT

| | |

I N THE WEST, the sky blazes protein-shake pink. But Kat can
outrun nightfall. The tilt of the earth. Fired by the excess of oxygen in the air, the applauding clap of the waves, she storms up the
steep rises and flies down the other side in a hail of small stones. She
speeds up when she passes *that* ledge. It still brings it back: her own
raging adolescent urge to release her grip and let Lauren fall that day.
To spark ruin. Immolation. By not doing it—swerving from that de-
structive impulse—did she just nudge it along the line? To the day of
the eclipse. And, for a stitch of time, she can see them all—Gemma,
Lauren, Flora, and her teenage self—pressing their flimsy solar viewing glasses to the bridges of their noses, their awed faces peering up
at the sky.

A few minutes later they're way behind her, thank god, and she's
panting along a jutting headland—long, thin, pointing like a broken
finger out to sea—with a sheer drop on one side, the hungry mouth

of the Atlantic beneath. She imagines her lungs swelling, juicy and red as sirloin. Out here, she needs no one. No one needs her. And there's a moment of pure exhilaration when it feels like she's flying, leaving all the crap behind. Dad roughly snatching the nude charcoal sketch from her hand. Angie's suggestion that the poisonous notes are Lauren's work: a double bluff? The work voicemails: "Kat, did you not get my last message? Call me back ASAP." She will call after the run. As soon as her head's straight.

As soon as . . . she winces. A stitch—she never gets a bloody stitch!—like a blade twisting under her rib. Her feet gain ten pounds. Flicking sweat from her eyes, she stops, and rips open an energy gel with her teeth. Tipping her head back, sucking the sweet gloop, she sees the sky glowering, banded with foxglove-violet. But she keeps going, outrunning her fear of standing still—and the rate at which her life consumes itself. And yet she's never far enough. Never reaches the point when it feels like everything won't be snatched from her. And she'll be thrown back to where she started.

Kat was eleven when she walked in from school and discovered Blythe dead on the floor, her head gored from a collision with the corner of the brass coffee table, an empty vodka bottle in one hand, her Dior scarf scrunched in the other. But then the body twitched. After covering her mother with a blanket to keep her warm, pressing a wad of toilet paper on the wound, she called the "emergency number": a close friend of her mother's, Xanthe, who lived in the same mews, grew up in a castle, and always stank of weed. Xanthe bundled Blythe into the back of a car, told Kat she mustn't breathe *a word* of it. She didn't want Blythe's career to go up in smoke, did she? To be splashed over the tabloids? Social services involved? Xanthe told her to call a sister and stay for a few days. Tell them Blythe had a last-minute shoot abroad, something like that, yah? And if there was any problem, let her know.

Kat didn't do this. Flora's house was far too wholesome and frenetic, all squealing blond siblings, and Annabelle still hated Blythe for the affair. Lauren lived in Oxford—Kat couldn't even point to it on a map—and Dixie would know something was wrong. Dad was in New York. And she couldn't possibly tell either set of grandparents.

So she stayed put, and slept with the Dior scarf scrunched under her pillow because it smelled of her mother's Hermès 24 Faubourg perfume. She learned how to survive—and own a secret. How to hold shame so close it became part of you: she was second on Blythe's list; after the booze. Not enough. And however much she loved her mother—and however much her mother said she loved Kat—she couldn't stop her drinking. Her mother had made a choice, and it wasn't her.

Blythe didn't come back for four days. No teacher guessed Kat went back to an empty house, cornflakes and pork scratchings, bought at a pub on Portobello with coins foraged from between the sofa cushions. Locally, no one batted an eyelid. The neighborhood was stuffed with glamorously dysfunctional families; the only sin was to be boring. And Kat grew up fast, learning lessons some people never did. How it was a bad idea to be dependent on anyone—or anything—ever. Why women need to make their own money. Rule their own lives. Control the room. Stay hypervigilant.

That summer, the summer everything changed, Blythe vanished on a bender: it would actually be her last binge—a heady mix of cocaine and booze—only Kat didn't know it then. She returned to their flat, skeletal thin, bloodshot eyes masked by sunglasses, and the next day she drove—just—to Rock Point—"You'll see the total eclipse, baby!"—and tooted the horn good-bye, leaving Kat standing on the drive in her denim cutoffs, carrying anger and sadness, like a suitcase of hardening cement.

But Kat's unpacked that bag long ago, alchemized it. And Blythe is twenty years sober. In London, Kat's feet don't touch the ground. Energy begets energy. And when her mind wheels like a mosquito in the dark—those biting micro-doubts about her life choices, the inevitable comparisons with her sisters—she reminds herself that Lauren's adrift rather than free. Flora's setup would be her nightmare: the suburban gated "community"; the inventory of food expiry dates stuck to the fridge; the dull husband. Kat's life is bespoke. It fits her exactly.

So why does it feel as if decades of catatonic fatigue are stiffening her muscles like lactic acid? Odder still; why is she craving a fucking *scone*? Cream first. Granny's strawberry jam, so sweet it strips the skin off the roof of your mouth. And Kofi. Oh god, Kofi.

Kat scrolls back to Kofi stroking her hair, whispering, "I'm so sorry," when the story of her childhood, and Blythe's alcoholism, poured out after particularly mind-blowing sex, the sort that cleaves your entire being open, leaves you changed, too alive. She sobbed as she came. He was the first person she'd ever told, all the grisly bits. She couldn't bear it, his tenderness: it felt like open heart surgery. She finished the relationship a week later.

Gasping, Kat bends over, hands on her knees, then crumples to a pad of heather. It feels like the first time she's sat down for years. Stripped by the elements—the lack of traffic, Wi-Fi, noise, the things that keep her afloat—she's like a boat stranded on the sand after the tide's gone out. The fight is too much. All her body hurts. Knees. Jaw. Fingernails.

She aches for Kofi. The person she was with him. But she murdered it, them. And she is alone again. And even though she knows it's more honest like this—we enter and leave the world alone, a cluster of atoms—the wanting is not rational. It is inside her. It is above, where the thick dusk swirls, studded with stars. In the sea's thunderous boom—like hundreds of whales thrashing their tails at the same time, beating out his name. She closes her eyes.

When Kat looks up again, night is stealing across the horizon. Fishing boat lights rock on a purple-black sea. In the metallic foggy half light, the cliffs have morphed into lumpy silhouettes. Part of her is stuck in childhood summertime, she realizes. This far west, it was never dark for long, and sleep always felt like a waste of time, a squandering of fun. It's different now. She checks her phone. No signal. Damn. She's mistimed it. Basic mistake. You must always have energy for both journeys—out and back; the crime, the punishment.

But her legs disagree. She tries to use the old visualization trick: sending out the mind first, the Usain Bolt of messenger pigeons. But it falls out of the sky. Her brain simply won't go forward. Instead, it keeps flicking backward to sultry hot days at Rock Point, when she could be a kid again, free from worrying about her mother. And then it lands on the secret that lives inside their last August here, like a grub in a sweet green apple. And it is this, she realizes, staggering up, she's doomed never to escape. No matter how fast she runs.

25

LAUREN

|||

2019

STEPPING THROUGH THE apple-green door in the dusk gloom, Lauren clicks on the studio lights. They buzz noisily, then flicker on. She's alone up here at last. Earlier she'd sought the same quiet commune, a return to the lost homeland of smells and feels. Maybe have a poke around, see if there was an old paintbrush or two from a pot or a rabbit skull from the shelves she could take back to London. The last thing she'd expected was to find Kat rifling through Dad's sketchbooks, furtively searching for something. Her "roof repair funds" line hadn't been entirely convincing. Lauren's pretty sure Kat's explanation to Flora would have been more honest. A reminder that in the archipelago of sisters she's still an island on her own, just as she always was.

Lauren catches her fragmented reflection in the various mirrors, the oil-dark glint of the windows. Seen from outside, the studio must be lit like a stage. Anyone watching the house—and the greasy mark on the living room window suggests they might be—will get an eye-ful. Will the sight enrage them further? Prompt another awful note. Part of her hopes it will. For the author to misstep and leak their identity anyway. Or snap down another piece of the puzzle; the August day her family can't talk about—"I just know what you know, sorry," Kat had said tightly—yet each turn of tide seems to bring a little bit closer.

They're leaving in two days, which doesn't give the note writer much more opportunity. And since the second note appeared—"I think you dropped something," Angie had said, revealing the crumpled bit of paper in her palm, and sending the blood rushing to Lauren's face—the atmosphere in the house has changed. Dad understands why she hadn't immediately declared it. "Let some stupid idiot hound us out? No way. You should have tossed that daft note straight into the fire," he'd said, leaving no doubt in anyone's mind he'd have done exactly this. But her sisters seem unnerved by her explanation. Lauren was aware of a silent interrogation in Kat's gaze as she tied her running shoes earlier. Doubt in the infinitesimal faltering of Flora's smile, despite her repeated thanks for rescuing Raff. Rather than drawing them all closer again, she's starting to fear that Rock Point, like an anvil, will push them apart once more.

But, as she just wrote in her letter to Gemma, the eclipse only took two minutes twenty-three seconds to change everything. A lot can happen in a couple of days. And time is mutable at Rock Point. Blink and it buckles. She lowers to the sofa, and she's pressed next to Flora's silky thigh again, Bowie's "Changes" pouring out of the hi-fi. Lumps of sea glass, smooth and bright as boiled sweets, stashed in her scout shorts' pocket. Sweat pooling behind her knees and in the nest of hair at the back of her neck as she absorbs every brushstroke, pencil scrape, and rag wipe. Inhales the paint, the turpentine, her sisters' salty, hormonal tang as Dad explains how "iron blue" paints are made from the oxidization of ferrous ferrocyanide salts. The cat-paw-quick movement of her father's sketching hand; his wire-gray gaze cast out like a fisherman's line.

Lauren now realizes that those summer hours, insignificant at the time—and whiled away—must have zipped together somehow, each a tiny tipping point. Before they're lost completely, she must try to examine each one. Go back and excavate. The ocean's coldest, deepest water is continually drawn up to the sunlit surface, a process essential for its nutritional health, life itself, Gemma explained once. And she must do the same.

Squatting next to the under-the-eaves cupboard, she drags out the picnic hamper blocking its entrance, pushes it against the wall and reaches for the box labeled "Photos."

Cross-legged on the floor, using the baggy crotch of her yoga leggings as a table, she flips open a packet, and gets a poignant glimpse of Rock Point before she arrived. Looking little older than eight or nine, Kat and Flora—angelic, with pigtails—are in Rock Point's garden, backlit by a honeycomb sun. Kat's arm is slung over Flora's shoulder. They already had each other. A private language. They didn't need another sister. They probably still don't.

Working quickly, aware she might be disturbed at any point, Lauren sifts through other packets: budgies, a long-dead dog, a stilted-looking dinner party, Dad as a punkish twenty-something, standing outside Rock Point with a girlfriend, Dad leaping off a rock into the sea . . . ah, *this* is what she's after. Studio photographs. The three of them sprawled on the sofa next to the birdcage in different lights and positions, all blurred moving limbs. She can almost hear Charlie saying, wearily, "For god's sake, just stay still for one *second*."

Lauren opens her phone, registering that it needs charging: the batteries drain so quickly in this house, as she does too, continually scanning for signals, trying to update who she was here once, who she is now. Eagerly, she flicks to a saved image of *Girls and Birdcage*, finished in Dad's East End studio months after the eclipse—when he could face picking up his brushes again—and working from photographs like these, that she's never seen before.

Her gaze switches between the photo and the portrait, trying to see what's left in, excised. Of course, the painting is a self-portrait more than anything else. The work of an artist at the peak of his technical powers—and a proud father. My DNA. My blood. My paint. He has forever stilled his daughters in the process of becoming, teetering on the edge of womanhood, blissfully oblivious to what was about to happen. Unaware they could have stopped it.

Unlike the gangly disorder in the photographs, he's imposed control, holding them, almost protectively, in a classical pyramid composition, with Flora wearing a sundress—the rich lapis blue of a Madonna's robe—in the center. On the left, Kat's bare leg sticks out, taut with youth, a perfect diagonal, and on the other side of the sofa, Lauren's younger self. Her eyes—dark, the paint ground into the canvas, like ink pushed into skin—are glancing out of the frame, as if watching something approach. The portrait is undoubtedly exquisite, in the way of a butterfly pinned to a board. But there is a strain that becomes more obvious when compared to the photos. Perhaps this is "the flaw" he's mentioned while resisting any more detail. Frowning into the phone's blue glow, Lauren still has the feeling she's missing something, and it's frustrating, like trying to guess at an image that won't download properly.

But it's never too late to see a familiar painting anew, she knows that. At the National Gallery she'll often return to favorite works after the public have left. The more you look, the more you see. An observer in a crowd. A memento mori hidden in the shadows of a bookshelf. Seeded with clues, mischief, the mistakes and revisions of its creation, rarely is a painting quite as it first seems. But *Girls and Birdcage*'s most obvious symbol, the birdcage, still dominates. Like an artist, or a canvas, it frames and contains, holds life captive for the admirer's gaze . . .

"Anyone seen Lauren?" Angie's voice, coming from downstairs. Not wanting to have to explain herself, she's hurriedly returning the packet to the box when a photo slips out, like the joker from a pack. She sucks in her breath. There it is, the moment after which everything was different; unbeknownst to them, everything was ready to unspool, like a curl of old-fashioned camera film sliding out of its canister.

It's daylight, the eclipse is over, but only just. All of them—bar Dad, the photographer: "my cosmic girls"—are standing by The Drop, beaming, windswept, still holding viewing goggles in their hands. Flora, her cheekbones bladed with glitter, wearing a sequin skirt—Lauren will never forget the star-shatter of that skirt—and Kat, kohl-eyed, looking at each other, not the camera. There's a complicit charge in their glance that makes Lauren shiver. And beside Lauren is Gemma, wearing her star-print dress, a dimple, a smile. Lauren brushes her finger lightly over the image, aching to reach back in time and pause them right there. Wipe out that morning as the moon's shadow did the sun, closing over it like a camera shutter. Going, going, gone.

26

FLORA

| | |

SNEAKY. BUT THE right thing to do given the circumstances. For Flora's own peace of mind, she must debunk Angie's awful—but not entirely dismissible—insinuation that Lauren is the author of the terrorizing notes. That she's been mentally destabilized by returning to Rock Point, this chaotic rummaging through their childhood Daddy has instigated. And Flora is trying to neutralize by working out some sort of calling-dibs system. Since no one else has bothered.

Most likely, Lauren's writing letters to a secret lover. Yes, that'll be it. Someone unsuitable. Married. After all, she heard Lauren chatting on the phone in her bedroom again. Flora can't help but feel miffed Lauren's not sharing such juicy intimacies. Although she'd never dare peel back her own bedsheets—different when you're married—the point of a singleton's escapades is the hilarity and discussion over a glass of wine afterward. Epic sex, bad sex, the men who never text, or text too often; all could be vicariously enjoyed by a married sister.

On the other hand, if the two notes *are* Lauren's work—and good people can do bad things, she knows this firsthand—at least it means there's no vengeful local, readying to burst into Rock Point at any moment, like Jack Nicholson in *The Shining*.

Checking that the landing's clear, Flora cracks ajar Lauren's bedroom door, enough to get a view of the desk in the corner. No letter pad now. No pen. It occurs to her that Lauren, sensing suspicion, has covered her tracks.

"Are you looking for me?"

Flora prepares her smile, then turns. "Yes! I am, Lauren," she fibs. "It's Kat. I mean she's fine, don't worry. She went for a coast path run and it seems she ran too far . . ." A small stab of schadenfreude. "Anyway, she's sensibly taken refuge in a pub. I'm off to pick her up in a minute. Would you come with? I'm a bit of a nervous driver in the pitch dark."

Lauren looks heartbreakingly pleased to be asked. "Of course."

Flora's phone beeps. "Ah, another Kat text. Hold on." She frowns, surprised. "She wants us to bring a scarf that's stuffed under her pillow."

Raff stubbornly refuses to budge so Flora leaves him watching *Toy Story* with her father, whom she gives an inventory of strict instructions: no sugar, no fingers near the parrot's cage, front door locked, and Raff in sight at all times. She waves to them from the drive, struck by how idyllic Rock Point's interior looks framed in a window: the gold firelight, the little boy, and his granddad. Then in stark contrast, she walks anxiously around her car, crunching on the gravel, using her phone's torch to cautiously check the tires. "Yep. Good to go."

The SUV smells of Flora's life: luxury leather and Diptyque Baies car diffuser, both artificial and cloying here. She reverses, grateful it's Lauren and not Scott sat beside her—"Reversing isn't your strong point, Flora. Let me drive"—but still imagining her foot slipping, hitting the gas, hurtling into the Atlantic. To her surprise, she manages it smoothly despite the sudden heavy downpour the wipers can't clear fast enough.

Driving down the lane, rain streaming across the windscreen, Ed Sheeran blasting—"Don't judge me, Lauren"—Flora's hit by an unexpected high, a whoosh of dopamine, as if the relief of Raff's safe return has only just registered. Also, satisfyingly, Kat has asked for her help—she *does* need Flora after all—and they're off to rescue her. This is what their Rock Point reunion should be about. Sisters. Weather. Bonding in outward-bound-like experiences, with a pub at the end of it. Finally, a fizz of light.

The pub's metal sign flaps in the wind. Inside, it's cozy and crowded, with low, wormwoody beams, a whiff of wet dog and spilled ale. The customers look like weather-beaten locals—not a Canada Goose jacket in sight. Heads turn as they weave toward a slump of muddy Lycra in the corner. "Met your match?" Flora doesn't enjoy seeing her sister like this. It disturbs the natural order of things.

"Never. I got beaten by the dusk, that's all." But she looks drained, slightly haunted, as if she's confronted more than the darkness out there.

"Your scarf, Kat." Lauren hands over the disintegrating, sordid-looking thing that Flora can't imagine Kat owning, let alone sleeping with under her pillow.

Kat presses it against her cheek, and closes her eyes for a second or two, just like Raff does when he loses and then finds his beloved doll.

"Are you hurt?" Lauren kneels beside her, exhibiting the sweet bedside manner that must make her a hit at the hospice.

"Only if a blister counts." But Kat looks away. And, more extraordinarily, there are bulbs of tears in her eyes.

In her adult life Flora has never seen Kat cry. She didn't cry at Granny's funeral last year, or Dixie's in the autumn, not even when Lauren stood up and gave that speech—"I hope you're swimming now, Mum, in the warm tropical oceans you loved, sunlit, weightless, free of pain"—and everyone else was in pieces. Yet here Kat is, broken by a run, a grubby scarf pressed to her cheek. And this brings with it the possibility that Flora imagines her sisters to be one thing when actually they're quite another; that perhaps *she's* not who she is perceived to be either, the entire Finch family one big case of mistaken identity. Or worse, a performance.

"Here." Lauren shucks off her puffer jacket and tucks it over Kat's knees. "Your lips are blue. Show me your fingers." After rubbing Kat's hands in hers, Lauren places them carefully under the coat, as if she were a toddler in a pram. "You need calories. What can we get you?"

"I'd murder a Coke. Full fat. A packet of pork scratchings."

"Pork scratchings?" says Flora doubtfully, checking that she's heard it right.

"Yes, and crisps," says Kat improbably. As they turn to the bar, Kat adds, "Don't drink, Flo. Not with these roads."

Flora's cheeks heat: she'd been about to order a glass of white. She can't see the point of being in a country pub without a drink in her hand.

But, astonishingly, a lime soda doesn't ruin the evening. Sat around the small wobbly round table, eating pork scratchings— delicious, who knew?—they don't talk about the notes or Dad or

Angie. Lauren doesn't ask difficult questions about the eclipse summer. Kat doesn't even check her phone, despite its continual flashing and buzzing.

And as they relax, old anecdotes resurface; stories they'd forgotten still tie them together in knots of cringing laughter. Dad's cameos outside their school gates, roaring up in his embarrassing sports car, the other parents staring agog. The time Kat's new headmistress invited Dad to give an "inspirational talk": "Bunk off whenever you can is my advice. I was taught absolutely nothing of any value until I went to art school." How he'd taken Scott to one side at Flora's wedding, and, prodding his chest with one finger, smiling like a mafia boss, said, "Treat my daughter like a goddess or I'll fry your bollocks for breakfast, okay?" (Flora had secretly *loved* that.) The year one of Dad's girlfriends—they think her name was Jemima, but it could have been Jane, or Jessie; he had a run of girlfriends with names starting with *J*—set up a chocolate fountain in his kitchen as a treat for them and it splattered all over a Damien Hirst spot picture; the silence afterward, as they all waited for Dad to explode, and he'd waspishly said it was an improvement. His impractical, un-parent-like two-bedroom Soho flat. Friends would ring the intercom at four in the morning. Its spare bedroom was the size of a broom cupboard; staying over as girls, they'd share it with a man-sized metal sculpture that looked like a dementor from Harry Potter. Flora revels in their rare togetherness, the Finch part of her life that has always made her feel so different to her other half siblings, who came from a different marriage, a different world. And she feels their sisterhood again, something of what was lost, found.

Then Scott texts: "Why aren't you replying to my messages? Where r u? I want to say good night to Raff." Flora's warm feeling vanishes. She dares not tell Scott she's in the pub. Nor can she risk him talking to her father, who will assume he knows about Raff wandering out to the cliff and mention it. "I better get back," she says abruptly, reaching for her coat. Lauren and Kat glance up, surprised, and then they too stand, pulling back, remembering their differences again.

Turning onto the unlit lane, it feels like they're leaving the sisters they could become behind, sitting at the pub table. And Flora wants to say this but doesn't know how, certainly not without digging up the reasons they've drifted apart in the first place, which reach all the way back here, to the unmentionable. And possibly beyond that to their mothers, she realizes; the seeds of resentment and jealousy that hers planted with her muttered asides and a certain pained look that'd pass across her face if Dixie's name was mentioned. But that's the problem with digging; there's always another layer and the soil is colder, rockier, and harder to work the deeper you go. And you can never be sure exactly what you might find.

The rainy night slides against the car, wet as a fish. A vehicle pulls out from the pub car park after they do, and she's glad of its company on these empty roads. Turning on the radio, Flora starts when the unmistakable riff of Bowie's "Changes" blasts out of the SUV's formidable speakers. In a fluster, she stabs at the settings with a finger, trying to switch to something less loaded, and making a point of saying it's the radio so they don't think she's played it on purpose.

"Leave it, Flora," says Kat, huddled under Lauren's coat in the passenger seat. "It's just a song."

They all know it's not, and Kat stating the contrary only proves this. But Flora tries to behave like it's no biggie too, tapping her fingers against the wheel as Bowie's vocals—and those studio sittings—travel up her spinal cord. Checking her rearview mirror, she's relieved to see that Lauren hasn't stuck her fingers in her ears and, when the chorus swells, actually mouths the words. Made of stronger stuff, clearly.

Flora tries to block out the song by concentrating on the narrow road, the high rocky banks on either side. In the mirror, that same car from the pub, not as far back as she'd like given the conditions. She's not sure if it's the car or the song but she takes a left turn far too hard.

"Easy," Kat mutters.

"Sorry." The car behind makes the same turn. Why is it coming up so fast? It's a twisty lane, too narrow to pass a car coming in the opposite direction, let alone overtake. Tailgating now. Dazzling fog lights. "Shit," she says, in a low voice. "We've got some sort of stunt rider up our backside."

The car flashes its lights.

"Maybe they're trying to signal there's something wrong with our car?" Flora's stomach is starting to cramp. She flicks off the music. "I better pull over."

"Don't. Don't stop," says Lauren with unexpected authority from the seat behind.

"Hold your ground." Kat reaches for the handle strap.

"Oh. Right. Yes." Realizing what her sisters are thinking, Flora pictures a screwdriver stabbing at Angie's tires. Their SUV slamming into the bank, then over the cliff, flipping as it falls. Raff left without a mother. Her palms, sweating, slide slightly on the steering wheel.

"Idiot." Kat twists around, trying to see the driver. "Probably drunk."

"Who is it?" Flora asks, her voice wavering.

"I can't see . . ."

"Oh my god. Are they trying to knock us into the ditch?" Flora slams the horn with the heel of her hand. "Back off!" There's a growl, and the car closes the distance between them, its headlights two blinding suns.

27

LAUREN

| | |

1999

THE SHADOW ON the sundial kept slicing right. But the late-afternoon garden was still, held, the air thick with the day's heat and the feathery dust that puffed out of the aviary cage every time a budgie beat its wings, its hollow toothpick bones.

Me and Gemma sat cross-legged in the powdery shade of the pines, sucking on cola ice pops, wondering what might happen if a blue budgie mated with a yellow one. Would their baby be green? Were parrots like paint? And then, even though it felt disloyal, I told her about my fall from the ledge that morning, trying my best to turn it into an amusing "you won't believe . . ." story, one of those mad Rock Point events, like the day of the ball gowns.

Gemma looked shocked. "But what if that boy hadn't shouted? What would they have done, Lauren? What? You've got to tell your dad," she whispered hotly. "I would. My dad would have *serious* words." She squinted at me, searchingly, trying to pick out the truth.

"Pete would never have done that to me, though. Not in a zillion years."

"Oh, Kat and Flora were just mucking about," I said quickly, not wanting Gemma to hate them. But my calves still had faint finger marks. And the thought of my sisters' return from St. Ives—they'd persuaded Angie to drive them in to go shopping—was making my insides slosh about a bit. "I found the bird anyway, that's the main thing." I sucked the last bit of ice pop, flattening the wrapper. "It's the coolest thing anyone's ever given me, Gemma." She looked so pleased I didn't dare tell her what happened just before she called round.

I never would tell.

Once my sisters had left with Angie, I curled up in a cane chair in the steamy conservatory among the palms and fed Bertha monkey nuts through the cage bars. Then Granny swept in, a column of flowing dress—the one with shells around the neckline that gave me the willies—with her misting spray can. "Hello, dear. Are you . . ." She stopped talking. Her eyes lit up. "Oh, gosh. May I?" She put down the can on the brick floor with a clink, took the corn bird, and turned it over in her hands. She'd collected corn dollies as a girl, she murmured, in a funny distant voice. Quite her favorite thing. All lost in the house fire that'd burned their beloved dogs alive.

"Dogs alive!" Bertha squawked. Bertha hated dogs.

Ignoring this, Granny carried on, explaining how the maker would have soaked the hollow stems in water overnight, so they didn't snap when woven, the incredible patience and skill involved. Something stopped me from saying it was Gemma who'd made it.

"So budgielike," she marveled. "You wouldn't mind if I held on to this, would you? Just to show Herb when he's back from bird watching," she called over her shoulder, already halfway into the kitchen. She put the corn bird on the kitchen dresser shelf, high, among the crockery. And there it remained, leaving me with a lost-something feeling.

Gemma's coughing cut short my thoughts.

I touched her arm. "Are you still poorly? Your mum . . ."

"I'm fine." But it sounded like she was holding a cough inside. "And I was yesterday too. Still can't believe Mum didn't wake me up when you called round. She's so overprotective. I hate it."

Growing up on the moor, Gemma seemed freer than anyone else I knew. And Viv sort of perfect. We sat in easy silence for a bit, listening to the hubbub of eclipse tourists outside the garden walls. My stomach rumbled: I'd barely been able to eat since the ledge fall.

"The birds are acting strange, aren't they?" Gemma knew birds.

I nodded. "The budgies sense the eclipse coming." They were bickering and jittery, darting around the cage. "That's what Grandpa says anyway."

"Hey, it's going to be all right." Gemma made soft clucking noises with her tongue. The budgies called back. It was like listening in to a private conversation. Gemma never wanted to talk to Bertha, though. Hated the idea of a parrot inside a house. Not everything about Gemma made sense. And with every August, a new bit of her was revealed: I'd yet to find a bit I didn't like.

"Funny, isn't it?" Gemma drew a blade of grass through the gap in her front teeth. "All this buildup for something that'll be over like . . ." She clicked her fingers.

"Two minutes." I leaned across and threaded a money spider out of her hair. "Look." I showed her the spider. "Good luck."

"You're the one who needs the money spiders. With sisters like yours," she joked, even though I knew she was enchanted with them too. That was the thing about Kat and Flora. However awful they were sometimes, they pulled you in. Because they were also funny, beautiful, and ballsy and you couldn't help but want to be around them, or ride in their wake.

I lowered the spider to the grass. "Will you come over and watch the eclipse tomorrow?"

Gemma didn't say yes.

"Kat and Flora want you to come." Possibly not true. Also, I needed to okay it with Granny first. But as I'd seen Viv talking to Dad earlier, I was hopeful. "Come on, Gem, we can both wear our star-print dresses."

She lost a fight against a smile then. The sun wove into her hair and right behind her eyes, making them sparkle, and she was all wonky teeth and freckles, with toenails grubby from the dry moor soil. "If you're sure that . . ." she began.

"Yes." Whatever the question was. *Yes, yes, yes.*

The sun dipped in the west. I had an idea. "Come inside the aviary?" I wanted to repay her for the gift of the corn bird, let her feel the gold-watch tick of a budgie's heart. "I can make them land on your arm."

"*Inside there?* After ripping your nan's dress?" She stood up, grabbed her rucksack, laughing, shaking her head. "No way, Lauren."

"Everyone's out. Apart from Dad, who is painting, which is the same thing."

The biggest risk was the budgies escaping. Flock birds, they'd follow one another. Freedom would be deadly, Granny always said. They'd be pecked to death by gulls, or frozen by the Atlantic gusts and drop out of the sky like fish fingers.

"Honestly, it's . . ."

Dad's voice drifted toward us. "Lauren? I need you."

Gemma's eyes bugged. She'd always been shy around Dad. The coughing started up again.

"You okay, kid?" Dad strode over in his paint-splattered jeans. He was bare-chested and had a pencil behind his ear. For a moment, I saw him as Gemma might, a famous painter, tanned and scruffy in that rich sort of way. "Shall I get you a glass of water?" His kindness was a relief. He wasn't going to be weird about me hanging out with Gemma, not like Granny. Whatever Viv had said to him had clearly worked.

"I'm heading back for my tea," Gemma said bashfully. "Thank you, Mr. Finch."

"Hey, it's Charlie." Dad swept his gray gaze over Gemma—and as he did something moved across his eyes, like a light just under the surface of water. He frowned, and an eleven formed between his eyebrows. What Dad's face did when he was really looking, melting someone down into shapes and light and lines. It wasn't unfriendly, but uncomfortable, like an optician's torch beam. And Gemma looked embarrassed, and I could tell that Angie's words outside the hermit's hut about me spending time with my sisters were streaking through her mind, every comment Kat and Flora had made about her being the cleaner's girl.

"Gemma made me a corn dolly in the shape of a bird," I said, trying to big her up a bit. She looked so small and skinny suddenly. Rock Point shrank her. "It's on the dresser. I'll show you, Dad."

His gaze slipped into a surprised smile. "Well, then you are a much better craftsperson than I, Gemma. I'd love to see it."

Shamefully, I felt a hot stab of jealousy. Gemma scuffed her transparent plastic jelly sandal in the yellowing grass and flashed a chuffed smile. "I better get back."

We watched her spring away. Dad continued staring even when she was gone. "Dad?"

He blanched, surprised, snapping out of a spell. "Sorry."

"Do you need me to come and help in the studio?" I said hopefully.

"No, no, not that. Angie's doing a shift later. I just want a quick study of your left hand, Lauren. Like this." He squatted down on an invisible seat in midair to give the impression of me sitting on the sofa, placed his left hand on his thigh. "Your sisters aren't back yet, are they? It'll be nice. Just the two of us."

I thought of Angie, her fingers touching all the studio things, soiling them, and I couldn't look at him. His betrayal hurt.

"I've got crisps?" he added, with a grin.

While Dad made coffee downstairs, I circled the hot, empty studio with a packet of Hula Hoops and inspected the shelves. Angie *had* tinkered with them. The skulls and sea glass were in the wrong places, the varnishes now above the gesso. I put a few things back where they were meant to be, my fingers trembly and angry, leaving greasy prints on the jars. Dad was ages.

"Sorry," he said, striding back in, raking his hand through his hair. "I got snared by your grandmother, who wanted to talk." Flushed, restless, like something had rattled him, he lit a cigarette and stood in front of the big wooden easel, narrowing his eyes at *Girls and Birdcage*. He beckoned me over and rested his elbow on my shoulder as he smoked. "Not much to see yet, I know. The paint takes so damn long to dry."

The layers of oils had to build gradually, the thickest paint over the thinnest layers—fat over lean, light over dark. But we were emerging as shapes on the sofa, like ghosts reversing back to life. Me, head at an angle. Flora, draped, relaxed, her contours soft like a cat's. Kat, boxy and strong, leg stretched out. I cocked my head on one side. No, we still didn't look anything like sisters, not even in the painting. Flora looked like her mum, as I did mine. Kat was more Dad-like, with Grandpa's nose. And even though he'd caught us individually, it felt like he could have rubbed one of us out and you'd not know she was missing. Or maybe it was something else.

"I knew you'd look at it like that, Laurie." He studied my face, reading my feelings about the painting. "You see these things, don't you?" He cursed under his breath. "I can't get it right. I can't . . . it's doing my head in. I never should have started this. I'm sorry. I'm really bloody sorry. I should just be swimming with you lot in the cove, like a normal dad."

It was a bit late for that. "But you hate quitting paintings," I pointed out, not wanting a normal dad.

"I know, I know." He groaned. People thought being an artist was easy. But it was a hard, physical thing. "It's just that . . ." He screwed up his eyes, and the muscles of his eyelids flittered. "The bones, you know."

I knew some painters started with a nude, even if that figure would end up fully clothed, just to get the anatomical details right. And I hoped this was not the problem here since I'd die of embarrassment. But I couldn't bear the thought of the sittings ending either. "It's probably just the eclipse, Dad. I mean, everyone's feeling funny. It'll be different once it's over."

He stared at me a moment, considering this, and then he put an arm around my shoulder and gave it a squeeze. "You are a wise little thing, Lauren Molloy. Just like your mum . . ." He stopped and looked so sad that I grabbed his hand. He rubbed the rough tip of his finger against my knuckles. "I am so proud of you, you know that? I am so happy you are in my life again, Laurie. And I'm sorry, I'm sorry that I wasn't always there. For you and your mum. I messed up."

Not knowing what to say, I stared at a glob of blue paint on the floor. My eyes went blurry and I had too many feelings that no words fitted.

"Right," he said eventually, releasing my hand. "Let's do this." He picked the pencil out from behind his ear, pulled out a stool and his sketchbook. "Sofa."

The soft brushing sound of pencil on paper made me think of Gemma's fingers weaving, determinedly tugging the wheat stems, creating something just as Dad was doing. My palm tingled, hot and angry, wanting it back.

"That'll have to do." He frowned at what he'd done, displeased, then stood up and put the sketchbook down on the trestle.

"I can stay longer?"

"No, you shoot." He lit another cigarette and stared out the window, his thoughts already elsewhere, slipping out of himself.

Bertha flapped her wings as I walked into the kitchen. When that didn't attract my attention or secure a nut, she squawked, "Don't ask the question, Pam!" in Grandpa's voice. I paused, wondering what this meant. Through the conservatory windows I saw the backs of my grandparents' deck chairs, the stripy fabric sagged by their bottoms; Granny reaching down for her cocktail glass on the lawn. I hadn't long.

I dragged a kitchen chair to the dresser, climbed up, and scoured the shelves, trying to find the corn bird, in case it'd fallen behind a plate or bowl. But all I found was one of Bertha's blood-red tail feathers, so I pocketed that instead.

28

FLORA

|||

BLACK ICE. A pileup on the A34. Heavy snow warnings. "When r u leaving?" Scott texts again. Unable to give him the answer he wants—"Now, darling! Miss u 2"—Flora curls up on the studio sofa, hugging her blossom-pink dressing gown over her knees, and watches Raff pick through a grotty old picnic hamper he'd found pushed against the studio wall. Her opinions on everything—and everyone, not least Kat, whose iron-hard shell turns out to have hairline cracks—are up in the air. Normally, she lays out her thoughts like a dinner table setting. But she doesn't know how she feels about anything anymore, her emotions untidy.

After last night's hair-raising trip back from the pub, she'd manically packed, vowing to leave at dawn and never to return to Rock Point, picturing not one individual with a grudge but a vigilante group—"*we* remember"—a huddle of shadowy locals with pitchforks, moving silently toward Rock Point in the briny dark. But she'd run out of energy at some point and realized she couldn't bear to leave without at least trying to fit the Swedish tall-case clock into the boot, as well as Granny's crockery and a pickle jar or two. Or maybe she just couldn't bear for anything to be so . . . final. To end on such a sour note. So she'd wriggled under Granny's patchwork quilt and held Raff in her arms, her dear defenseless mound, sucking in the sleeping boy scent of him, and woken contented—her child in her arms; just this—with the sea light dancing, disco ball silver, through the gap in the curtains. The relief came next: she could be upside down in a ditch and she wasn't. It took a second or two for the peril of the night before to fully land.

Her anxiety sharpening, Flora walks to the window, tightening the belt of her dressing gown. No sign of last night's malignity now. The winter sky is quilted, crisp and clean, the sea a dip-dye of Farrow & Ball blues. She feels bad, a bit bad anyway, for persuading Daddy not to go swimming with Kat and Lauren. Maybe she should have gone swimming too? Rather than balking at the cold and the idea of revealing the puckered sack of her belly in a swimming costume, she could have seized a chance to do something out of her comfort zone, an activity that would appall Scott, who'd know the exact statistical risk of death involved. As he'd certainly have called the police about the tailgating car, which she can't bear to tell him about until she's safely home.

The car's fog lights bore into her thoughts again. Even Kat's face was shiny with sweat by the time the car finally turned off, not taking the fork in the road that leads to Rock Point, but back inland, raging into the night. Afterward, disembarking on the drive, Kat and Lauren had hugged her, thanked her for getting them home safe, Kat saying that if she ever needed a top-drawer getaway driver for a bank robbery, Flora was now top of her list.

Just a drunk boy racer, her father insists. She wants to believe him. She really does. But it'd felt as if the past itself was closing in on her, trying to knock her off course.

In a funny way it's succeeded. Because now she's had to confront why, despite such horrors, she hasn't returned to her secure, lovely life: her hermetically sealed "smart" home; the rubber-matted play parks; the tennis club; the twice-daily pelvic floor squeezes because Scott says he can't "feel her" like he used to. Like before she had his *ten-pound* baby. Here, in this topsy-turvy time-travel house, she can see the world, her world, through her younger eyes again, and it makes her married life seem small and airless as a utility cupboard, however beautifully appointed.

And then, of course, there's Raff.

Something in her stroppy dear boy has settled at Rock Point: she can almost smell it on his skin. This is not the same Raff who collapses screaming to the pavement if she's forgotten his snack box. The Raff who overheard Scott hissing, "What's wrong with this kid, Flora? Why can't you control him?" Whom Scott and his mother discuss in terms of educational psychologists and empathy issues— whom she must constantly defend. There's nothing "wrong" with her boy. He has a streak of Finch, that's all. He'll grow out of it. (Scott: "Let's hope so.")

Her heart soft and full, she glances at Raff, still digging into the picnic basket, and is hit by a surging relief that he's not grown out of being himself. She marvels at the spinning orbit that is a four-year-old boy, everything so keenly felt, so physically inhabited; all that tumbling, colorful overspill of life awaiting him. Please let him have the life he wants, she thinks. Please.

"Mummy." His eyes shine. "Look!" He holds up a small skull.

Flora recoils. Rabbit? Hare? Lauren would collect skulls from the moor, scraps of fur hanging off the bone. Granny would say, "You are such a grisly little thing." But their father would declare them beautiful, and say Lauren had such a good eye, and display them next to her other finds, bits of sea glass and interesting rocks, razor clam shells, little triumphs of daughterhood. "Ew."

Raff pulls out a scratched Perspex arts award, what looks suspiciously like a nicked restaurant ashtray, and a fistful of plastic poker chips. "Birdie!" he says, peering into the basket.

"What?" But on some level, she already knows. It flutters in her chest. She experiences a dissolving sensation, a small falling away. And watches, heart in her mouth as Raff parts his cupped hands. Oh god.

That . . . that *thing*. The corn dolly straw bird! So that's what happened to it. Hurled back in time, Flora is sandy footed in the kitchen again, listening to Granny telling Lauren it's not good manners to give something to someone, then steal it back: Lauren vehemently denying it. No one believed her. Least of all Flora. But it was here all along. Granny must have found it after they'd all left and stored it away. She wishes she hadn't.

The bird can't have some strange malign power, can it? Just a bit of crispy old straw. If she threw it in the fire, it'd burn in seconds. "Put it back, Raff."

He hugs it possessively toward him. "Mine."

Flora feels slightly sick. "But you could take something else instead. Something even better! What about that sweet little skull?"

Raff buries the corn bird under his PJ top. "Birdie."

Oh, the witchy wicker against his butter-soft baby skin. "No, Raff. You see . . . the bird belongs to Aunty Lauren," she says, reluctantly resorting to the truth.

Raff frowns, confused. "Aunty Lauren hates birds."

"I'm not sure 'hate' is the right word," she says carefully, wondering how to deep-dive into this. "Most of the time when we grow older our worries get smaller, don't they? But sometimes—and not very often—our worries get bigger."

Raff nods solemnly like he understands this at least.

"Or we develop new ones. And that's what happened to Aunty Lauren." Her voice breaks dangerously. "She used to love birds."

He considers this, still gripping his prize.

"O-kay." She knows defeat when she sees it. "I tell you what. How about we pack it in your Spider-Man backpack now? Safely tucked away. And you can take it out again when we're back at home."

"Don't want to go home," Raff mumbles. And the mood pivots again.

Flora hesitates, part of her inclined not to ask the question, not wanting to know the answer. "Why not, Raff?"

His gaze slides away, a struggle chasing across it. "Daddy shouts."

"All daddies shout sometimes. Daddy loves you very much."

"But Grandpa doesn't shout, shout, shout. He doesn't shout at Mummy. Daddy shouts at Mummy."

Shame trickles over Flora like sticky hot milk. "Hey. All grown-ups argue. It doesn't mean they don't love each other." What else has he heard? Seen? She suddenly knows for sure she won't go home today. She'll blame the weather. But really, she blames herself. "So how much does Mummy love her Raff?"

His slow smile lights her up too. "Big as the world."

"That's right, Raff." She'd first heard the phrase that summer: Dixie to Lauren as they'd arrived at Rock Point, hand in hand. At the time, Flora had almost choked with jealousy. Her own mother's attention was always on the younger half siblings and her new husband, and Flora had felt as if her mother wanted her out of the house, out of the way. And because of that she'd played up, like teens do, slamming doors, creating arguments, refusing to talk to her stepfather, who'd called her "a royal pain in the arse." And she'd secretly vowed that if she became a mother she'd be more like Dixie. This vow was later joined by others: not to divorce; not to remarry; not to have too many children; not to repeat the mistakes of her parents. Whatever it took.

"Come on, Raff, let's go pack that bird away." Before Lauren returns from the cove. She cannot risk her sister seeing that bird, cannot imagine her reaction, the fallout.

On the landing below, ringing from Kat's room stops her. Kat surely hasn't left her phone behind. Normally it's grafted on to her palm. The call stops, then starts again, and Flora can see the phone flashing through the ajar door. It must be important, she figures, justifying stepping into Kat's room. When she sees the name of the caller, her heart leaps. Knowing she shouldn't, she clamps Kat's mobile to her ear and whispers, "*You.*"

29

LAUREN

|||

2019

WHO IS IT? Stepping back to get a better view, Lauren's bare foot sinks into silky, icy sand. She peers up, tracking the black dog along the rocky ridges until it vanishes from view. Her heart rises in her chest. She can't see the owner. But standing there in the cove, she can sense their gaze; a roving prickle against her cheeks, as if someone is aiming a laser pen down from the cliffs. How is it possible to be in such a remote, empty spot and yet feel so . . . *seen?*

London's busy streets and tall buildings are her safety net. A constriction that holds her in place. Here, she's exposed—and so are her nerve endings. Last night's driver careered through her dreams. Notes too; fluttering, falling, like frosted leaves, with Gemma, laughing, running, reaching out with porcelain hands to catch them. She'd woken in a knot of dusty blankets and, for a sleep-muddled second, there was Jonah, stood in her bedroom doorway, very still, like a monolithic moor stone. It wasn't him, of course. She's not certain anyone was there. If she dreamed the soft click of the door's latch too. And then at breakfast, she felt it again, a dark undercurrent beneath the homeliness of sun-faded chintz; a secret caught within Rock Point, the Finch family, like a brush hair in an oil painting, a tiny ridge under a varnished surface.

"Come on!"

Lauren whips around to face the sea and waves at Kat, happily bobbing about in the grotto-blue Atlantic as if it were a heated Roman bath.

"Get in!" Kat yells.

Glancing apprehensively at the cormorant perched on a boulder—no signs of imminent ambush—Lauren sheds her coat, revealing a dull navy swimming costume; her white, chicken-skinned body, ungroomed and unwaxed for weeks. Walking toward the water's edge, the curling catacomb tunnels of waves, she cannot believe she's even considering this.

A drowned person is skeletonized in about four days, according to Gemma, the daughter of a fisherman. The body is eaten from the inside out by shrimps, and then the bones bounce along the seabed until they are eventually ground down into fragments, becoming part of the beach itself. Not a nice thought. But when will she get a chance to swim—or connect—with Kat again? Especially since Kat's trying to get a flight this evening. Whatever lies beneath this place is flexing—they all feel it. She understands why her sisters might not want to hang around. And why she will stay.

With a warrior whoop, Lauren charges at the ocean, which shatters against her legs like glass. She screams. It's too cold to process, more like a burn, wiping out every other sensation, stealing her breath.

Kat's grin is enormous, the riotous grin of old. "Respect, Lauren!"

Lauren laughs, filled with a wild, painful joy. After the initial shock, the gasping, she surrenders to the deep tidal rock. But then her feet can't feel the bottom and the current lassoes her legs and panic bites like the cold. She plunges back to the shore and scrambles out, frozen but triumphant, buzzing, feeling as though a layer of skin has been scraped away.

"Back in, back in!" Kat rushes from the water, arms outstretched, and wraps Lauren in a wet bear hug. They fall to the sand, giggling, silly teenagers again. It's funny . . . until the moment it's not, and time pops like a cork from a bottle, and she's slipping out of herself, tipping from a ledge. She's in the aviary, her fingers rattling the cage door, trying to breathe. The sun is black, with a diamond-white corona. Beautiful and cruel, it's trying to make her look, but if she does it'll blind her, and she fights to not see, not remember.

"Shit, Lauren." Kat pulls her up. "I'm sorry." She grabs Lauren's puffer coat off a rock and drapes it over her shaking shoulders. "There."

"Thanks," Lauren manages, her teeth chattering, unable to explain that the morning of the eclipse sometimes feels like it's being lowered back over her, like some sort of cloche. "I'm f-f-fine," she manages, almost hyperventilating. The smile doesn't work, though. Her lips feel glued to her front teeth.

"You're not. Fuck, Lauren. Sit." Kat lowers too, lifts the side of Lauren's coat and they huddle under its warm wing, Kat's arm over Lauren's shoulder. It's the closest they've been physically for decades. As her breathing regulates and the shaking stops, they sit quietly, watching the shadow of a storm cloud move across the ocean's corrugated surface, like a shoal of fish. After a while, Kat says, softly,

"You need to get some help. I'll pay. For the bereavement therapist. It's the least I can do, Laurie."

"That's very kind of you. But not necessary. Really." She's protective of her grief, wants to hold it close, cup it in her hands, and keep it warm. It's all she has left. Kat wouldn't understand.

Grief may have stripped off a protective layer, but the issue is this place. On the train from London, the focus of her anxiety had been the aviary. If she could just face that, she'd be fine, Lauren had told herself, not realizing that the landscape itself would crack open memories, wispy recollections that switch course like bonfire smoke; that her father would reach through the decades, and, like a hand rooting in a box of sharp, dangerous objects, yank out Angie.

"It's not a big deal," Kat says. "Everyone has a shrink these days."

In Kat's world maybe. It was years ago when Lauren last saw Janet. Their sessions had been useful but also painful and utterly exhausting. She's no desire to do it again. "Bet yours is some sort of famous guru?"

"Oh, I'm too busy for all that stuff," Kat says with a brisk laugh. She stretches out one sinewy leg, digging a trench in the sand. "Work's my therapy. And it pays me, rather than the other way round. Far more sensible."

Before this week, Lauren would have believed this. But Kat had looked so vulnerable in the pub last night, sort of lost. Even if she's recovered today, reclaiming her strident Kat-ness, she still seems slightly less assured. "What about Flora?" Lauren asks.

"What you saying, girl? Flora has the perfect life! And perfect lives have the habit of falling apart if you examine them too closely," she adds with a wry smile in her voice but no malice. "And Dad, of course, well, Dad would much rather run starkers down the street than unburden himself on a psychotherapist's couch."

"If you're not cutting off your ear and posting it to a friend, you're hunky dory."

"Ha." Kat's laugh conducts down her arm. "Anything but the truth, eh?"

A chink opens in the conversation. Lauren knows she must try to push through it again. "Kat," she says carefully, picking up a razor shell, running a finger along its edge. "No one talks about what happened, which is kind of weird, right?"

"That's how the Finch family rolls." Lauren feels Kat's muscles tense. "Anyway, all families are dysfunctional, Lauren. You know, they have dark bits." Kat broods on this, then says, "We were all so ridiculously young, weren't we? So much a blur."

"Yeah. My memory of that day is shot." Lauren's bare feet are changing from scalded red to vein-blue. She shivers. "That's why . . ."

"Look, if I could click all the dislocated bits into place, I would, honestly." Kat stands up, showering sand. "Right. I need to check on the flight situation. Have you seen the weather reports? The beast from the east, they're calling it. So much snow. The rest of the country is gridlocked." She smiles. "And, no, I'm not running away. I'm just heroically screwed if I can't get back for the meeting, that's all."

"Have you earmarked anything? From the house, I mean," Lauren asks. Flora has organized a sticker system, involving yellow mini Post-it notes inscribed with the first letter of their names. "It's like pin the tail on the donkey!" she'd said brightly, thumbing an *F* to the blue tall-case clock. *L*s and *K*s are scarce. It's not that Lauren doesn't love Grandpa's brass telescope, his binoculars, or the barometer on the wall, but these things belong here somehow. Every item is loaded, poignant too. It feels a bit like robbing a grave. And she's got no space or storage in her rental flat either.

"Not much. The old maps. I like maps because they show you the route out," Kat says wryly. "I also feel like I should rescue Ugly Humphrey. But I probably won't because it's just a hideous stuffed fish, isn't it? Not actually a relative. Although anything's possible in our family." She starts patting down her coat pockets. "Bollocks. I've left my phone back at the house. First my phone, next my head, right? Jeez, this place, Lauren. What do they put in the tap water? Actually, let's not go there." She strips out of a sleek black costume without any self-consciousness, revealing an airstrip of pubic hair. Mid-towel rub, she looks up. "Is this about what Dixie said? When she was . . . ill?"

"Dying." Lauren hates the euphemisms. "Passed away," especially. As if the dead amble off down a sunlit country lane, when dying itself is so exhausting and physical—and binary. Lauren saw her own face reflected in her mother's dark eyes: where she belonged, where she'd always lived, just the two of them. And then those eyes shut, and they never opened again. She didn't look as if she was sleeping, like people said. She looked dead, very dead. And the world emptier and scarier. Her mother had definitely gone. "Yes, it's partly that." She fumbles inelegantly into her clothes, trying to hide her bush.

"Perhaps it was just the drugs talking, Laurie?" Kat says softly, as if addressing a child.

"Maybe." Lauren thinks of a baby bird trying to tap its way out of its egg, trapped within the very thing that protects it. "Do you remember how Granny didn't want me to hang out with Gemma anymore?" she asks, changing tack. "I was thinking about it earlier. I mean, that was odd, wasn't it? I've never worked it out. All these things that didn't quite add up that summer, I'd forgotten them until now."

Kat kicks a leg, hard, into her sweatpants.

"So you don't have an inkling what it was all about?" Lauren tries again.

"Nope. Sorry." Kat zips her coat, the conversation too. Fully dressed, they start picking their way over the hillocks of seaweed, scattering sand hoppers, and up the path, briny gusts blowing their hair into stiff walls. Near the hermit's hut, Kat stops suddenly and replies to a question Lauren hasn't asked: "I really don't have the answer, Laurie." And Lauren thinks, she's lying.

30

LAUREN

| | |

1999

THE QUESTION SUCKED the air from the living room. Angie, halfheartedly sweeping up sand by the sofa, stopped, and her green gobstopper eyes rolled upward to stare at Granny, waiting for her response. When Granny said nothing, Grandpa's hand swung to her lower back, the folds of her floral dress, releasing a familiar waft of her dressing room's smell. "I think it'd be just grand if Gemma joined us to watch the eclipse in the morning, don't you, Pam, darling? The more the merrier."

Granny pursed her mouth, like he was asking something else. *What*, I wanted to shout. *What?* It was stupid of me to seek permission in the first place, I realized. For trying to prove that Mum had brought me up just as well as Kat's or Flora's wealthy mothers. *And* that I hadn't sneakily thieved the corn bird from the dresser, which is what Granny had suggested: "It's unlikely to have flown away on its own now, Lauren, isn't it?" But I'd seen the hungry way Granny had looked at it earlier. Like the bird was *her* lost thing found, not mine at all.

I'd checked everywhere, running the bamboo end of a rock-pooling net under the dresser in case it'd fallen down the back. I suspected that one of my sisters had taken it, thrown it off The Drop for a laugh and sent it bobbing out to sea, where it'd join the cargo-spill of rubber ducks circling the world's oceans.

"Of course, it's all right, Lauren," Granny said eventually, with obvious effort.

I felt my bare toes uncrunch on the rug. Dad must have talked to her, corrected whatever Angie had said about me and Gemma in the hermit's hut. And yet the atmosphere was still prickly, her smile tight. "Thanks."

Granny lifted the leathery branch of her arm, her plastic bangles clunking. "Step up, Bertha."

With a beat of wings, Bertha swooped down from Ugly Humphrey's glass cabinet. Landing deftly on Granny's hand, she glanced around with jewel eyes, reading the room. I could tell she was about to speak, and she did: "A horrible dilemma, Herbert!"

"What nonsense," Granny said, with a small laugh. Grandpa tugged on his earlobe.

Something crackled. We all knew Bertha didn't invent things, just repeated them. There was a secret conversation going on in the house—and I wasn't part of it.

"Maybe Viv would like to come too, Laurie?" Grandpa said brightly.

I shot a triumphant glance at Angie, who tossed her hair, clearly irritated. Sand sprinkled out out of the dustpan. *See,* I wanted to say. The Heaps are welcome here. You were a cow to Gemma for nothing.

"And Gemma's brother?" Grandpa adjusted the TV aerial, which he'd extended with two wire coat hangers and sellotape. "What's his name?"

"Pete." He'd never come.

"And will you be joining us, Angie?" Grandpa asked, giving the aerial another waggle. "I hope so!"

"Watching it with my mates in St. Ives," Angie said.

Thank goodness, I thought. "What an atmosphere that'll be," he said. "And you know not to look directly at—"

"Oh, Herbert. Please." Granny spun on her heel to walk out of the room. "Just let Angie get on. The house is upside down."

"Well, that'll be Viv, won't it?" Angie muttered beneath her breath. Granny, whose hearing was sharp when least expected, whipped around, making Bertha spread her feathers. "I beg your pardon?"

"Sorry," Angie said, not looking sorry. "I shouldn't have said that. It's not my place to comment on your cleaner." She was sparking an angry energy that seemed to have burst out of nowhere, and landed, unexpectedly, unfairly, on Viv of all people. "And I know it's different down here, less choice and all that."

"Actually, the girls' mess is *your* job, Angie," Granny said crisply. "That's why I'm paying you." She raised one eyebrow. "Not to tidy up Charles's studio, more glamorous though that undoubtedly must seem."

Angie rolled her eyes. The moment teetered. Granny could have fired Angie there and then, or Angie could have said, "I quit," and everything would have worked out differently.

"Oh, and don't forget the girls' laundry and rooms, will you? The landing has a distinct whiff to it." Having had the last word, Granny turned and left the room.

Angie pouted. She hated doing any sort of housekeeping. "I feel like Marie Antoinette's lady's maid," she'd grumble, carting my sisters' laundry baskets down the stairs, leaving a trail of dropped socks.

I did as much as I could myself. Just as Mum expected at home. But my sisters treated Rock Point like a hotel. Flora was by far the worst, her bedroom floor a battlefield of knickers, wet bikinis, and sandy towels. My sisters never did see the mess they created.

"Don't forget about the sitting, Lauren," Angie said, and walked back into the hall, trailing resentment. I tried to work out what had just gone on, why Viv had pressed Angie's red button, why . . .

"Don't overthink it. It's just the discombobulating eclipse energy, Lauren." Grandpa walked to the window, his hands clasped behind his back. He folded back a shutter fully, revealing the sea and sky ablaze, as if from a distant fire. "Can't you feel it? It's in the air. *Disturbance*," he added with relish, absorbed by the view. "The temperature will drop and, if we're lucky, we'll see the moon's shadow *racing* toward us from the west, nine hundred meters a second. Like an explosion in reverse." He turned to me with intense lit-up eyes, looking just like Dad when a painting was going well. "Umbral velocity, Lauren. I've waited for this my entire life, you've no idea."

HEADING UP FOR the sitting, I paused on the studio landing, just outside the green door, surprised to hear Angie's voice, an urgent whisper that I couldn't make out, then Flora saying, *"No way . . ."*

"Oh, hi, Lauren," said Kat, loudly, like she was alerting the other two to my appearance as I walked in. They stood by the shelving, the glass jars winking behind them.

Angie still looked defiant. Kat and Flora smiled, too hard. I didn't understand. Why were they all here together? And why had their conversation suddenly stopped?

"Well, better get on." As Angie walked away, she hesitated, glanced back at my sisters, and a funny sort of look—doubt, or regret—flashed across her face, as if she wanted to say something else. She shut the door behind her with a click.

"What was that all about?" My heart was banging like it knew something I didn't.

"Oh, she was just looking for Daddy." Flora peered into a silvered mirror hanging from the wall, and I knew she was watching me too in the reflection. "Obsessed. You know what she's like, Lauren."

I wasn't sure why I didn't believe her. "Where is Dad?"

"Off buying fags." Kat put on a low male voice. "Don't ever smoke, girls. Disgusting habit. Right, where are my Camels?"

"But he's coming back, isn't he?" I needed to know. When he'd sketched my hand earlier, he'd sounded close to ditching *Girls and Birdcage*. Something had shaken his confidence in the portrait. I was worried.

"Why wouldn't he?" Kat threw herself on to the sofa, pulled one leg to her knee, and started picking at her blue toenail varnish.

I didn't feel close enough to even try to explain. Since the ledge, a biting unease had set in. I couldn't help but love Kat and Flora— and want to please them—and desperately want them to love me too, but I didn't trust them. All I wanted was the eclipse over, everything back on track, the summer to start again.

"Ugh. Split ends," said Flora, inspecting her hair, bleached almost white by the sun. She grabbed a pair of gluey scissors and shoved them toward Kat, stabbing them at her stomach playfully. "Trim it, Kat."

"Your dreamy, star child locks? Let me at 'em." Kat snipped

enthusiastically, not in a straight line. "Excited about tomorrow, Lauren?" she asked, looking at me, still scissoring.

I nodded, nervous about telling them. "Gemma's coming over too."

Kat stopped cutting, glanced at Flora. There was a tiny blue spark, like the flash of the scissors, where their eyes met. And it felt, for a brief second, like I was back on the ledge, the moment before I tipped.

"Well, I hope she's ready to party," said Flora, then started at her reflection. "Argh, Kat. Stop! Edward Scissorhands."

Dad appeared, an unlit cigarette in his mouth. He tossed his car keys onto the trestle with a clatter. "Christ, no new haircuts. The portrait is hard enough as it is. Positions. I know, I know. I'll be quick. And no sittings tomorrow. Not every day I get to watch an eclipse with my favorite human beings on the planet, right?" He picked his metal lighter from the lid of a highly flammable varnish, flicked it with his thumb, and the flame lit up his face, that new, unsettled frown. He didn't put on music this time. And the mood felt different, weighty, like something was pressing down on us all, waiting for release.

After a minute or two, Kat and Flora shared the CD Walkman, one headphone each, mouthing along to the lyrics. I tuned into the waves and the *whoosh-scuff-whoosh* of Dad's trainers on the floorboards. He stepped backward, forward again, like a boxer in a ring. His eyes narrowed into shark-gray slits, moving from us to the canvas, back again. He kept muttering beneath his breath, forgetting we were there, slowly vanishing into the painting.

Over his shoulder, I saw the studio door open, just an inch or two. A strand of hair curled around it. My heart sank.

"Only me." In the doorway, Angie again. Transformed. Her eyes shone, as if just being near Dad stuck emeralds inside them. "Sorry to disturb."

"Hey, Angie." Dad's painting hand froze, and he got a funny look on his face.

"Just to let you know, Charlie, I can hang on a bit longer later today." Her voice was velvety-soft now. She glanced at the sink, the mess of brushes, the squeezed worms of paint, and smiled. "And I might even tidy up a bit. So, we're all good, you know. For our session tomorrow, Charlie."

What session? What was she talking about? I held my breath, waiting for Dad to correct her. Angie's invasion to end. My sisters carried on mouthing along to the shared Walkman, unaware anything was wrong.

"Great." He touched his brush to the canvas.

I stared out the window, biting the inside of my cheek, trying not to think of Angie's hands all over the studio, trying not to cry. The sky was reddening in the west, the clouds like flames blown sideways. Grandpa's words about the eclipse—"an explosion in reverse"—streaked into my mind. And I knew what I had to do.

31

KAT

|||

THE DRESSING ROOM'S door is ajar. Peering inside, Kat's surprised to see Flora and Angie standing there, glaring at each other. The mood is charged, staticky. "You missed a great swim," she says. No one answers. The steamy smell of shampoo carries along the landing from Lauren's post-swim shower. "You haven't seen my . . ."

"Angie is wearing, no, *nicking*, our grandmother's clothes," interrupts Flora.

One hand on her hip, Angie turns defiantly in front of the mirrored dressing table, draped in a turquoise kaftan, embroidered with rows of shells around its V-neck. Recognizing it, a current of feeling—bittersweet—travels up Kat's spine.

"Hardly the heist of the century," says Angie.

A fedora flies across the small room, and Kat sees that Raff's digging in the wardrobe.

"We're clearing the house." Angie's engagement ring shatters light across the dressing table, where white ceramic hands, like discarded amputations, are still stacked with Granny's bracelets and necklaces.

"No, *we* are. Me and my sisters." Flora's voice shakes.

Raff flumps to the floor, cheerfully picking through a bundle of wardrobe swag.

"Granny's stuff feels quite personal, Angie," Kat tries to explain. Although it feels like this is bigger than the kaftan, that she's walked in on something else. Grabbing Kat's leg to steady himself, Raff stands up, slides one foot and then the other into a pair of patent heels, then clip-clops across the room, tugging a fox stole like a dog on a lead. The mood in the room doesn't lighten.

"Your nan's been dead a year. No one wanted anything until today," Angie says, missing the point. "I just wanted to choose a couple of things for the honeymoon. Thought it'd be a nice touch. You know, surprise Charlie."

"Oh god," Flora mutters.

Kat winces too, then thinks of her absent phone again. It feels as though she exists on two parallel planes—the beautiful mire of Rock Point, her urgently pressing real life—one foot stuck in each.

"You want everything, including your father, to yourself, Flora." Angie's voice is tremulous now. "Like you didn't want to share him with Lauren when you were younger." Her words ricochet around the room. "I haven't forgotten that either."

The "either" makes Kat's pulse skip.

"We *will* be talking to Daddy," Flora retorts fiercely.

Until now Flora has maintained a taut civility with Angie, but the gloves are off. Fascinating. Her edges haven't been entirely smoothed away by years of married life and to-do lists, as Kat feared. Deep down she's still Flora, her sister, her partner in crime, with whom she'd giggled until they'd wept, swam, squabbled, and schemed.

"But, of course, you've both already talked to him, haven't you?" Angie's name necklace trembles between her clavicles. "In the studio yesterday."

"Kind of." But all Kat can think about is the expression on her father's face as the nude sketch floated to the studio floor. The way he'd grabbed it, hidden it.

"You may as well know it'll take more than a few words from you—or spiteful notes for that matter—to kibosh our wedding," Angie adds.

"Er, what have the notes got to do with your wedding?" asks Kat, bemused, watching Raff do another joyful turn around the room.

"They're my unwelcoming committee, aren't they?" Angie pulls off some clip-on earrings—dangly gold peacocks—and slaps them down on the dressing table. "Rest assured you and your sisters are managing perfectly well on that score without them."

"Oh, please," says Flora.

"We didn't write the notes, Angie," Kat says levelly, finding herself in the position of peacemaker for once, trying to calm things down.

"Right. And the guy with the black dog, the dog Raff went outside to pat? Who always seems to be around whenever I go out of the house for a smoke?" Angie crosses her arms. "Well, you can tell him that I've dealt with London gangsters and seen off all sorts at club doors in my time, and if he's trying to intimidate . . ."

"*Gangsters?*" mutters Flora, horrified.

Kat's brain whirs. A new possibility presents itself. "Hang on, have you brought some sort of trouble with you from London, Angie? This guy, your tire . . ."

"Don't try to turn me into the villain of the piece here," Angie says quickly, maybe too quickly. Her mouth twitches. "Like your sister has."

There it is again. A more difficult conversation that Kat's surely walked in on.

"By the way, I knew you called me Monster back then too." Angie starts tugging Granny's kaftan over her head, revealing a hitched-up satin slip, a rounded stomach, and then, as she turns, a gecko tattoo above her hips, its ink greened by age. "I hated you all for that."

"Yet you still thought it a good idea to come back into our lives?" Flora says.

"Flora, it wasn't . . . an *idea*." Angie wipes her eyes, leaving a mascara streak. There's a smell of sweat. She looks vulnerable in the slip, smaller too. "I love your dad."

"You barely know him." Flora picks up Raff. His high heels dangle, then clatter to the floor. He clutches onto the fox stole.

Even Kat would never presume she knows her father, not really, not in the labyrinth of his heart. A psychological thicket, he's as lost in it as much as anyone, art his only pathway, his way of making sense of the world, his dead end, his way out.

"I do, Flora. I really do. We're two odd-shaped pieces that fit together." Angie puts the garment back on a hanger, then turns to face them, her face softening as she talks about their father. "North and south. Chalk and cheese. Soul mates."

Kat almost feels sorry for Angie then. Because her father has loved many women, all of whom likely believed they were his soul mate. And he was grieving Dixie when he started on this relationship with Angie. She wants to tell Angie it's a rebound thing, and yet she finds she cannot.

"I love every bloody cell of him, always have." A sob cracks in Angie's throat. "And I'll fight for him, okay?"

They listen soberly to Angie's feet thudding down the stairs, and it strikes Kat she's never fought for any relationship. Never been brave enough to risk failing in that fight, and she wonders how different her life would be if she had.

"Just before you came in," Flora whispers over Raff's head. "She brought up the eclipse, Kat. In front of Raff! She threw it back at me."

"Ah. I thought I'd interrupted something." Kat braces, waits for Flora to explain further. A gull flashes past the window, a shiny silver fish wriggling in its beak.

"What we told Angie about Gemma and Lauren." Flora's cheeks stain red. She cups her hands over Raff's ears. "That stupid . . . joke."

Kat steeples her fingers over her nose, thinks of her and Flora playing the new "help," and telling Angie that Gemma and Lauren were having "a thing." Idiotic. Mean. They didn't imagine Angie might mention it to Granny. Or did they? Is that what they secretly wanted? She's not sure anymore. Only that it feels close again. Like it might matter still. Less than an hour ago, when Lauren asked why Granny hadn't wanted Gemma around, Kat had managed to lie—a white lie, to protect Lauren from further hurt—but it was difficult, ugly doing so. It suddenly feels like there's far too much to unpack. Kat can feel herself bucking away, refusing to deal with it, hearing the call of work. "You haven't seen my phone, have you?"

"I heard it ringing out in your room," Flora says, turning away.

In her bedroom, Kat falls on it—her grown-up life, her real life, its validation—and frantically scrolls through the missed calls; the lawyer again, Blythe, her PA, Scarlett . . . hang on. *Kofi.* What the . . . ? A received call. Lasting eleven minutes, thirty-three seconds.

32

LAUREN

| | |

2019

LAUREN HEARS THE loose floorboard squeak outside her bedroom door. A second later, Flora bursts in, then stops, her gaze pinning to Lauren's fingers on the desk drawer's knob. "Oh. I didn't mean to interrupt . . ."

"You haven't!" Lauren quickly shuts the drawer; she'll write to Gemma later. "I just got out of the shower." But the ocean cold is still fizzing under her skin, lodged in her bones. She rather likes it. "Come in, come in."

Flora steps into the room, glancing around, as if mentally taking notes. She has a jangly, slightly manic energy. Her hair is disheveled, and it makes her look younger. "I'll swim with you and Kat tomorrow. A final hoorah on our last day," she says, her voice steely, as if trying to talk herself into it. "Before we all hit the road. It'll be . . ."

"Like the old days," Lauren says, smiling.

"Yes," says Flora less certainly. "Maybe it will."

Lauren unwraps the towel turbaned over her hair, pulls on her Fair Isle sweater. Emerging, she shoots Flora a puzzled smile. "You okay?"

"I just had a set-to with Angie." Flora flops onto the bed, kicks up her feet. The soles of her white socks are grubby, an unlikely sight somehow. "I spoke my mind, Lauren. I doubt I'll ever be forgiven."

"Reckon Angie can probably take it," says Lauren, intrigued. She digs a finger into her pot of Vaseline and balms her lips, noticing that the nail polish she applied in London has chipped, other parts of her too.

"I'm done, Lauren." Flora tips onto her side, props her head up on one hand. Her gaze grows bold, direct, no longer evasively fixed at a midpoint above Lauren's eyebrows. "I can't do nice and polite anymore. Maybe I'm not that nice person." She pauses. "Maybe I never was?"

Lauren sits on the edge of the bed, disarmed, unsure what to say. A breath of wind moves the curtain on its pole, a familiar childhood sound: cloth and air and metal curtain rings, weather working its way inside.

"I'm sorry, Lauren," Flora says quietly. "I'm sorry I wasn't the best sister."

"I didn't have any sisters, and then I got you and Kat." She lies next to Flora on the bed, as they used to, and it doesn't feel like any time has passed since those teenage summers, and she has to resist the urge to reach over and start braiding Flora's hair. "You weren't the sister I'd imagined, but I wasn't an only anymore either. And that was, and is, amazing to me. Honestly."

"That makes me feel very happy and totally wretched at the same time, Lauren."

Their father's baritone rumbles toward them: "Flora!"

"Eek. Listen to him. *Fuming.* This reunion has all gone wrong. And it's going to get more wrong." She flicks a button on the duvet back and forth with one finger, then looks up sheepishly. "You see, I answered Kat's phone while you two were in the cove. It was Kofi."

"Sorry?" Lauren thinks she's misheard.

"Kofi's name flashed up . . . I couldn't help myself. I know, I know," she says as Lauren winces. Kat will go ballistic. Kofi, even as a conversation, is off-limits.

"And Kofi told me . . ." Flora edges even closer, the sour smell of last night's wine on her breath. "Kat's been hiding something, she's . . ."

"Flora!" Charlie shouts again.

"We'll talk later." Flora pops into the room next door and tells Raff to stay put while she has a grown-up chat downstairs. "Will you come with me?" Returning, Flora reaches out her hand. "I'm going to need you on my side."

"I've always been on your side," Lauren says simply, letting her sister tug her off the bed.

––––––––

THE KITCHEN IS a Dutch interior painting, rich, full of shadows. Outside the windows, the late-morning sky is low and white, as if holding a belly of snow. Angie's and Charlie's interlaced hands are plinthed on the table, a declaration of intent. Also, bread. A jar of ruby-red jam. A brick of butter. The glint of Granny's tarnished silver cutlery.

"Sit," says Charlie, gruffly.

Lauren lowers to Grandpa's captain's chair—its seat polished from years of his thick corduroy trousers—and slides her hands along the smooth armrests, just as he once did.

"This discord has to stop. And stop now." Charlie looks crumpled, his shirt done up on the wrong buttons. But then everyone's been rapidly unpicked by the last couple of days at Rock Point, their edges frayed by salt and damp. Lauren didn't have so far to fall.

"If you look for my shortcomings, girls, you'll find them. Rest assured I have further untapped reserves." He pauses theatrically. "However, if you look for common ground—between yourselves and Angie—you'll find that too."

Kat snorts, leaning back against the butcher's block island, her fingers resting lightly on her phone, as if it were a gun she might have to pull at any moment. Her buoyant post-swim mood seems to have switched to something defensive and brittle, and involves frequent dark glares at Flora, sat nervously on the edge of the rattan sofa. Lauren shifts in her chair, suddenly wishing she were outside, stomping across the cliff tops.

"We all know this is not about who gets to take my mother's frocks home, only to later discreetly dispatch them at an obliging charity shop." Charlie drops a glob of jam on a bit of bread and mashes it in with the back of a teaspoon. "It's about the past," he growls. "Which we can't undo."

And won't discuss, thinks Lauren.

"I dare say those daft notes haven't helped the party mood either," he adds as Angie leans over and flicks a crumb off his shirt.

"Nor the slashed tire. Or the psycho driver, funnily enough," Kat says.

In the tightening hush, Lauren listens to the metallic *squeak-squeak* of Bertha's cage swing. Her thoughts tip back and forth, uneasily, heatedly to Jonah, the familiar stranger from the train whom she keeps spotting around and about, head down, hood up. She doesn't understand how someone she's just met has worked under her skin so quickly. Every time she looks out of a window, she cannot help but scout for him. The black dot of his dog. After today, frustratingly, she won't get a chance to find out what he's playing at. If he wrote the notes, or why.

"Whoever it is, whatever their motivation, it smacks to me of someone who is refusing to . . . to move on." Charlie takes off his glasses and squeezes the bridge of his nose, leaving fingerprint marks. He looks directly at Lauren. She's shocked to see that his eyes are rheumy with tears. "Your mother's death taught me a lesson, Laurie. For thirty-odd years there wasn't a day that went past when I didn't regret . . ." He stops; Angie is staring at him guardedly, as if she might not have heard him admit this before. "Well, spectacularly screwing up. But Dix died." He clicks his fingers. "And that's it. Grade four. Gone. No possibility of redemption. No rekindling."

Lauren blinks, astonished. Her parents, the most unlikely couple, only grew more unlikely as the years passed. Had he really fancied they'd get back together three decades on? Unimaginable. And yet, there was always a change in Dixie's eyes whenever Charlie's name was mentioned; a light that would come on, a light that didn't shine for anyone else. And she never did settle down, instead clinging to her independence, scared of being hurt and let down again. Lauren swallows hard, floored by the wastage: the union of her parents, which she'd longed for as a little girl, had been possible yet never realized.

"I won't make that mistake again." Her father turns and rests his hand lightly on Angie's cheek.

"Nice to know you loved our mothers too, Dad," says Kat frostily. Flora stares down at the floor, biting her bottom lip.

Old rivalries rush back into the room: a reminder that however much Dixie wanted Lauren to reach out to her sisters, a part of them will probably always pull away. A buried resentment, too deep to unpick.

"Oh, I did, of course I did," Charlie says, softly, sincerely. "You were all conceived with love. That's all that matters."

Kat raises an eyebrow. "Is it? You do let yourself off lightly."

"Oh, quit it." He's lost patience. "You would never interfere in each other's relationships."

"I don't know about *that*." Kat glances pointedly at Flora, confirming she knows Flora has answered her phone and spoken to Kofi. Flora colors. Lauren can feel the fractious energy forking between her sisters. And so can Bertha, who starts squawking.

"Huzzah." Kat smiles at her phone, reading an incoming message. "Confirmed. I'm on this evening's flight."

"But . . . but . . ." stutters Flora, aghast. "You'll miss our last night."

"What's this, Kat?" Disappointment crashes across their father's face. "When the hell did you book that?"

"Just now. Scarlett. My PA did." Kat knifes a look at Flora.

Charlie leans forward, palms spread on the table, a slighted patriarch. "It's bad manners to leave early, Kat," he thunders.

"Dad," says Kat, more affectionately. "You frequently don't turn up at all."

"Well, fine. Suit yourself." Charlie leans back in his chair and crosses his arms with a harrumph. "Have you fought out who gets what?"

"Post-it note system," says Flora with a sniff. "And we're going to need a man with a van to collect it all. I can't fit a tall-case clock in the boot."

For a moment, Charlie looks daunted. Doubtful even. Lauren wonders if the reality of clearing his parents' things has suddenly hit home.

"I know people," Flora adds. "Don't worry, Daddy, I'll sort it out." She glances at the dresser, mentally sieving something. "But I will wrap the crockery tonight. Take that with me tomorrow. You don't want any do you, Lauren?"

Lauren hesitates, torn. "No. You take it, Flora."

A percussion of little footsteps; Raff charges in, looking pleased with himself, his hands held behind his back.

"Why, hello, Indiana Jones." Their father's face erupts with a smile. "Now have *you* found any cool things to take home?"

Raff nods. Lauren makes a note to tell Flora she's raised a wonderful boy. A special boy. Whatever the legacy of this reunion, whether it brings them all together, or blows them apart, or ends up in a fistfight in Las Vegas, she's glad she came, just to have spent time with Raff, a tonic after weeks of being steeped in illness and grief.

"Raff has found a present," he says proudly, his chest swelling. "For Aunty Lauren."

"Me?" Lauren says with a surprised laugh. Her heart melts. She hears Flora murmur, "Oh, Raff. *No.*" Time slows. Flickering. Buffering. The William Morris tablecloth, the pea-green dresser, the moth-pale faces, all slip into a blurred slurry, everything reducing to Gemma's woven bird in Raff's palm. Then black.

33

LAUREN

| | |

1999

THIRTY-TWO MINUTES TO go. The eclipse was starting to feel like one of those things that might be more fun after the event, like Halloween, when you can talk and laugh about it and it's safely behind you.

Even in the honeysuckle air of the garden I felt scratchy, having been awake since dawn, when I'd sensed someone standing in my bedroom doorway, watching. Fuzzy with sleep, I'd glimpsed the door shutting again, slowly, softly, but not who was behind it. After that, I'd got up, sat on the desk chair by my bedroom window, and watched the first trickle of people, moving over the cliff tops like ants, carrying tripods, video cameras, camping stools, and rucksacks across a field. The invasion, Granny called it. Party time, said Kat.

I was ready for whatever was coming, having picked the tangle out my hair—cakey with salt, my scalp gritty with sand—and put on the star-print dress so me and Gemma would match, like we'd agreed. Only Gemma still hadn't arrived. And Kat and Flora had bombed upstairs after breakfast to rifle through their endless suitcases for the right outfit, as though everyone would be gazing at them, not the sky. They'd not invited me up. Not that I wanted to go. Not that I'd forgiven them for the ledge. And they knew it. I think they felt bad and resented me for making them feel bad. Something like that anyway.

I slid off the swing seat, landing on my tiptoes, and circled back to the aviary. I'd been outside a while by then. Being indoors felt wrong, as though it wasn't an eclipse coming but an earthquake, and plaster ceilings best avoided. But I'd kept one eye on the glass conservatory doors all the time, waiting for Dad to burst out, brushing through the palms and tall feathery grasses. That's what I wanted, really, just a chance to tell him that Angie was stealing my role in the studio, the world I loved so much, and I worried that if I was no longer useful to him, he'd vanish from my life as abruptly as he'd reappeared in it, like a genie sucked back into a bottle. All those things. But as Dad hadn't come to find me, it had started to sink in that he hadn't noticed what I'd done in the studio the night before, and things that felt enormous to me might be minuscule to him. Or maybe it was just that adults only saw what they wanted to see. They weren't big noticers.

Outside the garden wall, someone yelled, "How cool is that white house?" Then, a booming beat-heavy music started up, vibrating, hiccupping on the wind. The budgies were careering around the aviary. With their plumage stress-puffed, the yellow ones looked even more like the corn bird that I was still desperate to find. "Shush." I put my fingers to my lips. The budgies took no notice. My presence made them more nervous. Because I wasn't calm inside either. Birds could tell.

I'd wait for Gemma inside, I decided, slipping into the house. Bertha lifted a foot in hello. "Hi," I whispered, and sent thoughts through the bars of the cage, like paper planes; promises that the second dawn of the day wouldn't last long. "I don't know if I'm coming or going," she squawked in Granny's voice, making me smile.

"Lauren, you ready? The countdown begins!" Grandpa blew into the kitchen, his hair in a mad professor puffball. He'd been up for hours too, adjusting his pinhole camera, skipping between the TV news, the radio, and some live feed from astronomers on the internet, which kept freezing at important moments. Even the cloudy forecast hadn't dulled his mood. "To The Drop!"

"But Gemma's not here yet," I pointed out, as if he might be able to delay the eclipse until she arrived.

"Oh, she is! Upstairs with Kat and Flo. Been there a while. Go and herd them down." Something in my faltering expression made Grandpa double-take. He brushed the back of his hand against my cheek. "You'll always remember this day," he said gently. "It's like a memory you haven't had yet."

"I'm sure Lauren, like the rest of us, hasn't the faintest idea what you mean, Herb," said Granny, striding past, waggling her eclipse goggles, muttering, "I'm loath to trust these contraptions."

But I knew exactly what Grandpa meant. I always did. It was my sisters I didn't understand. And now Gemma. Why hadn't she come and found me?

On the first-floor landing, laughter rumbled down from the studio. My insides squeezed tight. "Grandpa says hurry up," I shouted.

There was a clatter of feet as Flora, Kat, and finally, Gemma, ran down the stairs, bunching up on the landing, stopping when they saw me. I sucked in my breath.

They were transformed. Snaky plaits crowned their heads, or

dangled, interwoven with colorful thread. Glitter streaked along their cheekbones. Face-paint stars and flowers. Flora's silver sequin skirt flung diamonds against the wall.

Even though Gemma was wearing the same dress as me, she was no longer Viv and Mike-the-fisherman's daughter, scrawny and freckled with curious mackerel eyes. Or my reliable friend. She'd shape-shifted much closer to my sisters. Switched sides. Kat and Flora had marked and claimed Gemma with their glitter, thickly applied, shedding from her eyelids as she blinked, like fish scales falling.

I stared and stared, then couldn't look at all. My throat tightened. "Why were you in the studio?"

"Best light." Flora finger-tapped the glitter on her cheeks, checking that it was all in place. And I knew that whatever happened in her life, she'd always sparkle; she was one of those girls, and I wasn't.

From the bottom of the stairs, Grandpa's voice. "Get a move on! The show's about to start."

Flora and Kat barreled downstairs. But Gemma hung back. "Don't be cross. I wanted to find you," she whispered. "But Kat grabbed me. They said I had to get ready. They made me . . ."

"Why don't you ever stand up to them? Why do you let them make you feel so. . . . so *small*?" The ugly words came out so forcefully Gemma backed away. The moment I'd spoken, I realized I was talking to myself, not her. That it was me who needed to stand up to my sisters, stop acting like I was the guest, had no right to be at Rock Point. I wanted to pull the words back inside. "I didn't mean . . ."

Gemma stared down the stairs where my sisters had just been, the air still ruffled by their presence. "No. You're right."

Grandpa called us again.

"Sorry," I said.

Gemma hesitated, teetering on the edge of leaving, going home, tipping the day, and our lives, in a new direction. Instead, she reached for my hand, threaded her fingers through mine, and without saying another word, we walked down the staircase together, ready to see the moon's shadow gobble the sun. A beautiful darkness fall.

34

FLORA

||||

LAUREN FALLS GRACEFULLY, soundlessly, like a dancer or a foal. There's a moment of stillness—a pinprick of shock—before everyone scrabbles to help, pushing aside the chairs. Kat barks something about the recovery position; Bertha shrieks. Raff bursts into tears. It all happened so quickly; Raff revealing the corn bird in his cupped palm; Lauren lowering to her chair but missing its edge, as if she'd completely lost all coordinates in time and space.

"Here, Laurie." Their father eases her to a chair. Holds her face in his hands, drawing a heart. "You okay, darling?"

Lauren nods gamely. She doesn't look fine. Her complexion has a glazy pallor, as if she's applied foundation four shades too light. Her eyes are enormous, flared to black holes.

Angie puts a hand over Lauren's shoulders. "Oh, babe."

A small shake of Charlie's head says, not you, Angie, not "babe," not right now. But there's no time to relish it.

A sob cracks in Raff's throat. Flora scoops him up and pats his upper back with the flat of her palm, as she winded him as a colicky baby. "Raff did the wrong thing," he whimpers. But it's her fault. What on earth was she thinking, letting him take that bird? But never in a million years did she think he'd return it to Lauren—at school, Raff's the boy who won't share—yet it seems she's underestimated her own son's kindness, his big heart.

"Let's have a look at you." Charlie tenderly parts Lauren's blue-streaked fringe, revealing a small swelling. "Do you think she needs to see a doctor?"

It takes Flora a second to realize her father is speaking to her. As the mother in the room, the responsible adult. She doesn't feel like one. Putting down Raff, she squats next to Lauren and peers into her sister's bottomless eyes. It's a bit like looking into a deep, muddy lake, where there may be a body floating under the surface. At first there's nothing, and a cramp starts to twist through Flora's abdominals, a fear of history repeating itself, but then, thank goodness, thank goodness, like the return of light after totality, she sees her sister start to spread inside them. Lauren points to the corn bird under the table, lying next to a pearl from Flora's broken necklace.

Acting quickly, Flora swoops down to pick up the bird, gripping it like a grenade. And it is really, an emotional one.

"I've waited a long time," says Lauren, her hand outstretched. "Out of everything in this house, this is what I want, Flora. All I want."

Flora hesitates. She daren't.

"Give it to her, Flora," orders Kat quietly.

"I never expected to see it again," Lauren murmurs, slowly turning the corn bird in her fingers. Her face seems to round, growing more girl-like; like one of those montages of a person changing through time. "It was like Raff was holding that summer in his hand," she adds. "I know that doesn't make much sense."

But it does, of course. It's the reason Flora didn't want Raff to show Lauren the thing in the first place.

"Well, it got back to you," marvels Kat under her breath.

"Where did you find it, Raff?" Lauren asks softly.

"Basket," mumbles Raff.

"An ancient picnic hamper, pushed against the studio wall. Granny, funny old thing, must have found it and stuffed it in there." Flora tries to sweep the subject away. Wishing she could do the same with the bird. Always was a bad omen.

"Remember how your nan blamed you, Lauren," Angie reminds her unhelpfully.

"But why would she do that?" puzzles Kat. They all look at Charlie, seeking answers.

A moment passes. "My mother was a complex lady," he says eventually. "Kept things close to her chest." He takes off his glasses and rubs his eyes. "A hoarder. A collector of things."

There's a funny buzz in the kitchen. A precarious hush. Flora doesn't like it. If they're not careful, they could all trip into that summer, as if through a trap door, one after the other.

"Say sorry to Aunty Lauren," Flora whispers to Raff.

"No, no. He's got absolutely nothing to apologize for." Lauren reaches across and squeezes Raff's hand. "Thank you for finding it. You are such a kind, wonderful boy, and I'm so, so happy to have it back."

Flora can see the tension drop out of Raff's little body, like when you snip the corner off a vacuum-packed bag of rice. A lump hardens in her throat: she's got so used to apologizing for Raff's behavior that to hear him thanked is overwhelming.

"Right. We need a brew, don't we, girls?" Angie fills the kettle.

"I might just go back to my room for a bit . . ." begins Lauren, holding the corn bird to her body, possessively, just as Raff had done.

"I'll take you upstairs," Flora says quickly, sidestepping the interrogation about the phone she fears is coming from Kat. "Dad, look after Raff." She waggles her fingers at Raff and smiles. "Nowhere near the cage, okay?"

———

FLORA VIGOROUSLY PLUMPS Lauren's pillows in a frantic attempt to make up for . . . well, everything. The night before, she'd stood in the doorway watching Lauren sleep, just as she used to do during Lauren's first Rock Point summer, letting the startling fact of a new sister settle into her mind. And as she'd done the night before the eclipse too, Flora remembers. She'd been so restless that day, unable to sleep, a feeling in her belly, a lightness, like something momentous was about to happen. Looking for company, she'd visited Lauren in the room next to her own but Lauren was fast asleep. Kat, across the landing, was half-awake too, so she'd crawled into her bed, and they'd woken a couple of hours later, sweaty, tangled; in a funny sort of physical way, their alliance strengthened.

"Lauren . . ." she begins, itching to tell her everything Kofi said on the phone. But Lauren's reaction to the corn bird—now eerily perched on her bedside table—is a reminder that she feels things more than others, the skin between her and the world—and that summer—thinner, porous. She can't risk more upset right now. ". . . rest."

"I'm honestly fine," Lauren protests.

"It's okay to let yourself be looked after, Laurie." Flora strokes her sister's hand. The nail polish chips break her heart. "You've been through so much. If you'd come to stay at Christmas, I'd have pampered you properly. I wanted to . . . I . . ." Something in Lauren's uncomfortable expression gives Flora pause. "I mean, I understand if you felt awkward." She digs herself deeper into a hole. "The disparity between our lives . . ." *Worse. Stop it.* "I hope you come next year anyway," she says, ashamed for listening to Scott, who kept saying how tricky and unbalanced it'd be, them having so much when Lauren had so little. That Lauren's grief would make any sort of festive joy seem indecent, which wouldn't be fair on Raff. But the last couple of days at Rock Point have made Flora wonder if Lauren hasn't secret riches of her own, and a freedom of which she can only dream.

"Flora, I spoke to Scott." Lauren hugs her knees. "He asked me not to mention it. But I get the impression you feel like I snubbed your invitation, your kindness, and I really didn't mean to."

The plummeting sensation is like one of those abrupt, hormonal dips in the second half of her cycle. "What did Scott say?"

Lauren pauses. "Please don't tell him I told you."

"What?" Flora's heart starts to thump.

"I called on the landline to ask what Raff might like for Christmas, and Scott picked up . . . When I asked about you, he explained you were trying to conceive. That you were run ragged, overcommitting to everyone and everything." Lauren colors. "When I mentioned you'd invited me over at Christmas too, he went silent. I asked what the matter was and he said, well, you know, he felt terrible for saying it, but it was probably best I turned down your invitation, given all the pressure you were under. If I didn't mind, which, of course, I didn't. Not at all. I totally understood. And the hospice wanted me for the Christmas shift anyway." She smiles ruefully. "It must be nice having someone looking out for you like that, Flora."

Flora hears only the roaring in her ears. Thinks of the drinks party they threw for his colleagues, who didn't go home until after midnight: the skinny woman in the gold lamé dress who asked her what she did all day. Her mother-in-law, the omnipresent colossus of Maureen—"Not a whole turkey, just the crown? Oh"—who stayed for *a week*. And she thinks of her little grieving sister, wearing cheap tinsel in her hair at the hospice. Flora wants to call Scott and scream down the line until his eardrums bleed. She also wants to crawl into a hole. "I'll leave you in peace," she murmurs, barely audible.

"Have I stuck my foot in it?" she hears Lauren asking, but she's already moving along the landing, tear-blurred, heart knocking in her chest. Unable to face anyone, least of all Kat, Flora rushes downstairs, slips out of the front door, through the moon gate and into the empty garden, where ghosts of old summers cartwheel across the lawn—and a hand slaps down hard on her shoulder.

35

KAT

|||

"YOU'VE HACKED INTO my life!" Kat draws hard on the cigarette she's nicked from Angie's packet, dragging its poisons into her lungs, not caring. "You answer *my* phone and tell Kofi I'm still in love with him. Even though you haven't a clue how I feel. Even though Kofi is six weeks from walking another woman down the aisle. You have crossed the fucking line, Flora."

"If I'd known Kofi was getting married, I wouldn't have said anything!" Flora yells and sobs, spittle flying.

The wind blows the cigarette smoke back in Kat's face, along with a faint odor of rotting fish. And it feels like they're in some sort of godforsaken tundra, all the flowers and the colors leached, salt-withered; the garden, everything, desiccated. Almost impossible to believe she, Flora, Lauren, and Gemma ever ran across a lush summer lawn, laughing, tripping over pilfered eighties ball gowns. Or a group of budgies bickered and chirped in the aviary, Granny watching her "little ladies" from her striped deck chair, afternoon gin cocktail in hand, a bowl of strawberries in her lap. Or that Grandpa's misshapen tomatoes ever grew in the greenhouse, sweetly breathing on its glass. And she feels scooped out by loss.

"Why wouldn't you tell your own sister something that major?" Flora asks, wounded.

"*Half sister.*" Kat knows this is the worst thing she could say. Just as she knew decades ago: if her sisters were "halves," she didn't need to tell them what was going on at home; as in a long-distance love affair, she could keep the truth of her everyday life obscured, her shame secret. All that mattered when they were together here was that present moment, lived with all their heart. She didn't want to think about the other stuff. She still doesn't.

And she hates, absolutely hates, that Flora now knows about Kofi's engagement, and her humiliation. It feels like there's no place on earth she can escape it. Not work, not New York, not even Rock Point. When Kat heard Kofi was marrying Sara—an old uni friend, now a midwife, deathly decent, perfect for him—she'd vomited on her shoes. Not even Angie's reappearance did that. "You had no right, Flora."

"But you looked so happy, Kat. The times I saw you together."

Kat doesn't know how to explain that she found that pure, simple happiness petrifying. She couldn't recognize herself in it. She couldn't control it.

"Scott never looks at me the way Kofi looked at you," Flora says quietly. "I just wanted to fix things for you, Kat."

"Life's not a fucking Coldplay song! I don't need fixing! Fix yourself first." She grinds the disgusting cigarette into the grass and storms off, wanting to lose Flora, wanting her to follow; a kernel of fear forming in her chest, as it had on her cliff path run. That realization that the world was a ball, alone in the godless vault of space, she just a speck. No one gets out alive.

"Fine. But can we sit? Let's sit." Flora gestures at the swing seat. "I'm at least twenty pounds heavier than you, and if this thing collapses, you're going down with me." The structure protests with a rusty squeak as they lower to it. "And, yes, there's a metaphor in there somewhere, Kat. I'm not as dumb as you think."

"Thanks for clarifying," Kat says, realizing she's comforted by Flora's thigh pressed against hers, as she was in the *Girls and Birdcage* sittings too. Human warmth. Just that.

They rock silently, edging closer, their noses and fingertips reddening in the cold. They watch a raven hopping across the lawn. Ravens are as clever as collies, Gemma said once. Such a Gemma thing to say. A moment passes.

"Kofi mentioned you were in some trouble at work," Flora says, cautiously.

Kat's startle makes the swing shake. Her mouth dries. She tries to rapidly process what this means, what Kofi knows. And how she can hide it from Flora.

"That was why he was phoning. To warn you, he said."

"How would Kofi even know . . ." Kat stops, realizing the obvious answer: *Scarlett*, her PA, his friend, the person who introduced them. Scarlett must have spilled the beans, traitorously. "Spring's defaulted on repayment of a loan. Happens all the time. I'll reassure the investors at the meeting." The seriousness of her last-chance saloon hits her again, and her stomach swoops. "I've pulled Spring out of bigger holes."

"How much is the loan?" Flora asks. As if she has any idea.

"Compared to Spring's potential? Teeny. This is a long burn, not a get-rich-quick scheme." She feels queasy. "And it's none of Kofi's bloody business."

"He was worried about you, Kat." Flora's voice is doing that soft maternal thing. She must resist it, stay on guard. "Apparently you've not returned important calls, Kat."

"The signal's rubbish." Kat can feel her defenses rising, sweeping around her like a cloak of steel.

"Scott's managed to get through."

"Scott could hunt you down anywhere, Flora. He's probably stuck a tracker to your handbag. And you know what?" Kat's blood pounds in her ears. "You've got so used to him controlling your life, you think it's okay to do the same to me. You do! That's why you answered my phone. And it's *not* normal, Flora. It's not normal at all."

She shouldn't have pussy-footed around this issue when they went for that wrung-out, bruised drink after Dixie's funeral; Kat had asked why Flora didn't have her own bank account and Scott saw every transaction, while keeping a personal account himself. "It's creepy and it's wrong," she adds.

"Scott is the father of my child," Flora replies weakly.

"Yeah, and you wanted a father figure, I get that." Kat can't help but be pleased to have Flora on the back foot and the magnifying lens away from Spring. "You wanted someone who'd offer you the security and constancy Dad never did. After what happened here, you wanted protection from risk. I get that too. But life *is* risk." She knows she's veering too close now but it's like standing on a cliff edge, that compulsion to jump off. "You're denying who you are. You've buried yourself alive, Flora."

"How dare you? You can talk! You can't even risk a loving relationship."

Kat flinches.

"And I know . . . I *know* you've always looked down on me. Boring, dumb Flora. Now more than ever. Here I am! Fat mum." She jiggles the back of her arms. "With bingo wings! And a bladder that . . . that leaked—*leaked!*—when I jumped on Raff's trampoline on Boxing Day. Yes, I peed myself."

Kat stares at Flora in disbelief.

"Match me," growls Flora, glowing with rage, looking more beautiful than ever. "Just flipping try."

And because she will *never* let Flora have the last word, and the raven is staring at her confrontationally, and she's done with the bullshit, Kat takes a breath. "The six months before that summer, the last don't-mention-the-war summer, Mum drank herself to oblivion most nights."

"What? Seriously?" Flora's heat dissipates. "I knew Blythe liked a party, but I had no idea. My god, Kat, why didn't you tell me?"

"I wasn't allowed. Too risky. Mum would have lost work. The tabloids . . . all that stuff." Also, it was easier to say nothing. She didn't want pity. Nor did she want people thinking badly of Blythe. "Back then, particularly that year—1999 was Mum's worst, the very bottom—Dad's flat and Rock Point were the only places I was free of it, allowed to be a kid. I didn't want to bring all that stuff with me." She remembers arriving at Rock Point that last summer, and the stifling fear that her mother would go on a bender and she, Kat, wouldn't be around to save her. Then the relief that she *didn't* have to look after her mother, and whatever happened would not rest on her shoulders. "But I guess it came out sideways."

"Oh, Kat," Flora whispers, a hand over her mouth. "I always thought Lauren had the rough deal. I'm so sorry."

"Mum's been dry for twenty years. The fallout from that summer freaked her into sobriety, I think. Silver linings and all that."

"You are crying," Flora says with wonder. "I haven't seen you cry."

"Don't tell anyone," she says, knuckling the tears away. Weirdly, she can't stop crying. Not just for herself but also for the girls they'd been in the painting. Time's refusal to damn well *stop*.

Flora slips an arm around her shoulders and pulls her closer. Oddly, Kat doesn't immediately want to shrug it off. And even though she needs to chase those calls, fire Scarlett, save her job, she has no desire to do these things either. She's caught in another deeper, faster slipstream. Rather than fighting it—she's always bloody fighting, swimming upstream, like a demented salmon—she leans her head against Flora's shoulder, feeling its warmth on her neck. And they sit like that, heads touching, rocking in the seat's creaking cradle. A moment passes, tender and strange, swelling with all the years they've been skirting each other's lives; scared of getting too close again.

"I think I might drink too much, Kat," Flora says eventually. "Not like your mother did. But you know . . . too much."

"Yep," Kat says, relieved Flora has also noticed. It's in the family. Granny was a functional soak too. All that gin.

Flora nudges her with an elbow. "Don't tell Scott."

"Me and Scott aren't exactly scheduled for a cozy tête-à-tête anytime soon, don't worry." Kat digs the toes of her trainers and the seat tips back.

"Kat . . ." Flora stops, bites down on her lower lip, tussling with something. "There's something else. Last month, I screwed up. I mean, really."

"What did you do? Put reds in the white wash?"

Flora draws a long breath. "I kissed someone in my book group."

"Bloody hell, Flo." Kat's feet lose their grip. Chains rattling, the seat flies forward. "Who is it? What's his name?"

"Louise," she breathes.

"Mind blown." Kat reels. "Tell me everything immediately."

"She lives at number nine. Moved in six months ago. Divorced. Her little boy plays with Raff sometimes. She's . . . really nice, just so nice." Flora drops her head in her hands. "Oh, Kat, what have I done?"

"Flora, what *haven't* you done?"

"I'm a terrible person."

"God, you might actually be as imperfect as the rest of us." She studies her sister, mentally reframing, feeling an enormous surge of love for her. "More importantly, did you really pee on the trampoline?"

"It was quite a high bounce."

They both start to crack up, laughing so hard the swing seat judders. As their hysteria draws to a breathless end, Kat marvels that they've spent so long hiding the truth of their lives. Then she realizes, with a sobering sensation, it's the secret they forged here twenty years ago that's pushed them apart as it's run through each day since. In each other they see too much of the worst of themselves.

"It was just there, wasn't it?" Kat says after a beat, pointing to where the raven tugs a fat pink worm from the earth; where they'd once thrown down a tartan picnic blanket on a daisy-studded lawn.

"It looks . . . so innocent." Flora stares at the spot, transfixed, then lowers her voice to a whisper, the collusion of old. "Doesn't it do your head in that we're the only two people alive who know exactly what happened here that day, Kat?"

"It'd do my head in a lot more if we weren't, Flo." The raven's wings spread. They watch it rise and rise, until it is just a tiny black dot in the huge white sky.

36

LAUREN

|||

1999

A DISK OF DARKNESS slid across the horizon. Not the eclipse. A rain cloud. Granny muttered, "For heaven's sake, do get out of the way," as if an inconsiderate person with a large head had just stood in front of her.

"Keep the faith, Pam," said Grandpa. A tree of sweat branched along the back of his check shirt.

I was starting to wonder if the experts had got the day wrong. Nothing was happening. The sun was still a glowing ball behind the cloud. And things were not working out as planned. Grandpa's cardboard pinhole camera had already blown over the edge and disappeared. My eclipse glasses were too big for my nose, so I had to hold them with my index finger or be *blinded for life*. And it already felt like we'd been standing at The Drop, gazing upward, for an eternity, our necks starting to crick.

My mind kept traveling to Mum. And my favorite fantasy: Mum

and Dad together, us a little family, living here at Rock Point. For them not to have had a big falling-out when I was a baby. For Mum to have given Dad a second chance instead of taking me traveling . . . I stopped because I was old enough to know that wishing for something didn't make it happen. Also, I knew Mum would be on Port Meadow at that exact moment, smiling, happy, with the friends who adored her, peering up at the Oxford sky. In a funny way it felt almost Christmassy: everyone doing the same thing at the same time. Only this was about darkness, not light. And not reliably the same, like Christmas. No one really knew what was about to happen next.

I think this was why Flora kept giggling—"I don't even know what's funny." Her sequin skirt shook in the wind, the tassels on her suede handbag beating against it. Dad's heavy frown deepened. Kat was fidgety. While Gemma was quiet, really quiet. I worried she regretted not watching this spectacle with Viv, and felt responsible for the eclipse's performance, like when you persuade a friend to shell out for the cinema and need the film to not let you down.

Just when I thought nothing would happen, Grandpa yelled, "Look west!" A rush of cold air. We turned our heads as one, searching for the umbral shadow he'd promised, the sweeping sooty wall of darkness. And there *was* something, there really was. A murky dimness, witchy, racing across the summer sky.

"First contact," Grandpa whispered. A murmur of oohs and aahs rose from the other groups of people on the cliffs.

Flora started to giggle more, flapping her hands, saying, "Sorry, sorry, I can't stop."

I understood. The eclipse was like a roll of feeling, a physical thing moving right through you. I could taste the metallic dusk light on my tongue, its pencil-sharpener tingle. It dimmed some more, as though the lenses in my eclipse glasses had changed. My scalp prick-

led. I felt swimmy. Time sped up. The sea to the west turned squid-
ink black and the temperature dropped, as if we'd fallen out of
August and landed in January.

Dad leaned over and whispered, gently, "All right, Laurie?"

"Yes," I mumbled even though it felt like all the rules were being
broken. Reversing. The ancient dead in their neolithic barrows
would be rubbing their eyes, sitting up and stretching; the smuggler's
shipwrecks on the seabed bobbing back to the surface, like corks,
sails hoisted.

"*Lauren*," said Gemma. Just that one word, a million packed inside it. The eclipse had stolen her breath too: her voice had a nasal
squeak to it. "Look."

"Wow," said Kat, impressed, possibly for the first time ever.

Dad just stood there, swaying in the wind, with his palms open,
as if he might catch the eclipse like a cricket ball.

"I've got a headache," muttered Flora, not giggling now.

"Me too. Our brains cannot process what they're seeing."
Grandpa patted Flora's shoulder with his trembling hand. "It'll
pass."

"The gulls! Good grief." Granny's bracelets clinked as she pointed
up. The birds were weaving out of the sulky sky, toward the cliff,
where they vanished. "They've gone back to their roosts. Heavens. I
hope Bertha and the budgies aren't in a terrible tizz."

"I'm going to die a happy man, a very happy man." Grandpa's
voice wobbled with tears.

"Oh, Herb, honestly. You silly old sod," said Granny.

We gasped as the clouds sailed apart, and there it was, just for a
shimmering, extraordinary moment, the blot of sun, a halo of light
around its edge, like chalk dust on black sugar paper. From the cliff
tops came the sound of clapping and whooping. My skin pricked,

electric with static. The day became night, the sun a hole in the sky. It was both the most beautiful and terrifying thing I'd ever seen in my life. And I already knew I'd never be quite the same Lauren again.

"Sublime," breathed Grandpa.

An eerie, fizzing silence grew. A pulse quickened in my temples. The world felt vulnerable and precious. Humans weren't in charge. There was no guarantee that you'd wake to cornflakes, or water would come out of a tap when you turned it. Needing to steady myself, I slipped one arm through Gemma's. The movement made her cardboard glasses slip. Panicking, she hurriedly shoved them back on.

"Totality." Grandpa's voice quivered. Tears rushed into my eyes, and I clamped Gemma's arm tighter. "This is it," he said. "It's yours. Take a picture in your mind, girls, and never ever let it go."

37

LAUREN

|||

2019

*C*LICK. LAUREN TAKES a photo of the corn bird and sets it as a screen saver. She's not losing sight of it again. Leaning over her desk, she starts to write quickly.

———

"DEAR G, DAD totally agrees your bird is the sort of detail an old master might paint, hinting at his tethered sitter's yearning for flight. But it hasn't flown anywhere! I don't think it's been exposed to UV in the last twenty years. The beak is bent—a crash landing in the kitchen, my bad—but the wicker is pliable and blond, as if woven last week . . ." In her mind's eye, Gemma's nimble fingers weaving, threading, working, the pink tip of her tongue poking out the corner of her mouth in concentration.

Lauren looks up at the bird. In a box. All this time. She still can't make sense of it. Did Granny—a woman who loved to show off her gewgaws—succumb to some sort of mad eclipse fever and hide it away? And when?

It also niggles that Flora didn't tell her about its discovery immediately. Further proof, not that she needed any, that she's viewed as a liability. This weekend, she's felt her family's guardedness, as if they believe they're a blurted sentence away from eviscerating her. But all she wants now is to fill in the blanks; "the full story" her mother talked about. It's starting to feel as if the note writer is the only person who might tell it, slip the truth into her pocket like a shiny new coin. And if not the note writer, then Jonah—unless they are the same person.

Will she see him again? She hasn't long. By tomorrow evening London will have closed around her, its sky slung like a sheet between tall buildings. And it will absorb her fully, drawing in her attention and energy: the crowds, the gallery, and the ongoing admin of her mother's death. She grabs her woolly scarf.

Catching sight of herself in the dressing mirror as she opens the bedroom door, Lauren starts. Dixie. She looks like her mother today, and surprisingly radiant, as if uniting with the corn bird has restored a vital trace element she's been missing.

"ONIONS!" FLORA EXPLAINS, not entirely convincingly, wiping her streaming eyes on a tea towel. "What's with the coat, Lauren?"

"Oh, I was popping out for some fresh air, unless you'd like me to help . . ."

"No, no. It's our last supper and it's mine. All under control." Flora shakes her head and starts dicing again. "Well, it's not actually. And it'll be late. But who cares?" she says improbably.

From the conservatory, Bertha starts to chirp, "Mind your fingers, Raff!" in Flora's voice. "Fingers!"

"Shut your beak up," Flora yells back. "God, that bird. Maybe we all get the pet we deserve, eh?"

Walking closer to the conservatory, Lauren meets Bertha's magisterial eye. The parrot slowly raises a bunched foot in greeting. "Hello, you," she replies, smiling. Bertha cocks her head, scrutinizing Lauren as if she were the wildlife, displayed and trapped.

"Hang on, did you just *talk* to Bertha?" Flora drops her knife to the board with a clatter.

It does feel like a shift, a tiny triumph. "God, I did."

"Maybe it was the bump on the head. Let me see." Flora's oniony fingers root through Lauren's fringe. "Gone. And where are your lines, for heaven's sake?" She nods at Raff, lying belly-down on the sofa, playing a game on the iPad, Granny's fox fur stole tucked under his arm. "The collagen thief."

"Why don't I take him out?" says Lauren. Flora does look kind of ragged, her eyes puffy. "Give you a break."

"Oh no, don't worry. He's a handful, really. And . . ." Nodding at the window, Flora whispers, "We don't know who is out there, do we?"

Lauren's mind flicks again to Jonah, like a compass needle to a magnetic north.

"Svalbard north of the Tamar!" Kat strides into the kitchen, her luggage wheels rattling on the flagstones. She's smiling, not snarling now: she and Flora must have sorted out their beef about the phone, which is a relief. When Lauren asked Flora what Kofi had said, she muttered something about getting the wrong end of the stick. Lauren's glad of this too.

"All flights tomorrow canceled. Just as well I've got a seat this evening," Kat says. "Are you okay taking the maps back for me, Flo? I can't shove them in here." She pats the side of her designer case and glances around the room, her expression wistful. "Funny to think this is the last time I'll see the kitchen that time forgot. You know, I may have one last scoot around the house to see if there's anything else I want."

"Do. Don't forget the Post-its," says Flora. "If you must go tonight, Kat, and I wish you weren't, I insist on driving you to the airport. You'll come, Lauren? I need my co-pilot."

"Absolutely." Lauren grins, happy to be asked.

"Great. Cancel the taxi, Kat." Flora glances at the door, lowers her voice. "But we still haven't decided what to do about Angie, have we? The Las Vegas wedding . . . Are we even invited? I mean, he hasn't made that terribly clear, has he? Or am I missing something?"

Lauren has been wondering the same thing. And how she'll afford the airfare to Vegas, let alone a fancy hotel.

"There's a pattern of missing information," says Kat, and something about the way she says this brings a colder, sharper mood into the room.

As if to block it out, Flora turns back to the worktop and starts slicing a stick of celery.

"On one level, Dad inviting us back here feels manipulative." Kat frowns. "Crafty even?"

Flora stops chopping. And something in Lauren seizes in recognition too.

"On another, just muddled. As in maybe he really has got too many heavy metals in his brain, his veins bunged up with paint." Kat sits down on a chair, agitates one foot.

"Or Daddy just wanted us here to have a lovely time," says Flora determinedly, cutting again. "Can we agree this is actually possible?"

Lauren nods. She prefers this version.

"I'd say the odds are very slightly stacked against it." Kat's phone starts to vibrate. Lauren notices that her sister silences it quickly. "Anyway, I've got to get back to civilization."

"Do you fancy a last walk first?" Lauren smiles hopefully. "Not far."

Kat glances at her phone again, worry streaking across her face. "I can't, sorry. I've got a few work things to straighten out."

"No problem," says Lauren, feeling slightly crushed. Stupid. It's just a walk.

Raff launches off the sofa and wraps around her leg. "Take Raff!"

"Lauren's not taking you. How about you chop some fruit for Bertha?" Flora picks an apple from the fruit bowl and offers it to Raff.

"Want to go walk," says Raff, shaking his head.

"I promise I won't lose him," says Lauren. This is a chance to prove she's a reliable loving aunt. Not a liability.

"Going with Aunty Lauren." Raff tucks a sticky warm hand into hers and glances up, grinning, making Lauren's heart swell.

"The boy knows his mind, Flora." Kat looks up from her phone and winks at Raff. "A true Finch."

Lauren watches opposing feelings fight it out on Flora's face. The clock on the wall punches holes in the silence.

"Oh, why not? He needs some fresh air. Long car journey tomorrow. But I warn you, Lauren, he's the world's slowest walker. You won't get far." Flora kneels and holds his shoulders. "Little man, you behave, okay? No running off. No sharks. No tantrum. Promise me, Raff?" She tucks a curl behind his ear. "Aunty Lauren is not used to tantrums."

"Raff is very, very good," he says.

Lauren squeezes his hand. She knows this is a big deal. "So, what do we need, eh? A coat and wellie boots?"

"A bit more than that!" Flora says, looking staggered. "Gloves. Hat. Snacks. Tissues. Wet wipes. First-aid kit."

"Arctic expedition," mutters Kat. Lauren, terrified she'll blow it, says nothing.

———

THEY'RE ALREADY OUT the drive when Lauren realizes she's left her half-written letter to Gemma on the desk in her room. She pauses, wanting to turn back and put it away, but Raff tugs on her sleeve and points up at the windswept moor. "King of the castle," he says, with a big grin.

"The moor?" she asks doubtfully. "You don't want to go to the beach? Really? Well, we could walk to the stones, if you want." She points to a field gate farther up the lane and taps the side of her nose. "Aunty Lauren has a shortcut."

Raff stomps his wellies. "And he marched them up . . ."

They belt out the song. It's the first time Lauren's sung since the funeral, and it feels a bit like joy. "And he marched them down again . . ." She stops abruptly.

In the distance, a man with a black dog, tail piped. Her heart skits.

Has Jonah seen her? Possibly not. He carries on tramping across the field, then lifts a leg over a stile to the moor. It's her last chance to speak to him before she returns to London. To ask if he knows anything about the notes: his expression will surely reveal the truth, even if he denies it. Would it be foolhardy? Irresponsible with Raff? There are other walkers around today. And if Jonah had wanted to hurt her, he'd have done it in the Heaps' deserted cottage already. "Come on, little man, this way." The draw is physical, hard to resist. They head up, up, up, toward Jonah and the stones, unaware of the looming wall of charcoal cloud far out at sea, starting to rush toward them.

38

LAUREN

|||

1999

THE COLOR BLED back slowly, like when you adjusted a telly. The birds sang out a second dawn. Although the day returned, it'd been pulled out of shape. I felt spacy. Gemma was very pale. Grandpa held the back of his head; a migraine kicking in. "Too much excitement in one day, Herbert. You're all at sixes and sevens. As am I, frankly. We need a stiff drink and a lie-down," Granny said, escorting him back to the house, leaving us with Dad.

But something was going on with Dad too. The way he was just standing there, gazing out to sea, his eyes unnaturally bright, like the eclipse's umbra was inside them. "I feel like Superman," he murmured, looking more like Jesus. He took a few photos of us—"my cosmic girls!"—then drifted away in a daze. The huddles of eclipse watchers began to pack up too. Dogs barked again. We sat down on the bench. We sat there for ages. Waiting for something else to happen. A sequin from Flora's skirt stuck into my thigh.

"So. Where's the party, Kat?" said Flora. Her face-paint flowers had smudged. "Because I see boring families. Old men in socks and sandals. I see a skinny dipper. Gross."

"Patience." Kat leaned back, waggled her foot, like Dad did. "I told you, I heard local boys talking."

"What if you misheard, Kat?" Flora blurted. We were all wound up. "And it's the wrong cove. A party could be literally going on right now—somewhere else!"

"Oh, the *drama*." Kat put the back of her hand to her forehead. "It just hasn't started yet, that's all."

Even if we did find a party—and I'd only been to the sort with balloons and paper plates—it suddenly felt like a bad idea. I wanted to be somewhere quiet and private to absorb what I'd just witnessed. "I'm going to check the budgies are okay." I stood up, swaying slightly, holding down my dress in the wind.

"I'll come." Gemma's voice skidded around, like the shock of the eclipse was still moving through her too. She peered under the bench, looking for her rucksack before realizing she'd left it at home.

"Well, we can't stay here, Kat. All dressed up. Just two of us. It looks loser-y. Let's head back for a bit." A knowing smile slid into Flora's voice. "Aren't you, like, *thirsty*?"

I felt something pass between them, all the whispered conversations in which I'd not been included. "Well, since we've been left to our own devices, it'd be rude not to," said Kat. "But first . . . Lauren, wait."

Kat wiped her thumb across her cheekbones, crusting it with glitter, then solemnly smeared it down the bridge of my nose, my cheeks, her fingertip a wand. "There. Now we all look the same." She tilted her head on one side. "You look so pretty. Doesn't Lauren look pretty?"

Gemma and Flora nodded in agreement. And I could feel the corners of my mouth curling. I knew I shouldn't be so easily won over. But it was a relief. As always with my sisters, it was impossible to hate them for long. I still wanted to be in their club. Still wanted to be them. I hadn't yet realized Gemma did too. "Thanks," I said quietly, trying not to look too pleased.

Kat put an arm around my shoulders, her skin cool and soft against my neck, and we were walking like that—half hug, half headlock—back to the house when Angie drew up in her car, kicking out exhaust and slamming on the brakes.

She dangled her keys from one finger and eyed us up and down. "Well, don't you lot scrub up nicely."

So did Angie. Platform cork heels. Eyelashes like palm fronds. A floaty black dress, cinched in with a gold braided belt. Replaying in my head, her comment to Dad yesterday: *"So, we're all good, you know. For our session tomorrow, Charlie."* Something ugly twisted in my belly.

"So, your dad . . . is he . . ." Angie squinted up at the studio windows. "Ah. Grand." She smiled. Her lip gloss glistened, syrupy in the sunshine. "I see him." Holding her windblown hair off her face with one arm, she turned to me, "Has your father said anything?"

I caught the pitiful hope in her voice. She needed his approval as much as we did. "About what?" I asked innocently.

Gemma, Kat, and Flora stared at Angie blankly.

"I smartened up the studio for him," Angie said. "As a surprise, you know."

"Don't think he's noticed," I said, enjoying this little bit of power.

Angie looked crushed, just for a moment, then tossed her hair and walked toward the house, leaving the front door swinging. Her shoes were hammers on the stairs.

"What was that all about?" asked Flora.

I shrugged, not telling.

————

FIRST, I CHECKED Bertha, who seemed unruffled by the topsy-turvy dawn and sang a lyric from ". . . Baby One More Time." The budgies were less happy. It looked like there'd been a pillow fight in the aviary. Feathers carpeted its concrete floor, and the birds were still restless. I pressed my head against the metal mesh wall. "Oh dear."

"Poor things," said Gemma, and smothered a small sneeze in her hands. "They must have freaked out."

"Hey, come on!" Kat called, and we turned.

My sisters had tossed a tartan picnic blanket on a sunny patch of lawn. Flora lay on her belly—her skirt sparkling, surely visible from space—chewing a blade of grass. Kat lolled next to her, legs kicked up, her face flat on one arm, her fingers twiddling with a hank of Flora's hair. Beside them were beakers and a big bottle of lemonade. My mouth started to wet. I'd barely drunk or eaten anything all morning. We joined them.

Outside the garden's walls, a distant boom. Then another. Heavy fast beats, rising and falling on the wind. Kat's head bobbed up. "The sound system! Told you!" She slapped Flora's bottom, then nodded up at the house. "Granny's and Grandpa's bedroom curtains are closed. I think it's time, don't you?"

The music started to build.

"I'll be mother." Flora sat up, cross-legged, not caring that she was flashing the gusset of her knickers. She poured the lemonade into plastic beakers. "Here you go."

I took a thirsty gulp, then spat it out onto the grass. "Ugh. What *is* that?"

Flora creased over in laughter.

"You tricked me," I said, wiping my mouth with my arm. I was back on the ledge again, starting to fall.

"If it's safe for Granny." Kat sniffed her own glass. "From her drinks cabinet, that's all, Lauren. Keep your hair on. It's a Finch alcopop. We could charge good money for this."

I pictured my grandparents' collection of sticky bottles, the duty-free liquors that reminded me of the chemicals on Dad's metal studio shelves. "But . . . but we're not allowed," I stuttered, horrified, enthralled.

Gemma held her beaker away from her body, warily.

"You won't snitch, will you?" Flora stroked the top of my bare foot in little circles with her finger. It felt nice.

"I'd never snitch." The acrid smell of the drink mixed with the fresh green smell of the grass.

"Gemma?" Kat raised an eyebrow. "If you tell Viv, I swear . . ."

Gemma shook her head, then flashed a slightly pleading look at me that said, let's get out of here, but I ignored it, my sisters exerting a stronger pull.

"Down in one?" Kat said, like she did this all the time. "Who's game?"

It was like seeing a needle approaching a balloon. I knew I couldn't stop it, that the day was about to spin in a new direction, hurling us out of childhood into a more exciting place. I also knew that if I joined in, I'd prove myself equal. A Finch sister. Not just Dixie's daughter, the gawky kid they resented. Finally, I'd belong.

"*Go,*" hissed Kat.

Squeezing my eyes shut, I tipped my head back, trying not to retch as the liquid burned down my throat.

Flora and Kat wiped their mouths on the back of their hands.

The only person who hadn't touched her drink was Gemma. "The smell." She coughed, shuddered. "Ugh."

"The smell is much worse than the taste," Flora lied.

"Sip, sip," Kat and Flora chanted. I wanted to tell them to leave Gemma alone—Gemma looked upset—but the garden had already started to wobble at the edges.

With no warning, Kat reached across and roughly shoved the beaker to Gemma's mouth. Gemma whacked it away, knocking over the lemonade bottle and sending its contents fizzing into the grass.

Kat and Flora yelled and laughed and scrabbled for it.

Gemma shot me a glance. It carried a question. But for once, I couldn't read it. Her eyes were a puzzle of silver and gray and green and they made me feel woozy. The music boomed louder. *Bouff-bouff.*

"You don't get off that easily, Gemma," Kat said with a hard-eyed smile.

Everything started to ripple. New sensations pinballed about my body. Then nausea roared up in a huge brown wave. "Need the bathroom." I held my hand over my mouth.

"I'll take you." Gemma scrabbled to her feet and took my arm.

"No, no." I pulled away from her, not realizing she probably wanted to escape too. I suddenly wanted Mum so badly it squeezed the air out of me. If not her, no one.

The journey to the downstairs toilet took forever. I got there just in time. Afterward, I slurped cold water from the tap, then sat on the toilet seat, my eyes closed. I'm not sure for how long: time tunneled away.

Back in the garden, the others stopped talking when they saw me. The atmosphere had changed, although I couldn't work out how, or why. But I didn't want to throw up anymore, and that was all that mattered. A new zingy boldness swept through me, a feeling that I could do anything. I'd passed through a door I hadn't even realized was there, leaving the square, childish Lauren Molloy behind, and I wanted the others to see this too. "Who wants to come inside the aviary?" I sounded confident, cocky. Like someone else.

"Oh, get you." Kat's voice slurred. "Good little Laurie, breaking Granny's ten commandments."

"You're not catching me in there." Flora lay back on the blanket, hands behind her head, and sighed at the sky. "Real-life corn birds. All that poo!"

We laughed. The air was sweet with honeysuckle. It wasn't just Flora's skirt, we all shimmered in the sunshine, our eyes full of light. Radiant, perfect. Gosh, we were beautiful. Even me. "Gemma?" I could barely speak for smiling. "No one's around."

Gemma ran her palm over the top of the grass and shook her head. A ladybird landed on her knee, like a drop of blood.

"Why not? Bet your mum has secrets too," Kat said.

The salt air twitched. I hadn't the foggiest what Kat was talking about. I only knew that Gemma loved those budgies and summer would soon be over, and we'd not see each other for another year and go back to writing letters, which wasn't the same.

"I dare you, Gemma. Or are you scared of Granny?" Kat carried on teasing. There was affection in her voice—we were all a bit scared of Granny—but I don't think Gemma heard it.

"Shut your cakehole." Gemma jumped up, eyes flashing. And she seemed taller, a whole lot fiercer.

"She roars!" Flora clapped, delighted, swiveled to her side, head on elbow. "Again, Gemma! Tell Kat where to stick it. No one ever does."

"And you can shut up too," hissed Gemma.

I'd never loved Gemma more intensely than at that moment. Even Kat and Flora were staring at her with a new respect.

"I'll do it, Lauren," Gemma said, visibly steeling herself. "The aviary."

I was thrilled. Careful not to let any budgies escape, I unbolted the aviary door, opening it just a crack. Gemma and I slipped in soundlessly, one after the other, like fish into a tank, another world, sending the birds into a frenzy. Feathery fluff kicked up under our feet and sent nutty dusty bird smells whirling, catching in our throats.

"Stay still, very still, so we don't spook them," I instructed quietly.

Standing with our backs to the garden, I resisted the urge to turn around when I heard a metallic noise. Out of the corner of my eye, a flicker of movement; Kat and Flora running toward the moon gate. After that, it all happened so quickly: the sneeze rising through Gemma, her desperate red-faced struggle to hold it in; me noticing that the aviary door had been bolted from the outside; Gemma's sneeze exploding, turning the aviary into a spinning cyclone of birds, feathers, dander, and dust. A wheeze. A whistle. A scream.

39

LAUREN

||||

2019

RAFF'S WHOOP IS pure and high, a choirboy's note. He runs into a boggy puddle, stomping his wellie boots. Lauren laughs with him, carried along by his joy, and when she looks up again, Jonah's vanished. Sunk into the earth like the drizzle.

Well. There goes her last chance. And now the moor is empty again, it's almost as if Jonah never existed; that he clambered out of her head on the train journey from London, forged by her muddled emotions about this place—and her need for answers.

Enough already, she tells herself firmly. The trail has gone stone cold. She's out of time. Raff has walked far enough. The upright stones loom on the horizon. Beyond them, if she squints, she can just make out the Heaps' cottage.

"You're a trooper, you know that?" She squeezes Raff's gloved hand.

"Very fast," Raff agrees.

"Let's march home then. Ready?" Lauren adjusts his beanie, tugging it down over his ears. She's enjoyed his company so much—"Who lives inside the rocks?" "Why doesn't the buzzard fall out of the sky?"—but in the last few minutes frozen gusts have started rolling across the moor like barrels. She's never known Cornwall so cold. Or so sepulchral, stripped back to its beautiful bones. Within it, the abstracts of Ben Nicholson, Patrick Heron, Peter Lanyon; all those artists who've fallen into this place, poured it out in paint. And in the stones, Barbara Hepworth's sculptures. Lauren says a silent good-bye, feeling an unexpected wrench, and they turn and walk, the bracken wetly slapping their trousers. The sky dims abruptly.

Raff points up. "Uh-oh."

Not an eclipse this time. Dark vertical columns advancing, carving through the air. Seconds later, the load is dumped with a roar and a rattle. The hail bullets their faces and bounces off the ground.

Raff screams. "It hurts! Make it stop, make it stop!"

Sheltering him inside her coat, she desperately looks around for somewhere to wait it out. But the moor is so exposed. Raff is sobbing now. The hailstones grow bigger, more frantic, like pearls dropped from a great height. Seeing no other option, she picks up Raff and starts to run toward the Heaps' cottage. It always was a refuge for her, a place of shelter. Her eyes stinging, barely able to see a foot ahead, she lunges at the front door. They're in. After the ferocity outside, the cottage's stillness has a vacuum suck, its hush broken by the hiss of hail on the windows. Raff's whimpering fades.

"That's better, eh?" Lauren plants him down on the floor, plucks off his gloves, and rubs his hands. "There. Warm pinkies."

Raff peers around the decrepit living room with astonished owl eyes. He's never seen grot like this. Something scuttles along the skirting, a flash of brown in the jaundiced light. Lauren hears the *plink, plink* of an unseen drip. Another sound, a scuffing in another room, like claws on stone. She tries not to think about what that might be.

"I'm going to phone Mummy, tell her where we are." No signal. Turning her back on Raff, she walks to the nearest grimy window and tries to punch out a text message. Won't send. Lauren imagines Flora at Rock Point, anxious now, trying to phone, not getting through, regretting ever trusting her irresponsible sister with her precious child. "Come on, come on," she mutters, trying again.

"Doggy!" Raff announces delightedly behind her.

Confused, Lauren turns. Raff is stroking an actual dog, black and glossy as a pool of oil. "Raff!" She runs toward him, squelching on the mulch of carpet, and pulls him away, onto her hip. A thin wire of fear starts to pull, a possibility. Raff reaches for the dog. She steps back. "We need to leave."

"Why?" growls a male voice. "I'd say this is as good a place to meet as any."

Panic rises in her chest, spreads its wings. Someone is emerging from the back of the living room, out of a doorway to the kitchen. Black coat. Hood. She recognizes his shape and heft. Those coat hanger shoulders. And the dog, the bouncy pup who'd knocked her flying on the beach. "Jonah?"

Another step into the room. He flips down his hood. A stranger's pale, pinched face. Flinty, sharp eyes. Not Jonah. Her mistake dawns; she's misidentified Jonah, likely countless times, wanting it to be the handsome man from the train, willing it to be him, seeing what she wants to see, all the while missing *this* man, letting him hide in plain sight. And this is the dog Raff must have patted outside Rock Point, not Rocket. Oh god.

Lauren freezes as he tramps the short distance across the room with a casual territorial swagger. Then he leans back against the peeling wall, arms crossed, positioned between them and the front door. He's built like a barn. She's trapped.

Lauren's terror has a ferric taste now. She has a sharp moment of lucidity, a realization that—once again—she's slipping out of the everyday illusion of safety. A bad decision, wrong time, wrong place, all it takes for your life to change. Lauren understands this better than most, the crack that can fissure, yawn open, cast you from one world into another. Did she really think she could come back to Rock Point and emerge unscathed? It hasn't finished with her. What started years ago is not yet done. She deserved this. If she screams, the hail and wind will smother it, even if anyone was there to listen, which they're not.

It almost defeats her.

But Raff's little heart patters against her own, and she knows, without any doubt, she'd fight to the death to keep him safe. Lauren also knows her fear is not an irrational phobic response. Not this time. This threat is real and human. She cannot have a panic attack. She must breathe. Think. *Escape.*

The man's eyes narrow to silvery slits. "Surely, you remember me?"

40

KAT

| |

THE GUST ALMOST knocks Kat off her feet. She steadies by squeezing her core muscles tight and cautiously leans over the edge of The Drop. A sprinkling of rare Cornish snow has replaced the hail; light as volcanic ash, blown into a frenzy by the wind. Still no sign of Lauren and Raff.

She's quite sure that Lauren—slight but strong, knowledgeable about this landscape—will keep Raff safe. Flora doesn't share this confidence. And there's no lift to the airport—the last flight to London—until they're back. Or at least until they get through on Lauren's phone, currently bumping straight to voicemail.

Kat has tried every local taxi number, and none are available for hours: she's begged, offered to pay double. A signaling problem and snow farther up the line has screwed the trains. Angie, who never was in any hurry to leave, hasn't got her car fixed. Her father's sunk a saucepan of mulled wine and, despite insisting otherwise, is unfit to drive.

Worse, Scarlett has just emailed: the meeting has been rescheduled—to a breakfast meeting in E1 tomorrow bloody morning! The board members have done this on purpose, Kat's sure of it. Knowing she's stuck in Cornwall, a good chance she won't make it back in time. And if she doesn't swagger into that meeting, polished, on form, it'll be much easier to offer a scalp—hers—to the shareholders: change at the top, they'll be able to say, saving their own skins. She can picture them now, edgy from the deprivations of detox January, maxed up on their credit cards after Christmas, petrified of losing their posts. All the "yes" people switching sides. Kat's loved Spring, given it everything, and is starting to realize it doesn't love her back. But she'll be damned if she makes her dispatch easy.

There's still time.

The coast path is a gum of mud, rock, and snow. But she reaches the hermit's hut, the best vantage point, like a royal box over the auditorium of cove and cliffs. As she stands by its ruined walls, memories of the eclipse summer blow through her: she and Flora running, laughing, toward the sound system on the beach that day; in her peripheral vision, an incongruous splash of brilliant yellow, giddily free, lost on an Atlantic gust. When another budgie flew past, she'd known—in that highly sensitized part of her tuned by Blythe's blotto binges to sense danger—that something was wrong, very wrong.

And she feels it again at a lower level, a dull warning buzz. A second later, her mobile rings in her pocket. "Found them?"

"No. I've got a bad feeling, Kat. I shouldn't have trusted . . ." The line keeps cutting, and Kat has to redial three times. Flora's anxiety pours out in staccato bursts. "Scott keeps calling too." A sob wracks her voice. "What do I tell him?"

"Nothing. Not yet." Kat hunkers down on a stone, talking into the crook of her arm, trying to keep out the roaring wind. "It's snowing, but not heavily, and they've not even been gone that long. Where are you now?"

"Pub car park."

"Right. Here's the plan. You drive back to Rock Point. Wait for them there. I'm on my way down to the cove. Tide's out. I'll check the cave too."

"Christ. The cave! Yes, yes, check. They could be sheltering there. Thank you, thank you."

"And as soon as we find them, you'll drive me to the airport?" She hates herself for mentioning it. Sounding so self-absorbed. "It's just I'm toast if I don't make . . ."

"Oh, bugger, yes. Sorry. I know Spring's your baby, Kat."

"Raff is far more important. I'll find him and Lauren. Hang in there."

The hail has drilled holes on the dry upper beach. Sloshing over the shallow ribbons of water that pour down from the cliff walls to the sea, she steps into the cave. It's darker and deeper than she remembers. "Lauren?" she's shouting when something wet and warm—*alive*—licks her hand and she gasps.

"Rocket!" A man runs across the beach. "I'm so sorry. She's in training. Sit, Rocket. No, *sit*."

"Don't worry." She strokes the dog, who pants moist meaty breath. "Listen, I'm looking for a woman—early thirties, smallish— and a little boy? He's about this high. You haven't seen them, have you?" she asks, and he shakes his head. "Oh, and the woman, my sister, she's got this blue streak in her fringe."

His expression immediately changes. "Lauren," he says quietly. Reading her surprise, he explains they've already met. Says his name is Jonah.

Kat scrutinizes him more closely. Tall. Black dog. Check, check. And yet there are lots of lone male walkers. Even more black Labs. The notes have made them all slightly paranoid. She's not a paranoid person. And she refuses to be intimidated. But she stands a little taller all the same.

"You wouldn't happen to be Kat?" Jonah asks cautiously. "The wild swimmer? Lauren mentioned you."

"That's me." Odd Lauren hasn't mentioned him, though. He's not unattractive. "Lauren took Raff for a walk," she says, answering his unformed question, impatient to get on. "The hailstorm blew in. I was hoping they might be sheltering in the cave." Her mobile rings. Keeping a wary eye on Jonah, she takes the call. "Flora. Any news?"

"Oh, Kat, Kat, I just got back and rushed to Lauren's room, thinking they might be there—Dad and Angie are out looking too now—and . . . and . . ." Her voice cracks, the line shredding again. "She's unstable, Kat! She's a total fruitcake . . ." Flora cuts out.

Kat stares at her phone, with a sinking feeling. She redials, mouths "Sorry" at Jonah, who is doing a very bad job of pretending he's not listening. Even the dog is staring, its tail sweeping a fan in the sand. "What? Flora, you're seriously saying the letters Lauren's been writing the last few days are to *Gemma*?"

"I'm sorry to butt in," Jonah says. It's the gravity in his voice that grabs her attention. A glint of alarm in his eyes. "I've an idea where they might be."

"One sec, Flo," she says, pressing the phone to the shoulder of her coat—Flora's voice faint: "Is someone with you?"—and following Jonah's intense gaze to the cliff top and beyond, where frozen sky meets cold, cold earth.

41

LAUREN

Birthmark." The man's finger circles his hollow, unshaven cheek. "But I'd have recognized you anyway. You haven't changed that much, Lauren."

The sound of her name on his chapped lips. Lauren's mind scatters. She cannot think who he is. What he wants. She must get past him to the front door. Or the kitchen door that leads to the garden? Surely his route in. But this living room is so small, and he so large, he could be on them in moments. She should have pressed that emergency stop button on the London-Penzance train carriage wall while she still had the chance. *Mum*, she keens. *Mum*.

But Dixie can no longer save her. And no one's coming anytime soon since no one knows where they are. And this is her fault for not mentioning visiting this place, worrying about looking a freak. She's messed up in every possible direction. Raff's breath lands in little warm puffs on her neck, a reminder of what's at stake.

She tries to draw up courage from deep inside, where it's always lived. And she can almost feel her mother beside her then, a warm current in the cold dead air of the room. *You stood by that aviary, Laurie, you are stronger than you know.*

The dog starts to nose Raff's dangling feet. "Can you call your dog back?" Her voice shakes.

"Patty." The man clicks his fingers and the dog trots obediently to his side. He strokes its head with gentleness at odds with the rest of him, while pinioning Lauren with a caustic gaze. "Have I changed that much? Lost my boyish looks?"

"I really don't know you." There's something about this man that suggests he hasn't got much to lose. That life has not been kind. Her heart is banging so hard he must be able to hear it. And smell her fear.

"Oh, you do." A pulverizing stare. "Come on, Lauren."

She edges toward the kitchen, careful to keep the disintegrating sofa between them. But her legs are like jelly, and every muscle flex, every movement, seems cartoonishly exaggerated in the fleshy air. The cottage a terrible inversion of the happy, warm place it used to be.

"I'd offer you a cuppa, but the kettle is on the blink." A smile plays at the corners of his mouth. "It's me, Lauren. Me, Pete. Gemma's brother."

Pete. Lauren's knees buckle. The decades thrash back. The walls brighten into Battenberg cake yellows and pinks; Viv's laughing in the kitchen, her phone receiver crooked under her chin. Lauren blinks away the déjà vu. Yet Pete remains. It's like being stuck in a nightmare, trying to run away but unable to lift her feet.

It is Pete Heap. But it is not Pete Heap. The years have etched their way across his features and given his face a Dickensian, pinched quality. But the silvery-blue of his eyes is the same.

As a boy, Pete was watchful, with a big goofy smile when it broke. She'd liked him. At times she'd even wished he were her brother because he was funny—teasing, rather than cruel—and sweetly protective of Gemma. And, in a way she sensed rather than fully understood, he was more of her world than Kat and Flora, in the same way that her mum was more like down-to-earth Viv Heap than Kat's and Flora's mothers. But that connection no longer exists. The shock of him threads down her spine. Any relief that this menacing man is Pete—someone she once knew, liked—melts away. "What . . . what are you doing here?"

"I was walking this one." He ruffles the dog's ears. "Smelled that hail coming we did, didn't we, Patty?"

Lauren thinks of his mum Viv saying something similar years ago about smelling rain. Viv, lying on her towel in the front garden, lithe, oiled, and brown, hair piled on her head, not looking like a cleaner. The memory frays.

"Check it out." He nods to the window. "Snowing now. I can't remember the last time it snowed around here. Pretty, isn't it?"

Nothing is pretty. Through the grimy window the snow looks gray, like dying moths. The collective noun for moths, an eclipse, she remembers randomly, her mind seeking its own escape route. "Pretty," she agrees weakly, holding Raff tighter, as if her grasp might protect him.

Pete stomps his feet to keep out the chill. "I like to check in on this place, time to time, you see." His conversational tone belies the fact that he is blocking their exit. "Can't help myself. Houses are never just bricks and mortar, are they?" His mouth presses into a line and his eyes spark. "You'd know something about that too, I guess."

Lauren nods, trying to pretend this is normal, that she hasn't worked out that Pete must have seen them enter, then stolen in round the back. The scuffing sound was surely the dog's claws on the kitchen floor. A gull swoops down and settles on a windowsill outside and its cold avian eye meets hers. Nothing happens. Lauren is already in a fight-or-flight state, heart racing, mouth dry, only this time it's a threat her rational brain understands too. And the gull's relative power shrinks. She'd swap its presence for Pete's in a heartbeat.

"This cottage will be buried before too long," Pete says, punching his hands deep into his coat pockets. "Ground's going to open right up and suck it down."

Raff yawns and rests his head on her shoulder, staring at the dog, who thumps its tail wetly on the carpet.

"Foundation's shot." Pete nods toward a wall, with a jagged crack like a lightning strike running up it. "Old tin mineshaft collapsed below."

Lauren pictures a sinkhole gaping open beneath them, vanishing without trace.

"Health and flipping safety." Pete strides to the damaged wall and pats it affectionately, like a farmer might the flank of a favorite old cow. "Forced us out years ago. Oh yeah, and burglars broke in. Bust the locks. Couldn't find anything worth nicking, obviously."

"That's terrible, Pete." She must keep him sweet, keep talking. Get him on her side. He's moved from the front door now, no longer blocking it. "How is your mum?"

Just for a moment, his face softens. "Bearing up, you know."

Her heart aches. She considers telling him about all the letters she's written to Viv over the years, then thrown away, having lost her nerve to send them. "And your dad?"

He's silent. Lauren notes how he's inherited the net-hauling bulk of his Kernow forefathers. Her mind trips to a ring net, its circle tightening, bagging its catch. White and red entrails swimming on a boat deck. A fisherman's blood-spattered oilskins.

"Long time dead," he says eventually.

"I'm sorry." With Pete now having moved, Lauren can draw a line between her and Raff and the front door. She may just have a chance. "It's great to see you again, Pete. But we should go." She tries and fails to sound casual. Four big steps. Five. "Raff needs his tea."

He narrows his eyes at Raff and mutters, "Yours?"

Raff shyly buries his face into Lauren's neck, sticky with snot from his dripping nose.

"Nephew." Lauren searches for a smile, but her mouth is too tense and won't work properly.

"Which sister?"

"Flora's," she says, quietly, and instantly regrets it, without knowing why.

"Sure, looks like a Finch."

"Everyone in the house is going to start wondering where we are and come looking, aren't they, Raff?" she says, although she knows no one's knocking on a deserted cottage door in the middle of a snowstorm anytime soon. And Pete probably does too.

Raff pulls on her earlobe for attention. "Hungry."

"Oh yes, a snack. Good idea," she says. "Let's see what Mummy packed." Lauren twists and manages to rifle in her bag. Pete's eyes bore into her as she pulls out a box of raisins. Pretending to look for more, she goes back in for her phone and tries to stab 999, hidden by the rucksack.

"Leave the phone, Lauren."

She freezes, terrified.

"Nice your sister has got a family of her own now. Nice motor too. And how grand that you all held on to the fancy house all those years so you can tootle back whenever, eh?" His smile twists. "Some people get all the luck, right? Some people get to forget." A vein pulses in his neck. "I'm not one of those people."

"Pete . . ." she says, precariously, not knowing how to begin. She glances at the nearest window. A hard kick might do it. But she can't push Raff out there on his own. If she doesn't escape with him, he'll be lost in these conditions. "I am so, so sorry."

"Are you? Are you really? Champagne! Woo-hoo!" The mood shifts dangerously. "The evening you arrived, I saw you all, clinking glasses. All lit up in that big house. It made me want to retch. The little people can be forgotten. A few lines in the local newspaper. You lot kept your names out of it, didn't you? Bad-boy artist didn't fancy that sort of press. Not that bad, right?"

Lauren's heart knocks against her ribs. Her quickening breath scrolls white into the room.

"Shame it wasn't one of you golden girls." He fights a suppressed sob. "Or the mad redhead."

Lauren inhales to speak. But she doesn't want to pull the thread that holds her together: the story she's woven around herself, protective and comforting as a silky cocoon.

"Why *my* sister?" His face is savage with sadness. "Why my Gemma?"

The floor seems to tilt to one side. She survived. Gemma did not. And now it is her turn. A different cage. A different fate. Helplessness engulfs her. But then there's Raff's cold fingertips again, tapping her cheek, a reminder of the vulnerable little person she must save, as she didn't save Gemma. She surges toward the front door. And she's there, almost out, the rush of freezing air on her face. Snow-flakes starring her black coat sleeve.

The beam of Pete's arm falls, barring her exit. "Not so fast."

42

LAUREN

| | |

1999

GEMMA SLID DOWN the aviary wall. Legs extended, stiff and straight as a string puppet's. Her heels scuffing the fluff and feathers on the ground into a dune. She was making funny noises, like she was trying to suck in air through a straw. As I bent over her, calling her name, asking what was wrong, the budgies panicked further, the frantic beat of their wings catching in our hair. Time went mushy. My arms and fingers started to prickle, as if a thistle were being rolled over my skin. My jaw clamped. My vision tunneled until it was just two beams of torchlight. An underwater silence.

Then I was somewhere near the aviary roof, looking down through the leafy shadows, swinging ropes and perches, the feather-flashes of yellow and green. And I could see myself, crouched on all fours, kneeling next to Gemma, who was slumped, bent over. Glitter on our cheeks. My lips were moving, although I couldn't hear what I was saying. And Gemma's stomach was sucking inward with effort—the dress bagging at the waist. Her lips turning blue. I watched myself crawl on hands and knees to the aviary door, reaching up, fumbling, sticking my fingers through the metal grid, trying to undo the bolt from the inside. It took years and years, and then it was sliding open, and we were saved.

I crawled outside, slipped back into my skin again. I cried out but no one came. No one heard. The house's bedroom windows were blank, curtains half-drawn against the heat. But on the top floor, the studio window, just for a second, *Angie*. Naked, a nude in a frame, her head thrown back, her hands star-fished on the glass, her breasts squished. She looked straight at me, covered her breasts, and turned away. Then fluttering past, over my head, a bolt of yellow; a budgie, another, and another—flock birds!—*free, free, free,* soaring into the summer sky.

43

LAUREN

|||

2019

EATHERS," PETE SAYS heavily, his breath a cone of white. He is crouching against the closed front door, back slammed against it, his arms slung loosely around his knees. The dog trots in a circle, then curls down beside him, a black question mark. "We had to be careful. Always had foam pillows and cushions and whatnot."

Lauren nods, unsure if Pete is softening, or if she's started to sympathize with her captor. How long have they been in here? She daren't try to look at her phone again to check if her battery has drained in the cold, or if there's a signal. Outside the window, the snow still whirls, phosphorescence against the darkening sky.

"Are we in trouble, Aunty Lauren?" Raff's breath smells, heartbreakingly, of raisins, which he's now finished.

"No. We're having an adventure, remember?" She must keep Raff calm so that he doesn't provoke Pete. She tries to smile. She wants to scream.

Raff repeats the soothing words "an adventure" and drops his chin back onto her shoulder, satisfied for now. His trust kills her. Her arms throb with his weight. But as long as she's holding him, warming him, he's okay.

"If we'd lived in a polluted city, Gemma would have been much worse, Mum used to say." Pete stares into the mid-distance, speaking less to Lauren than himself, the way people do when they're sorting through their childhood, dusting down the things that might make sense of it. "Mum wanted her to stay in Cornwall always." A grimacing smile. "Gemma, of course, had other plans. Big plans." Unexpectedly Pete looks up and smiles, a disarming flash of genuine warmth. "Hey, you know how herring gulls are born with their eyes open?"

Lauren nods, a bit of fear shearing away because curled inside this ornithological fact, like a hibernating tiny creature: Gemma.

"My sister was like that."

"She was!" Lauren almost forgets her peril, then catches herself, aware of being lulled into a false sense of security. "And she knows . . ." She forces herself to correct the tense, a knife twist from present to past. ". . . knew so much about birds. She loved birds, Pete." She needs him to understand how it happened. But it's a fine line. Pete's got his narrative, and you can't just kick those sorts of stories down, the ones that live inside you. You must dismantle all the moving parts carefully, reassemble them.

Lauren and her therapist did months of such "work." (Lauren hated that word, as if feelings neatly clocked in and out, rather than rioted in her head in the middle of the night.) But even though the sessions made her less anxious, she didn't want to give up her story. It was precious, so she held it tighter, more secretively. It was she, Lauren Molloy, who hadn't been able to breathe. Lauren who'd almost died. She and Gemma had both survived. They were like a child's butterfly picture, where you paint one half of the paper and fold it together to make a mirror image.

One night, a year later, maybe two, Dixie overheard her talking out loud to Gemma. Lauren was mortified. But Mum took off her shoes and lay next to her on the bed and they'd stared at the stick-on glow stars on the sloped eaves ceiling. It's fine to talk to people you miss, Laurie, she'd said. I do it all the time. Love doesn't die. Nor do souls. We just change state into a sort of beautiful dark matter. The physicists haven't been able to prove it yet. But they will. I promise they will. Just because something isn't understood doesn't mean it doesn't exist. Lauren had needed to hear those words. And she clung to them.

As the world texted and emailed and messaged, she wrote longhand, continuing as the loyal pen pal she'd been, writing letters to Gemma and the letters Gemma would have sent her. The more she wrote, the more alive Gemma became. She grew older. She had a full, wonderful life. The job she'd wanted, an environmental scientist, based in Greenland. A favorite painting: Dürer's *Young Hare*. The mosaic, Gemma adored that too, which is why Lauren's found such solace in it, sticking each fragment of glass to the board. Beauty out of broken things.

"Ironically, her worst sensitivity wasn't to feathers but horses." Pete's voice spikes into her thoughts. Yet again he swings between being Gemma's brother, the boy she once knew, and a monster, conjured up by bleak moorland itself. "So, our eye was off the ball. And Gem's asthma was usually all right in the summer. Under control. Like, she wouldn't have been expecting . . ." He screws shut his eyes. "Fuck."

A moment passes. "We only found this out after she died, Pete.

She never told me about any of it." Her voice breaks. "I never even saw her use an inhaler."

Gemma hadn't shared the things that would have saved her. This will always torment Lauren, who'd obsessed about it in the months afterward, raking through the past for clues, finding them: Viv's spotlessly clean house; Gemma's wheezy "summer colds"; the distance she kept from the aviary, and why she rarely came inside Rock Point, refusing to go anywhere near Berthingham Palace, despite her fascination with birds. And the little rucksack. Hidden inside, of course, her inhaler.

"So it's Gemma's fault?" he snaps, brittle again.

"No!" Lauren's heart crashes in her chest.

"Why *would* she tell you and your sisters? Gemma wanted to be like you, don't you understand?" In the small space, his grief feels blistering, corrosive. "Didn't want to be the sickly cleaner's daughter, you lot looking down your noses with your money and your celeb dad and snotty nan. Didn't want to be known for what was *wrong* with her. Singled out. Adults didn't understand. Mum didn't. But I did. I got that."

Lauren opens her mouth in protest. Then closes it again. She gets it too, despite her grown-up self knowing that no one would ever have judged Gemma, not even Kat and Flora, who were far too self-obsessed to have given it more than a moment's thought. But it's different when you're young. And a little voice tells her Pete needs to be heard. And while she may not have power or size on her side, she does know how to listen. It's the only escape route she's got.

So she nuzzles Raff's curls and reminds herself that when she worked on the National Gallery's information desk, she dealt with all sorts of oddballs. People carrying the frustrations of their lives

like folded umbrellas, seeking the generosity of great art, its surfeit
of feelings when they couldn't bear to live with their own. Trying to
make art mean what they needed it to mean. And volunteering in the
hospice too, she's learned when it's better to speak and when it's better to say nothing—and never to tell anyone things are fine when
they're not. "Tell me more about Gemma, Pete."

He looks slightly distrustful at first, then cautiously pleased.
"Well, she was nervous about the eclipse. It freaked her out, you
know. She'd had these nightmares about it in the days beforehand.
Like she knew." He stares down at his hands, looking vulnerable,
almost boyish. "I know it sounds nuts."

"Not at all," she says, and sees his shoulders drop. "She was the
most intuitive person."

His face lights up. "Yes, that's it, that's the right word. Intuitive."
He taps his head. "Stored that one. Thank you."

Lauren dares to feel a bit of hope. Psychopaths don't feel, do they?
And Pete is all feeling.

"The worst thing? We argued that morning." He stoops with despair again. "I didn't want her watching the eclipse at yours. Like we
weren't good enough. So she ran off. Forgot her rucksack. Although
we didn't realize until . . ." His voice drifts.

"I know," Lauren says quietly.

"Do you? What else do you know?" He bristles again, his eyes
start to blaze dangerously. "You see, a mate from school, on his way
to this party on the beach, he was there, right there that day. He
passed your sisters on the coast path. Heard them talking about what
they'd 'done.'" He makes quote marks with his fingers. "Going to tell
me what that might be?"

Lauren lets out a small mewl beneath her breath. Had Kat and

Flora been talking, or worse, laughing, about the bolting of the aviary's lock? She has no appetite to share that detail here, not with Flora's little boy in her arms. "Flora and Kat nicked booze from the drinks cabinet," she says, knowing this information is already out there. "We drank a bit in the garden. But Gemma didn't have any, I promise. She wouldn't touch it, Pete."

He watches her carefully. "Were you there the whole time?"

"I . . ." She'd been sick in the loo. And so much of her memory of that day, and the days that followed, has holes. Rips. Blind spots. Not atypical, she was told after many scans. Most likely she'd suffered a psychogenic non-epileptic seizure, the doctors told her. Set off by the trauma of witnessing Gemma's asthma attack, primed with the nervous excitement of the eclipse, her brain's nerve cells had discharged a firestorm of sudden, excessive electrical signals. And this was why she could only recall snatches of the whole. Why she'd been outside herself. As if it'd been Lauren who'd lost consciousness. Lauren who'd died. If she'd tried to draw the scene—her therapist had earnestly suggested this; Lauren refused—it'd be patched with streaks of shadow, empty blooms of light: negative space. The shapes of the bits in between.

"I miss her," Pete says, and Lauren releases her breath, glad he's not pushed her for an answer to his question. He stands slowly, pressing his spine up along the door, like a bear rubbing against a tree. "Every Christmas. Every time I see this . . . this look in my mum's eyes." His pain like glass dragged across her skin. "Every time someone gets a new niece or nephew. Like you, mate." He nods at Raff.

Lauren hitches Raff up her waist. Wishes Pete weren't staring at him, his expression unreadable. She's still not sure which way this will go. But it feels as if attempting escape might be as perilous as staying put.

"When a woman scientist pops up on the news, I think, that's Gemma's job. The world needs Gemma. *I* need her. She's not just some . . . some statistic. She was my little sister. She was everything. And if I could have died instead of her, I would."

"Pete, I am so, so sorry." Her voice chokes with tears. "But we need to leave."

"You don't want to hear about the notes first?" He sounds put out, like a kid whose attention-seeking mischief is being ignored.

"It was you," she says hoarsely, realizing the first note—"*We know what you did*"—was a double bluff. Not only was Pete not a "we," but he also tried to scare them away by pretending to know something he didn't.

"You know, Lauren, about a year after it happened, I sent a letter to your nan," he says, not done. "Respectful. I just wanted an apology. Something." Lauren cannot bear what's coming. "She didn't reply. She didn't even fucking reply."

"That's inexcusable." Granny should have known better. Lauren wonders if she froze in the headlights. Granny never was the same after that summer either. "It was you who tried to run us off the road too?"

"Hardly. You in that tank. Me in my little crap car." He laughs, mirthlessly. "Just a warning. To give you a taste—a teeny fraction of the stress I feel having your family back here. And to give you a bit of a scare, get you to sell up. Leave us in peace. Finally."

LEAVE. "Hard with a slashed tire."

He looks genuinely puzzled. "What slashed tire?"

"Want to go home," Raff whimpers, and Lauren decides to leave the subject of the tire alone. It feels like they're in an airlock, the oxygen running out. She tries to smile. "How about we meet and talk again another time, Pete?"

If her voice quavers, he doesn't seem to notice. Instead, he's surprised. Pleased even. "Really?"

"For sure." Her adrenaline is surging again, her muscles tensing, priming; she can taste freedom.

"I want to hate you, Lauren. I really want to hate you. But you're all right. Gemma always said you weren't like the others." He rubs his cheek, roughly, like he might want to smack it. "Shit, I've screwed this. I wasn't going to hurt you. Please believe that."

"I do." Lauren cannot afford to trust him. She can see each footstep, the route she could take. A small room. A short distance. *One. Two. Three.*

"Want Mummy." Raff starts to sob.

"You'll see Mummy soon, Raff, very soon." But the fear in her voice is obvious now.

"I'll walk you both home. Make sure you get back safely. It's rough out there. Don't look like that! I wasn't planning to keep you here all this time. I just wanted to say my bit and leave." He sounds confused, as if trying to work out his own behavior. "You see, it's your gestures, your voice . . . You've got so like Gemma."

Lauren reels. But her feet burn, ready to run. She thinks of the budgies. Anything caged can escape if it's brave enough, reckless enough. Seizes its opportunity.

"I don't want you to go. For her to go. That's why I kept following, watching." Pete drops his face into his huge hands and peers out between his fingers, a lost heartbroken giant. "After it happened, as a kid, I used to try and make deals with God. Like, just let me have one more swim with my sister, one more boat trip, one more laugh. It never happened, obviously. Then there you were. Grown up like she'd have grown up, and it . . . I could pretend you were her."

It's an involuntary reflex, that surge forward. And she's moving, across the room, into the kitchen, grabbing the back door's handle and waggling it fiercely up and down.

"Locked." Pete stands in the kitchen doorway, the dog peering out between his legs. "I came in up there."

Lauren sees it now, the gaping window, just above the kitchen unit. Despair roots her to the spot. "I'm not Gemma, Pete," she whispers, fastening her hold on Raff.

A door elsewhere in the cottage slams. Pete startles, mutters something under his breath.

"Hello?" A woman's voice, firm and kind. "Pete, love, are you in here? It's me, Mum."

44

FLORA

|||

"CALL YOURSELF A bloody four-wheel-drive!" Flora accelerates hard. Mud spatters across the windscreen, and the SUV pitches out of the furrow and rocks across the open field like an overladen cattle truck. In the far west, red pools on the horizon.

"Out that gate." Jonah points from the passenger seat, a stinky black Lab in his lap. "And . . . left," he adds, with exactly the sort of male measured urgency that makes Flora panic and take the corner far too sharply.

"Wacky Races," Angie mutters from the back, squished between Charlie and Kat.

Flora mutters, "No one asked you to come," loud enough to be heard.

Incongruous in her leopard-print fake fur and silver boots, their father pinioned to her arm, Angie had flagged down Flora in the lane. Kat gabbled an explanation of sorts out of the car window.

Angie insisted they get in: "All hands to the pump!" But Flora caught Daddy's expression when the Heaps' cottage was mentioned, the way the color drained from his cheeks. Since then, he's barely said a word, staring out the window, his glasses misting, and tapping a fingernail anxiously against one tooth. If she had less to worry about right now, she'd worry about him.

And Jonah? Flora keeps shooting him pointed glances, wanting him to know she's got him in her sights. While he may appear earthy and sincere, she knows men are adept at hiding their ugly sides. When she met Scott, he was so softly spoken she couldn't even imagine him raising his voice. Also, Jonah fits the description of the lurker too closely for her liking. What if it's a trap?

"Pull up," says Jonah, softly but brusquely, a few minutes later.

The start of a track—narrower than the SUV—the Heaps' weeny cottage at the end of it. Unlit windows. A sunken roof snowed white, straight out of one of her Scandi noirs. Hard to believe Lauren had stepped inside such a bleak place, and on her own, a couple of days ago—as Jonah insists, says he saw her there—and didn't mention it. But then Lauren never said anything about her letters to Gemma either. She has a whole secret life going on, surreptitiously moving inside her. Writing notes to dead people. Chatting to them too: her sister's phone calls, overheard through the bedroom wall, have taken on a sinister tint.

Flora throws open the vehicle door and stumbles toward the cottage, shouting Raff's name. Kat scissors straight past her, Jonah too.

A few seconds later, Lauren and Raff appear out of its front door, blinking into the grainy dusk light like hostages. Flora sucks in cold air, pure joy. Lauren, who is carrying Raff on her hip, places him on the ground, and he runs up the track toward her, arms outstretched.

"*You!*" Overwhelmed by an avalanche of love and relief, she sweeps him up, kisses his cheeks all over. He smells gloriously, blissfully of Raff. "Let me have a look at you. Are you all right? Hurt?" She inspects him for damage. Finding none, she marvels that Raff, who loathes the cold and wet, is not a sobbing mess. "Mummy loves you so much," she says, picking him up, wanting never to let go again.

A tearful, exhausted smile. "Big as the world."

Flora's heart explodes. She clocks Lauren, still hovering uncertainly by the cottage door. The nose of a parked small white car. Then, rushing down the track, not one black dog but *two*. Leaping and circling around each other, a mirror image. She can't make sense of them. She can't make sense of anything.

"We went on a big adventure, Mummy." Raff presses his cold face against her neck, as if trying to nuzzle under her skin. "Ice balls fell out of the sky. A dog came. We met the BFG."

"Oh, Raff." This is the sort of place that would stoke any kid's imagination. Not in a good way. "I swear I'll turn gray overnight," she says, as her father and Angie catch up, Dad ruffling Raff's hair.

"Finches don't go gray until well into their fifties, my darling Flo. Raff's okay. It's okay." Charlie circles an arm around her. It feels solid, safe, exactly as a dad's arm should. Angie edges forward a little, as if she wants to join in too. "By tomorrow it'll be another family anecdote with which to horrify your husband," Charlie adds, his gaze softening, fixing at a point over her shoulder. Flora turns to see a tiny dark figure, walking toward them in a snow-globe whirl.

"I'm so sorry, Flora," Lauren says, approaching, looking devastated.

Flora's stomach starts to cramp. Charlie removes his arm from her shoulders and takes Lauren's hands, mottled and purplish, and rubs them. His little Lauren; Dixie's precious child. And even now, in this hurricane of giant feelings, Flora feels a diminishing spike of childish envy. "Why didn't you call?" she asks, tightly.

"We've been worried sick, Lauren," Angie says.

"I tried to call. But I couldn't. Look, can I explain back at Rock Point?" Lauren nods down at Raff. Her trembling undermines Flora's anxious anger. "But I kept him safe, I really did." Her voice breaks. "I honestly can't tell you how sorry I am, Flora."

Before Flora can swallow the lump in her throat and say anything, Kat starts shouting, "Dad!" They turn to see Kat frantically beckoning Dad inside the cottage, then darting back in.

Her father doesn't move.

"Babe?" Angie rubs his arm. "You look like you've seen a ghost."

Flora follows his sightline; a flash of scarlet in the cottage doorway, as if someone else has just moved out of view. Jonah, perhaps, who is yet to emerge from the building. Without a word, her father starts a solemn march over the thin crust of snow, his head bowed. Like he knows what's waiting for him.

"Stay with Aunty, Raff." Flora hands her little boy to a stunned Lauren, a gift of trust. "The car isn't locked. Emergency Twix in the glove compartment. Blankets in the boot. Angie, it's warmer in there. You go too." She needs to see this place for herself.

Walking toward the cottage apprehensively, Flora spots ivy growing up the inside of the windows. It makes her feel peculiar, slightly queasy. The scarlike crack on the wall too. Behind every house refit—all that consumption, the desire for the shiny and new—there is a primal aversion to this. Decay. Rot. The brutality of it. Plaster and stone: skin and bone. Dust to dust. We are all a breezeblock or a brick from mud and worms.

Stepping inside, Flora gasps, struggles to process what she's seeing. A woman in a smart red coat. Gray-blond hair. Groomed. Late fifties. She's holding hands with a man half her age: huge, grizzled, looks like a squatter, with the angry gaze of a cornered bull. Her father, standing opposite, next to a sober-faced Kat and Jonah, is slackmouthed, staring at this woman. Like a bomb has gone off in his brain.

"Flora, this is Viv. Viv Heap," says Jonah, shifting uncomfortably.

Viv. Flora cannot risk looking at Kat. There's nowhere left to hide. In this cottage, the past gapes open. It feels like they've both been plucked out of 1999 and reassembled in some sort of domestic dystopia.

"And this is Pete." Jonah perseveres with gentle formality. "Viv's son."

Flora doesn't recognize Pete. She barely knew him. But Viv is still very much Viv, Granny's cleaner, Gemma's mum; an older, stouter version, dignified but weathered, fine grooves of grief etched around her eyes and mouth.

The hush is unbearable. "I'm Flora," she blurts, nervously filling it.

"Yes, wow. So grown up," says Viv with a hard-to-stomach warmth. She doesn't need to say, unlike Gemma who never grew up. It hangs in the swampy air.

"So, you knew Pete was here, Jonah?" Kat asks, pulling her coat tight. "How?"

Jonah shoots Pete a sidelong look. "We bumped into one another earlier, out walking the dogs. Got chatting, you know. Pete was heading up to the moor to check in on this cottage, as he likes to do. He was . . . a bit agitated about you all being back." Jonah clears his throat, as if this might be a huge understatement. "When Kat said Lauren was missing, I just thought . . . well, I thought it might not be ideal if they bumped into each other, that's all." He shifts on his feet awkwardly. "And I gave Viv a call."

At this Pete bows his head, like a little boy who's been caught red-handed doing something he shouldn't, his mother called in.

"I'm not sure I understand," says Flora, trying to collect herself.

"Flora, it seems Pete gave Lauren a bit of a fright," Viv answers with one of those steely but soft voices, a natural authority, like a popular no-nonsense teacher. "But we've talked it out. Cleared up the misunderstanding."

"What sort of fright?" Flora asks uneasily, concerned about what Raff might have witnessed.

Silence draws around them, no one daring to speak. Viv and her father seem to be locked in wordless conversation.

"Pete surprised Lauren in this cottage, where she and Raff were sheltering from the hail," says Jonah carefully.

"I bet you followed them, didn't you?" Kat says fiercely to Pete, who stares guiltily at the floor.

"Excuse me, Pete didn't hurt anyone." Viv dares Kat to take another swipe at her boy. "He wouldn't hurt anyone, Kat."

Flora stares from Kat to Pete, shocked, bewildered. A thought is trying to take shape. But it keeps bumping into Viv's and Pete's existence, living proof of that summer, everything she and Kat thought they'd left behind, neatly tucked away in another millennium. Viv *here*. In a red coat.

"Viv's right," says Jonah.

Flora frowns at Jonah. Not unlike Pete, is he? Dark coats. Hoods. Six-footers. With black dogs. From a distance, on a cliff top say, or outside in a storm. Yes, easily confused. Close up, the similarities end, one radiating a rugged wholesomeness, the other damage.

"I was at school with Pete," Jonah adds.

"People change," says Kat sharply, and Flora thinks she's not changed that much, after all. Kat's still the person you want on your side.

"And life can be hard. He's all right, Kat. He's the same Pete," Jonah continues steadily. "I moved back to Cornwall last year and we were reintroduced by the dogs, weren't we, Pete? Our dogs are littermates, you see. Sisters. Bred by a lady up the road."

Kat shakes her head disparagingly. But Flora's glad to have the matching dogs explained at least. Her father still looks dumbfounded by it all, though, and is staring at Viv.

"It was an unforgivable way to go about things, and Pete's sorry." Viv is clearly the sort of mother who'll always stand by her son, however difficult or wayward. Flora can't help but respect this: she'd do the same. "Aren't you, Pete?" Viv prompts.

"I am sorry," Pete says, although the apology seems to be directed at his mother rather than them.

"Gemma wouldn't have wanted any of this, Pete," Viv says firmly.

Gemma: the name shatters the fetid icy air, its aftershock traveling over their faces. Her father covers his mouth with his hand, his composure almost collapsing.

"The notes were Pete's work, Flora." Kat is the first to recover.

Dear god.

"I just wanted you all to go away, clear off back to London," Pete says sulkily.

"You tell the police that." Kat sticks her hands into her pockets. "And why you wouldn't let Lauren leave this cottage. She must have been completely terrified."

Pete grimaces. "I didn't mean . . . I know how it looks."

As what Lauren must have gone through sinks in, she adjusts in Flora's mind. Her brave little sister.

"Look, it's your call, Mr. Finch, Kat, Flora, but can I just say, Pete's had a very tough time," Jonah says. "He's recently lost his job. Divorced. And it's been difficult for Pete, seeing you all back at Rock Point after twenty years. Stirred up a lot of feeling. He could do with being cut a bit of slack, just saying."

"There'll be no more notes, we can promise you that," Viv assures, cutting off Jonah with a tone of finality. She adjusts her fluffy gray scarf, tucking it neatly around the lapels of her coat. "Lauren says she's happy to leave it."

"I agree with Lauren. We won't be taking it any further," Charlie says, finding his voice. "No more bullshit, okay, Pete? Or you'll be in those Truro police cells before you know it."

"No more," agrees Pete, relief draining over his face. And Viv's.

Charlie raises his hand in a goodbye gesture. Flora slips her arm inside Kat's—it's all too much, she needs that arm—and they follow their father out of the cottage. Already the flouring of snow is melting; their footprints will soon vanish, any trace they've been here. But the cottage will leave a more indelible mark.

When they're a few steps down the track, Viv calls, "Charlie?"

Their father turns, slowly, like an old man. He's aged ten years in ten minutes.

"Thank you for going easy on him." Viv stands in the cottage's doorway, her arms crossed against the cold, the wind blowing her hair off her face. "I know you lost someone that day too, Charlie."

45

LAUREN

| | |

1999

DAD'S FACE DREW into focus, scrunched, shadowed, like how he'd look old. Above his head, a murmuration of starlings, swelling and shrinking, a fishing net in the sky. No wire roof. I was out of the aviary. But I couldn't work out how.

Mum. I wanted Mum so, so badly. Where was she? It was time to leave Rock Point and go to St. Ives. Wander down the sandy cobbled lanes to Barbara Hepworth's Sculpture Garden, my mother's favorite place, chatting at a million miles an hour, filling in the August days we'd been apart. Then Porthmeor beach with a cone of salty, vinegary chips, our feet bare in the warm top layer of sand, Mum's toe rings glinting.

Voices rinsed over me. But not Mum's. The edges of things were smudgy. My teeth and jaw ached, like I'd been grinding. My dress was soggy, weirdly stuck to my knickers. Trying to clear whatever it was that sat between me and the world, I rubbed my eyes, saw a lemonade bottle fizzing into the grass; Gemma's face, full of glazed wonder. *Gemma.*

I twisted around. It was okay. Gemma was still inside the aviary, propped up against the wall, one hand resting in the pillow of feathers on the concrete floor, her palm upturned and her fingers curling inward, as if holding out food for the birds. Other people too. Green uniforms. Flashes of high-vis. Radio crackling. Words, calm, urgent: *"Blood pressure dropping."*

Gemma emerged on a stretcher, a plastic mask over her nose and mouth, like a snorkel. Dad stumbled up, away from me, his face contorted; he was calling out for Angie to come and help. But Angie couldn't be found. Dad beckoned over Kat and Flora, who were stood by the swing seat, stunned and still. "I'm going with Gemma to the hospital. Look after Lauren."

Walking over, they looked scared. It dawned that I was the one scaring them. The flashes on Flora's sequin skirt stuck pins in my eyes, and I had to look away.

Flora whispered to Kat, "She's wet herself."

I smelled it then. The urine. The disgrace.

"It's only wee." Kat put an arm around my shoulder. "It doesn't matter, Lauren. Honest."

I wanted to scrub and scrub until my skin peeled away.

"We're sorry about locking the cage." Flora's voice sounded froggy. Her eyes were red-rimmed and full of tears. "We're sorry we . . ."

Kat elbowed her to shut her up.

Outside the garden walls, a whirring, an engine roar. I glanced up: the sun cut into strips by the pine branches. Then, a helicopter rising, red as a robin. Had the eclipse happened? Any of it? There were holes. Floating blobs of black. Bits I couldn't remember, slipping around the bright bits I could. No one mentioned Gemma, because

Gemma was fine. Gemma was flying. Kat took my hands and pulled me up and I mumbled something about needing a shower.

"Don't go inside the house," said Flora. "We're not allowed . . ."

They called out but I kept running.

In the conservatory, Bertha was glaring, spreading her wings, threatened, territorial, as if I were a stranger. She looked exactly the same, but also completely different. Not friendly anymore. The house wasn't the one it'd been earlier either. And I knew without understanding, everything had changed. The tall clock chimed at the top of the stairs, ringing out like a bad fairy's bell. Bits of Gemma's glitter sparkled on my hands, my dress. "What have we done?" Bertha squawked in Flora's voice. "What have we done?"

I stumbled away, into the kitchen, knocking over a chair.

In the entrance hall, I stopped, blinked. My head emptied. Grandpa was sprawled at the bottom of the stairs, one yellow-socked foot on the lower step, blood glistening in his hair. Granny was kneeling, bent over him, holding his hand. "Help is on its way, Herbert," I heard her say, her voice distant, muffled. "The child needed the air ambulance. Hang in there, darling."

Grandpa looked dead. He was stargazing the ceiling. His teeth were scattered across the flagstones. My heart wouldn't accept what my eyes were seeing.

"Grandpa has had a fall." Granny didn't look up. "Lauren's right here, Herb." She stroked his hair, pressed his hand to her mouth, kissed it. "I got muddled, darling. What a moppet I am! Same frocks, you see. Looking out the bedroom window, it was impossible to tell which was which. I'm so sorry for giving you a fright, dear."

Outside, a vehicle door slammed. From the conservatory, Bertha called, *What have we done?* My heart was a wet boom in my ears.

"Oh, you silly old goat, rushing down the stairs in your socks.

Now, you mustn't worry. Gemma's in good hands. Gemma will be just fine. And the budgies too. As soon as you're back on your feet, you can go out with your binoculars. They can't have flown far."

Two policemen strode through the front door, without knocking. I slipped upstairs, away from myself, the girl I'd been before. In my bedroom, I stamped out of my dress and knickers, leaving them puddled, stinky, on the rug, my sandals in the middle so it looked like I'd vanished, sucked through the floor. After the shower, my skin sore from the loofah, my mind still fuzzy, I nudged open the bathroom's blind and peeked at the world beyond. *Oh.* Me and Gemma! There we were, sitting on a crooked hawthorn branch; two budgies, happy and bright as lemons.

46

KAT

| | |

"DEADLY SERIOUS, SCARLETT." Kat can barely hear her PA over the wind. Fifty-five minutes after returning from the Heaps' cottage—a lifetime ago—she's sat on the stone porch step, her mother's ragged nineties scarf scrunched in her lap, her phone pressed against her ear. "Someone needs to resign if Spring's to survive. Sorry, the line . . . I've just sent the email. What . . . ? It's been *leaked*?" Kat tries to imagine the unleashed chaos. But she's already moving away, her margins re-forming. "No, you're not fired, Scarlett. Ha. And don't take any shit from anyone else, okay? Right back at you. Bye."

She drags a finger over the phone screen—ablaze with notifications—until it goes black. Kat's not sure who she'll be without Spring. But she wants to find out. Resting her chin on her knees, she fixes thoughtfully on Jonah and Lauren, standing by The Drop, silhouetted against a giant silver moon.

Oh, Lauren. Even when they were young, she had a different range to her daily experience in the way a bee can see a prismatic spectrum of color humans can't. And this holds true now.

So, Lauren's kept a hallucinatory Gemma alive in her mind all these years? Kat's not shocked, not really. The rest of the family has also spun fantasy narratives. What else is Flora's perfect marriage and—hard to admit it—Spring, a house of cards she's stacked higher and higher, as if the bull market hadn't already ended. As for Dad. He doesn't seem to live in real time either. At Dixie's funeral he'd sobbed as if they'd been together weeks, not decades, earlier. The sketch he'd snatched from Kat's hand clearly had a raw emotional power undiluted by the passing years—and one he'd rather bury than understand.

Unlike the rest of them, Lauren's climbed right into the void and shined a torch into its shadows. By writing to Gemma, she's kept that summer's dark, pulpy heart beating, while Kat's refused to look it in the eye—as she struggled to meet Viv's earlier, and occasionally Lauren's too. She's not sure which approach is the greater dissemble. All she does know is that in the Heaps' cottage, there she was, not thrusting forward—congratulating herself on how far she'd come—but slam-dunked back to where she'd started. Forced to acknowledge that the past lives on like the wrong tense in a Word document, constantly underlined, needing to be addressed. And she never has. *They* never have. Damn it.

Holding the scarf in her fist, Kat strides, head bent into the wind, to The Drop. Lauren and Jonah, a few meters along, the other side of the hawthorn, are still so absorbed in conversation they don't seem to notice.

Kat peers down at the rocks, wet coal-black beneath. The waves smashing and grinding against them, shattering into mercury drops.

She holds the scarf between forefinger and thumb, watching the tattered silk writhe in the wind, then soar over the edge, carrying with it the shame and secrets of her childhood, sucked into the vast roaring night.

Back in the house, she sits at the bottom of the staircase, all the stories locked inside it, and licks the salt off her lips with the tip of her tongue. She feels different. Lighter. *Sharper.* For the first time since she returned to Rock Point, she sees it, allows herself to go there. Grandpa's limp foot on the bottom step; his yellow sock and hairless ankle; the spatter of blood on the wainscoting; the gore on the flagstones.

"Oh, it's you." Angie bursts out of the living room, and her smile falls. "Sorry, I was hoping it was Charlie. I'm worried, Kat. He's still bunkered up in the bedroom," she says in a hushed voice. "Just lying on the bed, a million miles away, staring at the ceiling. Has been since we got back. I can't reach him. I mean, I know it's been a heavy day, but . . . it's like there's something else. I don't know. He won't talk to me." She wrings her hands. "Do you think he's all right?"

Seeing Viv and Pete again has tossed everything up in the air. Everyone has landed in different places, no one the same person they were at lunch. "He's processing, I think." But what exactly, Kat's less sure.

"I guess." Angie looks unconvinced. "And are *you* okay? I heard you missed your flight. That's a bummer."

"Oh, reckon I was destined to miss it." There she goes, sounding like Lauren. Irrational. Even Angie is looking at her strangely. "Grandpa was lying just there." She points to the flagstones under her trainers. Angie blanches. "It looked gruesome," Kat adds. "And I was wondering why Dad didn't stay with him, wait for his ambulance."

"Well, Gemma was a kid."

Kat stares at the spot on the floor, lost in thought. "Yeah."

"May I?" Angie's leatherette trousers squeak as she lowers beside Kat. "Look, about that day," she says abruptly. "I shouldn't have bolted. It was a shitty thing to do."

"Yep." In running away, Angie had proved she was Monster.

"When I saw Lauren and Gemma in the aviary, you know, from the studio window, I thought they were messing about. Well, I wasn't really thinking at all, to be honest. But then all hell broke loose and I . . . I panicked. Thought I'd be blamed. You know, my fault for ignoring the girls, doing what I was doing with Charlie. I should have raised the alarm. I desperately wish . . ." Angie stops, nervously fiddles with her engagement ring, and her mohair sleeve tickles the back of Kat's hand. A moment passes. "Kat, I knew the police were coming, and I was totally paranoid about the police that summer. Been in a bit of a tight spot in London. Fallen in with a bad crowd. That's why I came down to Cornwall in the first place. To lie low." She takes a breath. "Nothing to do with the eclipse."

"I think you came here to meet Dad. You knew his name. His work."

"Well, that was a factor. Charlie was a bit of a god back then," she acknowledges with a shrug. "I was an unemployed ex–art student, looking for a way out . . . that's not a crime, is it?" She knocks her knees together, apart again. "I suppose I shouldn't have seduced him."

"Oh no." Kat rolls her eyes. When will the middle-aged get it? "*Dad* had the power. He was in his late forties. You were in your mid-twenties—being paid to look after his daughters! Gross." She doesn't even feel disloyal for saying it.

"Always liked an older guy." Angie picks a bit of fuzz off her jumper.

"You do realize '99 was the year the Tate exhibited Tracey Emin's *My Bed*? Mum took me to see it." Kat remembers saying, provocatively loudly, "It's like your bedroom after a bender, Mum." Blythe had turned on her Manolos and pretended not to hear. "And there was Dad behaving like a cheesy, iffy *Austin Powers* walk-on. He'd get canceled today. Seriously."

"Whoa. Not fair," Angie protests.

"Isn't it?" Kat thinks of all the other women who've slipped through their father's sheets—and studio—over the years. Not least Dixie. "Look. You weren't the first, Angie," she says, as kindly as she can manage.

"Oh, bloody hell, I know *that*." Angie's nostrils flare: Kat's struck a weak spot. "Still. Those life studies he squirreled away tell quite the story, don't they?"

Kat sits bolt upright, the hairs on her arms prickling. Hang on, hang on. Her brain grabs at a new possibility, a pattern in the jumble of confusing Dad data. An asterism in a seemingly random crackle of stars.

47

LAUREN

| | |

2019

Lauren wants to roll up the Titian-starry sky, take it back to Whitechapel and hang it on her flat's gray wall. Also, the sea. The snow. The smell of wood smoke, wet granite, and clean salt cold. The fishing boat's light winking on the horizon. The ladder of moonlight on the water. Jonah's dog, Rocket, warm and bulky, leaning against her leg. Her heart full, full, full.

Her elation might be the relief of vanquished terror. But she's pretty sure it's also connected to the fact that Jonah is standing closer than he was ten, five, two minutes ago. And the rare feeling that she's in exactly the right place at exactly the right time. "Did you really recognize me on the train?"

"Obviously, I did think, what are the chances?" He shoots her a sidelong glance, like he can't stop staring either. "The Finch sisters made quite an impression back in the day." A moment passes. "You, especially."

A stomach swoop of pleasure. "Oh, I was invisible next to Flora and Kat."

"Not in a ball gown on the cliff top."

It slides together, easily, like something oiled. Of course. Jonah's familiarity has nothing to do with a resemblance to a figure in a Renaissance painting but a face she viewed through a different sort of frame years ago, one made of stone, empty of glass: the hermit hut's window. She suggests this, tripping over her words, before drawing to a breathless stop, and feeling stupid for imagining he'd ever remember.

"Sorry for gawping." He sounds shy now. "You were the loveliest girl I'd ever seen."

Her stomach flips again. "You shouted at my sisters," she says, her throat locking. "When they dangled me from the ledge."

"What can I say? Some heroes have acne and really bad hair."

"Thank you, Jonah," she manages, overcome by the wonder of life, the way it seems to circle on a track that plunges mineshaft deep, then out into the sunshine again. How it comes at you so fast. And before she can process what's happening, he's reaching across and, with a gentleness that kicks her heart into her hips, traces the tip of his finger over her cheek. "This is why I remembered you."

His finger is on her birthmark. A charge passes through her.

"A swallow. You came for the summer and flew off again. It's perfect."

She hopes he cannot see her eyes filling. Dares not blink in case the tears fall. And she doesn't know how to explain that since the eclipse, she's grown up feeling imperfect, guilty, fractured. Even the bits that time had mended were broken all over again by Mum's death. But right now, it feels as though they're starting to move together, like a slow-motion film of a dropped plate played back-ward. And she's quite sure he'll kiss her—please, please—until he whips his hand away. And whatever it is that hums between them—chemistry, an intimacy she cannot explain, bearing no relation to the depth of their acquaintance—is left unexplored. She sags with a quiet, absurd devastation. Jonah must have been politely waiting to leave for the pub ever since Viv dropped him at Rock Point: sweetly, he'd wanted to check that she and Raff were okay. But she's kept him here, yakking on. This pause in the conversation feels like a natural point for him to attempt an exit.

"Gemma was the first young person I knew who died," Jonah says instead, taking her aback. "It changes how you see the world. You don't go back to the person you were, do you?"

Lauren knows then, without any doubt, she could fall head over heels in love with this bearish easygoing man, who seems to have her mapped. And this sweet, sharp realization makes her feel unsteady and vulnerable. She shoves her hands deep into her coat pockets, as if her heart were in her fingertips, safer in there.

"I think about it still, Lauren."

She can't help it. She loves the sound of her name on his lips.

"That moment I saw this exotic yellow bird, flying really low." He makes a gliding gesture with one hand, and a silence stretches. "Passed your sisters too." Something about the way he says this. "Just after."

"You're the friend Pete mentioned, who overheard my sisters talking about something they'd done that day, aren't you?" He confirms this with a nod and Lauren shivers, nothing to do with the cold. "So what . . . what *did* my sisters do?" Her voice comes out strangulated.

"Look, they didn't say—as I've told Pete a few zillion times." A moment passes, tightly woven, where strands of that last summer meet. "He's always latched on to it, I'm afraid."

"I don't blame Pete. Of course, he wanted to know. I do too, Jonah. I really do. My sisters haven't been exactly transparent." Her frustration burns, and she hears it in her voice. "No one in my family is."

"But your sisters were so young," he says gently. "Whatever they did, it's over now, Lauren."

It'll never be over for her. Maybe one day, if she ever gets to see Jonah again, she will explain how she's lived two lives, one for her, one for Gemma, inhabiting them both. How part of her even wanted the bird phobia—she let it take hold, fed her own fear—because if Gemma had been more scared she'd not have let Lauren persuade her into the aviary. Not died so horrifically young. The earth would have Gemma helping save it, and Viv and Pete would never have been hurled into hell.

"After you left the cottage today, Viv said pretty much the same to Pete," he says after a beat, rumpling Rocket's ears, his hand brushing against her coat. "She desperately wants him to get on with his life."

"He's lucky to have a mum like Viv." Lauren will never forget how Viv Heap strode into the cottage earlier and took her hulking angry son in her arms, patting his back, transforming him into a boy. "She asked if I'll meet her tomorrow at the station for a coffee before my train leaves. I'm not sure it's a good idea. Do you think . . ."

"Go," he says without hesitation. "She's a very cool lady."

"But will Pete mind?" She doesn't want to risk poking the beast again. A snowflake lands on her eyelash, a blob of white.

"No doubt he'll have something to say about it. He's at war with the world. But he won't do anything more to upset Viv. Not now," he says in a way that makes her wonder if he's had words too. "It was good of you not to call the police on him, Lauren."

"How would that have helped? He needs closure."

"And a bit of luck for once." He smiles, such a big smile, and she wishes she could climb inside it. "Right, well. I'd better be . . ." And he pauses: held within it, a question.

Lauren hears Mum saying, "If life throws you something beautiful, take the gift." Her heart smashing in her chest, she slips her hand from the safety of the coat pocket—the cold gap of air between them, not very far at all—and threads her fingers into his, shyly, tentatively at first, checking for resistance. He tightens his grip and, without needing to say anything, pulls her close, right up against his body into his warmth, a sky thick with stars, the world falling away at her feet.

48

FLORA

| | |

A WOOLLY BLANKET wrapped over her shoulders, Flora peers out the living room window. Caught in the rectangles of light, snowflakes whirl like fireflies. Farther away, by The Drop, are two figures, one huge, one small—Jonah, Lauren—standing close, very close indeed. It must be cold out there.

Turning, Flora warms her hands by the fire, flipping them over like pieces of toast so they're evenly done, then pulls the best armchair—Post-it noted *F*—toward the comforting bake of heat. Sinking into the horsehair cushion . . . well, it might just be the most comfortable armchair she's ever sat upon. The whole house seems unexpectedly luxurious tonight. She forgives it everything. Watching the fire, sipping her glass of mineral water—after a short, vigorous tussle, she turned down the wine—it feels as though the muddle of the last few days, and two decades, is starting to resolve with its own dream logic. She's quite sure the Heaps' cottage has held up, fighting inevitable collapse, just so the two families could cross paths again. To press the Finches hard against everything the Heap family has lost. And Viv. Oh, Viv.

After Gemma died, Flora couldn't bear to think of the cleaner who scooped their carelessly discarded bikinis from the floor. The mother who must have been utterly broken. Nor did she dare think of Pete, who'd lost a sister. Lauren's breakdown—although no adult ever named it, fearful it would be catching among teen girls, like suicide or anorexia—was a warning of what happened if you dwelled on dead people rather than parties, festivals, and boyfriends. Grief was gluey and dangerous. You could get stuck in it.

Despite her determination not to think about that summer, it must have simmered somewhere inside, she realizes now. Reducing, intensifying, like a salty sauce forgotten on a stove. Changing her consistency in unforeseen ways.

But if there was a precise instant that she'd turned into the sort of woman who'd marry a man like Scott, she'd been oblivious. All Flora knows is that *before* she'd been fearless, desperate to explore the world. But she'd settled too young, having not explored herself; grateful for a stable, steady man, reassuringly unartistic. And since Raff's birth, whenever her life has started to feel like a cage—which sounds so spoiled; it *is* so spoiled—she's thrown herself into "projects," wallpapering, tweaking and organizing, setting up fundraisers and class WhatsApp groups, striking away misbehaving thoughts, like jobs on a to-do list. Creating endless small problems so she can solve them. But her subconscious has proved less obedient. Night after night—trapped beneath her luxury goose-down duvet and the clamp of Scott's meaty calves—she'll dream of flight. Arms outstretched, soaring above fields and twinkling cities, like the little boy in *The Snowman*.

"Flo?"

She glances up from the fire to see Kat, wearing black and a funny jagged energy, her hair wet at the front, like she's been outside. "Oh, sorry. Miles away. Hi."

"Is Dad down yet?" Kat asks, the question loaded in a way Flora doesn't understand.

"Reading Raff a bedtime story." Flora suspects he's taking refuge in Raff's company and using it as an excuse not to come downstairs. "He still seems pretty shell-shocked to be honest."

"So do you."

"Well. A bit of a day." Flora pulls up her feet, tucks the blanket over her knees, and smiles weakly at Kat. "It's got me thinking."

"Uh-oh." Kat perches on the coffee table. "Be careful, Flora. I started thinking and ended up resigning."

"You did? Wow." Flora dares hope her interference has not been a *total* disaster. By talking to Kofi, at least she's forced Kat to reveal a career crisis she'd needlessly hidden from her family, who love her irrespective of her job title, or Spring's share price. "What will you do next?"

"Not sure." Kat cracks her knuckles. "Chew into my savings. Have an identity crisis. Take some time off. See what bubbles up."

"You've changed." She can't even see Kat's phone.

Kat looks surprised then, as the comment settles, cautiously pleased. "And you?"

Flora's married life spins past. The empty cot in her nursery. The Tiffany-blue utility room where she can cry alone, muffled by the whirr and thump of the washing machine. Scott tickling Raff, aeroplaning him in his arms. Her wedding vows, which she'd meant, really meant, every word. Her heart twists at the irreconcilability of it all. ". . . I've had enough buggering on, Kat."

Kat smiles. "You want to bugger off?"

"Not from Rock Point. Or anyone here." It is hard to imagine the person she'd been, or pretended to be, three days ago. "I don't really know how to explain it. But it's like the woman who lives my life back home, does her Kegel exercises, cooks meals for when Scott gets back from work, which is so much more important than mine because it's paid, right? It feels like she's not actually me, just some sort of . . . *doppelganger*."

"First Lauren," Kat says wryly. "Now you."

"I mean, is it greedy to want to feel one hundred percent *in* my own life? Like when we were teenagers, Kat. Remember? Remember how we felt? Is it selfish to want . . ." Louise from number nine slips into her mind. The way she'd dropped her novel to the floor as they'd kissed. The unexpected softness of her mouth. How she'd tasted of M&S Brie parcels and Prosecco. A sweet explosive joy. Blushing, fearing Kat might read her thoughts, she glances down at her wedding ring. It'll always be too tight. "There are too many lies in my life. And I honestly cannot bear one more day of them."

Kat reaches over and squeezes Flora's hand, her heart. She can feel Kat's blood—Finch blood—pumping under her skin. "Well, there's a way to fix that," Kat says.

"No more lies?" Flora asks cautiously, seeing Kat wince as she absorbs the implications. "I've realized it's all a . . . a tangle, you see, Kat. Inseparable. The summer, that day, it's like the hairy knot in the middle. We've made it unsayable. But it doesn't need to be, does it?" she appeals to Kat, who pulls away her hand. "We could tell Lauren. *Everything*. Tonight. We could, Kat. Don't shake your head. It's created a wedge between the three of us. Hung over us all these years."

"So, we get to leave with armchairs, maps, and a disinfected conscience, and Lauren returns to her grim Whitechapel flat with Gemma's weirdly missing straw bird—like, what *is* the story there?—and a bout of fresh trauma." Kat crosses her arms. "I don't know, Flora.

I mean, I get it. I've had enough of the bullshit too. And if it's any consolation, which it isn't, I've a hunch our deceit isn't the biggest, or worst. Not in this family. Dad is the virtuoso. Dad set the example years ago. Subterfuge as the Finch signature. The holding pattern."

"But we're adults now, Kat." It feels necessary to remind herself too. "I'm a mother. Like Viv. Seeing her today, it . . . just got me." Suddenly hot, Flora shucks off the blanket. "And . . . and . . . well, isn't the truth important?" Part of her wills Kat to say something clever. Truth relies on perspective. It's relative. If you lived a life of pure, sheer truth, it'd be blinding, untenable, and every family would kill one another over Sunday lunch.

Kat squeezes the bridge of her nose and nods. "It's fucking everything, Flora."

"Thank you." She exhales long and hard. That's it then. Agreed. Her belly already feels less bloated, as if whatever her body has been holding on to is starting to dissolve. "I think Lauren has an inkling anyway. Apparently, Dixie, on her deathbed . . ."

"I know what Dixie said," Kat cuts in. Ominously, her leg is now jittering, her foot pedaling in midair. "And Dixie wasn't talking about us, or she'd have confronted us long ago. No, Dixie was trying to tell Lauren something else. A secret." She leans forward, hands intensely clasped. "*Dad's.*"

"Oh."

"Think about it, Flora. Out of all our mothers, Dixie was the only one he'd have confided in. The only one he would have trusted . . ."

They hear the front door bang, followed by a high-pitched excitable squawk, which signals one person only. Kat stops talking.

Lauren seems to blow into the living room on a snowy gust. Pink-cheeked. Her eyes filament-lit. Sitting down on the window seat, biting down on her lower lip, she looks as if she's got a delicious secret of her own. Not like a woman who's recently been held hostage in a derelict building. Unless Flora's very much mistaken, Lauren looks like a woman in love.

She will dig for juice later. Before she loses her nerve, she's got to do this. "Lauren, there's something we should have told you about the morning of the . . ." Her words fade as her father and Angie— holding a large tray—appear in the doorway. She rearranges her face. Forces a bright smile. "Hi!"

The parrot starts to caw, the racket louder than normal.

"We've had to move Bertha's cage into the kitchen," Angie explains. "Too cold in the conservatory tonight." She lowers the tray to the coffee table, the nibbles bowls and glasses chinking, red wine sloshing in a decanter. "Just to warn you, Lauren."

Rather than growing rigid with fear, Lauren seems to weigh her feelings about this. "I think I might be getting used to her. Just a little bit."

"Told you so! She'll be nibbling your earlobe in no time." Charlie collapses to the sofa, then shoots a funny, knowing smile at Flora. "You were in full sail." Flora's heart sinks: he heard. "Don't let us stop you," he adds.

She hesitates, struck by doubt, unable to bear the thought of her father's dismay. His crashing disappointment in her as a human being, a sister, a daughter.

"Oh, we'll talk later," says Kat briskly, fooling no one.

"I'd like to know." There's surprising steel in Lauren's voice. She flicks her blue-streaked fringe out of her eyes, as if to see them more clearly. And Flora can hear a slow drumbeat, which isn't the waves, or her heart, but seems to be coming from the house itself, as if it were a sentient thing.

"Well, go on," says Charlie coolly. And a bit of Flora flares: *he* has a history of hiding things too. The dates of their birthdays attest to that, secret lives run in parallel. Then blame twists inward. Whatever sort of screwy blueprint their father has laid down, it doesn't get them off the hook. It just doesn't. She shifts, unsure where to begin.

"The jar. Start with the jar, Flora." Kat reads her thoughts; finally, they're in sync.

"That morning, before the eclipse started," Flora stutteringly explains. "Me and Kat were doing the face paint in the studio. I . . . I took a jar of rubbing alcohol from around the sink. One of the jars Daddy warned us about." She cringes at that attempt to appear sophisticated and edgy to Kat. But also, at her father's inept warnings— that he took no notice of himself. The studio was a place of misrule. Funny stories about artists licking paintbrushes. Bones crushed to make paint. Fume highs. You never knew what to take seriously. "And I slipped it into my bag."

Charlie looks up with a dazed jerk: "What the hell would you do a dumb thing like that for?" Angie places a quieting hand on his arm, and he shakes it off.

"The plan was for me and Kat to take it to the beach party. But . . ." Flora contorts her mouth around the damning words. "We didn't sniff it. Gemma did."

"Gemma?" Lauren's laugh is mirthless, disbelieving. Her eyes are huge, dilated, flecked by firelight. Flora thinks of the studio mirrors, how they'd reflect the pots and jars, gleaming apothecary potions. "No," Lauren says, quieter now.

"Later that day, in the garden, while you were in the loo being sick." It's too ugly for Flora to polish. "She did, Lauren."

"But you didn't tell the paramedics," Lauren says, hand over her mouth as it starts to sink in.

"No," admits Flora heavily. They'd panicked. Thought they'd

poisoned Gemma. "I threw the jar into the greenhouse. The tomatoes." That sweet, earthy smell of growing tomato vines still makes her feel sick.

"We didn't tell the police either." Kat bows her head, looking wretched. "You. Anyone. We were terrified. And we were cowards. I . . . I knew how it'd look, Lauren. Rich girls, cleaner's daughter. The optics . . ." Kat's voice trails away.

"*Optics?*" Lauren stares at them in appalled astonishment. Their father makes a deep guttural noise that comes from his belly, not his throat.

"We've been haunted by it ever since, Lauren, not knowing if it'd made a difference to . . ." Flora stutters, her eyes filling with tears, trying not to sob and make it about her. Even though it is about her. Kat. Everyone in the room. Pete and Viv too. Gemma's death knitted their lives together as it pushed them all apart. It was, and will probably always be, the defining moment of Flora's. The pivot. The before and after.

Questions crowd into Lauren's face, and Flora braces. "Gemma was so . . . so sensible," Lauren says in a low voice. "Why would she do something like that—and when I wasn't there?"

Flora catches Kat's fever-bright eye, and her determination to tell the rest of the story starts to crumple.

Their father covers his face with his wrinkly artist's hands. No one moves or speaks. It's like a painting, Flora thinks, a ghastly Finch family portrait. From the kitchen comes the sound of Bertha limbering up, chirping, clicking, then squawking. Flora stiffens. Bertha says it again, unmistakable now. And Flora will always hear it, a talking, screeching parrot that refuses to forget—and can perfectly mimic a human voice. Flora's own.

49

LAUREN

| | |

2019

BERTHA'S SQUAWK RIPS into time as if it were a sheet of newspaper. And Lauren is stumbling through the conservatory on quivery colt legs again, her dress wet, stinky, smudged with Gemma's glitter, and Bertha is shrieking, *"What have we done?"* in a posh girl's panicked voice, echoing through the years.

Finally, Bertha quiets. The memory flicks off, and Lauren resets; the past and present overlie each other, more gently. Her grown-up sisters have simply whipped away a dustsheet from a shapeless lump of furniture she's walked around for her entire adult life. Look! *Here* it is! Yet she senses other things too, still covered, shoved into corners. And conducted along the window seat, up the buttons of her spine, Lauren feels the vibration of gigantic waves that have traveled across miles and miles of mountainous winter seas, their energy building, finally hitting rock. The violence of a tide turning.

"Excuse me, folks. Something to add." Angie sticks up her hand.

"I spring-cleaned the studio the night before, as a surprise for Charlie. Binned those manky old jars by the sink, dug out some new ones, diluted the alcohol down to safe levels so they wouldn't combust, or trash his hands. He had fingertips like barnacles." She clears her throat. "Look, I've done a fair bit of recreational experimenting in my time, and I honestly don't think that new mixture would have done much."

"Oh, thank god," heaves Flora. Kat tips her head toward the ceiling, muttering under her breath.

With a rush of light-headedness, a scattering sensation, Lauren twists to face the window, the night. Hanging in the indigo sky is the same fat white moon that slipped its shadow, like a card trick, between the earth and the sun twenty years ago. Should she do the same? No one ever need know that after Angie finished her studio reorganization, Lauren furiously, territorially moved everything back to its *proper place*; including those jars, which she remembers scooping out of the waste bin. Clearly, neither Angie nor Dad noticed. Their mind on other things.

"Lauren?" Flora's voice swims toward her. "Do you hear what Angie's saying?"

Lauren also hears the call of a different future; one without her sisters' guilt. Torment over things that cannot be changed, whose impact will always be uncertain. It was, she realizes, sickeningly, the way many small decisions, words, and events were strung together that created the deadly circuit. Not one thing.

"Lauren?" Flora says again, more pleadingly. "Say something."

"Feathers and dander brought on the asthma attack. And if she'd had her inhaler . . ." Lauren collects herself and turns. "Pete was clear about that." Her voice snags on his name, his loss, his need for his sister.

"Speaking of Pete." Angie's eyes dart nervously. "Poor bloke. I don't want him to take the rap for everything. And since we're laying our cards on the table tonight . . ." She gnaws on her lip, leaving a trace of lipstick on her front tooth. "I did it. The tire."

"Why the hell would you do that, Ang?" stutters Charlie, shocked. Lauren feels only relief that it wasn't Pete's work.

"I drove all the way down here—*seven* hours!—and you wanted to turf me out after one night? No, sorry, babe." Angie wiggles her hips, bearing down on the sofa cushions. "Anyway, I wanted to stay. Show your family I wasn't Monster."

"Interesting way of going about it," Kat says, catching Lauren's eye and fighting a smile.

"Enough. My blood pressure is about to punch through Rock Point's roof." Charlie takes off his glasses, rubs his eyes.

"Drink some water," instructs Flora.

He takes a gulp of his wine instead. "Let's call it a night."

"Really? We're done, are we, Dad?" Kat says in a pointed way. No smile now.

Charlie fumblingly refills his glass. The wine overspills, trickling down its stem. Lauren's aware of an odd undertow in the room. Too many moving pieces.

"Lauren," Flora says urgently, interrupting her thoughts. "A couple of days before the eclipse, Kat and I caught Angie rifling through Dad's personal sketches in the studio. And Angie told us she'd seen a study of Viv."

"Nude." Kat studies their brooding father, watching his reaction.

"Don't be ridiculous," Charlie snorts.

Viv. Lauren feels that fragmentation again, a tinnitus buzz, the summer a swarm of bees, constantly reshaping as she tries to grasp it.

"I wasn't one hundred percent certain it was Viv, Charlie," Angie backtracks.

"You saw this drawing too?" Lauren asks her sisters. She can't believe it. She won't.

"No. You interrupted us." Kat looks away, palming her cheek.

Lauren's insides clench. She knows what's coming. Sees it written on her sisters' stricken faces. "But you told Gemma."

"When you were in the bathroom, and you were gone ages. We teased Gemma about her mum," Flora says hoarsely, wiping away a tear on her sweater sleeve. "Awful, awful, awful."

It starts to slot together with a sick sort of sense; the screw-you fire in Gemma's eyes; Gemma shouting at Kat and Flora. Humiliated, she'd have done anything to prove herself. Sniffed from that jar then—angry, defiant, possibly high, not thinking straight—seeing off their dare and, disastrously, gone into the aviary. *Bitches.* "What did Gemma ever do to you?"

"You preferred Gemma to us," Kat says quietly.

"You were our sister, not hers." Flora sniffs back tears. "But you acted like . . . like the opposite."

Anger rises through Lauren, a wave of heat. She's not buying it. "But you two didn't want another sister! You didn't want *me*."

Charlie drops his head to his hands with a "girls, please," and a suppressed sob. The burning logs pop. The flames stretch and leap yellow, and in them Lauren sees streaks of cadmium-yellow paint, budgie feathers, late-summer sunbeams. A bonfire of past and present.

"I internalized my mother's bitterness toward Dixie and Blythe. But I already had a bond with Kat," Flora says. "You . . . you just appeared!"

"And it was obvious Dad still loved your mum, Lauren, which is why our mothers hated her, and you were his little pet, his cute art pixie, who'd follow him up to the studio. But he was ours first." Kat grimaces. "Fucked-up sibling logic."

Sibling logic. Those two words—unqualified by "half"—leave a glittery tail, like a sparkler's loops of light. Lauren softens very slightly, grateful for their honesty at last. She turns to her father. "If you loved Mum, why did you behave badly?" In her pleading voice she hears the little girl who just wanted her parents to be together, who had to accept her mother's line about things not working out, things not meant to be. "And what was it, exactly? *What* did you do, Dad?"

Sweat starts to wax her father's forehead. "It's not the right moment to discuss it, Lauren."

"It's hard being honest, Dad," says Kat. "Ugly. Painful. But me and Flora managed it. So did Angie. She could have let Pete take the blame for the tire, but she didn't."

"You did say no secrets, Charlie," Angie says, looking at him askance.

Her father starts to look hunted then, the women in his life circling, ready to swoop and bring him down. "It'll be of no surprise to any of you, I'm ashamed to say." He seems to shrink as he speaks. "I was unfaithful."

Lauren sucks in her breath. Although long suspected—Dixie never denied it, nor offered up details—this confirmation still hurts, and it hurts right inside her ribs, her heart, as it would have her mother's.

"You know what, Dad? It's a miracle me, Flora, and Lauren have any sort of relationship at all." Kat's voice shakes, the wound hers too. "We are sisters *despite* you, not because of you." Tears roll freely down Kat's cheeks. "And we will always look after one another, despite you too. I will make damn sure of it."

"I am very, very happy to hear that," Charlie says heavily as Flora pulls a tissue out of the sleeve of her sweater and hands it to Kat. "And to all your mothers. You are a credit to them, all of you, you really are." He gets up with an "oof" and prods a glowing log back into the fire. "Do you want to know the reason you're here, right now at Rock Point?" He turns, waggling the poker at them like a long paintbrush. "Dixie."

An unstable hush falls.

"Reuniting you all at Rock Point was your mother's idea, Lauren." His expression animates as it always does when he speaks of Dixie. "A way of healing. Moving forward, she said. Dix called me, not long before she died."

"Mum did?" says Lauren numbly. Wind blasts down the chimney, sending sparks flying and smoke curling over the mantel, a perfect scroll, like the one on her mother's violin.

"Yes. And she hated my house clearance idea!" His cheeks are flushed now, filled with life, heat, passion. "Forbade me to do it until you'd all been back one last time. I was under strict orders to put that old birdcage back in its spot by the studio sofa. *Not* to cover the aviary. She wanted you to face that aviary again, Lauren. Frankly, I wouldn't be surprised if she orchestrated the bloody parrot being dumped back at my flat."

"But all my life she tried to protect me from triggers," Lauren says, struggling to process this, or imagine such a conversation between her parents. Her sisters look equally staggered.

"Yes, and she came to rather regret that approach in the end, Laurie. She wanted you, Kat, and Flora to spend time together, as you know. I did tell her it was a high-risk proposition, inviting you all back here. That you were all so busy, wouldn't come anyway. She said it was a risk worth taking. And that I just needed to make it happen." He smiles, lightening for the first time that evening. "You don't argue with Dixie Molloy."

"She sounds like quite a woman." Angie bristles. "Did she plan our meeting too?"

"Oh no. That night was written in the stars, my love," he says, hurriedly. Although Lauren wonders if he does put it it down to Dixie magic. "*I* wanted you here, Angie. Let's bring it all to Rock Point, I thought. Smash the past like a piñata! It's what Dixie would have wanted," he adds, less certainly. "Anyway. Here we are. It is what it is." He reaches for his glass and raises it. "To Dixie."

Lauren listens to them all chanting her mother's name—*Dixie! Dixie! Dixie!*—and she's not quite sure how they've leaped from Gemma to her mother, the total eclipse to this winter fire, only that everything in her life seems to be connected by gossamer threads and if you touch one, another bit trembles. And the next moment, Kat's standing, saying, "And now we need to circle back, Dad. Finish what Dixie started." And those threads start to shake.

50

KAT

|||

KAT HATES BEING wrong. Today she wants to be spectacularly wrong. If her hunch is right, her father lives with a secret
so big it'd crush most people. It'd be like trying to breathe with a
boulder lying on your chest. But Charlie Finch is not most people.
He's a Finch. He's an artist. He has an ability to detach from his
subjects; to see human beings as arrangements of form and flesh in
space; volume and light; a technical challenge to be solved. And if he
can't solve a problem, he can paint over it, destroy it—or hide it in a
neglected studio for years. *The brighter the light, the darker the
shadow*, she can still hear him saying that.

"Kat, what's going on?" says Flora anxiously. Angie's face, her
slack mouth, asks the same question.

"Before she died, Dixie tried to tell Lauren . . ." Kat begins.

"Leave it, Kat," Charlie cuts in too sharply, giving himself away.

"I want to know, Dad," Lauren says. Kat can almost see Lauren's mind streaking after her own like a hare through the grass.

"Can I borrow you a moment, Lauren?" Kat stands up and walks toward the colder air of the hall, darker places. She waits by the door, her heart starting to pound, unsure if Lauren will follow.

"Don't get dragged into this, Laurie," Charlie warns.

But Lauren walks across the room determinedly. In the hall, she peers up the staircase, as if instinctively understanding where they must go next.

"Wait!" Flora thunders up behind them. "I'm not being left out of this one, thank you very much." And they ascend together, up to Rock Point's paint-spattered messy heart.

———

LAUREN QUICKLY FINDS the key to unlock the bottom cabinet drawer: it was always kept in the cranium of a rabbit skull displayed on the shelves, she explains, dipping in two fingers and plucking it out.

"So, what are we hunting for?" Flora crosses her arms with a shiver. Winter has crept deep into the studio tonight.

"Bodies," Kat says, half joking, flicking through a jumble of documents: letters from galleries, invoices, old exhibition invitations. At the bottom, she pulls out a sheaf of drawings. "Bingo," she murmurs, pulling out the charcoal sketch her father snatched earlier in the week, and a clutch of similar ones beneath it. She slides them to the trestle, the charcoal nude on top. Lauren switches on the swing-arm lamp.

"Can you identify the model?" Kat asks, not wanting to steer them.

"Viv?" Lauren says weakly. "I think it could be Viv."

Flora rests her chin on Kat's shoulder, frowns down. "No. I don't see it . . . actually *maybe* . . . But she's a lot younger here."

Now Kat's seen Viv in the flesh again—although not this much flesh, and decades later in the gloom of an unlit cottage—it seems so obvious. The tilt of the nose. The curl of the mouth.

"More than one sitting." Lauren starts sifting through the other sketches.

In all of them the rapport between sitter and artist is palpable. And while Kat's used to their father's nudes—the ick factor never quite going away—these seem, well, intimate. She takes a sidelong glance at Lauren, checking she's okay, that this is not too much. "Go back to the first sketch, Lauren. There. Look." She points to the left-hand corner. "I thought it was 1980. But that's a loopy six, isn't it? 1986." She raises an eyebrow. "Do the math."

"Really not my strong point," says Flora.

"The year I was born." A shadow slides over Lauren's face. "Oh. Oh no."

"You've lost me," says Flora.

"I suspect we've been misled, not lost," Kat says, squeezing Lauren's hand.

———

DOWNSTAIRS IN THE hall, Kat pauses, walloped with doubt, wondering what the hell she's doing. It's Lauren who nudges her forward; Lauren who pushes her into the light.

Their father is on the sofa, huddled against Angie; his hand laced in hers and resting on her knee, like a nervous boy and his mother in a dentist's waiting room. Man-child. He never grew up, Kat realizes.

The art world celebrated this. Granny passive-aggressively encouraged it, outsourcing his parenting to Rock Point summers. Grandpa just wanted his difficult, baffling artist son to be happy, and for no more family fallouts.

"Well?" Their father's gaze moves slowly from one of them to another, seamlessly, like a pencil between points without lifting from the paper.

If he didn't want "the full story" excavated, he shouldn't have brought them back to Rock Point, Kat thinks, trying to shore her conviction. Subconsciously, perhaps he wants to come clean, and Dixie knew this too. Yes, that's it. Still. Anything could be true at Rock Point. This could blow up in her face. Nerves make her movements exaggerated, clumsy, as she places the drawing on the coffee table, forcing him to face it. The firelight licks over the sinuous lines of waist and hip and hair, eerily bringing the sitter to life. "Viv. We think it's Viv."

Any emotion that flickers over her father's face is quickly controlled.

"Ooh." Angie leans forward, tapping a tooth with a fingernail. "Maybe I did get it right the first time." She turns to Charlie, awaiting an explanation. "You never told me."

Their father tries to smile. Hold it together. Thinks he can bluff it, Kat realizes, with a heavy heart. He's going to make this difficult. "Oh, long time ago," he says with forced mildness, still trying to stamp out the questions like small fires in dry scrub. "If I remember rightly, we did a few sessions while I was at Rock Point on a peace mission, trying to patch things up with Mum after our estranged hiatus, when she'd been scandalized by her portrait. Among other things." Like his affairs and the out-of-wedlock children she had to explain to her friends; Granny had refused to meet or acknowledge

Dixie and baby Lauren. She'd hated Blythe too—before Dixie took the crown for most unsuitable girlfriend—and wanted her son to stay married to Annabelle. "Viv was on the life model carousel," Dad adds.

"Clearly," Angie says, then, bluntly, "Did you screw her too?"

He opens his mouth to deny it, then closes it again, and for a second or two he looks quite trapped, caught in a cage of his own making.

"The date, Dad," Kat says gently. It brings her no pleasure to see her own father squirm.

Glasses steamed up, he takes them off, rubs the lenses on his denim shirt. He doesn't need to look. The date must be etched on his heart.

"I'd have been a baby." Lauren's voice trembles. "And you and Mum were together. So . . . that's it, isn't it? The thing that made her leave you."

"Oh, Daddy." Flora stares at him horrified, his godlike status crumbling. "How . . . how foul of you—and Viv!"

"Viv didn't know about Dixie, or you, Lauren," he says, correcting this quickly. "It happened just the once, a late-night session. Not that that makes it . . . you know." His face sags with sadness. "It was the worst mistake of my life. I confessed to Dix . . . I thought if I was honest . . . But, no. That was it. Lesson learned."

Lauren walks to the fire, her back to them; taut, sharp shoulder blades visible under her thin black sweater, and rising.

Flora huffs into the nearest armchair, ripping off the *F* Post-it note, balling it in her hand, and throwing it to the floor. "Then you employed Viv, a decade or so later, as a housekeeper. Ugh."

"No, Flora, I really didn't. Viv stuck a leaflet through the letterbox . . ." he says: Kat thinks, another note, the irony. He wipes sweat off his forehead with the corner of his shirt. "I wasn't in Cornwall at the time."

"So, Granny never knew you'd had a . . . a thing." Lauren sits on the fender, small, brave, the conflicting emotions they're all feeling—disgust, pity, love—streaking across her face.

"Oh, wait a minute!" exclaims Flora, bolting up in the armchair. "I think Granny guessed. *'A most terrible suspicion!'* Don't you remember? Bertha would call it in Granny's voice, and it'd send Granny into a right fluster."

But Kat wonders if Granny—mind like a trap—suspected something else. She pictures Viv in her red coat—*"I know you lost someone that day too, Charlie"*—and Dixie dying, trying to tell Lauren a secret, and she readies to plunge into the family's deepest, coldest waters. "Dad, should we talk about the corn dolly bird?" As her words settle, something in their father's face seems to rearrange itself, surrender, open like a door. "It wasn't Granny who took and hid that bird, was it?" Kat adds softly. "It was you."

51

LAUREN

| | |

2000

PUMPKIN, THE RESCUE cat, kept most birds out of our backyard. Only the same bold robin appeared every morning, a ball on stick legs. I was sure it was the same one I used to feed cornflakes before that August. He flew down and perched on the brick wall, head cocked, watching me through the kitchen window, like an unwanted friend who refused to accept that the friendship was over.

An associative fear, Janet the therapist called it. Not as disabling as many phobias—dogs, for example, or crowds; I was lucky, she said, since birds kept their distance. But if a pigeon strutted too close, I'd physically recoil, even though I knew it made no rational sense. My mouth would dry, my heart start fluttering like a trapped thing.

I never had another seizure like the one in the aviary. But it always felt as if I could. Like there was a blister-thin layer between normal and the other place. But Mum wouldn't let me take the pills: she didn't believe in "big pharma" or medicating children, she told the doctor.

"You'll beat this, Laurie," she'd say, lying beside me on her futon where we then both slept, stroking my hair off my face, trying to feed me hope in little pipette drops. "It's okay to feel sad, okay? We'll find our way out of this, we really will."

But Mum had purple shadows under her eyes too. She took compassionate leave from her TA job at the local primary and started homeschooling me again. Between lessons on algebra, Leach pottery, and suffragette history—Mum played fast and loose with the national curriculum—I read and read, tumbling out of myself and into the pages. Sometimes I'd look up and Mum would be standing in the doorway: she'd smile brightly but something in her eyes was flinty and frightened. I'd never seen Mum frightened before.

My fault. I was crushed by guilt for not being the "old Lauren" or strong like Kat and Flora, who visited us in Oxford, now awkward around each other but otherwise the same. Kat whispered, "Do you blame us?" And I shook my head: I blamed myself. And I was embarrassed that I was "ill" and that their glamorous, warring mothers were squeezed into our Jericho kitchen, forced together by crisis—the crisis being me—and talking in hushed voices over Mum's courgette cake. I longed for them to leave. Tiredness sat in my bones.

Every couple of weeks or so, Dad's car would growl down the narrow, terraced street, and our neighbors would nosily appear at their windows. He always brought a stash of new books for me and, for Mum, a food hamper from Fortnum & Mason, which Mum was very cool about until the moment he left. She'd then fall on it excitedly, unwrapping the cheeses and sniffing, transported. I loved seeing my parents together; such a rare sight normally. I loved the way Dad would make Mum laugh. Tease her about the tea: "Are you trying to kill me with calendula?" He'd pick up her guitar and start strumming. Beg her to play an Irish tune on the fiddle—"Just one, Dix!" She'd try not to look pleased, refuse flat, then say, "Oh, go on then." Dad would look so happy, eyes half shut, listening, and I'd curl beside him on the sofa, inhaling the studio smells on his shirt, listening to the percussion of his heart, yawning, rubbing my eyes. Not wanting to sleep.

Sleep meant nightmares. They were mostly about birds—Bertha, flying off with one of my fingers in her beak—and the eclipse, the sun with a parrot's bite taken out of it. Trying to stay awake, I'd build alternative Augusts in my mind, all ending with me and Gemma hugging good-bye and promising to write, Grandpa waving at the window, his binoculars around his neck. Or I'd sit on the stairs in my nightie, listening to Mum chatting on the phone: "We're just about hanging in there, Becca"; "Poor thing still can't remember, Lou"; and mutterings about the patchiness of NHS mental health services. Waiting lists. Then one night I heard her say, "Hello, Viv, it's me again. Just checking in. How are you doing, lovey?" I didn't know how they could bear to speak—one mother with a daughter, one without—and rushed back to my bedroom, hands over my ears, wanting to die.

Then spring blew in. Daffodil shoots pushed up in our patio pots. I returned to my own bed. School, half days at first, then full. At the weekends, Mum took me to museums. Baby steps, she said. Oxford, then London. There, we'd meet Dad, who'd take us around galleries for an hour or so.

"Feeling chipper today, Laurie?" he'd ask. I'd nod, even though I always felt like I'd mislaid something precious but couldn't work out what it was. But I didn't want to waste time talking about the broken stuff. "A greatest hits tour," he called it, arm outstretched, hailing a black cab. He wanted to show us his favorites: Da Vinci, Gentileschi, Rembrandt, Freud, Bacon, Rego, and Auerbach. Point out their geniuses, failings and tricks, revisions and mistakes. They all screwed up at some point, he'd say, and I was never sure if he was talking about their lives or art or himself. Or if he was talking to me or Mum. I wanted to live in those huge, soaring windowless galleries, without the worry of sky. Walking and talking. Eating sticky brownies in gallery cafés. Sitting on smooth oak benches between my parents in front of huge paintings until the colors started to waver, or the sitter winked.

In the National Gallery one day, when Mum was in the ladies', we stood in front of Gainsborough's *The Painter's Daughters Chasing a Butterfly*. This is my favorite painting, I declared, relieved to have finally found one; like when you get a best friend.

"Oh, excellent choice, Laurie." He leaned forward, his hands clasped behind his back. "*Girls and Birdcage*," he said after a while. "Well, what do you think? Shall I finish the damn thing, or destroy it?"

The question was too important to answer straight away. I studied the little girl lunging after the butterfly, the big sister holding her hand. And I thought of my first day ever at Rock Point and Kat and Flora, helping me down the rocky beach path. The driftwood bonfire they built, and the marshmallows they carefully toasted for me, stacked on a stick, making sure I didn't burn my fingers. It made me feel warm inside.

"I haven't been able to work on it since . . . well, you know." His voice went funny.

"Finish it, Dad. It's good."

He did. And it was. It was beautiful. A few weeks later he sold it. When I asked Mum why Dad hadn't kept the painting, she was separating a stringy ball of pizza dough on the kitchen table. The bronze autumn sun was pouring through the kitchen window, making her nose stud glint. "I'm not sure he knows himself yet, Laurie. But he'll tell you one day, when he's worked it out. Here, catch." The ball of dough met my palm with a satisfying slap, a puff of flour. We laughed and, without saying another word, started to knead the dough into life.

52

THE GAZETTE

| | |

4 FEBRUARY 2019

The swimmer pulled from the sea near Zennor last month has been named as Charles Herbert Finch of Soho, London, a celebrated portrait painter with links to the art community in St. Ives. Mr. Finch also owned a home in the area, where he was staying at the time of the tragedy, and had gone swimming on his own on 7 January, without informing his family. He was pulled from the sea by local hero Pete Heap, who an eyewitness says risked his own life to rescue him. Despite attempts to revive Mr. Finch, he was later declared dead at the scene. The family has expressed their enormous gratitude to Mr. Heap. Sixty-eight-year-old Mr. Finch, who had health issues, suffered a cardiac arrest shortly after getting into the water, according to the coroner's report. "Like his beloved daughters, I am devastated by Charlie's loss," said his fiancée, Angela York. "He was the great love of my life, a wonderful father and a unique artist. We don't know why he went swimming—we'd already warned him against it—only that he was a huge character who always liked to do things his own unpredictable way. And he hated being told what to do. Charlie died as he lived in a place he'd loved since he was a boy. He would have been moved by the great kindness the community has shown his family since, and how they have taken him, and his work, to their heart." There will be a memorial service at St. Senara's Church, Zennor, on Thursday at 10 a.m. Mr. Finch's funeral is due to take place at St. James's Piccadilly next week. Angela York said, "Everyone is welcome. We want both occasions to be a joyful celebration of Charlie's colorful life and work and ask that mourners don't wear black."

53

LAUREN

|||

Rock Point

24 DECEMBER 2019

SCREAMING AT THE stabbing cold, Lauren runs up the beach, spraying water and sand. Jonah catches her like a rugby ball, belting his arms around her waist. She presses against him, wet, laughing. Desire tugs at her, lodges deep inside.

"Out the shot!" Precariously balancing on a small boulder, Flora grabs a photo of Kat and Kofi smooching in the swell. Proof of her matchmaking triumph. If Flora had not answered Kat's phone that day, she likes to tell everyone, Kofi would never have known Kat was still in love with him—"I mean actually god-awful *sick* with love, Kofi. *Poleaxed* by regret," she'd said, going all in—and he'd have not called off his wedding, nor been at the airport, waiting for Kat to step off the plane.

Hearing her own mobile ring from the pile of coats and bags, Lauren wipes her hands, digs it out with cold-clumsy fingers. "He wants to do it now? No, no, not a problem." Flora glances over quizzically, jumping down to the sand when Lauren mouths, "Grandpa."

They've not had great success with FaceTime. A food-stained jacket lapel comes into focus. "I'll just adjust the wheelchair," says the care home nurse. And there's Grandpa, wizened and toothless, with a confused smile.

"Hello, Grandpa!" they call, and swing the lens up the beach to Raff, tossing a ball for his new puppy. Grandpa's smile grows wider before he jabs a finger at his screen, turning it off.

"Bye then," smiles Flora, who'd taken some convincing it was Grandpa—not a married lover or a fantasy Gemma—she'd overheard Lauren calling almost a year ago. Lauren had hoped her return to Rock Point—telling Grandpa all about it, every day—would send beams of light into the unlit room of his dementia. It hadn't, not really. She suspects she's still the only granddaughter who regularly phones him. Partly, she understands this. He's no longer the grandfather they once knew. Another painful loss Kat and Flora can't bear to dwell on—and avoid talking about. Most of the time, he hasn't the foggiest who anyone is: "Lauren? Lauren Bacall? Wonderful!" But he's always happy to meet her anew, so she'll persevere. Just not right now. She yelps at the time on the screen; the way Rock Point hours slip like sand. "Jonah, we need to shoot," she says, kicking her legs into her jeans.

IN THE DECEMBER sunlight, Rock Point glows white, a sugar lump on the angelica-green cliff top. The red tissue streamers that Flora's wrapped around the porch posts wriggle in the wind. Either side of the front door, two large hurricane lamps wait for the drop of dusk. Inside, the hall is warm and smells of cloves, pine, mulled cider, wood smoke, and soggy dog. The flagstones gleam like river stones—Flora's been down on her hands and knees with some sort of fancy wax. There are plans for a stair runner, hard-wearing enough to take their guests, who arrive in eight weeks, Kat having bullishly accepted bookings before the house is anywhere near ready. Their first artist in residence—Ida; funny, clever, pierced like a pincushion—will move into Dad's studio next month. It's the only room they've barely touched.

Pete, who calls Lauren "my unexpected piece of luck" and feels like Lauren's too, has been extremely busy, and very polite about Flora's decorative flourishes and Kat's tight budgets. Overseeing all the work, he's called in favors from builder mates, who must transport materials and equipment to a cliff top through lanes little wider than a bed. It wasn't easy when the house was built in 1841. It isn't easy now.

Logically, Lauren should feel more stressed. But when has logic ever ruled Rock Point? She feels herself again. And love. She feels so much *love*. Splitting her time between a new job at Tate St. Ives and Rock Point, her head buzzes with plans. They'll kick off with an exhibition of her father's sketches before they go to the Royal Academy. After that, it'll be mostly local artists and makers. "An art B&B with a boho vibe," Flora's feeding to Instagram, which means it's very much not Claridge's and the showers take a while to run hot, but it's fun and informal, with hearty breakfasts around a communal table, an honesty box by the bar, a fire pit in the garden—a built-in semicircular bench where the aviary once was; a hub of warmth and light—spare wellies by the door, and dogs are welcome. And, yes, it's run by three sisters.

The roles are still being worked out. So far, Kat does the financial stuff, often remotely from London. Flora comes back and forth, her life in flux until the divorce is finalized. But Lauren's rooted. Lauren isn't going anywhere. When it's just her and Jonah, they'll sit on the bench by The Drop, talking, huddled under a blanket, his hand sandwiched between her thighs, watching the sun melt over the horizon.

When it all gets too intense—Kat bellowing at the crypto markets on her phone, Flora weaving foliage garlands around the banisters, Raff's puppy biting the baubles off the tree—Lauren laces her walking boots and hikes three miles south. At Viv's, one cup of tea can last three hours. Every conversation folds and stretches into another. And Viv's a good sounding board, Lauren's discovered, filling a tiny bit of the vacuum her mother has left. It was Viv who said, "You know, Lauren, I really don't think Dixie would have sold Rock Point."

Her father must have felt the same. In his last incendiary will—"saving his most explosive firework for last," as Kat says—written a year before he died, and not updated, he bequeathed Rock Point to her mother. Since Dixie could not claim it, the house was dissolved back into his estate—which was divided three ways. They all agreed the only sensible thing to do was sell Rock Point as soon as possible. Before the roof blew off. But then Lauren said, "What if . . ." Flora said, "Why not?" And Kat was already at her laptop, fingers flying across the keyboard, crunching numbers.

A shriek. A squawk. A seagull's perfectly imitated battle caw.

"Uh-oh, she's off again," says Jonah, as he rummages for the chili to dress the crab. Since Flora rearranged the cupboards, no one can ever find anything. But there are lists stuck to the fridge, every holiday meal and snack detailed. The utility room is stacked high with provisions. As Kat says, they could be trapped for weeks and still put on ten pounds. Lauren just hopes they can survive until Boxing Day without World War Three breaking out over the dinner table.

Another squawk, more plaintive this time.

"I'll go." Lauren kisses Jonah—he tastes of sea—and shuts the French doors carefully behind her.

Berthingham Palace is nestled in the conservatory's flourishing jungle—Kentia palms, Monstera, and fiddle-leaf fig—and well positioned to project nutshell missiles at any passing dogs. "Hello, you."

"*Silent night*," Bertha sings.

"Extremely unlikely, I'm afraid." Lauren opens the birdcage door, knowing she has a million things to be getting on with—not least showering and changing—but wanting to settle Bertha first. "Step up."

Bertha swoops to her hand with a pouf of air, a flash of scarlet tail feathers. She's lustrous, fully plumed now. The stress plucking has stopped. But Lauren's gained more from their reconciliation—tentative at first, taking place in incremental steps over many months, twice a week, with the help of a new therapist, who'd asked, "After all our work, Lauren, where do you want to be?"

A car toots its horn outside. Displeased at the prospect of another visitor, Bertha spreads her wings. "Sorry. Back you go." Lauren secures the cage door and rushes to open her own, holding it against the wind, puzzled by the sight in the drive.

Above a large, flat wooden box, a flume of vermillion hair whips in the wind. Beneath it, silver ankle boots. "Eight hours! Eight flipping hours it took me to drive here. Happy bloody Christmas."

Lauren helps Angie into the hall. The package is suspiciously shaped.

"I wanted it to be a surprise. But it's a bit of a bugger to hide, babe. Where shall we put it?" They shuffle into Grandpa's old study, now a library, with his telescope examining the vault of sky, and Ugly Humphrey in a sparkling glass case on the teal-blue wall. Lauren helps lean it gingerly against the shelving. "So, you remember Yana, who's renting the smaller studio?" Angie asks breathlessly. By carving up Dad's East End studio, Angie, its new manager, has reduced the rents, opening it up to artists otherwise priced out of the area, yet cannily increased the yield. "Well, she called me a couple of days ago. Said she'd found one of Charlie's paintings behind a panel at the back of the storage cupboard . . ."

Cutting her short, Kat shouts, "We're back!" and bursts into the room with the others, carrying the wind in their coats and hair. "Ooh, what's that?" Jonah drags away Kofi to help him work out another pudding—reports are coming in of Annabelle's lemon tart disaster—leaving Flora, Kat, Angie, and Lauren to stare at the package warily, as if it might detonate. "Unless you're actually three witches, it's not going to unwrap itself," says Angie.

With shaky fingers, Lauren unclips the wooden case and carefully pulls away the acid-free tissue and foam infill with deft gallerist's hands. And there it is. Everything they knew about Charlie Finch, as a father and an artist, is reversed, turned upside down, like the image in a pinhole camera.

"Bloody hell," says Kat.

Lauren's spellbound. The beautiful savage truth, all occlusion gone. It's the light returning after the shadow. It is half-squeezed metal tubes of paint, her father's Camel cigarettes, Bowie pulsing out of a paint-splattered speaker, turpentine, linseed oil, and rag wipes. Dad in his knackered Dunlops, sinewy and nimble, stepping back and forth from the easel. And it is them.

The painting is not *Girls and Birdcage* but its livelier, smaller sister. With none of the original's troubling sense of incompletion or stasis, here the brushstrokes are looser, more energetic, as if Dad had splashed down the oils in a fever dream. His young sitters—struggling to stay still—seem to find this hilarious, their suppressed laughter surely directed at the old male artist himself. The studio sofa can barely contain them: Flora, Kat, Lauren—and Gemma, the corn bird cupped in her hands.

"It's . . . it's the answer to the question no one knew to ask." Kat's voice breaks.

"And the birdcage has gone," murmurs Flora.

"Hasn't it? In every way. I think it's his masterpiece, I really do, don't you, Lauren?" says Angie. "It's flawless. And . . . look." She tilts the painting away from the wall, revealing the scrawl on the back: "*Four Daughters and Straw Bird*. Charlie Finch, 2005."

Lauren keels at the date. Six years after Gemma's death; he'd have retreated from public life, leaving gossips to carp. He was old news. Over. Her father would have known this painting was brilliant, that it would have shut up his critics, probably restored his crown. Yet he hid it all these years. Had he lived longer, he'd have shown them, she's sure about that. Instead, it feels like a gift from the grave, as well as a bittersweet reminder that Gemma never knew they were sisters, nor that Pete's late fisherman dad, Mike, wasn't hers too.

Mike brought Gemma up, lovingly, as his own, long after he and Viv split. And it became ever harder to undo that. Viv also admitted she got a job at Rock Point so she could see the Finch family up close, work out if she could ever trust them with Gemma's soft heart. Incensed by Angie and Granny's attempts to distance Lauren and Gemma, she'd told Charlie the bombshell truth that August: the result of their one-session stand was Gemma. When Gemma died—given the fragile mental state of Pete and Lauren—they agreed not to risk further trauma by revealing this to anyone else. Except Viv broke that vow by confiding in Dixie, with whom she'd struck up a kinship after that August, and Dixie . . . well, she changed her mind about telling Lauren too late.

The sound of multiple cars pulling up. Car doors slamming. Voices.

"Shall we cover it? Show everyone later," Kat suggests hurriedly. Lauren agrees—they can't accost Viv and Pete with this straightaway—and rests the cardboard back over the painting. The doorbell rings. A snag of collective self-doubt holds them still until Flora says, "It'll be lovely, come on," and strides across the hall in her black boilersuit, throwing open the front door with a dazzling hostess smile.

Viv. Pete. Blythe. Annabelle and her newest husband. Louise and her little boy. The living room turns into a frenzy of voices and barks, clattering heels, waspish asides, hoots of laughter, and competing clouds of expensive perfume. It starts to melt at the edges in a fairy-light blur. Slipping away from the clamor and back into the library, Lauren tips the cover from the portrait again, sees how the paint gleams where the hog-hair bristles of her father's brushes finally, finally caught the light. And she knows what she must do. No one will notice. Not if she's quick. As a champagne cork pops, she rushes up the staircase, the foliage garlands brushing her legs, her steps quickening until she's at her little desk, her black pen hovering above a white sheet of paper. She has one last letter to write.

ACKNOWLEDGMENTS

| | |

I'm enormously grateful to everyone who helped *The Birdcage* hatch from an idea in a scruffy notebook to an actual novel over the course of a pandemic. The editorial steer and unfailing encouragement of my editors, Tara Singh Carlson and, in London, Maxine Hitchcock, meant everything. Also, Ashley Di Dio, Clare Bowron, and the fantastic team at G. P. Putnam's Sons. My wonderful agent, Lizzy Kremer, as well as Maddalena Cavaciuti, Alice Howe, Margaux Vialleron, Kaynat Begum, Imogen Bovill, Sam Norman, and everyone at David Higham Associates. My friend Sacha Newley, for talking to me from his studio, via Zoom, about the painting process. Chloe Wood, for answering so many questions about galleries and art on our dog walks. Gregory Lander, for sharing his knowledge of the African Grey. (Many parrots, including the extraordinary African Grey, are now in danger in the wild, due to loss of habitat and the illegal wildlife trade: there's information about what we can do to protect them at the World Parrot Trust: www.parrots.org). The stellar novelists Sarah Vaughan and Claire Douglas, for reading the first proofs so generously, so quickly. My brood—Oscar, Jago, and Alice—I love you very much. You've been troupers throughout. This novel would have been impossible to write without you, Ben. "Thank you" doesn't begin to cover it. Last, not least, my readers, for the messages, reviews, and encouragement—and for liking my dog posts!—thank you. I hope you enjoy this novel too.